PENGUIN BOOKS

DRIVE ME
wild

Carly Robyn writes contemporary romances with heat, heart, and humor. When she's not writing or reading, you can find her spending time with her family, scrolling through TikTok, exploring Chicago's restaurant scene with friends, watching a Grand Prix, taking a million pictures of her dogs, or binge-watching anything true crime related while drinking a Diet Coke.

Follow her on social media for updates: @carlyrobynauthor.

T0322260

ALSO BY CARLY ROBYN

Drive Me Crazy
Ella & Blake's story

DRIVE ME
wild

CARLY ROBYN

PENGUIN BOOKS

PENGUIN BOOKS

UK | USA | Canada | Ireland | Australia
India | New Zealand | South Africa

Penguin Books, Penguin Random House UK,
One Embassy Gardens, 8 Viaduct Gardens, London SW11 7BW

penguin.co.uk
global.penguinrandomhouse.com

First published in the United States of America by Blue Dog Press 2024
First published in Great Britain by Penguin Books 2024
001

Printed and bound in Great Britain by Clays Ltd, Elcograf S.p.A.

The authorized representative in the EEA is Penguin Random House Ireland,
Morrison Chambers, 32 Nassau Street, Dublin D02 YH68

A CIP catalogue record for this book is available from the British Library

ISBN: 978-1-405-96928-4

www.greenpenguin.co.uk

MIX
Paper | Supporting
responsible forestry
FSC® C018179
www.fsc.org

Penguin Random House is committed to a
sustainable future for our business, our readers
and our planet. This book is made from Forest
Stewardship Council® certified paper.

For Lauri.
My guardian angel, forever and always.

AUTHOR'S CONTENT NOTE

This book is written in a light and humorous style but does include explicit language, references to the death of a parent (past, off-page) and a main character who was adopted as a newborn. It is a slow-burn, open-door romance that portrays sexual content and is meant for readers 18+. Please take note!

The focus of this work is on the fictional characters and events within the Formula 1 racing world, and deviations from the current Grand Prix schedule and tracks are intentional for storytelling purposes.

PLAYLIST

Adore You | Harry Styles
the boy is mine | Ariana Grande
Friendship? | Jordy Searcy
Always Been You | Jessie Murph
I Can See You (Taylor's Version) | Taylor Swift
Love On The Brain | Rihanna
Wild Nights | Corey Harper
Belong Together | Mark Ambor
So High School | Taylor Swift
Boss Bitch | Doja Cat
Easier Said Than Done | Plested
BED | Joel Corry, RAYE, David Guetta
Dirty Thoughts | Chloe Adams

"Love is friendship that has caught fire."
-Ann Landers

1

JOSIE

I'M SURROUNDED BY BALLS. Big balls, tiny balls, oddly shaped balls. White balls, orange balls, dark brown balls. So many bloody balls. Even when I was in a relationship, I never had so many goddamn balls around me. Two balls are more than enough... this is overkill.

Turning to my best friend, I shoot her a panicked look. When I asked her boyfriend to pick up a few props for our photoshoot, I didn't think he'd buy an entire sporting goods store. What does he possibly think I'm going to do with an athletic cup meant to protect a man's groin?

"Do you think it's enough?" Blake asks, running a hand through his tousled hair. "Or should I get more?"

Ella and I both give him a resounding, "No!"

I kick a basketball out of my way, so I don't trip and accidentally break something. I've been assisting Ella while she restarts her podcast, and I can't exactly sue for worker's comp for simply helping a friend.

"This is more than enough," I quickly reassure him. "Thank you, babes."

Glancing around the photo studio Ella rented, I start

mapping out a game plan. A white backdrop covers one wall while exposed brick makes up the others. A few windows close to the ceiling let in gorgeous natural light that will be great for what I have in mind for her podcast cover and promo photos.

I hand Blake a white ceramic mug featuring the *Coffee with Champions* logo emblazoned on the front. "Do you mind filling this up with some coffee? There should be some in the kitchen area. I want to get some photos of El holding it."

Plus, I could use another cup.

He shrugs. "Yeah, sure."

McAllister is one of the top Formula 1 teams and, as part of their marketing team, I've learned a lot. Not only do I know how to engage an audience and capture someone's attention with a thirty-second video, but I also know that Blake—the driver who does not like being told what to do—will happily jump through any hoop if it involves his girlfriend.

He leans down to kiss Ella like I'm not in the room—an intimate moment I'm awkwardly included in simply because of proximity. *Ugh.* The two of them are great together, but I'm a freshly single woman, and their lovey-dovey cuteness is a constant reminder of that. Of Andrew. Of the lease I just re-signed on my one-bedroom flat after backing out of moving into Andrew's place.

Nope. Not going there today. Or ever.

I pull out my phone and connect it to Bluetooth so we can listen to some music while we work. I'm the de facto DJ and the automatic aux holder because, objectively, I have the best taste in music.

I'm not sure where my love for music comes from. Definitely not from my parents, who think Justin Bieber was in One Direction. Maybe from one of my birth parents, although I'll never know for certain. Fun perk of being adopted, I suppose; my past is just as mysterious as my future. Which is also probably why I used to be obsessed with astrology—it gave me a frame of reference for my quirks and preferences my parents can't take credit for. Scorpios like music that makes them feel deeply and connects them to their emotions: check.

I click on my playlist titled "cigarettes and sex." It's filled with angsty songs that you want to scream along to at the top of your lungs. The kind of songs that let you get out your energy when you feel like a badass. Also, the kind of songs that will force apart a couple who are kissing in front of you.

Joan Jett and The Blackheart's "Bad Reputation" does its job, and Ella and Blake *finally* stop kissing. Her cheeks are completely flushed, although I'm not sure if it's from desire or embarrassment. If you had told me a year ago that this Formula 1 fuckboy would now be the king of PDA, I would've thought you were high.

"Great song choice, Jos," Ella compliments me, her cheeks still pink. "I swear you're a musical savant or something."

I throw her a quick thanks before turning to Blake with a wide smile. "Coffee?"

He rubs the back of his neck guiltily before disappearing from the room. Ella and I begin setting up the sports equipment, rearranging and taking test shots to see what looks best. Unlike the McAllister drivers, Ella listens when I give her simple directions—no eye rolling, mumbling under her breath, or flat out refusing. *Cough, cough, Blake*.

"Remi texted me again," Ella says casually. "About getting your mom on her podcast."

I swallow back a groan. Remi Baxter is the host of my favorite podcast, *Dating and Dildos*, and is now Ella's mentor in the indie podcasting world. When Ella told her my mum is *the* Caroline Bancroft, London's leading sex therapist, she nearly had a heart attack.

There's a reason my mum has a seven-month long waiting list just for a consultation—she's the best in the field. That doesn't mean I want her spouting sex advice to millions of people, especially because she tends to "anonymously" use *me* as an example. God knows why. Most of the sex I've had is… vanilla. Not bad by any means, but it certainly wouldn't be featured in the Kama Sutra. I've never had sex in a position called the *Himalayan Hump*, or anything elusive and bendy like that.

"Nope," I confirm. "The reason I love her show so much is so I can hear someone *other* than my mother talk about sex and dating. And if there's even the slightest chance the word *dick* comes out of her mouth, I'm vetoing it. On the list of things I hope to *never* experience, that's in the top five. Top three, if we're being completely honest."

I love my mum. I really, truly do. But sex to her is a normal dinner conversation. *Please pass the rolls, darling. Oh! And by the way, have you had an orgasm today?* When other kids were learning about the birds and bees, I was learning about breast cancer screenings and boundaries. I'm grateful she's open about these types of things, but it can be a lot sometimes. I still have post-traumatic stress from when she taught a safe sex class at my school and demonstrated how to properly put on a condom using a banana. She kept repeating that it wasn't an accurate representation of a man's size, and I still can't eat the yellow fruit to this day.

"Can I at least tell her you'll think about it?" Ella asks, picking up a stray tennis ball. "Pretty please?"

I start singing the chorus of Megan Trainor's "NO" in response. There's no way in hell I need my mum making it anymore obvious to the world that her love language is vibrators.

I only stop my private concert when a brilliant idea strikes like lightning. "El, let's do a test shot of footballs and American footballs. I think it'd be a cute double entendre to have both."

Her eyes light up with excitement at my suggestion. "Don't tell Blake I said this," she lowers her voice conspiratorially, "but your talents are *seriously* being wasted at McAllister, Jos."

Shrugging in response, I grab a ball and position it by the chair Ella will be sitting in. She's not wrong; I can do my job in my sleep at this point. McAllister isn't the most creative when it comes to their marketing, but leaving my position isn't part of the plan. I may be restless at work, but a breakup is enough upheaval for the foreseeable future. My only plan right now is to focus on myself. Figure out who the hell I am outside of a relationship.

I shoot her a pointed look. "Who else would put up with your boyfriend if I left?"

She laughs and lightly tosses a rugby ball at me. "He's been on his best behavior lately."

Blake's the greatest Formula 1 driver the sport's ever seen, but his grumpy—and sometimes hostile—attitude is notorious. Ella softens his tough exterior and makes him much more amenable, though, and everyone and their mother is thankful for that.

"I know, I know." Taking a deep breath, I quickly admit, "I talked to Rhys about possibly implementing an influencer program."

I went through my eighteen-slide presentation with my boss in a conference room called *Supportive*, ironically enough. McAllister's meeting rooms—both in the paddock and our offices outside of London—are all named positive adjectives that are supposed to "inspire and motivate" us. *Teamwork. Apathy. Agility. Flexibility*. It's eyeroll-inducing to say the least.

Ella drops a ping-pong ball. *Why the hell did Blake get ping-pong balls?* "Look at you, you little confrontational… lady. Wait, that sounds weird. Assertive boss bitch…? Yeah. I like that."

"Hardly a confrontation," I admit. A mouse scares me more than McAllister's director of marketing does. "And all he said was that he'd think about it."

"Hey, that's better than when he flat-out rejected your 'fan-in-the-stand' takeover idea," Ella reminds me. "If anyone can pull this off, it's you, Jos. You single-handedly made McAllister blow up on TikTok last year. That takes talent."

I blush from the compliment. "We'll see. Not getting my hopes up. Can you pass me the football behind your left foot, please?"

Ella grins at me, her dimple popping. "You mean the soccer ball?"

I slap my hands over my ears. "Blasphemous!"

Blake bursts into the door, an overflowing cup of coffee in one hand, his phone in the other. I expect to receive third-degree burns from him handing me the mug, but instead, he slips his phone into my open palm. "For you." He rolls his dark eyes. "An *emergency*."

There's only one person who'd be calling Blake simply to talk to me: McAllister's other driver, Theo Walker. He's the sunshine to Blake's moonlight, and I mean that in the most bromantic way possible.

I walk to the other side of the room so I can hear him over Blake's deep voice telling Ella something he learned about coffee beans from a *BBC* documentary.

"What's going on, Walker?" I ask as his face comes into focus. If Adonis and Casanova somehow reproduced, Theo Walker would be their love child. He's objectively gorgeous with his navy-blue eyes surrounded by dark, curling lashes women pay to replicate, espresso-colored hair, and a jawline that's always covered in stubble. And don't even get me started on his abs… They're so defined, you could grate cheese on them. "Blake said it's an emergency."

My tone is teasing instead of worried. Theo's emergencies are not *real* emergencies. They're usually him asking which photo of himself he should post on social media or whether eating a family-sized bag of crisps in one sitting will make him sick.

He sticks out his lower lip into a pout. "It is! And you've been neglecting me."

"I've been a little busy to answer your five million texts." I pan the phone over to where Blake and Ella are huddled in the middle of the set with balls surrounding their feet. "You're quite needy. You know that, right?"

He shrugs as if this isn't new information. "Tell Blakey Blake I always knew he liked playing with other people's balls."

I wait a moment before turning the camera back on my face so he doesn't see me swallow back a laugh. "You have five seconds to tell me this so-called emergency before I hang up on you."

"Do you know how to delete a text?"

I crinkle my brows together. "You've never deleted a text?"

"No, I have," he reassures me with nod. "But can you delete one once you've sent it? Like how you showed me that unsend feature on Gmail?"

"No, not if it's already delivered."

Theo tips his head back and releases a string of swear words—some of which are Australian slang I'm unfamiliar with. "You're supposed to know how to do this shit, Jos."

Apparently, being an Adobe Photoshop wiz translates to anything and everything technological. "Texting isn't the same as the social media algorithm, babes."

"You're a millennial, though," he argues with a groan.

"You're a millennial, too!"

This makes him pause. "I'm actually a Sagittarius."

A smile breaks across my face. Theo's only a few years older than me, but maturity-wise, he's a lot younger. "Why do you need to delete a text?"

"I accidentally sent Andreas a rather… risqué photo of myself," Theo mumbles just loud enough for me to hear. I throw my head back as I laugh. Theo's done a lot of idiotic things, but sending McAllister's team principal a dick pic tops them all.

"How do you accidentally do that?" I howl, clutching my stomach.

He huffs loudly and narrows his eyes at me. "In my defense, Andrea and Andreas are only a letter off. I obviously didn't mean to send it to *him*."

I usually don't bother learning the names of Theo's "women," because by the time I do, he's already moved onto someone else. The only way to tell his revolving door of lady friends apart is by which flat tummy tea or hair vitamin they're promoting on the internet.

"Wow," I say, shaking my head. "You continue to surprise me, Walker."

His deep chuckle reverberates through the speaker on Blake's phone. "I like to keep you on your toes, Bancroft. What'd you do last night? Get wild and crazy at a pub? Didn't see any stories on Instagram."

"Probably because all I did was order in sushi, drink wine, and binge-watch *MasterChef*. Did you know that you can use Coke in a marinade? I guess the acidity tenderizes the meat or something."

"They televise that? It feels illegal…"

It takes me a minute to catch onto where his head is at. "Not the *drug*, you bloody idiot. The fizzy drink! Coca Cola. Pepsi. Christ, Walker."

He shrugs his broad shoulders. "Sounds just as illegal. Why are you staying in on a Saturday night? You're freshly single, Jos. You're supposed to be living it up, not acting like a fifty-five-year-old divorcee, watching cooking shows to impress your dinner guests."

I stick my tongue out. "I'll have you know that I—"

"And by living it up, I meant getting laid, princess," he clarifies, cutting me off. "Dicks galore and all that. There are plenty of fish in the sea, myself included."

"Sushi is technically fish," I remind him, grinning at my cleverness. "Now, was that it? I've got people to see and things to do."

Things that don't involve discussing my sex life, or lack of one.

His lips curl like flames. "When I get back to London, can I be one of the things you do?"

"Absolutely not."

Before he can see the smile tugging at my lips, I end the call. I'd like to say I'm completely immune to Theo's charm, but who am I kidding? We've always enjoyed a flirtatious friendship under the keen awareness that it'll never go further than that. I set boundaries when we first met, and Theo's respected them for the past few years. I've always had a boyfriend, and he's always had, well, like two to five women at a time.

I don't want him to read into any suggestive banter with my newfound single status. Now is the time for me to fall back in love with myself, not a man. That means no bananas for me —metaphorical or not.

2

THEO

IT'S PROBABLY NOT the best idea to Google the dictionary definition of a fuckboy when the woman I just slept with is still in the room. I mean, sure, I have no desire to be in a serious relationship, but that doesn't mean I'm against love or anything. I simply enjoy the female body way too much to commit myself to only *one* at this point in my life. Don't get me wrong, the women I spend time with know the score; I'm careful to never make promises or set any expectations whatsoever, so it's clear that I'm not interested in anything long-term or meaningful.

I'm too focused on my career to handle the delicate nature of being in a relationship right now. I want someone to yell at me to fuck them harder, not yell at me for being late for a dinner date. How can I stay at the top of my career if I'm not fully focused? I want to win another World Championship, and I can't do that if I'm distracted because I'm texting my girlfriend back. So, for now, love can take a backseat to lust.

Thankfully, Jenna—the brunette who just gave me a blowjob that included moves I've only seen in porn—is on the same page as me. She's probably the longest "relationship" I've ever had, although we've never done anything outside the confines of my California king. She's a traveling consultant, but I'm on her "to-do" list whenever she's in London. We have mind-blowing sex a few times a year, that's it. If only all women were as casual as Jenna.

"You don't leave until Tuesday, right?"

"Mm-hmm." She's already back in work-mode, typing away on her phone at rapid-fire speed. There's nothing professional about her outfit, though. She's wearing tight leather pants that fit her shapely legs like a glove and a silky blouse that's now missing a few buttons, thanks to my eagerness to get her naked.

"We can grab drinks or something before you leave." I quickly add, "If you want."

She flicks her gray-blue eyes away from the screen, focusing on me for the first time in ten minutes. *A true fuckboy wouldn't notice the color of her eyes, right?* "Theo. You're a sweetheart, but don't make this weird. You don't need to buy me a drink to guarantee you'll get laid the next time I'm in town."

I snort loudly. Apparently, wanting to know more about Jenna than her Instagram handle and last name is one step too far in our arrangement. *It's not like I asked her what her blood type is.* I like sex with a little bit of an emotional connection—which may be my problem—but at the end of the day, sex is sex. I'm not going to argue with her.

"Can I order you an Uber, at least?"

Her eyes are back on her phone as she slips on her shoes. On her way out of my bedroom door, she says, "Nope! Later, Theo."

"Bye," I call out, but she's already gone.

I throw on some clothes and make the thirty-minute drive to McAllister's headquarters. The first Grand Prix is still a month away, but McAllister's owner, the aptly named William McAllister, insisted Blake and I come in today. I had to leave Australia a week early because of his "exciting" news. He doesn't use positive adjectives very often, so I'm equally intrigued and suspicious.

I flash my badge at the front desk—as if security won't recognize me—and make my way to the cafeteria to grab some breakfast. The long hallway leading from the lobby to the café is lined with photos of drivers, past and present. My photo is directly across from my dad's, and it's like looking at myself fifteen years in the future. My dad drove for McAllister until his MS progressed to the point where him driving was dangerous, but it was his biggest dream to have me drive for his team. A knot in my stomach forms as I brush my fingers past his picture. I quickly walk toward the cafeteria, not wanting to linger and let myself spiral down a rabbit hole of missing him.

Already in line to order a coffee is an arse I'd recognize blindfolded. I've only been crushing on Josie since the day I met her. I fight the urge to palm a cheek in each hand and instead tap her on the shoulder like a gentleman.

"G'day, gorgeous."

Josie immediately swirls around, her pouty lips making a perfect "O." She somehow makes a gray sweater and black jeans look sexy. It's like Levi's used her measurements to custom-make those pants because they cling to her like a perfectly wrapped present.

"Walker!" she squeals, pulling me in for one of her organ-crushing hugs. "I thought you didn't get back from Melbourne until next week. What're you doing here?"

"Change of plans," I manage to cough out as she squeezes the air out of me.

"I wish you would've told me." Releasing me from her arms, she goes to readjust the clip her blonde hair is held back in. Not that I mind being pressed up against her tits, but it feels nice to breathe again. "We could've done the video shoot for the—"

I groan and cover my ears. "Can you at least let me get some caffeine in me before you start badgering me?"

She sings the opening chorus of Cee Lo Green's "Fuck You" in reply. Josie's quirk of responding in song lyrics never fails to bring a smile to my face. I probably wouldn't find it so adorable if she had a shitty voice, but her vocals are decent enough that I wouldn't boo her off the stage at karaoke.

She stops singing and gives me a quick once-over. "So, what're you doing here? Do you have a meeting?"

"With the big boss himself," I reveal.

Josie wiggles her eyebrows. "I thought you were going to say with Andreas. Getting in trouble for sending a beauty shot of your balls and what not."

"My balls *are* beautiful," I inform her with a cheeky wink. "I can show you—"

"And look at the time!" Josie's hands fly up as if hiding from my words. "I'm late for a meeting!"

Looking down at my watch, I realize I'm the one running late. I quickly grab a chocolate chip muffin and matcha latte and make my way to the conference room called *Innovative*. Josie claims that McAllister must have hired some inspirational speaker on shrooms to name the rooms in this place.

Blake's already seated when I walk in. His dark hair is messy, per usual, making it look like he just rolled out of bed, although I'm sure he's been up for hours.

"Morning," he greets me before doing a double take. "You look like you had a rough night."

"The sex was rough"—I shoot him a wink—"but the night was great."

Blake rolls his eyes as if he wasn't doing the same exact thing about a year ago before his girlfriend Goldy—my nickname for Ella—domesticated him. It's for the best, but I could live without his judgmental attitude at the moment.

"Any idea what this meeting is about?" Blake asks as I sink into an open chair.

I shrug. "Fuck if I know."

"Maybe they're telling us we don't have to go to so many damn sponsorship dinners," Blake says, his eyes lighting up.

Blake despises small talk and schmoozing, but Formula 1 is pay-to-play. If we expect our sponsors to pay upwards of two hundred million pounds a year to let us race, then we have to play their game like we're show ponies. I don't mind going to the events. People telling me how great I am? Don't see a problem with that.

I take a bite into my muffin and audibly moan. *Fuck.* If I had to decide between a repeat performance of this morning's blowjob or this muffin, I'd choose the muffin. No hate to Jenna, that's just how good it is.

"Want some?" I ask Blake, flicking a crumb off my pants. "It's really good."

He shakes his head. "I already ate, but thanks."

I fight the urge to ask if he ate his girlfriend for breakfast. Blake's sense of humor doesn't quite allow me to poke fun at him and Goldy.

"Suit yourself," I say with a shrug.

When the door opens, I expect William to walk in, but what I don't expect is the man who once threatened to ruin my life to waltz in behind him. A chocolate chip goes down the wrong pipe and I start coughing. The way I'm hacking up a lung sounds like I've been smoking for thirty years.

What the hell is James Avery doing here?

"You okay, mate?" Blake questions, half-rising from his seat. I know he's certified in the Heimlich maneuver, but he'll crack my ribs if he tries that. Holding up a hand, I wave him off.

"Wrong pipe," I choke out. "No dramas."

It takes me another minute before I can actually breathe again. Breathe is a very loose term, considering I'm near hyperventilating. I haven't seen Avery in a few years. He's sporting a small beer belly now, but other than that, he looks the same—like a piece of shit with ears and eyes. I absent-mindedly touch my left eyebrow. The small scar that runs through it is courtesy of good 'ol Avery the asshole. A part of my life I'd rather not relive.

"Theo, Blake," William finally says. "Meet James Avery."

Hearing his name aloud makes my stomach drop out of my ass, through the floor, and land all the way in the depths of hell. That's where all my memories of this fucker are kept.

Blake stands up and sticks his hand out. "Pleasure to meet you."

"You as well, Blake," James says, pumping Blake's hand. "Can't believe it's taken me this long to meet the Formula 1 legend."

Does he want Blake to take out his dick so he can suck it, too?

Blake waves off his comment like it's no big deal that he's won six World Championship titles. It's the entire reason his biography is the damn talk of the town—scratch that, the *world*. The release party is a few weeks away, and while it hasn't even come out yet, no one will quit chattering on about it. *Blake this. Blake that.* McAllister has two drivers but apparently, only one of them warrants attention right now.

"Walker," he says curtly, his lips pursing together as if my last name makes him nauseous. "It's been a long time."

Not long enough.

I nod and mutter, "Avery."

Blake watches me, trying to gauge what the fuck is going on. Unfortunately, we have an audience and I'd need about six uninterrupted hours to get into that, anyway. William and Avery sit opposite of Blake and me at the table. When William starts talking, it quickly becomes clear what he's going to tell us. I'm not religious, but I pray to God I'm wrong.

My prayers go unanswered.

Turns out, I should've made a deal with the devil.

FOR THE THIRD time in a row, someone bangs on the bathroom door. It sounds like a jackhammer doing the cha-cha-slide against my skull. Can they not hear me emptying the contents of my stomach? *Rude*.

"It's Blake," a familiar voice calls through the door.

As if I wouldn't recognize who it is after twenty years of friendship.

"I'm a little busy," I weakly call out. I thought I was done throwing up, but then the realization that I've been sitting *on a bathroom floor* with my face centimeters away from a toilet seat that *hairy arses* have sat on hits me. "Or is that not obvious enough?"

I make an exaggerated gagging noise and will him to leave me alone. I miss the old Blake who would just buy me a beer and let me sulk in silence. Domesticated Blake does *feelings*.

"Open the goddamn door before I kick it down," he growls.

Okay, well, sometimes *he does feelings*.

I shrink at the sound of his voice. It would make any dog's tail sit snugly in-between its legs. Given the fact that Blake's single-handedly cost McAllister thousands of dollars in repairs thanks to his hot-headedness, I don't doubt his threat.

I flush the toilet before standing and opening the bathroom door. Blake squeezes his imposing frame into the small crack I've left him. Now I'm nauseous and claustrophobic. *Lovely*.

"What the hell was that?" he demands, poking me in the chest.

"What was what?"

He narrows his dark eyes at me, not amused. "Let me reenact. William says, 'I'm pleased to announce that James is our new CEO. We wanted to introduce you before the press release goes out.' Then I go, 'Welcome to the team.' And then you projectile vomit matcha and a half-eaten muffin all over the table."

If Blake ever quits racing, he could easily make a name for himself in Hollywood with that performance. Maybe be the next Bradley Cooper.

I sigh loudly. "Why are you asking me what that was if you *clearly* have a grasp on it?"

Running his hand through his hair, he glowers at me. "Are you done being an asshole?"

"Are you mad you're not the biggest asshole in the room for once?" I snap. My head is pounding, and I'd like to talk about literally anything but *this*. When I see Blake's jaw start to tick, I briefly worry about my safety.

"Out with it, Walker." He sighs after a moment. "What's going on?"

Like ripping off a Band-Aid, I blurt out, "James Avery wants to murder me."

Blake's deep laugh fills the otherwise silent room. He thinks I'm kidding. I really wish I was.

"I'm serious, Hollis," I say nervously. "He's threatened to kill me."

Numerous times, actually.

When he finally calms himself down, he tilts his head at me, his brows harrowing tighter. "Okay, humor me. Why does he want to kill you, Theo?"

"I dated someone he knows… and let's just say, it didn't end well."

I don't mention that the person happens to be his daughter, Christina. That period of my life is one I don't like thinking about, because every time I do, guilt wraps around me like an ugly scarf. It's the reason I never told Blake what happened with her.

Christina Avery and I were not on the same page. Hell, we weren't even reading the same novel. She was annotating a Nicholas Spark's romance, and I was listening to a Stephen King audiobook. She's the entire reason I triple-check with anyone I sleep with that they're cool with casual.

He leans against the door and releases a deep breath. "You think he holds a grudge?"

"Yes," I say without hesitation. Of course he holds a grudge. I not only fucked his daughter, but I fucking broke her heart.

"Okay, well, it's not like the CEO goes to all the Grands Prix. Out of sight, out of mind, you know? He shouldn't give you too much trouble."

If only it were that simple.

"My contract expires at the end of the season," I remind him with a tight smile.

Up until now, I haven't given it much thought. I've been delivering consistent wins and points for McAllister since they signed me. Hell, I won two World Championships with them. But now, the new CEO, who once promised to ruin my life like I ruined his daughter's, has a say in whether they renew my contract or not. And I bet he's going to push hard for the *not* option.

"Fuck, Walker," he swears.

"Why do you think I just spent twenty minutes on the bathroom floor, mate?"

I like being rock-hard, not stuck between a rock and a hard place.

"On a scale of one to ten, how bad are we talking?" he probes, his chiseled jaw tensing. "Seven? Eight?"

I take a moment to think about it. "Probably thirteen."

Blake slams his fist against the bathroom door. The harsh

sound reverberates against the tiled floor, and I'm surprised the wood doesn't split in half. Or that Blake's hand doesn't break.

I worked way too hard to get here to let Avery ruin it. At McAllister, you're the best and everyone knows it. There's no way to be forgotten, but there is a way to be replaced, and there's no way I'm letting that happen. I just have to prove why I deserve to be here. Because I do. My dad knew it and I know it, too.

3

JOSIE

BLAKE AND THEO'S race weekends are planned down to the minute. Press conferences, strategy sessions with team management, time in the garage, practices, media interviews, meeting their fans. If something runs late or needs to get moved around, it throws everything else off.

That's why I'm desperately trying to get them back on track as we film content for our YouTube channel. I don't want to be the reason Blake's late for an interview or Theo misses a meet and greet. Or God forbid they're late for lunch, which is the one free hour they have to themselves to decompress. I always try to schedule more time than I think I'll need given Theo's tendency to get sidetracked by anything and everything and Blake's habit of grumbling.

"Name the two chicanes at Monza," I say for the third time in a row, not bothering to hide the annoyance in my voice. I'd usually have one of the guys explain what a chicane is—a tight succession of corners in alternating directions—but it'll be a miracle if I can even get them to play the game.

Neither of them respond; they're discussing a Porsche driver's performance during the first practice of the day. I walk up to the table positioned in front of their chairs and smack the buzzer resting on it. The loud noise stuns them both quiet. *Finally*. I'm one of the only people who has the patience to deal with Blake and Theo for long-form content, which is why I tend to handle all things video-related.

"Now that I have your attention," I say sweetly, placing my hands on my hips. "Can one of you name the two chicanes at the Monza Grand Prix?"

Blake slams the buzzer before Theo even registers the question. There's no way in hell Blake knows what the chicanes are called. Most drivers know the breakdown of the circuit by numbers—second chicane, third straight, first corner. Theo's one of the few drivers who knows everything by its actual name. It's rather impressive.

I wave my hand to indicate Blake can give his response. "Okay, first we've got chicane one, which is…" His voice trails off as he tries to come up with an answer.

"Variante del Rettifilo," Theo supplies. He doesn't bother hiding his enjoyment at having the upper hand. They may be best mates, but if there's a chance to show off or outdo one another, they're going to take advantage of it.

"Which is what I was going to say if you had given me more than five seconds to answer." Blake narrows his eyes at his driving partner. "And your Italian accent is rubbish."

Theo shrugs. "The second chicane is Variante Ascari, although I'm sure you knew that, too, right, Blake?"

"Sod off," Blake retorts, glaring at Theo.

I groan into my hands. We're going to be here all afternoon if they keep this up. Theo and Blake get into a heated discussion about what the chicanes at other Grand Prix tracks are called, so I take my phone out to answer some emails in the meantime.

My stomach tightens when I see a new text from Andrew.

ANDREW CAFFREY

> Hey! Just wanted to say good luck at the first
> Grand Prix.

Whose ex is nice to them when they're blindsided by a breakup after a two-and-a-half-year relationship? Mine, that's who. Guilt rolls through me in crashing waves. The issue is that Andrew didn't do anything wrong. He didn't cheat on me, there was no type of abuse; we didn't have some explosive fight that made us crash and burn.

I just couldn't be in a relationship where I stopped having a life outside of it. So much of me was tied up in us that I stopped listening to my needs and only focused on his. I didn't know how to be independent while still allowing myself to depend on him. I forgot who *I* was.

My fingers hover over my screen as I debate whether to answer. Guilt gains the upper hand, and I type out a quick response.

JOSIE BANCROFT

> Thanks. I appreciate it!

"Jos." Theo's voice pulls me from my thoughts. I glance over just in time to see him lean back in his chair, the hem of his shirt lifting to reveal a happy trail and toned stomach. "You look stressed."

I slip my phone into my back pocket and paste on a happy face. "All good, babes."

Theo shoots me a movie-star smile. "I've offered before, and I'll offer it again, but I'm more than willing to help you relieve that stress with a good old-fashioned fu—"

He's cut off as Blake smacks him in the back of the head. I'm an only child, but if I ever had an older brother, I'd want it to be Blake. He's overprotective to a fault. I appreciate it, although any man within three meters of Ella probably does not.

"Not happening, Walker." I laugh lightly, ignoring the way his arm muscles flex against his shirt. "I'm not looking to get emotionally entangled with anyone right now, thank you very much."

"Emotions?" Theo releases a deep laugh that sends goosebumps up my arm. "Orgasms only, baby girl. Just pure, raw sex. That's the Theo Walker promise."

Blake groans loudly and lays his head on the table. "I promise to knock you out if you don't shut the bloody hell up."

Theo's face twists up in disgust. "Do you know how many germs are on that table, mate? Do you know the last time this thing was cleaned? Probably in the nineties."

For someone who's made out with half of the female population, he's surprisingly germ-adverse. We only have forty-five more minutes before lunch and Theo acting like he's the president of the Department of Health isn't helping speed things along.

"Focus, please," I say while snapping my fingers like I'm in a musical production. "Next question."

We're wrapping up when my coworker Wes waltzes in. Her bleach blonde hair is tied in double buns and freckles dance across her high cheekbones. Blake glares at me as if I've committed some huge act of betrayal by allowing her to enter the room. Wes is brilliant but after a not-so-fun incident last year involving an exploding can of LaCroix, a German sausage, and the phrase "the devil's twin brother" being thrown around, the two of them rarely work together.

I ignore him and greet her with a warm smile. "Hi, Wes."

"'Ello," she replies, her Essex accent giving her already melodious voice a slight lilt. "How goes it?"

"Oh, just lovely." I look toward the door, where Theo and

Blake elbow one another to leave the room and get to the cafeteria first. "How was your meeting?"

"Well, it was in *Teamwork*, if that's any indication." Wes snorts and rolls her baby blue eyes. "Did you see the TikTok AlphaVite made?"'

"Yes." I sigh begrudgingly as we head downstairs to grab lunch. "It's trending."

If I sound bitter, it's because I am. I may have gotten McAllister over twenty-five million views on TikTok last year, but then I was told we should spend our energy and budget on other platforms. Management simply sees the numbers, and right now, the numbers are great. No need to fix what isn't broken and all that bullshit. If Thomas Edison didn't experiment with carbon filament, we'd still be using candles instead of light bulbs. But what do I know, right?

"Just means we have to work harder to *drive innovation*," she says, mimicking McAllister's tagline. "Although the only thing I'll be driving is a pen into my eye if I have to hear Rhys say that one more time."

I grin at her as we enter the cafeteria. Nearly every seat is filled with bodies wearing McAllister's cherry-red color, each side conversation louder than the next. The one person wearing blue sticks out a like a sore thumb—even more so because their shirt boasts the lightning-looking logo of Alpha-Vite, one of McAllister's biggest competitors.

"Grab us a table?" I ask Wes, nodding toward the door of the motorhome. "Gonna go say hi."

I weave my way through engineers and mechanics holding trays of sandwiches and salads and sidle up next to Lucas.

"Staking out enemy territory?" I tease.

Lucas Adler's three-musketeer status with Blake and Theo is the only reason him being here isn't raising any red flags. No one so much as bats an eye when he wanders in looking for his friends. If Everest—another top Formula 1 team—driver

Harry Thompson walked in on the other hand… that'd be reason to worry.

"Ah, my favorite McAllister employee." Lucas's olive-green eyes twinkle with amusement. "Although don't tell Dumb and Dumber."

I laugh at his nicknames for the McAllister drivers and pull him in for a quick hug. "How was your winter break? You went back to Boston, right?"

The opening lines to "Boston" slip out before I can even consider stopping them.

He chuckles and runs a ring-clad hand through his dark blonde locks, which have the obnoxiously perfect amount of volume. "For a bit, but then I went to Monaco. How are things with you? Blake said you've been helping Ella out with her podcast."

"Mm-hmm. It's been a lot of fun. The most fun I've had working in a while, actually." A dash of color flushes my cheeks at my admission. "Not that working for McAllister isn't fun, but Blake and Theo are like drunken toddlers who need constant care and attention. Can get a bit exhausting, you know?"

Lucas chuckles before taking a sip of his water. "Oh, I know. Theo called me at three a.m. for Tums because he ate one too many shrimp cocktails at the party last night."

Yep. That sounds about right. I roll my eyes at Theo's predictability. "He eats those things like he's never seen food before in his life. I don't know how many times I have to remind him that his mouth isn't a vacuum."

"It's Theo," Lucas says simply. "He's… well, he's him."

"Amen to that." I tap my McAllister-branded water bottle against his AlphaVite one. "But yeah, it's been nice to change things up a bit. Learned more about your beloved American baseball than I ever wanted to, but I'll survive."

"Are you interested in freelancing?" Lucas asks with a head

tilt. "A buddy of mine is looking for a marketing consultant. I can name-drop you if you're interested."

"Oh," I state dumbly. "Um… maybe? I haven't really given it a thought outside of *Coffee with Champions*. And that's technically not even freelancing because I'm not being paid. Not that Ella won't pay me, she's insisting on it, but I'm not about to take money for helping her with something I genuinely enjoy doing, you know? I want to see her succeed. She can pay me in pints of ice cream or jugs of iced coffee. I'm easy. Not like sexually easy. I mean, I've had a one-night stand before, but I'm not like putting up posters advertising my tits. But no judgement if that's what people do, or want to do. Free the nips, right? I, uh… meant easy as in go with the flow."

I exhale sharply to catch my breath. "And I'm going to stop talking now. Thank you for attending my TED Talk."

He waves off my mortification with an affectionate grin. "Ah, how I missed your long-winded tangents, Jos. I'll keep you posted once he starts seriously looking for someone, though. I—"

His voice falters and I follow his gaze to find Theo and Blake walking into the cafeteria. Theo's hitting Blake's arm repeatedly with a can of sour cream and onion Pringles… that his hand is stuck in.

Let the season begin.

POINTS, podium wins, pussy. What more can a Formula 1 driver want? Well, besides all those things with McAllister. It's only the first Grand Prix of the season, but I may need to go out and purchase some scuba gear because I know I'm going to be swimming in all three.

The sounds of clanking metal, purring engines, and mechanics jostling one another greet me as I walk into the garage. I'm going to be late to a meeting with a few McAllister race engineers, but it's been some time since I've seen part of the team, and I want to make sure I greet everyone. *A good impression makes a lasting impression.* That's what my dad always said. When people think of McAllister, they think of me and Blake, but in reality, we couldn't do what we do without the mechanics, engineers, and countless employees who work tirelessly to build and baby our cars.

"Walker!"

The voice sends a chill up my spine and I briefly debate playing dead. I've managed to avoid Avery all weekend, but it seems like my luck has run out. He's in front of me before I can even think of an escape plan. The fabric of the McAllister shirt he's wearing is taut against his stomach, and the way the veins in his neck are pulsing makes it seem as if they're about to explode like a geyser.

"G'day," I say, trying to come off neutral. "How goes it?"

My skin crawls as his eyes give me a once-over. Between his snarled lip and the creases in his forehead, he looks like an angry bulldog. "Spent the morning going over driver stats, and I can't say I'm surprised by what I saw. Looks like Blake has the upper hand on you with more wins, points, and sponsorship interest. Some may say that McAllister's success is completely dependent on him."

Every one of my muscles seize up. I'm used to people pitting Blake and me against one another. Formula 1 is a sport where your teammate also happens to be your biggest competition. You're working together to win the Constructors' Championship but competing against one another for the World Championship title. Just because I'm used to being compared and evaluated doesn't mean I like it, though, and especially not coming from Avery.

"Some may also say that without my point aggregation and aggressive defensive technique, McAllister wouldn't be where they are today."

"My job isn't to defend your driving," he says with a smirk. "It's to make decisions that benefit the team as a whole. And just because your dad was a McAllister legend, doesn't mean his son will be, too."

My knees buckle as I fight the urge to lunge forward and smack the shit out of him. Hit him so hard that I send him all the way back to Milan and away from me and McAllister. But I don't want another cut eyebrow and black eye. I'm a lover, not a fighter. Granted, that seems to be the issue. It's why it looked like I got punched by a fucking boxer rather than a middle-aged man all those years ago.

"Don't *ever* speak about my dad," I spit out. "You'd be lucky to be a quarter of the man he was."

We stare each other down, slowly sizing one another up. Do I get why he hates me? Sure. I probably wouldn't like me either if I were him, but I can't change the past.

"Oh, I'm lucky." As he takes a step closer to me, his spicy cologne floods my senses. "But only because I know this will be the last season McAllister has to deal with you."

And with that, he's off to terrorize someone else. *Fuck.* He can't really do that, right? I puff out a deep breath, pushing all thoughts of Avery into a corner labeled "panic about it later." There's nothing worse than distractions during a race week-end, so I focus on my breathing as I jog to the conference room in the motorhome. Through some sleuthing, I've confirmed that Avery will only be at a few of the twenty-two races this season, so at least I can avoid him face-to-face for the most part. I just need to keep my head down. That'd be a lot easier if I didn't love being the center of attention.

I'M YELLING into my headpiece when Russell barges into my suite. I keep my eyes on the screen, desperate to find a way to salvage this game. It's hopeless. My "teammate" keeps getting killed while reloading more ammo. *Call of Duty: Black Ops 4* isn't as fun when the people you're stuck playing with are newbies.

"This game is chalked thanks to you," I growl into my headphones before shutting off my Xbox. Gaming is my go-to way to de-stress before a race, but it feels like every inch of my skin is agitated. I'm glad I'm not live-streaming this game on Twitch, which I tend to do a few times a week, so my followers don't catch on to my piss-poor mood.

I lean against the plush couch in my suite and close my eyes. Maybe I need to get into yoga or meditation or something. Russell coughs in case I somehow missed his muscular frame blocking any direct sunlight from spilling through the window.

I slowly open my eyes and sigh. "Yes?"

"When's the last time you ate, Theo?" He narrows his moss green eyes at me.

"Probably the last time you jerked off." I scratch my forehead before throwing him a grin. "So sometime last night?"

I've known Russell for years. His father-in-law owns Pegasus, otherwise known as my biggest—and favorite—sponsor. Without their support and backing early on in my career, I wouldn't be where I am today. When I achieved every junior driver's dream of signing with a Formula 1 team, I brought Russell on as my performance coach. Our long-term working and personal relationship means he's used to my raunchy language and doesn't so much as bat an eye. When I told him about the time I got rug burn on my balls during sex, he simply asked if I needed him to get me ointment. I must have some redeeming qualities, though, because I'm his daughter Rosalie's godfather.

"The race is in a few hours," he reminds me, ignoring my comment. "You need to eat something now because you won't have time between the press conference and heading to the pit."

"Oh." I chuckle. "That's why I have a press conference in a bit. I thought it was to discuss the weather patterns over the Baltic Sea."

I spy a tray of food on my desk—an egg white omelet with red peppers, spinach, and feta, turkey bacon, and an English muffin with seedless grape jam. I let out a low whistle. "What would I do without you, Russy boy?"

"Die of starvation," he deadpans, pulling out a chair to sit.

We both know he's right. Russell's responsibility as my performance coach includes handling my diet and meal plan.

Not to mention my daily routine, personal logistics, sleep patterns, travel arrangements, and pretty much anything else. If you combine a personal assistant, physiotherapist, confidante, and friend, you've got Russell.

"Well, cheers, mate." I shove a piece of bacon into my mouth and savor the taste. It burns my tongue, but I suck it up and chew. "Appreciate it."

He waves off my thanks and launches into my schedule for the rest of the day. I tune him out because I know he'll repeat the same exact speech every hour for the rest of the day.

"I met Avery earlier," he says, snapping me out of my daze.

There're no lengths Russell won't go to in order to help me stay in the best frame of mind possible, and he knows the issue of James Avery has been eating at me. He's one of the only people who I feel comfortable sharing those details with.

"Do you now know what I mean when I said he's the lovechild of Stalin and Mussolini?" A sour taste fills my mouth. "He puts the dick in dictator."

"He may be a dick," Russell agrees, "but he's got to have a good work ethic if McAllister hired him."

I grumble to myself, knowing I can't deny that Avery's good at his job. Back when I lived in Milan while driving for Ithaca, James was the CEO of some major hedge funds. Since then, he's had a few other high-profile jobs, so it's clear he has the credentials and experience. *Unfortunately*.

He doesn't care about Formula 1, though—he just follows the money. Considering McAllister's nickname is McMoney to its sponsors, it's honestly no surprise he found his way into a high-ranking position. And a bonus of his latest job is that he can ruin my career.

"Don't focus on him," Russell warns me, running his hand through his chestnut-colored hair. "Focus on what *you're* the best at and you'll be fine."

"I don't think making a girl come in less than five minutes is going to help me much today, but thanks for the advice."

He pinches the bridge of his nose and shakes his head. "Win the race today and you'll have plenty of women lining up for you to do just that."

He's right about that.

MONZA'S the fastest track on the Formula 1 calendar. It's made of long straights and tight chicanes with engines being in full throttle for most of the race. The aerodynamics are relatively low, which means the grip is low, too. Drivers put a premium on good braking stability and traction, which is why I'm starting the race on medium tires.

I wish I could capture the smell right before the final gantry light goes out at the start of a Grand Prix. It's a mix of grease, burning rubber, and nervous sweat. It's all of Formula 1 bundled into one specific, adrenaline-fueled scent that reminds me why I love this sport so goddamn much.

I keep my eyes transfixed ahead of me, listening to each *thump* of my heart. The sound of twenty engines roaring flood my ears as the gantry lights flick off. I peel forward, sweeping over the asphalt beneath my tires.

My starting grid position is P3, but I quickly crowd Alpha-Vite driver Mateo Bertole going into turn one and maneuver myself to P2, directly behind Blake. No surprise that he started the race in P1. I hold my position for the first twenty laps, except for when Lucas nips past me for second. I'm able to maneuver around his left side to reclaim the position as we blister down the main straight. This is my favorite part about driving—the feeling of complete control as I maneuver my car toward a win.

Every vibration from my engine pulses from my head to my toes. I feel every bump and groove of the circuit, every bit of speed I gain. I don't mind it as it helps me stay in tune with my car. For everyday folks, it gets uncomfortable within the first five minutes. I took Josie out in a double-seater last year, and after three laps, she was yelling that it felt like she was trapped inside of a vibrator. It's the first and only time I've ever gotten a semi while driving a circuit.

The pit crew doesn't disappoint when I make a stop at lap twenty-four to swap out my medium tires for hard ones. A quick and clean pit is essential to holding my position, and I'm in and out of the pit lane in two-point-four seconds. My body arches backward as I change gears and speed up to re-enter the race. Thompson and an Ithaca driver speed past me, but they're both a lap behind me, so I'm not worried.

"You've got Bertole six seconds behind you," Andreas tells me through the radio. "Full throttle after this turn, Walker."

If my eyes didn't have to be on the track ahead of me, I'd roll them. Full throttle? No fucking shit. What do they think I'm going to do? Slow down to be courteous?

"Copy that, mate. Thanks."

The deep blue paint of the AlphaVite car glistens in my mirror, the sun illuminating the color. A thrilling three-lap battle between Bertole and I kick off as we head into the Variante della Roggia. It's a surreal feeling knowing that few in the world have experienced speed like this. Only those of us lucky enough to drive for Formula 1 share the combined goal of taking a circuit lap as quickly as possible, performance over-riding every other factor, facing every twist and turn without compromise.

The edge of my elbows press against the cockpit of my car as I take the turn at a heart-lurching speed. Bertole drives off the track, heading into the chicane, and my chest expands with pride. Aggressive defense is my specialty.

As we near the final ten laps, dots of sweat bead on my forehead. A podium win fringes on my ability to keep Bertole and Lucas behind me. I lock my eyes ahead, melting into the seat of my car as I will it to go just a fraction faster. Flexing my gloved fingers against the wheel, I navigate the intense drop in speed around the next corner. My body pitches to the side as I hit 4Gs of force.

Eight minutes later, I'm driving over the black-and-white-checkered line right behind Blake, securing a second-place win and eighteen points. I point a finger in the air as I cheer into my radio.

This one's for you, Dad.

5

JOSIE

MONEY MAY NOT BUY HAPPINESS, but it buys you the ability to host an exclusive event at SoHo House in London. The members-only club costs an exorbitant amount in annual membership fees, but the type of people it caters to can afford it. Blake's been a member for years and insisted it be the venue for his book release party.

His publicist fought him on it—wanting somewhere with the capacity to hold more than two hundred people—but Blake put his foot down. Although he's opened up about his mental health and anxiety, he prefers the shadows to the spotlight, and SoHo House offers the privacy and security he wants. The irony that he wants a "small, intimate" party for a book that quite literally shares his life story, with whomever wants to read about it, isn't lost on anyone.

I've only been here once before, for Lucas's birthday dinner last year, and I've been dying to come back ever since. Situated in West London, there's three floors of club space, a rooftop pool and terrace, and some of the best cocktails I've ever had. I'm usually a wine girl, but their signature drink, the Picante De La Casa, is to die for. It's a fired-up version of a classic margarita, with added chili for extra bite. I've tried recreating it based on copy-cat recipes online, but it's not the same.

I'm ordering my second—okay, maybe it's my third or fourth, whatever—cocktail of the night when a familiar voice causes my entire body to freeze. Turning to my right, Andrew comes into focus. I notice he's wearing the tie my parents bought him for his birthday last year. It makes the emerald specks in his eyes pop.

He's at the other end of the bar, standing next to his friend as they order drinks. *What in the bloody hell is he doing here?* Well, I know he's here because he was invited, but that invitation was obviously revoked when we broke up. Well, apparently it wasn't obvious enough because here we are.

The scent of bergamot and birch announces the presence of someone next to me. It's floral, spicy, and distinctively Theo. He lightly places his hand on my lower back. "Whatcha lookin' at, Jos?"

I don't answer, still debating what to do: approach Andrew and say hi or abort the entire situation and hide in a corner somewhere. It's not like we ended on bad terms, but an occasional text is much different than seeing each other in person. I may be over him, but that doesn't mean I'm ready or willing for us to transition into some sort of awkward friendship. One where we shoot the shit and pretend we didn't used to spend all of our spare time together.

Theo turns his head to see what I'm staring at and, without another word, he's guiding me away from the bar and through a crowd. Looks like we're going with the *abort the situation* option, and I can't say I'm too upset about it.

"Want me to go back there and knock him out?" Theo asks with furrowed brows. "You don't even need to give me a good excuse. Happy to do it just for fun."

Theo's never been shy about his dislike of Andrew. But

then again, Andrew wasn't shy about despising Theo, either. Stupid male egos at their finest.

"No punching necessary. I'm fine," I say with an eye roll. "Just caught off guard is all. Didn't expect to see him here."

Theo cups one of his hands behind my head, pulling me against him. I bury my face in his chest, letting the familiar scent of his cologne calm me. He's always had this effect on me, and his presence is more calming than any relaxation tea blend I've tried.

"Let's get out of here," he suggests once I've stepped back. "There's a pub around the corner that's great. Also, have I told you how gorgeous you look tonight?"

His eyes rake over my body, the curve of his grin unconsciously widening as he does. There's no doubt that Theo's a flirt, but his compliments are as genuine and honest as his smile.

"Thank you." I curl my fingers into the material of my dress to stop myself from tugging at the delicate necklace I'm wearing. "We can't leave, though. It's your best mate's party. He needs you here."

Theo's eyes finally focus back on mine. They're such a specific shade of blue, I don't think Van Gogh could accurately capture their beauty. "Blake doesn't need me. He has hundreds of people here to celebrate him. Just like always."

Maybe it's the Picante De La Casas talking, but an undertone of frustration marks his words. Theo's always been the Robin to Blake's Batman; the lovable sidekick that everyone adores. *Is it possible there's some tension I don't know about?* Shaking my head, I focus on the conversation.

"Well, even if he doesn't *need* you here, he definitely wants you here," I reassure him. The two of them have been inseparable since they were kids.

Theo shrugs as if it doesn't matter either way before swinging his arm over my shoulder. "No one will notice we're gone. You look like you could use some greasy food and a cheap drink, and in case you forgot, your ex-boyfriend is here."

We end up at a semi-crowded pub a few blocks away from the launch party and snag a high-top table toward the back. A group of nearby women don't bother hiding their appraisal of Theo and eye him like he's a piece of choice steak. I swear the man has a fan club everywhere he goes.

I order a tequila soda the moment our server swings by our table. What I really want is a glass of wine, but I don't think mixing liquors is in my best interest right now. Theo requests a lemon drop martini and a basket of chips.

"Not in the mood for a beer?" I laugh, knowing full-well his penchant for fruity cocktails. He genuinely enjoys them. We were once out at a dive bar in São Paulo, and he asked for a pina colada. At least he's comfortable enough in his masculinity not to care what he orders. It's an admirable quality.

"Nah." He shakes his head, the corners of his mouth twitching up. "Why would I choose to drink carbonated bread water when I could get drunk in half the time on something that tastes like candy?"

Conversation between us is easy as we finish our first round of drinks. Soon enough, that one drink turns into two. As our new cocktails appear in front of us, Theo's eyes widen to cartoon-like proportions at something on his phone.

"Everything good?"

"Yeah." He chuckles while shaking his head. "Some chick just AirDropped me a photo of her tits."

Slyly tilting his screen so I can see, he shows me the AirDrop request he received. She either has the world's best plastic surgeon or she's one of God's favorites. How can they be so symmetrical and perky? My boobs are fine, but this random woman's breasts are straight up stunning.

"I-I cannot believe someone just did that," I stammer after tearing my eyes away.

Theo's eyes twinkle with amusement. "I know this may be a foreign concept to you, but some women actually find me rather attractive."

There's no way I'm walking into that trap. Obviously, I think Theo's attractive. I have eyes.

"But she can clearly see you're here with *another woman*. What if we were dating? Is she trying to poach you away? It's just disrespectful. Does she not know girl code, for Christ's sake?"

Theo seems enthralled by my outburst. "I doubt she thinks we're dating."

I place my glass down on the wooden table so aggressively that liquid spills onto the already-sticky table. "Why not? I'm dateable. I'm *very* dateable. Hell, I'm the full kit and caboodle. I'm not just a Sunday morning kind of girl; I can be a Saturday night kind of girl, too. Like I can give you a blowjob that would impress a porn star *and* make you an award-winning breakfast in the morning. Would you like references?"

"Okay, slow down there," Theo says, holding his hands up in surrender. "No references needed. It has *nothing* to do with you, princess. Promise. It's all me."

"That's the oldest line in the book, Walker!" I throw my hands up combatively. "Am I not attractive enough to warrant your attention? Sorry that my—"

"Whoa, whoa, whoa." Theo's brows pull together in a frown. "I just meant that I don't exactly have a reputation for having girlfriends, Jos. It really has nothing to do with you. If anything, she feels threatened that I'm out with a gorgeous woman. Oi? I know you're very dateable, don't worry. I'm sure she's just familiar with how I tend to *date*."

I take a big sip of my drink and silently thank the bartender for giving me such a heavy pour—even though I should've cut myself off about two drinks ago. What in the world has gotten into me? I'm actively trying to *not* be dateable so I can avoid a relationship and here I am, complaining that Theo, of all people, doesn't think I'm girlfriend-material.

"You don't date," I remind him. Theo goes through women faster than he can drive his car. He's made it crystal clear to anyone who will listen that his lifestyle doesn't leave room for anything significant. Whereas I crave commitment and stability, he craves sex and random women AirDropping him nudes. Water, meet oil.

He tilts his head. "Yes, I do."

"Babes, I've had leftovers that've lasted longer than any of your so-called relationships." I throw a chip at him, and it bounces off his arm and onto the floor. "You don't date; you fuck around."

Theo scratches his chin in thought. "Relationships are a distraction."

"From what?" I laugh. "Video games?"

"Yes." He laughs. "And my career. That comes first. Always has, always will."

"That's where you're wrong, Walker. It shouldn't be a distraction; it should be an *addition*." I hit him with the opening lines of Deon Jackson's "Love Makes the World Go Round."

Theo takes a sip of his martini, his lips puckering at the sour taste. "You still feel that way, even after your breakup?"

"Yes," I answer automatically. I love love. It's probably why I tend to fall fast and hard and can't really remember the last time I was single. Pet names, morning cuddles, late-night phone calls, merging friend groups and meeting one another's families, slow sex filled with words of adoration, steamy sex filled with grunts and groans. All of it. "Even if they're not your person, you still learn about yourself. What you need in a relationship, what you're looking for."

I already know what I need *in* a relationship. What I don't know is what I need to be happy *out* of a relationship.

Theo nods before placing his hand over mine and moving his thumb over my knuckles. "How're you doing with all of that? I mean, I know you're okay because you're better than your douche canoe of an ex, but how're you *actually* doing?"

I roll my eyes at the dig. There's no need for me to defend Andrew, although I wouldn't call him a "douche canoe."

"I'm doing fine," I admit truthfully. "It's more the adjustment of being alone."

"You're never alone." I'm expecting him to say something cutesy like he'll always be there for me but instead, he says, "With the amount you talk, angel, I'm sure there's more than enough thoughts going on in that pretty little head of yours to keep you company."

"Pot calling the kettle black."

He chuckles into his drink, small bubbles dancing across the top. "Let's play truth or dare."

I roll my eyes. *Is he twelve? Does he want to play spin the bottle next? Seven minutes in heaven?* "You can't be serious—"

"Truth or dare," he says, taking a long sip of his martini. Theo's nosier than a middle-aged woman eavesdropping at a salon. I wouldn't go as far to say he's a gossip, but he *loves* being in the know. I can see the questions bouncing around in his head.

"Truth," I decide after a moment.

"What are your boobs named?" He says it so quickly that there's no way he hasn't been thinking about asking me this the entire night. It's also not the first time he's asked me this. He's under the impression that all women name their boobs. I have no idea who gave him this idea, and why he won't believe me when I tell him he's clinically insane.

My arms immediately cover my chest in a protective manner. "I change my mind. Give me a dare."

"I *dare* you to tell me what you named your tits," he replies without missing a beat.

I mutter under my breath. Stubborn may as well be his middle name. I guess I should be happy he didn't ask me to divulge details about my breakup. He's been surprisingly respectful about it, no prying or unwarranted questions. Yet.

"There's no rule clarifying that a dare can't be a truth, just so you know," he justifies with a cocky grin. "So hit me with your answer, Bancroft."

His eyes momentarily flicker down to my chest.

"My *breasts* do not have names," I huff. At this point, I debate making something up just so he'll drop it. I bet whoever Airdropped him named her boobs something like Athena and Aphrodite.

"C'mon. You're telling me you didn't name your boobs? I'll tell you what I named my balls to even the playing field if you want."

I fight the urge to dump the entire basket of chips over his head. Why would I want to know that? I already know his dick is named Theo Junior, and that's bad enough. Especially when he talks about it in the third person.

"It's a wonder I've been able to resist your flirting for so long," I mumble with an eye roll.

"No need to resist me any longer now that you're single, babe." He swipes a chip from the basket and pops it into his mouth. "I'm here to service you in any way you please."

I stick my tongue out. "Gag me."

"If you're into that kind of thing, then sure." He throws me a wink that makes my stomach twist. *Or maybe that's the tequila?* "I choose truth, by the way."

Ignoring his comment, I wrack my brain, trying to think of a good question. Theo's an open book, so I feel like there's not much I *don't* know about him. There's no good reason I should know that Lola Bunny from *Space Jam* was his sexual awakening or that he once took a Viagra because he was curious and wanted to see what it felt like.

I finish my drink with a hearty sip. "Okay, why are you so obsessed with boobs?"

"Not all boobs," Theo clarifies quickly. "Just yours."

I flag down our server, desperate for a refill. I don't have the capacity to fight off Theo's flirtations without a little more liquid ammo.

6

JOSIE

I PRESS MY LIPS TOGETHER, *desperately trying to swallow the scream of pure pleasure building. Theo gently presses his fingers against me, rubbing slowly in soft, pressured circles, matching the pace of his unhurried thrusts.*

"Let it out, baby," he coaxes. "I want to hear every sound you make."

I shoot up as if I've been electrocuted. The sudden movement makes me nauseous, a hangover announcing its presence. I'm really hoping I'm only having a sex dream and not replaying last night's events in my head. I sneakily peek an eye open to see if I'm alone in my bed. No. No, I am not. According to my now-confirmed, actually very real sex dream, this means that Theo and I had sex. Everywhere. On the kitchen table. On the couch. On the floor. On my bed.

Bloody fucking hell.

How did the night go from telling Theo that I didn't name my boobs to letting him lick and tease them for hours? Damn tequila. I check the time on my phone and cringe at the brightness of my screen. It's only five thirty a.m. Rolling over, I grab Advil from my nightstand and quickly dry swallow two pills.

I take a moment to look at Theo as I snuggle back under

the covers. It's not that I've never noticed how great his body is —he walks around shirtless enough—but I've never allowed myself to truly appreciate it. Now that he's naked and in my bed…? I'm studying him like he's the Mona Lisa and I'm a graduate student writing my dissertation on da Vinci.

Every muscle in his long, lean body is sculpted to perfection. It's like someone took a block of marble and chiseled it down until Theo Walker emerged. I fight the urge to run my hand over the curve of his back. There's something extremely vulnerable about seeing a grown, naked man sleeping soundly, completely unaware that my childhood stuffed animal is hidden under the pillow his head is resting on.

Shutting my eyes again, I will my body to fall back asleep. I'm drifting off when a warm body spoons mine from behind, a muscular forearm wrapping itself around my waist. Theo's hand crawls up my stomach, finally resting once my left breast is sitting nicely in his palm. I can't help but let out a quiet laugh. Even while asleep and snoring softly, he's still a boob guy.

Theo licks the valley between my breasts, groaning in appreciation. "I'm naming your tits Tom and Jerry."

My laughter turns to whimpers as Theo glides his tongue over one nipple, while gently toying with the other. I arch my back, thrusting them upward and further into his mouth and hand.

I open my eyes a few hours later to find a handsome face inches from mine. How is it humanly possible that Theo looks good hungover? The morning light gives his long body and sleek muscles a warm glow. He's so gorgeous, it's painful. Or maybe that's just the hangover. I don't know at this point.

"Morning, princess," he greets me with a lazy smile. "Sleep well?"

A lightning bolt travels straight down to my core at the memory of that smile looking down at me as he rocked into me over and over again.

"Mm-hmm," I mumble. "Do you know what time it is?"

Theo glances down at his watch—the only item on his body besides his socks—and tells me it's nine-fifty-five a.m. I hop out of bed like someone lit a fire under my arse and quickly grab jeans and a sweater from the top of my clean laundry pile. He watches me with interest, clearly unbothered by the entire situation. Glancing at myself in the mirror, I notice the hickeys covering my chest and neck like a constellation.

"Fuck," Theo moans before biting into my neck. He pumps into me with long, greedy strokes that make my body buzz as if I've just had four consecutive energy drinks. "You were so worth the wait, baby. So goddamn worth it."

"Christ." I peel off the sweater and exchange it for a turtleneck. "Are you a vampire?"

He grins, clearly pleased with his handiwork. "Have somewhere to be?"

"Yes." I spray some perfume on my wrists, rubbing them together. "Brunch with my mum, then filming a teaser video with Ella for her podcast later."

"Ohh! What're you going to tell Goldy about my dick?" Theo asks, clasping his hands behind his neck. "That it's everything you've imagined and more?"

My eyes bulge out of my head. He's huffing paint if he thinks anyone is finding out about this. *Ever.* I'm locking this in the vault and throwing said vault into the Thames River. Focusing on myself does not include sleeping with one of my closest friends, and the last thing I need is unsolicited opinions or commentary from anyone.

"First of all, don't flatter yourself. I've never imagined your dick, babes. And second, Ella won't be hearing anything."

"Don't girls talk about this sort of thing?"

"Theo," I tell him in all seriousness, "last night was fun, but it's staying between us. Seriously."

He pouts like I've just taken away his favorite toy, so I spin around on my heel and narrow my eyes to reiterate how serious I am. It's hard to avoid looking at his dick, which is still on full display—and is just as perfectly sculpted as the rest of his body. I never thought I'd describe a penis as beautiful, but his really is. *Ugh.* Theo needs to leave sooner rather than later so I can freak out over this entire situation in private. Why can't I even do rebound sex right? Have I learned nothing from listening to *Dating and Dildos*? Rebound sex is supposed to be with some random bloke I meet at the bar, not someone I genuinely care for and enjoy spending time with. That's how feelings develop.

"Who cares if people know?" he continues. "It's just sex. Not a big deal."

"Agreed." I shake my head. "Not a big deal. So no one has to know about it."

"Wait… Holy shit." He sits up and blinks in a puzzled fashion. "Are you embarrassed?"

His jaw springs open when I fail to correct him.

"Sleeping with me is *embarrassing*?"

"I don't like being one of your… bimbos." *Bimbos? Who says bimbo anymore?* "And I don't want people to make a *thing* out of this. It happened, but it's done, so things are going to go back to normal now."

God knows how we can ever go back to normal after sex that makes me want to sing Drake's "Best I Ever Had," but now is not the time to dwell on that. I search my floor to find his briefs. He needs to cover himself up because I'm dealing with too much right now to also deal with *that*. Clothes are strewn all over my floor in a haphazard manner, but I finally find them under the dress I wore last night. I avoid eye contact with his nether regions while I hand them over. "Can you put these on, please?"

"Are you kicking me out?" he asks in wide-eyed surprise. "Seriously?"

"Did you want to stay and cuddle?" I laugh with an eye roll. "Yes, I'm kicking you out, Theo. Although you're making it hard."

"You make me hard."

I lick the inside of his left thigh, watching as he twitches with antici-pation. Teasing him, I take my time committing the shape and feel of his balls to memory. When I finally take him in my mouth, he shudders deeply and runs his fingers through my messy hair.

"Clothes." I shove his pants at him. "Now."

I'm too focused on the way his butt looks to care about his grumbling as he tugs on the rest of his clothes. Now I understand why he refers to himself as a fine piece of ass. I'm not one to objectify a man's body, but here I am, practically drooling over Theo's squeezable butt. I'm never drinking tequila again because it's taking the full blame for how the entire night unfolded.

Theo finishes getting dressed so I can look in his direction without blushing. Well, sort of. I don't think I'll ever be able to look at him again without the image of his forehead creasing in concentration and his eyes darkening in pleasure. *Nope.* He needs to leave immediately.

"Don't feel weird, Jos." He winks at me. "Now we just know what the other looks like while finishing. No harm, no foul."

A familiar tightening grips my stomach as my breathing gets caught in my throat. Oh, God. How is it possible to orgasm so many times? The gasps slipping through my lips are borderline hyperventilation.

"You going to come for me again, baby?" Theo asks, dusting his lips against my collarbone. "Such a good girl."

"How do you know I wasn't faking it?" I challenge.

I've faked my fair share of orgasms over the years, although last night was not one of those times. Most guys I've slept with either are too focused on their own selfish pleasure to care if I finish, or they turn into an arse once they realize that they haven't made me come at all. Enter the big, fat, fake O.

"Well, I'm assuming you weren't having an exorcism." He smirks. "So you tell me."

I groan into my hands as my stomach sinks. "Christ, Theo, way to not make this weird."

"You're really that bothered by this?" A frown crosses his lips. "All right, well, we can, uh… pretend it never happened."

"Yeah?" It's pathetic how hopeful I sound. "Really?"

"Sure." He shrugs. "It's going to be hard, though."

"Why?"

He smiles disarmingly and a new flush of desire heats my skin. "You may act like an angel, but last night you rode me like the devil straight on her way to hell."

I'm stunned silent. He chuckles and brushes his soft lips against my forehead. Now why did he have to go and do that? I'm a sucker for forehead kisses. One-night stands aren't supposed to give you forehead kisses, boyfriends are. Theo's neither of those; he's my friend. Except now, he's a friend I've slept with.

"See you at the race next weekend, angel." Theo shoots me a knowing wink before the door closes with him on the other side of it.

He's right about one thing. I'm definitely the devil because the thoughts I'm having about last night are ensuring my entry to Hell.

7

THEO

I'VE EXPERIENCED a lot of weird morning afters. The one chick who claimed she was pregnant hours after we slept together. The one who refused to leave my house, and I had to call my security team to physically remove her. Oh, then there was the one girl who claimed we were married in a previous life and had to renew our vows in this one.

I thought I'd experienced everything until the pure horror on Josie's face when she realized we slept together—that's a new one. I know she enjoyed it. Hell, she more than enjoyed it. She wasn't faking it when she told me I fucked her like no one else ever had. So why the hell did she act like she had committed a cardinal sin? She didn't want another round; she wanted me to get the hell out of her apartment.

It's been two weeks, and I still haven't stopped thinking about it, about *her*. I can't get her out of my head. The image of how goddamn sexy she looked with her head thrown back, jaw slack with pleasure, as she rode me. How her tits fit perfectly in my palms. How she blew me with such enthusiasm, it's a wonder I lasted more than a minute. The award-winning noises she made have been playing through my mind on repeat. *Fuck.* Would I be down to sleep with her again? Abso-fucking-lutely. But I'm almost sure she'd rather never watch *MasterChef* again than have a repeat performance. I just don't know *why.* It was phenomenal sex.

Now I have to watch her run around the pit garage, snapping photos on her camera, wearing a skin-tight McAllister shirt that accentuates every curve. She's somehow acting as if nothing happened between us. As if she hadn't begged me to thrust harder.

"Theo," our team principal, Andreas, snaps for the third time in a minute. "Pay attention."

I peel my eyes away from Josie and apologize with a charming smile. It won't work on him, but it will work on the engineers. Andreas is only impressed by wins so unless it's a Grand Prix and I'm on the podium, it doesn't matter to him.

"Not a problem." An engineer smiles back. *Suck on that, Andreas.* "We were asking about the steering. You mentioned it seemed off in the practice run."

Formula 1 steering wheels are complicated. With over twenty switches, dials, and paddles, it's easy to make a mistake. People can't use mobile devices while driving, but we can operate a steering wheel with insurmountable settings while driving at insanely high speeds. Go figure. It wasn't my fault I was off in practice, though, since there was an alignment issue. Not enough to affect me noticeably, but enough that I wasn't one with my car, which I need to be to meet the standards I've set for myself. The team gets to fixing it while I head to my suite.

I play some *Call of Duty: Vanguard* to distract myself. I need to take my mind off Josie and there's no better way to do that than by loading up a virtual AK-47. I'm about halfway through my second game when my phone starts ringing. I'd usually ignore it since I'm in the middle of playing, but it's from my younger sister, Charlotte. If she's having an emergency and I miss the call because of a video game, I'll never forgive myself.

"Everything okay, Char?" I ask as soon as I answer the phone.

She groans theatrically. "Yes. Why does something have to be wrong whenever I call you?"

"It doesn't." Although I wouldn't be surprised if it was, given the situations Charlotte gets herself into. "You know I worry about you. I just wanted to confirm that everything's good. How have you been feeling?"

"I've been feeling fine. And I haven't added any new arrests to my record, so…"

I nearly fall off the couch. "*New* arrests? Has there been a *first* arrest I'm unaware of?"

Ten different terrifying scenarios run through my mind: drug bust, kidnapping, robbery gone wrong. How did she get bail money? Who was her one call? Why am I just finding out about this?

"Gotcha." She laughs, clearly pleased with herself, and the familiar sound pushes away any panic. "That's what you get for being such a worrywart. I'm more than capable of taking care of myself, Theodore. Stop babying me."

"It's my job to worry about you, kid."

"Well then, consider yourself fired."

If people think I'm outgoing, it's only because they haven't met my sister. I swear she puts speed instead of sugar into the five cups of coffee she drinks a day.

I prop my phone between my ear and shoulder. "What's up?"

"Eh, not much," she reveals. "Mum and Richard are driving out to campus to have dinner with me later."

"Nice. Enjoy."

Charlotte clucks her tongue. "Don't be like that."

"Like what?"

"God, you're annoying," she groans. "You love Richard. And you haven't cared about any of mum's other boyfriends, so it's clear you just don't like *them* dating."

An annoyed scoff slips through my lips because there's truly nothing more annoying than my little sister not only calling me out on my shit, but being right about it, too. Richard was my dad's best friend and manager back in his racing days. He became somewhat of a mentor to me, someone I could joke around and share a beer with.

But now, he's someone dating my mum.

I toss my controller next to me and sigh. "What's your point, Char? Do you want me to do a little jig and have confetti shoot from my arsehole in joy?"

"Be happy for them, Theo," Charlotte instructs, as if it's as simple as snapping my fingers. "I don't know why you're making things more difficult than they have to be."

"How am I making things hard, Charlotte?" I snap, my hands curling. "They're the ones who changed all the dynamics when they got together."

"You know what they say," Charlotte answers in a sing-song tone. "Change is the spice of life. Wait, that doesn't sound right. I think… it may actually be *variety* is the spice of life. But whatever, the sentiment still stands."

"Who's the *they* that says that?"

"Huh?"

I snort back a laugh. "Who says variety is the spice of life?"

"Oh. I don't know… People."

"So you don't actually know who says it?" I press, knowing the more I tease, the more flustered she'll get.

"What is this? The Spanish Inquisition? Stop asking me so many questions. You know I've never been good at tests."

I ignore her sage advice and latch onto a familiar topic. "How'd that test from last week go, by the way? The one you were stressed about?"

Charlotte spends the next twenty minutes chattering on about some professor who's an absolute terror and dedicated to making her life miserable. She only stops speaking when she realizes she's running late—an ongoing habit of hers—and has to get ready for dinner, which takes at least an hour.

"Be safe," I remind her. "We'll talk again soon, yeah?"

"Course!" she says. "And Theo? Call Mum. She misses you."

"Mm-hmm."

Not a yes. Not a no. Things between my mum and I have been strained since I cut my trip to Australia short back in January. She knows it was work-related, but I was more than happy for the excuse to get away. Richard had just moved in with her, and I didn't exactly enjoy not feeling at home in my childhood house. Having someone living there who wasn't my dad, but had always acted as somewhat of a father-figure, wasn't my idea of fun.

Picking back up my controller, I swap out my AK-47 for something a little bigger. Time to blow up some shit.

I SWEAR Blake is a grandpa trapped in a thirty-year-old's body. For a full year, he thought CRM were the initials of the person who helped with our marketing. His mind was blown when he learned it stands for customer relationship manager. I'm honestly surprised he doesn't sign his name at the end of each text he sends.

Right now, I couldn't be more thankful for his inability to grasp the importance of hashtags. His questions pour a bucket of cold water on any horniness I may be experiencing due to staring at Josie. She's spent the meeting typing away on her computer and completely oblivious to the fact that my dick is acting like she's the North Star. It's not like this is the first meeting I've been in with Josie—we've sat through hundreds of them together and I've never once had this issue. I *so* do not need to be getting hard while someone drones on about reaching a different target demographic.

I screw around on Instagram for a bit to distract myself, scrolling through the messages of the many beautiful women who've slid into my DMs, but it doesn't help much. When my manager texts me, I'm eager to strike up a conversation. Anything to make my eyes stop wandering back to the blonde sitting across the table from me.

MARTIN THE MANAGER
Just landed.

THEO WALKER
I thought you didn't fly in until tomorrow morning! Welcome to Portugal, honey.

MARTIN THE MANAGER
Surprise! Meet at my hotel room after practice?

THEO WALKER
Your hotel room?! Martin... are you going to put the moves on me? I've never been into men, but if you put on a wig, maybe I'd consider it.

MARTIN THE MANAGER
I wouldn't touch you with a five-meter pole, Walker.

THEO WALKER
Yet you want to meet in your hotel room!? Don't deny that you love me. Everyone does. :)

MARTIN THE MANAGER
I want to meet in my hotel room so no one witnesses me yelling at you for failing to mention you have an issue with James Avery.

A cold tremor runs through my body. I can list on one hand the people who know *all* those details: Russell, Christina,

James, Blake, me. Apparently now it's more, although I don't know what Martin is aware of. *Fuck fuckity fuck fuck.*

THEO WALKER

Be there by two-thirty.

The moment my manager opens the door to his suite, I start asking more questions than a reporter during a press conference. "What did Avery say? Did he tell you I'm a horrible driver? Because it's absolute bullshit. He's just trying to ruin my career. Did he say something to you? Or did he say something to William? I don't get why he's talking about me at all. It's rude to talk behind people's backs."

Martin's eyes widen behind his tortoise-shell-framed glasses. "Um, hello to you, too, Walker."

"Hi." I push past him and walk into his suite, collapsing onto the couch. A knot of nerves sits in my stomach, and I pray my manager says something to unravel them. "How'd you find out?"

"Find out what?" Martin heads into the small kitchenette and turns on the Nespresso. "Right now, all I know is that James Avery doesn't seem to like you very much. Care to tell me why?"

"He's blowing things out of proportion." I push my open palm into the cushion beneath me and the material makes a weird whoopee-cushion-like noise. "I dated his daughter. We broke up. End of story."

Martin sighs dramatically as he waits for the machine to pour his coffee. "Please expand on the story, Theo. I need to know what I'm working with here. Now is not the time for you to suddenly get all shy and skimp out on the details."

"Why do you assume it was me who did something?"

"Because I know you," he says like this should be answer enough. "And you have a reputation for accidentally getting women to fall in love with you and then breaking their hearts.

Have you never wondered why the tabloids switch between calling you *Walker of Shame* and *Wet 'n Wild Walker*?"

I open my mouth to say something before deciding against it. I'm certainly not going to fill the silence by digging my own grave.

"Listen, I get it," Martin says to soothe me. "You're young and you want to have fun. But you have to know that, sometimes, fun may bite you in the ass."

I rest my head against the back of the couch and groan. "It was a few years ago, Martin. I told her from the beginning that I didn't want anything serious. She just—"

"Thought she'd be the one to change you."

I nod solemnly. More so now than ever, my career is my main focus. You don't work your whole life toward something to not give it your all. I told Christina I wasn't looking for a relationship, and that Formula 1 would always be my number one priority, but she—and pretty much every woman I've ever dated—never took it at face value. Instead, it was a challenge. What she heard was, "I'm not looking for a relationship *right now*" and "My career is my number one priority *behind you.*" No matter how many times I repeated myself, she could never grasp that I was taking the whole "honesty is the best policy" thing very seriously.

"Was it just a bad breakup?" Martin presses. "Run of the mill, dad-hates-boy-who-broke-daughter's-heart thing?"

"Yes," I lie through my teeth. There's no way I'm getting into the details of how things actually went down. There's nothing *normal* about her faking a pregnancy and then me having to file a restraining order. "Regular breakup."

"Okay." He removes his now-steaming mug from the counter, pressing it to his lips. "I can work with that."

I tap my fingers against my thigh. "What did Avery say?"

"Nothing," he admits before taking a sip of his coffee. "I

met with Andreas to see where McAllister's head is at regarding contract negotiations."

I draw in a deep, audible breath. Contract negotiations usually don't happen until a bit later in the season, but I'm appreciative that Martin's being proactive. Always good to get a quick pulse check, especially when the body may as well be a cadaver.

"Don't act so surprised." He shrugs. "You pay me well because I'm good at my job, Walker."

Pay him well is the understatement of the year. I'm the reason he can send his kids to private school with enough left over to buy his and her Ferraris for him and his wife.

"Anyway, Andreas gave me the impression that Avery was going to pussy-foot around and draw things out longer than necessary because of *you*," Martin continues. "I asked Russell if he knew anything, and he said I had to talk to you about it."

"Oh."

"Yep. So I wanted to get ahead of any drama," Martin says. He runs a hand over his bald head, the smooth skin gleaming under the harsh hotel room lights.

"I wish I could rub your head."

Coffee dribbles down his chin as he opens his mouth. "What the fuck?"

"Like a crystal ball. That way I could predict the future of my contract negotiations," I explain with a grin. "Martin the Fortune Teller has a nice ring to it, eh?"

He laughs deeply, shaking his head. "You're weird, Walker."

If the paparazzi called me *Weird Walker* instead of my other names, I probably wouldn't be in this fucking situation.

8

JOSIE

RACE WEEKENDS ARE EITHER SO hectic that I forget to drink water for extended periods of time, or so calm that I could head back to the hotel for a quick catnap and no one would have any idea.

Today is a shitstorm worthy of a tornado report on the local news.

The morning starts off normally, but quickly devolves after Blake crashes his car during morning practice. Unexpected rain hit while the cars were out and he took a turn too quickly, forcing it into the overrun and barriers. The team has to rebuild it in time for qualifying tomorrow, or he'll start at the back of the grid.

Then Theo spent thirty minutes during a live interview with SkySports discussing why his spirit animal would be a red fox. Is his assessment accurate? Yes. He makes some good points. Is it necessary? Absolutely not, and now his team is running way behind schedule.

I head to the conference room for some semblance of peace and quiet. I set up a few Instagram and Facebook ads for our newest line of merchandise before typing "must-see landmarks in Le Mans" into Google. The French Grand Prix is still weeks away, but tons of Formula 1 employees and team members extend their stay in France and head to Le Mans to attend the 24 Heures du Mans, the world's oldest and most well-known endurance race, the next weekend.

Although researching the city of Le Mans as a kid is what initially led to my interest in motorsport, I've never actually visited—never felt the need to. I may have been born there, but the only thing French about me is my love of wine and cheese. Other than that, I'm crumpets, tea, and "All Hail the King" through and through.

But according to the internet—and of course, I believe everything I read on the internet like the millennial I am—connecting to my birth city will give me a better sense of self. So I'm going. It's time for me to explore my French beginnings, outside of my love for charcuterie boards.

I've been creating a guide of all the things I want to do once I visit. I'm busy making a reservation at a cocktail bar I discovered on Instagram when Theo appears in the doorframe. The blue shirt he's wearing makes his eyes pop and hugs the contours of his muscles, highlighting the work he puts in at the gym every day.

"Hey," Theo greets me, head cocked tentatively. "Can I come in?"

I give him what I pray is a casual and cute smile. "It's a free country, babes."

"Bahrain is actually a constitutional, hereditary monarchy," he says matter-of-factly. "According to Blake."

I shake my head and smile. Blake knows a little about a lot, thanks to his love for watching documentaries. "Well, it's a free conference room at least, so you may do as you please."

The smile on his face widens. "What about *whom* I please?"

Nope. I can't let a few orgasms get in the way of my favorite sparring partner. I start singing "Thank u, next" by

Ariana Grande, and a low chuckle rumbles out from Theo's chest. He once told me I've got more songs in me than a jukebox.

As he makes his way over, I quickly switch tabs, so it looks like I'm doing actual work. Theo settles into the chair to my right because, of course, in a conference room with ten chairs, he has to pick the one where I can smell the masculine deliciousness of his cologne.

He rests his large hand on my forearm. I hate that my mind automatically thinks of the magic he can do with those fingers. "Are you annoyed with me?"

My brain short-circuits as his hand torches my skin. "I'm annoyed with you quite often. You're going to have to be more specific, Walker."

He snorts and sweeps his hand from me, as if the simple touch wasn't making my heart forget to beat.

"I don't know. Haven't seen you much since the last race, and I wanted to make sure you're not avoiding me after..." he lowers his voice, "you know."

If I'm avoiding you, it's probably because every time I look at your lips, I imagine them pressed against mine.

"We're good," I reassure him. "No dramas, mate."

He grins at my use of an Aussie phrase. "Glad you can still joke around with me."

"Just be glad I found your dick to be more than adequate, or the jokes wouldn't be merciful."

The words come straight from my G-spot, up my throat, and out of my mouth before I can stop them. *Abort. Mayday. Code red. Phone a friend.*

"More than adequate, eh?" He turns his chair to face me, triumph gleaming in his eyes. "Tell me more."

I nervously giggle because apparently, I'm a teenage girl with a crush on her friend and not a woman who knows she can't blur the lines of an important friendship, no matter how more-than-adequate his dick is. "Aren't you supposed to be at a press conference?"

"Nope." He drums his hands against the table. "Got pushed back an hour thanks to Blakey Blake."

"What'd he do?" Blake gets extra grumpy when he has back-to-back interviews and, honestly, I don't blame him. How many times can reporters ask the same question but disguise it as something new? And ask about Ella in an interview? You're pretty much blackballed from ever asking him anything ever again. "Cuss someone out? Flip a table? Throw a water bottle at a reporter?"

"Goldy had a phone call with a lawyer that Blake wanted to be there for." Theo scratches the five o'clock shadow that perpetually marks his jaw. "Very nicely asked if we could move some things around."

I nod in silent understanding. Ella's testifying in the case against Conner Brixton—the man who assaulted her a year and a half ago—and Blake's been her rock through the pre-trial hearings and never-ending calls with her lawyer. "Makes sense."

Theo smiles, a row of white teeth showing. "What're you working on?"

Before I can answer, he turns my computer so he can see my screen better. *Okay, nosy.* It's a good thing I wasn't stalking his Instagram or anything embarrassing like that.

"Why are you emailing James Avery?" His voice is unusually distant. "Do you work with him closely?"

I take my laptop back to see what he's looking at. It's an email I received earlier in the morning. I don't know if it can be considered an email, considering the message is written in the subject line: *Please send report of website traffic from last quarter.*

"He sent that to the entire marketing team," I point out. "It's not like we're having a one-on-one email chain about something top-secret."

"Have you met him?" he asks, a sudden note of contempt creeping into his voice.

"First Grand Prix," I respond. "He came to a marketing meeting and introduced himself. He's... interesting."

Theo's back straightens immediately, his face suddenly tightening. "What'd you talk about? Did I come up?"

"Yeah, I told him your national security number and blood type," I tease with an eye roll. "No, you were not a topic of conversation, Walker. The world doesn't revolve around you."

He nods to himself, running a hand through his hair. "Okay. Cool."

"Are you okay?" I gently nudge him with my elbow. That's the only physical contact I'm allowing myself to have with him. "I just told you the world doesn't revolve around you, and you didn't fight me on it."

He chuckles. "Yeah, I'm good. Avery is just... well, he's not good news. Let's leave it at that."

"He seems kind of creepy," I admit.

Theo tilts his head at me, waiting for me to elaborate.

"Wes said he asked for her number so he could 'text her if he had any immediate questions.'"

Theo leans back in his chair, a frown playing on his lips— the lips I can't stop staring at. *Ugh.* "He was like that back in Milan, too. He likes his women legal, but young."

Wait, what? Theo knew Avery before when he was driving for Ithaca?

I don't get a chance to press him further because Theo grins at me, making any coherent thoughts I may have fly out the window. "Want to play video games with me tomorrow night? And before you say no, I promise to give myself some sort of a handicap to even the playing field."

"Is the handicap that you play with your toes instead of fingers while blindfolded?" I ask incredulously. "Because that's the only way I'd stand a shot of winning."

He laughs low in his throat and pinches my cheek. It's a

friendly gesture that reminds me that we are indeed *friends,* which means I have to stop looking at him like he's a Playgirl pin-up. "C'mon, Jos. *Pleeaaseeeeee?* Pretty please with a cherry on top? I don't want to play by myself."

I ignore the double entendre. "Can't you ask Lucas or Blake? Harry? Mateo? Or literally any other human who actually enjoys video games?"

"Aww." Theo pouts his lip. "That's so cute that you thought you were my first option. Of course I already asked them. They're busy."

I smack his arm. "Rude."

"What if I throw in the promise of ice cream?"

"Aww," I mimic him. "That's cute that you thought ice cream wasn't already part of the deal."

He throws his head back as he laughs, exposing the paleness of his neck in comparison to the rest of his bronzed body. "Does this mean you're in?"

I rest my chin in my hands. Do I want to spend my Saturday night playing video games? No, not particularly. But I do want to re-establish the boundaries of our friendship, and this is the perfect opportunity to do so. Plus, my only other option right now is to third-wheel Ella and Blake. Again.

"Easy games only," I concede, lifting a brow to show my seriousness. "And no yelling at me if I do something wrong."

"It's a date, princess."

I absolutely hate the feverish rush his words give me. Theo does sex, not dates. There's nothing wrong with that, except sex between friends is never *just* sex. I've seen *Made of Honor.* And *Friends with Benefits.* And *13 Going on 30.* Hell, I even went to Katz's Deli, which is where they filmed the famous orgasm scene in *When Harry Met Sally,* when I went with Ella to visit her friend Poppy in New York.

"Purely platonic, Walker," I warn him.

"Or strictly sexual," he challenges with a playful grin. "Come over around eight?"

"Yeah, I'll come." My cheeks heat at the innuendo of my words, so I quickly add, "To your hotel room."

Theo doesn't miss a beat. "I thought you said this was purely platonic, Bancroft?"

He winks and my ovaries explode like fireworks. *Keep it together, Josie.* Leaning back, he flashes me his signature smile, and it immediately feels like I'm burning up in the tropics.

A man with charm is a very dangerous thing...

A FEW HOURS before qualifying on Saturday, I meet Wes in McAllister's motorhome. Albie, McAllister's head chef, made his famous toasties for lunch and to say I'm excited is an understatement. If I had the metabolism to eat this for every meal, I would.

"Do you want to do dinner tonight?" Wes asks, twirling her platinum blonde hair around her finger. "We can go to that Mediterranean restaurant you were telling me about?"

As a foodie, I essentially moonlight as a Yelp page in every city we visit during the season. "Wish I could, but I promised Theo we'd hang out."

She doesn't respond, giving me a look instead. There's no way she knows we slept together. *Right?* My breath catches in my throat as I contemplate my options. Deny it? Own up to it? Pretend to faint to get out of the situation? I bit my tongue to stop myself from singing Shaggy's "It Wasn't Me."

"There's sort of a bet going on..." Wes finally tells me with a guilty smile. "Whether you and Theo are going to get together."

My hands smack the table so loudly, people sitting around us turn to see what's going on. "Between who?"

"Uh, everyone." Wes laughs. "Wouldn't be surprised if some of the team principals are in on it."

I glare at her through my shock. "That is completely absurd!"

Absurdly accurate but absurd, nonetheless.

"Oh, c'mon, Jos! The two of you have always been close," Wes rationalizes. She shoots me a wide smile, revealing the slight gap in between her teeth and the two dimples at the corners of her mouth. "This would've happened ages ago, but you've just always had a boyfriend. First there was Jason, and then Andrew... Wait, didn't you date someone between them? His name started with an R?"

"Robbie," I grumble. We only dated for a few months, but things got intense way too soon, like they always do. "He was never an official boyfriend, though."

"My point remains." Wes rolls her eyes and takes a bite of her sandwich. "You're always dating *someone*. You're a relationship girl."

Tell me something I don't know.

"And there's nothing wrong with that," she clarifies. "But maybe it's time for you to have a little fun. Go for the guy who doesn't want to settle down."

I hate that everything she's saying makes perfect sense. And if it were anyone but Theo, I'd probably jump on the idea. But adding sex to our friendship would dip us dangerously close to relationship territory when that's the last thing Theo wants and the last thing I need. Our friendship is more important to me than some temporary sexual desire.

"You just want us to get together because you've got money on the line," I tease, hoping to steer the subject away from Theo. "And I'm not giving you that satisfaction, babes."

I start singing The Rolling Stones' "You Can't Always Get What You Want," although I'm not sure if I'm telling her or reminding myself.

9

THEO

I TOP the times at all three practice sessions and keep the momentum going through each segment of qualifying. Blake comes behind me in second, having finished just 0.001 seconds after me—a frustratingly narrow margin for him. He seems okay with it, though. Ella's mellowed him out in the best way possible. His performance has never been better, and his attitude doesn't make mechanics cry and engineers shake in their boots. It's a win for everyone.

The two of us head to the press conference that's held for the drivers in the top three starting positions. Lucas is already there, chatting with some reporters. The race has only been over for thirty minutes, but the silver rings he wears are already back on his fingers. While I have a partnership with Adidas, Lucas has one with Gucci. He's been in Vogue for his style more times than I can count, but he's the least conceited person I know.

"Nice job out there," he congratulates me. "You too, Hollis."

"Thanks, Adler," Blake and I say simultaneously.

"You guys do know each other's first names, right?" Josie

says, appearing at Lucas's side. Her camera is hanging around her like a necklace. "You're not just awkwardly using last names as a cop out?"

I point my thumb at Lucas. "Of course not. This is Larry, and this," I wave my finger in front of Blake, "is Bill."

Josie's laugh is soft and sincere. My dick twitches underneath my race suit like it remembers the sound and wants to say a nice hello. *Christ.* I need to jerk off before she comes over later so I'm not too tempted to try anything with her. But if something were to happen on its own—like we end up playing with one another instead of a game—I would be all for it.

She chats with us for a little before disappearing into the sea of reporters and journalists. Lucas, Blake, and I sit at a long table, ice-cold water bottles and microphones stationed in front of each of our seats. The Formula 1 logo looms behind us, just in case anyone forgot what this press conference is for. The questions are low pressure—reporters inquiring about the condition of our cars and the track, any concerns, or predictions we have about the upcoming race.

"Walker!" someone from SkySports shouts. As soon as I make eye contact with him, all the other voices in the room quiet. The steady drone of the air conditioning buzzes as I wait for the question. "How do you feel about securing your second pole position of the season?"

I lean toward my microphone, interlocking my fingers in front of me. "Some people like missionary or doggy-style the best… I'm not going to lie; my favorite position happens to be pole."

The room erupts into a chorus of laughter. Press conferences tend to get boring after a bit, so I've made it my personal mission to liven things up a bit. A sex joke here or there never killed anyone—at least, I don't think. I'll have to ask Ella, whose true crime and mysterious death knowledge is alarming.

"In all seriousness," I continue, "it feels great, but as you know, it's truly anyone's race tomorrow. Every driver wants to deliver a win, regardless of where we start on the grid."

JOSIE, being the most punctual human on the face of the planet, knocks on my door the moment the clock switches from seven fifty-nine to eight p.m. I wonder if she sets an alarm in the morning or if she's one of those people who naturally wakes up at the same time every day.

"You ready to get your arse kicked, Walker?" she greets me. "I've been stretching my thumbs all afternoon."

I open the door to my hotel room, letting her pass by me. She's wearing a matching beige sweatsuit, her blonde hair hanging loose around her shoulders. Is it a Netflix and chill sort of outfit? My guess is no, but a man can dream.

"I'd rather you spank my arse than kick it."

Josie swivels her head and looks at me. "A naked woman isn't going to pop out from behind the curtains, is she?"

It takes me a minute to realize what she's insinuating. It takes me another minute to realize that Josie's the only person I've slept with in the past few weeks. Not only that, but I haven't even tried to sleep with anyone else. And it's not like there weren't options, because trust me, there were. I'm not a sex addict by any means, but I do get laid on a regular basis. And it's been over a month since I last slept with someone. *What the fuck?* I'm not concerned that I haven't had sex in a few weeks; I'm concerned that I don't care.

"Don't worry," I tease with a grin. "I threw her out before you got here."

"Ah." She smiles but it doesn't quite reach her eyes. *Fuck.* I wasn't trying to make her uncomfortable. "Well, I appreciate it."

Before I can tell her I'm kidding, she plops onto the couch. "So what're we playing?"

I toss her the case of the game. I'm on the cover of the newest F1 racing game, alongside Everest driver Harry Thompson and Ithaca driver Frankie Talmud. It doesn't come out for another few months, but they sent me an early copy. I'm not a bona fide beta tester, but I do give them thorough feedback. If a game with my face is going to be sold, it damn well better be the best game out there.

She bursts out laughing. "Obviously, you're going to win! That'd be embarrassing if you didn't, Walker. It's a video version of what you get paid millions to do in real life. That's like Mary Berry losing a baking competition or something."

"I haven't played this yet!" I protest. "But we can play something else if you want."

I list a bunch of games. *League of Legends, Hearthstone, Fortnite, World of Warcraft, Arena of Valor.* Josie stares at me as if I'm speaking ancient Egyptian. "What about *Super Smash Bros.*?"

She combs her fingers through her hair. "Isn't Super Smash Bros. the name of that micro-brewery out in Kensington?"

"You're kidding," I say with a hollow feeling in the pit of my stomach. *Please tell me you're kidding.*

"Of course I am." Her easy-going laugh alleviates the tension in my neck. "God, you should see your face, Walker. It's like I told you I ran over the family dog."

Relaxing against the comfortable couch cushions, I let out a satisfied sigh, glad that I don't have to end our friendship immediately. I get to work setting up my PlayStation while Josie scrolls through her Spotify to find a playlist for us. She has playlists for every mood, situation, feeling, and thought. I have no idea what types of songs should be on a playlist called "crying in the shower" or "dancing in my room at two a.m." but somehow, she does. She claims she's not bilingual, but she knows music better than I know English.

Josie's still choosing a playlist when I finish readying both controllers and choose the right settings for the game. "Christ,

Bancroft, are you sorting through the damn national archives?"

"Found it!"

A Khalid song flows through the surround sound system, and Josie smiles to herself. She relaxes next to me, our thighs brushing against one another, and she starts asking questions—what buttons control which part of the car, how accurately aspects like understeer and DRS are represented in the game. It's hotter than any dirty talk I've ever experienced.

"Want to make a bet?" I query, my eyes twinkling.

"The last time we made a bet, I had to eat a hot chili pepper and spent the night tossing," she reminds me with an eye roll. "So, no."

"You won't spend the night praying to the porcelain God with this one," I promise. "If you win, I'll tell you a secret. If I win, you tell me a secret."

Josie toys with the buttons of the controller, familiarizing herself with it. "You do realize I'd be setting myself up for failure, right?"

"Nu-uh," I argue. "You're playing as the *best* Formula 1 driver—me—and I'm giving you a thirty-second head start. Plus, I told you I'll pause the game at any time to help you."

Josie's blonde eyebrows lift thoughtfully. She's not one to make rash decisions, so I dig my heels into the patterned carpet as I wait for her answer.

"I also got cookie dough ice cream," I blurt out a minute later. Patience isn't a virtue I have.

"Well, why didn't you lead with that? It's a bet. Best three out of five?"

For someone who's not super competitive, Josie is very well-versed in smack talk. I pause the game a few times to double-check that I'm hearing her correctly. I'm not sure if some of the things she's saying are made up or just extremely British, and I make a mental note to double check with Blake later.

"Why do you like the F1 game so much?" Josie asks after the first round is over. She stretches her legs like we're about to go for a run. "Doesn't that defeat the purpose of work-life balance if you're playing your job during your downtime?"

I keep my eyes focused on changing the settings so the track acclimation doesn't affect the optimal racing line. "When my dad got really sick, he couldn't come to the track as often, so he bought it for us to play together."

As far as most things go, I'm an open book. Want to know what razor I use to shave my pubes? I'll send you the link. Curious about my gym routine? I'll have Russell send over a detailed workout regime. Dying to know what cologne I wear? I'm not going to gatekeep the information. I don't mind sharing my life. The more people know me, the easier it is for me to make a name for myself and for people to remember me.

But my dad? That's a different story. Talking about him is like pouring gasoline on my heart and leaving a lit match in my lungs.

"Who was better?" Josie's question brings me out of the fog. "You or him?"

"He kicked my arse almost every time," I admit with a chuckle. "He was the best at everything he did."

Josie opens her mouth to say something but decides against it, instead sitting back on the couch. "Ready for game three?"

It turns out, she's the one who's not ready for the third game. She loses, horribly. The effort is there, but the quick combination of braking, cornering, and acceleration is not something Josie exceeds at via a video game. I give her props for not trying to knock my controller out of my hand, though, because I'm sure she wanted to.

"Secret time," I announce happily after having kicked her cute ass. "Hit me, Bancroft."

She smacks my arm. "Like that?"

I shake my head and chuckle. "Nope. Tell me something juicy." I hum the *Jeopardy* theme song as Josie takes her sweet time thinking of a secret.

"What if it's not exactly a secret?" Josie asks while tilting her head. "More just something not a lot of people know."

Hmm. I shrug. "That works."

She takes a deep breath before releasing it slowly. "Andrew wanted to move in together. Well, he wanted me to move into his condo. He owns it already, so it wouldn't make sense for us to have rented somewhere else, but yeah."

Oh. I was expecting a secret, like she used to match the rubber bands on her braces to her outfits. Not *that*. I'm not the type of bloke who gets flustered, but right now, my cheeks are taking on the hue of wild cherries. The one topic Josie and I tend to skirt around is her relationship—*former* relationship, I should say—probably because I didn't like Andrew and he didn't like me. My dislike stems from the knowledge that no one will ever be good enough for Josie. His dislike was that I shamelessly flirted with his girlfriend and rubbed our friendship in his face more than necessary. *Oops.*

"You weren't ready for that?" I ask once I get my voice back.

"I only owe you one secret," she reminds me with a wink. "And I'm pretty sure you owe me ice cream."

Josie bounces happily in her seat when I return with a bowl piled high with cookie dough ice cream. She's easy to please. Some women want diamonds, some want designer purses, but Josie just wants a bowl of her favorite comfort food. It's probably why our friendship works so well. I don't have to pull out all the stops or try to impress her. She's happy to spend time with *me,* and she's even happier when there's dessert, too.

It's nearly midnight when we decide to call it a night. Even though I have to be up in less than seven hours, I don't want Josie to leave. I want to kiss her—gently, roughly, slowly, desperately, sweetly. It's all I can focus on. It's all I've been able to focus on. I feel like a drug addict because one hit of Josie and I was hooked, and I've been desperate to get my next fix ever since.

Before she opens the door to leave my suite, I stop her. "I want to see you again."

"We see each other all the time, babes. That not enough?"

"That's not what I meant." I brush my fingers against her cheeks, which are rapidly turning pink. "But you knew that."

I meant I can't stop thinking about the way you kissed me like you were dying of thirst and I was water. I meant I'm desperate to spend an hour between your legs until you can't handle any more pleasure. I meant I want to feel you come on my cock while you moan my name, begging for more.

Josie's eyes widen and she starts singing Justin Bieber's "What Do You Mean?" I can't help but let out a loud laugh. Her ability to pair a song to every situation is impressive. Doesn't matter if it's an obscure song from the seventies, or a Top Ten hit on the radio.

"I mean," I continue, "that I want to fuck you until you can't stand straight. And I say that with the most utmost respect."

Josie's uncharacteristically quiet. I'm starting to wonder whether I laid all my cards on the table too soon when she finally says, "But we're friends."

"Friends are supposed to have fun together," I point out, my eyes dwelling on her lips. "And we had a lot of fun."

My dick agrees. We haven't even done anything sexual tonight, and my balls ache for her touch.

"Sex will only complicate things, Theo. I don't want either of us to end up getting hurt." Her voice is slightly apprehensive. I'm not sure what to make of it, and I don't know if she does, either. "Let's just stick to friends, okay?"

She blinks her chestnut-brown eyes at me, silently asking

me to agree as if I could ever say no to her. I haven't stood a chance at that since the day we met. I tuck a loose strand of hair behind her ear and nod. "We'll always be friends."

Her lips spread into a smile that would make any grown man fall to his knees. I would know because I have to lean against the door to support my weight the moment she leaves my suite. I'm not sure what's going on with me. I hate doctors, but I'm seriously starting to think I need a neurologist to examine my brain.

10

JOSIE

IT WAS a lot easier to keep Theo in the nice, tiny friend box I'd created for him when I didn't know he wanted to sleep with me again. I mean, Theo's always wanted to sleep with me and has made that abundantly clear since the day we met. But I thought it'd be an itch he'd scratch and then forget about. Apparently not.

As much as I hate to admit it, it's all I've been thinking about since we left the last race. *He's* all I've been thinking about. The feel of his large hand against my hip. The way his eyes light up with desire when he looks at me. The rough stubble gracing his jaw.

This is not part of my plan.

The plan is to focus on myself, not on Theo telling me he wants to fuck me until I can't stand straight, which I have no doubt he can do. The man exudes sexual energy like it's cologne.

"Are you okay?" Ella asks. We're sitting in the pit garage, watching Blake and Theo do final checks on their cars before the Spanish Grand Prix. "You keep staring into space like you're having some sort of fortune-teller vision."

I rest my head against her shoulder. "Just tired."

"You can talk to me, you know that, right? Breakups are always hard."

My breakup with Andrew isn't the issue. The fact that I'm already crushing on someone else is. Especially because that someone else just so happens to be Theo—my friend, her friend, her boyfriend's best friend. Talk about complicated.

"I appreciate it, but I'm okay, El. Really."

"Mm-hmm." Ella studies me, tugging her lower lip between her teeth. I know she doesn't believe me. "Okay. Well, my offer stands."

"Thanks, babes," I say. "I'm going to watch the race from the stands with Wes. Do you want to come?"

She shakes her head and grins. "And deal with Blake's security team? No, thank you. I'll see you at the event later, though, right?"

"Yup!"

I locate Wes in the motorhome and the two of us make our way to the stands situated by the starting line. We trudge up the concrete metal steps, side-stepping strangers sitting shoulder to shoulder in their favorite Formula 1 team's gear. I've always loved the camaraderie between fans—people who might not meet, otherwise connecting, all because they love the same team.

We find our seats and settle into the hard plastic. My feet tap against the floor, crushing discarded popcorn and smushed peanut shells as we wait for the race to start. A hush comes over the crowd as the gantry light start to flick on. The moment the final light goes off, indicating the race has begun, the announcer's voice booms through the loudspeaker.

Theo shows great pace right away, and his launch is so good that he doesn't even need the slipstream Blake's car gives him. He aggressively nudges his way into the corner of the first turn, forcing Blake to pull back and concede the lead. The two of them duke it out for the next sixteen laps, pushing and pulling to take the front of the pack.

During lap twenty-four, a Catalyst driver cuts too close to Theo, forcing him to clip the curb with his front right tire. He loses control of his car and slams into the barrier, front-first. The screech of metal sliding against the barricade makes the hair on my arms stand up.

I've seen almost every Formula 1 driver crash. No matter how minor the crash is, my heart still skips a beat, my breath catching in my chest as I wait to find out if the driver's okay. Theo's crash isn't the worst one he's been in, but it's not a good one, either. Not that there's such a thing as a good crash.

The camera switches between Andreas in the pit garage, standing between engineers, and Theo's car, metal pieces surrounding it. *Shit*. I adjust the volume on the radio earpiece I'm still wearing so I can hear what's going on.

"Theo?" Andreas asks through the radio. "You okay, mate?"

"Well, I just got hit by a car going 170 kph," Theo responds, his breathing heavy. "So I've definitely been better, Andreas, but your concern is appreciated. Almost makes me forget that it feels like someone just smacked my head with the back of a frying pan."

"Safety car will be there shortly. Can you get out on your own?"

There's a pause. "No. It's like someone sticky glued my arse to the seat. I am *not* having a very good time right now. I'd like a refund for this ride."

I snort in response. Theo's radio recordings are legendary for how ridiculous they can be.

I watch the safety car swarm his wrecked car from the jumbotron. As soon as they get Theo out of his car, he swings his foot at the tire before bending over, his left arm gripping his right shoulder. These drivers don't care as much that they've slammed into a barrier as they do that their cars are ruined and their chance at a win is dashed. Now that fans know Theo's okay, the screen switches back to the race.

I wait a few minutes before texting Ella.

JOSIE BANCROFT

How's Theo doing?

ELLA GOLD

He's currently having a screaming match with Russell because he's refusing to go to the medical center.

Getting Theo checked out after an accident is akin to getting a toddler to agree to a flu shot. It's always a fight. The last time Theo went to the med center was when Blake was in a bad crash last season, and he was worried. Theo's insistence that he's "fine" after every crash is not only stubborn, it's plain stupid. Formula 1 cars may have all the best safety features, but there's no telling the internal damage a crash can cause.

JOSIE BANCROFT

Sounds about right. Does his shoulder seem okay? He grabbed it when he got out of the car.

ELLA GOLD

He keeps rolling it back and grunting. I'll have Blake talk to him once the race is over.

I sink into my seat and force my attention back to the race. I'll just have to trust that Russell and Blake can convince Theo to take care of himself.

SLINKING OUT OF THE CAB, I power walk into the nearby hotel the party is being hosted at. Blisters form on my feet and my Spanx are dangerously tight under my silky dress, making it hard to move my body, let alone breathe, but I have a certain driver to yell at.

Under Russell's strict instructions, Theo is supposed to skip the event and take it easy tonight. Ice his shoulder, take some pain meds, and go to bed early. I know this because Blake grumbled about Theo's bedrest all afternoon. He hates attending parties without his driving partner because it forces him to talk to McAllister's sponsors on his own.

Thanks to social media and Theo's inability to *not* post what he's doing, I know he's here and is already two drinks in.

The party planners go above and beyond for each Grand Prix gala and event, constantly one-upping themselves, and this one is no exception. The room is filled with the usual who's who, but it's easy to locate the Australian in question. He's leaning against the bar, chatting with a few other drivers, who I'm sure are worshipping at his feet. Theo prefers to be the center of attention, so wherever there's a crowd, he'll most likely be in the center of it.

My heels click against the shiny floors as I make my way through the crowd. Gorgeous white marble stretches as far as the eye can see and crystal chandeliers glisten in the soft lighting, illuminating the glamour of the event. I grab a flute of champagne off the tray from a server circulating through the crowd, careful that the golden bubbles rising to the top don't spill over the edge of the glass.

I take a swig of my drink as I approach Theo's gaggle of admirers. "What are you doing here?" I demand. All four men turn to stare at me, their black dress shoes gleaming despite the soft lighting of the room.

"Enjoying the party," Theo says, talking loud enough so I can hear him over the live band. His eyes roam up and down my body as if there's no one standing next to us. I'll positively die if he can see my nipples hardening under his gaze. "New dress?"

I glower at him. "You're supposed to be taking it easy tonight."

"It's not like I'm skydiving, Bancroft. I'm simply enjoying a drink," a smile pulls his mouth to one side, "in the company of a beautiful woman."

Although my insides turn to mush at his words, my face stays stoic.

Theo sighs. "Gentleman, do you mind if we finish this conversation later? It appears I'm in trouble."

The drivers slowly disappear into the crowd. One of them accidentally bumps into Theo as they walk away, causing him to shut his eyes and grit his teeth. The pink liquid in his martini glass sloshes out of the glass and onto the floor. Rolling his shoulder back, he grimaces. His whole "I'm fine" routine is being poorly executed.

I touch his arm gently, my exasperation dissolving into concern. "Theo? Are you okay?"

"Hmm?" He opens his eyes and stares at me as if he had no idea I was there. "Oh, yeah. I'm good, angel. No dramas."

"I'm going to find Russell," I decide, trying to keep the worry out of my voice. "You need to see a doctor."

"Don't, Jos." He grabs my arm as I walk away. The pleading tone of his voice makes me pause. "Please."

Theo's eyes search mine in a silent petition to just let it go. Leaning against the bar, I release a deep breath. He could have a torn ligament, a strained shoulder, a minor concussion, a stress fracture.

"Jos, please." His hand moves down my arm until his fingers are intertwined with mine. "He'll want me to get scans and I can't do that. I *won't* do that."

Fireworks glow inside me from the feeling of our hands clasped. How can a simple touch extort such reactions from me? *Reactions Andrew didn't even come close to eliciting.* I don't know what to make of it.

"I haven't been to a hospital since my dad passed." His voice is barely above a whisper. "And I don't want to go to one now."

A desire to wrap him in my arms overwhelms me, but I'm not sure I can handle that type of intimacy with Theo anymore, so I squeeze his hand, hoping he knows I'm here for him. He absentmindedly strokes his thumb against my palm. I feel a fluttering in my throat and press my free hand against it. *Maybe I should pick up yoga to learn how to control my breathing better.*

"My dad always joked that when he wasn't at the track with me, he was in the hospital, wishing he was at the track with me," Theo says, his lips turning up a fraction of a centimeter.

"I'm sure you had tons of stories to let him live vicariously through you." My voice is gentle because Theo rarely talks about his dad unless someone asks him a direct question. When he does bring him up on his own, it's shrouded in pain so deep, I don't even think he realizes it's there.

"He was the one who travelled with me to every competition, every meeting, every practice. Every time I wanted to go karting to practice more. Then his MS progressed, and he couldn't anymore... too susceptible to infections."

Words bubble up in my throat but fail to come out. My heart breaks for him.

"McAllister was his dream for me," Theo says quietly. "I had a red racecar bed growing up and everything. Went to the Australian Grand Prix each year, decked out in our colors."

I've seen the photos—they're hung up in one of the hallways at McAllister's headquarters—of a young Theo and his dad, wearing matching McAllister hats and grins in front of the track. They took the same photo every year until Theo's dad passed away.

"He said besides marrying my mum and having his kids, McAllister signing me was the happiest day of his life."

I squeeze his hand. "He'd be proud of you, Theo."

His formally calm face is disrupted by the hard tightening of his jaw. "What if I wasn't at McAllister?"

Um, what?

Before I can ask him what he's talking about, his familiar lopsided grin appears. "It's cute how worried you are about me, Jos. I wouldn't mind seeing you dressed up in a sexy little nurse costume for some role play."

I'm equally impressed and confused at how quickly he switches topics. He has skillfully mastered the art of saying something serious, but following it up with a wisecrack to deflect.

"Of course, I worry," I say, dutifully ignoring the nurse remark. "I'd be a pretty shitty friend if I didn't."

He cocks an eyebrow. "You're not a shitty friend; you're the *best* friend."

The liquid in my stomach swirls. I've only taken a few sips, but I can already feel the burn. Right now, I'd prefer that burn over the one on my face. The way Theo's looking at me, appraising my body like I'm a piece of art, is making my cheeks redder than the lipstick I want him to kiss right off me. "Yep. Key word being *friend*."

I'm not sure I've ever thought about a friend while using my vibrator, but there's a first time for everything.

"C'mon, Jos," he says with an amused laugh. "You're going to stand there and tell me the sex wasn't amazing? We both know it was."

"I don't remember," I lie. My cheeks reach tomato-like proportions, and I untangle our fingers, suddenly hyperaware that my palms are sweating. What the hell are we even doing holding hands? Friends don't hold hands, unless the other one is so drunk they need help walking. "We were drunk."

"Not drunk enough to ignore how good our chemistry is in bed, angel. Though, I'm than happy to prove you wrong and have a re-do while sober. I think we'll enjoy ourselves immensely." He leans back against the bar, propping up an elbow. "It's not like we won't be friends just because we have sex."

Sex with Theo won't necessarily ruin our friendship, but it will change our dynamic in some way—it already has. I can't even look at him without imagining his lips grazing my neck or the muscles in his back flexing as he thrust into me.

I ping-pong my gaze around the room to avoid eye contact. "You know what else I enjoy? Appetizers. Have you seen a server passing any out? Man, I could go for a flatbread right now. One with fig, goat cheese, and honey would be divine."

"You'll cave eventually, Bancroft," Theo promises. A cold thrill goes down my spine as he trails his fingers against my exposed skin, almost taunting me to whimper. Tonight was not the night to wear a backless dress. "I have a great dick. Some have even called it 'more than adequate.'"

I'd like to bury myself in a cave and not come out for about eighty years, so Theo's "great dick" will be wrinkly and completely undesirable. I notice Lucas walking by and latch onto his arm like an octopus. Nothing like a cock-block decked out in Gucci.

"Lucas! Hi!" My voice is so enthusiastic that he stumbles back a step. "Great race earlier! Congrats on the win."

Pink accentuates the taut angle of his high cheekbones. Lucas is a rare breed of Formula 1 drivers: he's humble to a fault, always congratulating everyone else before accepting praise on his own behalf. Theo and Blake tease him mercilessly about his aversion to talking about his successes.

"Thanks, Jos." He runs his hand through his styled hair and shoots me a beyond-adorable grin. Moving his eyes to Theo, he says, "Tough break out there today, man."

"Shit happens," Theo concedes with a shrug. "Could've been worse."

"Yeah. You could have a sore shoulder that makes you

wince in pain anytime you move it." I shoot Theo a cheerful smile. "And we wouldn't want that, would we?"

The shadow of a frown appears. *Point for Josie.*

The two of them chat about the race, discussing the impressive second place podium win a Catalyst driver secured. I scoot closer to Lucas, causing Theo's hand to land back on the table with a soft *thud*. Avoiding any direct physical contact with him is the only way I can, hopefully, keep my common sense from turning into an insatiable craving. But the issue with cravings is that they don't just go away because you think they should, and I've been craving Theo more than a double-scoop of chocolate chip cookie dough ice cream with gummy bears on top.

11

THEO

THE MONACO GRAND PRIX is the slowest and toughest race to win. It's also one of the highest-pressure races since you've got everyone from Sebastian Stan to Serena Williams in the paddock, watching and waiting for you to either cock up or win. What's ironic is that the Monaco track isn't super exciting for the drivers. There are virtually no areas to pass or overtake —it's not impossible, but it's rare. Unless a crash occurs, a pit stop goes horribly wrong, or something happens with your car, the grid formation stays consistent throughout the race.

As the lights go out, I unleash my power unit's full torque, giving me enough muscle in my rear wheels to maintain my P2 position as we head into the first lap. Besides a few upsets during the race—Blake's tires wore heavily during the final few laps and my engine nearly overheated—McAllister secures two podium wins. Blake may be my teammate and friend, but it sure as hell feels nice to come ahead of him every once in a while, even if it's only by 2.17 seconds.

The celebrations have already begun by the time I shower and change. I bounce around to a few yacht parties before ending my night at the annual Dom Perignon after-party. It's so exclusive that they don't even reveal the address of the event until an hour before it starts. Not every driver gets a de facto invitation, so it's always a crap shoot who will be there. McAllister, and now AlphaVite, are the only teams with a standing invitation for their employees.

This year's party is being held at a massive estate on the outskirts of Monaco. I have no idea who currently owns the property, but I'm almost positive Elton John did at one point.

I make my way through the twists and turns of the expansive home, passing marble statues of women holding jugs and egregiously expensive art that looks like it was drawn with crayon. When I finally make it to the backyard, I'm greeted by the quiet drip of an ice sculpture and the blaring sound of animated conversations. Hollywood directors sip on good quality wine while models and actresses take selfies and mingle underneath the charming lanterns scattered across the party.

I mill around, chitchatting and accepting congratulations on my win, before spotting Lucas and Harry tucked away at a corner bar.

"Evening gentlemen," I greet as I order a cocktail from the bartender.

Lucas barely gets a "hello" in before Thompson is talking my ear off. It's his third Formula 1 season, but his first year at this party and shell-shocked doesn't begin to cover it. His cheeks are flushed baby pink with excitement, and his amber eyes light up like a carnival ride as he spots celebrity after celebrity.

"Is that Sydney Sweeney?" he guffaws as the *Euphoria* actress waltzes past us. His jaw is nearly touching Lucas's Valentino slides. "I'm ninety-nine percent sure it is. I've had a crush on her since… well, forever."

A knowing grin pastes itself on my face as I sip my cocktail. The glitz and glam of Formula 1 hasn't jaded him in the slightest. He's just happy to be here. It doesn't hurt that he worships the ground Lucas walks on, giving my friend a nice confidence boost.

"You should go talk to her," Lucas encourages. "I'm sure she's impressed with your driving today."

"Yeah?" Thompson tears his gaze away from Ms. Sweeney. The way his body angles toward Lucas in a bid for approval is sweet. "You think so?"

I nod. "Hell, even I'm impressed."

Harry downs the rest of his drink and looks at us with the confidence only a twenty-four-year-old with just a few seasons under his belt has. "If you'll excuse me, gentlemen."

"He's precious," I tease Lucas, nudging him with my elbow. "He's like your puppy."

"Ha, ha, ha." Lucas flips me the bird. "You're just jealous you don't have a groupie."

"Technically, I do," I say back. "Blake's low-key super obsessed with me."

My driving partner's been parked at a nearby table with his manager, Keith, talking about God knows what. If the devil works hard and Kris Jenner works harder, then Keith works the hardest of all. That man is legendary and manages some of the top athletes in the world. He offered me representation when I first joined Formula 1, but I didn't want to sign with the same person as Blake. The two of us compete enough, so the last thing I needed was to compete for a manager's attention, too.

"Where's his better half?" I ask, realizing I haven't seen Ella all night. Or Josie, for that matter.

"Talking to Zach Lavine."

I tilt my head. "Who's that?"

"He plays for the Bulls," Lucas says, as if that points me in the right direction. "Chicago's basketball team."

Ah. The only American sports teams I know are from Boston. The Red Sox, Braves, Celtics, Bruins, and finally, the

New England Patriots. Lucas is from Massachusetts, and his hometown team loyalty runs deep.

"Oh, that's cool."

Lucas takes my comment to mean I want to hear about this Lavine fellow's career stats and highlights. I half-listen to what he's saying for the next thirty minutes before excusing myself to the bathroom. Josie is still nowhere to be seen, so I shoot her a text as I make my way past a group of models reapplying their lipgloss.

THEO WALKER

> Where are you, princess? Want to see your gorgeous face.

JOSIE BANCROFT

I'm looking for umbrella!

Walking out of the bathroom, I head down the spiral staircase that leads back outside to the party. It's a gorgeous night, with diamond-like stars breaking through the midnight-blue sky. There is absolutely no need for an umbrella.

THEO WALKER

> It's not raining.

JOSIE BANCROFT

For a drink. Cute baby umbrella.

A voice memo follows her latest text, featuring a slurred version of Rihanna and Jay Z's "Umbrella."

THEO WALKER

> You want a drink umbrella? Why?

JOSIE BANCROFT

Yes. And purple.

THEO WALKER

> Purple? You're not making any sense, angel.

JOSIE BANCROFT

> Do u have a purple lighter?

If I had a suspicion that Josie was drunk before, this confirms it. Her pet peeve is when people don't type out the full word. "U" instead of "you," "R" instead of "are." According to her, unless you're disassembling a bomb or at a funeral, there's no reason you can't spend an extra five seconds to type out the entire word. I once texted her "thx, u 2," and she threatened to block my number.

JOSIE BANCROFT

> NVM. Located.

THEO WALKER

> Why do you need a purple lighter and a drink umbrella?

I wait for three little dots to appear to indicate she's typing, but they don't show up. It's another two hours until I spot her. The white sequined mini dress she's wearing hugs her figure in a way that makes me jealous.

She's chatting with Russell and Sam—Blake's performance coach—waving her arms wildly as she talks. Both men are laughing at whatever she's saying and a jolt of jealously slithers down my neck. Russell's no worry, but Sam? He's a single, handsome dude in his thirties, who's looking at Josie the same way I do—with intense attraction. *Nope. No, thank you, kind sir.*

"'Ello, gorgeous," I say, sidling up next to Josie. Turning to the two men, I nod. "Russell. Sam."

"Walker!" Josie squeals loudly. "Hi!"

Just then, the song the DJ is playing switches to a remix that Josie must like because, without a word, she's dragging me to the packed dance floor at the edge of the lawn. *Bye, Russell. Bye, Sam.* The hanging lights above us change color, pulsing to the music. Sweaty bodies are pressed together, but the only one

I'm focused on is Josie's. She's grinding against me like we're at a Vegas strip club and I won't pay up unless she performs. *Fuck, I want her.* Despite the drinks I've had, my dick is hard and ready to party.

"Your eyes are beautiful," Josie tells me, her words slurring together. She snakes her hand up and around the back of my neck, and my heart skips a beat when she presses her forehead against mine. "Like the ocean."

Lust swells inside my chest as she runs her nails against my scalp. It doesn't take a detective to figure out how drunk she really is. Her lips are so close to mine, I can almost taste the vodka on them. This is way more than a buzz; this is blackout. Her eyes are glazed over, her movements sloppy and loose.

"I think we should head back to the hotel," I announce, channeling the maturity of my inner-Lucas. Josie needs water and her bed. I fucking detest vomit, but I'd rather she do it in the privacy of a hotel bathroom than at an elite, private party.

She responds by leaning forward and tracing her tongue against my lower lip. My vision momentarily goes blurry. No one's paying any attention to us, but the boldness of her actions surprise me. Someone went from "we can't ruin the friendship" to "let me lick your lips in public" very quickly. If she wasn't so drunk, I'd be thrilled.

I gingerly remove her hands from my neck. "C'mon."

"To your room," she clarifies.

"To my room," I repeat dumbly.

"Mm-hmm." Her lips brush against my neck, leaving a trail of kisses. "Then I want you to fuck me until my throat's sore from screaming your name."

Excuse me? All the blood rushes from my head and goes straight to my dick. I'm getting harder by the minute. I don't even realize I've stopped dancing until Josie swats at my hip.

"You're drunk, Jos," I finally say. Almost all her body

weight falls against me. I'm pretty sure if I took a step back, she'd tumble to the ground like a wilted flower. "Very drunk."

"I was drunk the last time we slept together," she points out.

Fair fucking point. But we were both drunk then, and right now, she's hammered and I'm tipsy at best. As much as I want to spend the night between her legs, she's not in the right state of mind to make that decision. If we sleep together again, she's going to be dead sober so she can damn well remember me making her come, over and over and over again.

"Well, if you're still horny tomorrow, we can discuss it then."

"I will be," she says without hesitation. She leans forward like she's about to tell me a secret. "I get wet just thinking about you fucking me with your perfect co—"

"Nope!" I practically shout. I need her to stop speaking before the tent in my pants becomes too obvious. "Let's get you to bed. We can talk there."

"Your bed?" A small frown plays on her lips. I love how she's looking at me like I'm a present waiting to be unwrapped.

"Sure, Jos," I concede, not sure how else I'm going to convince her to leave. "You can sleep in my bed."

She mumbles something about how we won't be doing much sleeping, but I tune her out and stay focused on getting her out of here in one piece. Wrapping my arm around her waist to keep her upright, I walk us toward the front of the party. If I wasn't worried about Josie toppling over, I'd enjoy the envious looks of every male we pass. Are they surprised I'm pulling the hottest chick here? Well, I would be pulling her if I wasn't quite literally pulling her into an Uber.

The ride back to the hotel is a testament to my willpower. Josie wasn't kidding when she said she wanted me. I momentarily blackout when she tells me she got herself off thinking about us having sex. I didn't know such dirty words could come out of someone with such a sweet smile, but I do know that my blue balls may kill me.

Josie's stripping the moment we're in the privacy of my hotel room. "Unzip me, please."

At least she's a polite drunk.

She piles her hair on the top of her head and waits for me to do as she asks. I quickly slide down the zipper, fighting off the urge to skim my fingertips down the curve of her spine. I hand her a clean shirt from my suitcase, desperately keeping my eyes trained on the wall behind her and not the teardrop shape of her breasts. When I'm certain she's dressed, I finally look at her. She's staring at me with a frown, her lower lip jutting out. It's the sexiest goddamn pout I've ever seen.

"You don't want to have sex with me anymore," she says in a resigned voice. "Why?"

"Of course I do, Josie." I sigh. I cannot believe I'm having this argument. "Why do *you* want to have sex with *me*?"

Besides the fact that I'm extremely handsome, wildly hilarious, and talented as hell, of course.

"You're my favorite banana."

I tilt my head, unsure how a conversation about us having sex has anything to do with a banana. Josie hates bananas; she stares at them like they're the reincarnation of an evil spirit. "Um, okay. Good for me, I suppose."

Josie starts mumbling the chorus of "Good 4 U," which adds zero clarification. I walk over to the mini fridge and pull out a water bottle that probably costs ninety bucks. Handing the bottle over to Josie, I watch as she slowly takes a few sips. She's going to be miserable tomorrow morning when she wakes up to a mariachi band performing inside her brain.

After drinking half of the bottle, Josie wipes her mouth with the back of her hand. "Do *you* like bananas?"

I let out a confused laugh. "Yes."

"What kind?"

Maybe I'm more drunk than I thought, because the look Josie's giving me makes me feel like an idiot for not understanding what in the bloody hell she's talking about. Is there more than one type of banana? Does she mean ripe versus unripe?

"We can revisit this conversation in the morning," I suggest, because I'm too tired and confused to dig for more.

I strip down to just my briefs before leading Josie to the bed. She snuggles into the quality comforter and eight-hundred-thread-count bedsheets. No, the hotel doesn't provide Egyptian cotton sheets and a newly dry-cleaned duvet. I bring my own because the thought of random people having slept in this same bed just a week ago makes my insides squirm.

"Theo?" Josie mumbles a few minutes later.

"Yeah, Jos?"

When she doesn't answer right away, I assume she's fallen asleep, but then I hear her tired voice. "You're my favorite."

A curious flutter stirs in the pit of my stomach at her words. Soft, deep breathing indicates that the alcohol has lured Josie into dreamland so there's no need for me to respond. I'm not sure if I'm relieved or disappointed she didn't get to hear that she's my favorite, too.

12

THEO

JOSIE WAKES me up at the goddamn arse crack of dawn by aggressively tapping my shoulder. I barely slept last night because she kept tossing and turning, accidentally rubbing against me, so I burrow deeper under the covers and ignore her. This doesn't deter her. Instead, she just sneaks back under the covers and continues to poke me.

"May I help you?" I mumble, keeping my eyes shut.

"Did we have sex?" Her voice is raspy, adding another level to her sex appeal. "Or did I just wake up wearing your T-shirt for fun?"

My eyes fly open but it's dark, so I push the covers down. Josie's honey blonde hair cascades around her shoulders and her pouty lips part in anticipation. The covers are over my waist so she can't see my morning wood, but there's no chance it's going away anytime soon with her... well, with her existing. Especially in my bed, wearing my shirt, giving me *that* look.

"For fun," I confirm reluctantly. "You tried to sleep with me, though. Said you wanted to lick every inch of me like a lollipop."

She buries her head into a pillow. "That's mortifying."

"It was sexy as hell," I reassure her. "I had to jerk off at two a.m. just to give myself some relief."

"I don't need to know those sorts of details, Theo."

"It's only fair since you told me you get yourself off to the memory of us having sex." There's no keeping the satisfied smirk from my face. That little nugget of information does wonders for one's ego.

"Please check my pulse because there's a chance I may die of embarrassment."

I place two fingers on her inner wrist. "You're alive and well, baby."

"I may be alive, but I am definitely not well," she grumbles. "I hope you know there's no chance of me licking you like a lollipop this morning."

"What about this afternoon?" I trail my fingers up and down her back. "I'm a patient man."

Liar, liar, pants on fire.

The noise she makes is half-grunt, half-groan. "The mere thought of a dick is making me nauseous, so no."

Well, at least she won't be sleeping with anyone else, either. Not that I have any claim over her or anything. I'm the one who told her she should be sowing her wild oats and sleeping around now that she's single. I wish there was a Brita filter for brains to stop all the stupid shit from coming out of my mouth.

"You were pretty drunk last night, Miss Bancroft," I tease softly. "What, the twinkling lights of Monaco got to that pretty little head of yours?"

She makes some sort of grumbling noise. "The damn scavenger hunt."

Ahhh. That explains the purple lighter and drink umbrella at least. "What scavenger hunt?"

Josie lifts her head and stares at me. "We play every year,

Walker. You just usually get wasted and leave with some wannabe influencer forty minutes into the party."

Ouch. She's not wrong, though. Last year I slept with some bat-shit crazy girl Blake had fucked way back when, then passed out in Leo DiCaprio's yacht afterward. You know I'm hammered when I double-dip into Blake's dirty laundry.

"Who plays?"

"The teams are different every year, but it's usually people from marketing, operations, engineering, and a few finance guys."

How have I never heard of this scavenger hunt? Why aren't the drivers invited to play? Blake's not exactly Mr. Party People, but I'm the dictionary definition of a good time. Which probably explains why Josie wanted to sleep with me last night.

"The list is on my phone if you want to see what else we had to find," she tells me, shutting her eyes. "My passcode's one-one-two-one."

"Your birthday? Seriously?" I scoff. "You don't even like your birthday!"

"It's easy to remember."

"It's also easy to hack, princess."

She reopens one of her eyes to glare at me. "Unlike you, I don't keep nudes on my phone. If someone wants to hack me, all they'll find is food porn, endless playlists, and a grocery list."

We'll see about that. I grab her phone from the bedside table, where it's been charging all night. *You're welcome*. My eyes zero in on the text messages on the screen. It's not snooping since these just so happen to be here.

ANDREW CAFFREY

Saw you on TV! It was a great race.

WES (THE BEST COWORKER EVER)

> Can we boycott champagne for the rest of the
> season? There's a man in my bed and I can't
> remember his name...

The text from Wes makes sense, but the text from Andrew, not so much. Why is he still texting her like they're friends or some shit?

I try to ignore the heat prickling my skin as I read through the scavenger hunt list. Purple lighter. Two signed business cards. *Are Josie and Andrew getting back together?* Cocktail umbrella. Two different brands of beer caps. *It's none of my business if they are. It's not like I know shit about relationships.* One monogrammed flask. *Fuck that. Yes, it is my business. I'm her friend.* Photo licking the ice sculpture. Wine label from the nineties. *But if we're just friends, then why does the thought of her getting back together with her ex make me so mad? If we're just friends, then why can't I stop thinking about her day and night?* Selfie with a celebrity holding up something that says McAllister. Three different colored stirrer sticks. *Don't overthink, Theo.* Mini dry shampoo. Baby blue scrunchie.

"Some of these are hard," I note when I've finished reading the items.

"Mm-hmm," she mumbles. "Losers have to chug a bottle of Dom."

I toss Josie her phone, but she just watches it land by her hand, making no move to grab it. Her eyelids flutter, trying to stay open and fight off the extra hour or two of sleep her body wants. It's clear she's too tired for much of a conversation, but she's in my bed and I love pillow talk—it's my second favorite kind of conversation after dirty talk. Curling up on my side, I tuck my knees up so they're grazing hers.

"I'm sorry you lost, princess."

She opens her eyes to look at me and the muscles in my throat tighten. "I won."

"Oh?"

She buries her face into my chest. Mumbled words flow out of her mouth, but I can't understand a single one. Tilting her chin up, I politely ask her to slow down.

She twirls my chest hair with her fingers before finally saying, "My trip got cancelled."

"Your trip? What trip?"

Josie glances up through thick lashes. "Promise you won't freak out?"

"If you're going to a sex show in Amsterdam without me, I'll most certainly—"

"Not Amsterdam."

"Because you promised me," I remind her.

"You will be the one to accompany me to an infamous sex show. I know, Walker. Promise still stands."

I brush away a piece of hair that's fallen against her cheek. "So why would I freak out?"

"Just tell me you won't," she says.

The questions rattle around in my head like loose change in a piggy bank as I nod.

She exhales deeply. "I was going to Le Mans after the French Grand Prix."

My legs jerk in surprise, banging against Josie's. Her face crumples in discomfort, so I rub my hand against her silky-smooth thigh in apology. So much for hoping my morning wood goes away anytime soon.

"You were finally going to go?" I stammer out. I've been encouraging Josie to visit her birth city for years, but she's always brushed it off, saying it'll happen eventually.

"Yes," she says simply. "Finally felt ready to."

Josie doesn't talk about her adoption a lot, if ever. The fact that she's technically French never fails to blow my mind. The only reason her British parents adopted a baby from France is because they first met in Paris and her mum wanted to "adopt a child that was conceived in the same country their love was conceived in." Hence, their *un petite croissant*—her mum's words, not mine—is a byproduct of the world's most romantic country.

"That's amazing, Jos," I murmur. "I'm so proud of you."

"Well, I'm not going anymore," she states. "So, the only thing that's amazing is the fact that I'm not puking my brains out after drinking my body weight in champagne."

"Why aren't you going anymore?"

She curls her hands between the pillow and her cheek. "The AirBnB I was supposed to stay at accidentally double-booked themselves, and I don't feel like paying an arm and a leg to find another accommodation this late in the game. Plus, I found out the guy I bought the ticket from is some sort of scam artist. I even double-checked to make sure he was legit, but apparently, I didn't look hard enough. That's what I get for buying something through a Facebook group." She sighs deeply. "Not the end of the world. I can always go next year."

"But you wanted to go this year."

"Yes, but it's not like I'm expecting to run into my birth mum walking down the street. Another year of waiting to go won't kill me."

The softness of her voice pulls at my heartstrings. The overwhelming urge to wrap her in my arms and hide her away from the world is so intense that I forget to breathe. I sneak her hand away from the pillow and intertwine our fingers, liking the intimacy of having her this close. "It's a possibility, though. If I went with you, I'd be able to pick your mum out of a crowd immediately."

Josie raises her eyebrows. "I highly doubt that."

"Genetics are the only reasonable explanation for your amazing ass," I inform her. "And I'd recognize your backside in a lineup, nine out of ten times, babe."

Her pink tongue shoots out at me. "What is it with boys and butts?"

Wrapping my arm around her waist, I pull her flush against me. Warm legs tangle together like a pretzel, but my body breaks out in goosebumps.

"Boy? Baby, I'm all *man*." Trapped between us is my hardness, desperate for attention it's not going to receive. Given her provocative performance last night, I know she's still horny, and this *man* has no intention of letting her forget it.

"Only boys have to convince women they're men." Josie challenges me with a look of deliberate nonchalance. Once again, my willpower to not devour her lips in kisses that'll make her writhe is tested. "I'm going to go back to bed, but if you need to relieve yourself in the bathroom again, feel free to do so. Will you wake me up in an hour or so?"

She shoots me a tired smile before burrowing underneath the comforter and turning so I'm spooning her with my hard-as-concrete dick nestled against her ass. *Yup.* Definitely going to relieve myself. I hear a soft giggle from the bed as I make my way to the bathroom.

Cheeky, cheeky woman.

"Hey, Jos?" I ask before shutting the door to shower.

"Mm-hmm?"

"I feel weird even having to ask this, but do you suddenly like bananas or something?"

"No." She lifts her head and makes a face. "I still think they're gross."

Interesting…

Josie's already fallen back asleep by the time I've showered, so I grab my phone from the nightstand and head into the sitting area. There's a text from Jenna. *Shit.*

JENNA (FROM BERLIN)

I'm in town next week. You around?

For the first time in forever, the idea of having sex with Jenna sounds… meh. My cock doesn't twitch in anticipation or do a happy dance, especially not when there's a sweet blonde sound asleep in my bed.

THEO WALKER

Nah, I'll be in France for the Grand Prix.

At least I don't have to lie to her. I lay down on the couch in the suite's sitting room, but instead of checking Instagram—aka my normal morning routine—I text Martin to see what connections he has in Le Mans.

13

JOSIE

A SWIRLING LAYER of clouds interrupts the sunny weather of Marseilles, France. I slip my sunglasses onto my head, the glaring sun no longer making me squint. It's a few hours away from qualifying, but I cross my fingers that any undesirable weather stays away so McAllister has a successful qualifier. The Circuit Paul Ricard has traditionally been a McAllister stronghold, with Blake and Theo taking first and second place victories in each edition the past few years. But this year, Harry Thompson's impressive practices have spectators pegging him to take pole, so the pressure is on.

I'm up on the rooftop of the motorhome finishing some work when my phone rings. I groan when I see it's my mum calling because I really don't want to talk about my cancelled trip to Le Mans. Does it suck that I was finally doing something for myself, only for it to tatter quicker than an old blanket? Yes. But the race happens every year. I'll go next year. Maybe.

Knowing she'll phone the police if I don't get pick up or call her back in the next hour or so, I bite the bullet and answer. Her sing-song voice greets me almost immediately.

"Hello, my darling. How's Marseille?" She pronounces the

city name in a near-perfect French accent. A perk of being bilingual and having lived in Paris for a bit. *"Beau et étonnant?"*

I laugh. "Speaking to me in French is not going to make me magically understand it."

We all have our strengths, but learning languages is not one of mine. I accepted this years ago, although it seems my mother has not, as she still insists on sneaking in French phrases here or there to see if I've miraculously become fluent.

"Context clues, Josephine," she clucks jokingly. I cringe at her use of my full name. *Josephine Violet Bancroft.* It sounds hoity-toity, like it should belong to a long-dead poet who wrote about her adulteress husband or one of Marie Antoinette's ladies-in-waiting. It's the reason I exclusively go by Josie. According to my mum, if she wanted to call me Josie, she would have put that on my birth certificate instead of Josephine.

"Yeah, yeah," I mumble. "Marseille is good, though. Did Dad watch the practice earlier?"

My dad may not understand what I do for a living—I'm pretty sure he thinks I just scroll through Instagram all day—but he's insanely proud, nonetheless. He watches every practice, qualifying round, and race, not because he loves Formula 1, but so he can try to spot me anywhere in the background. He's managed to locate me a few times and then proceeds to text his friends to brag.

"He hasn't left the recliner all morning," she tells me.

I chuckle. "Tell him I'm in a white McAllister shirt and flower-patterned skirt."

"I'll let him know. And I'm sorry about Le Mans, love," my mum says, her voice softening. "Maybe we'll go on a family trip there over the summer?"

If you go to Le Mans, you go for the 24 Heures du Mans endurance race. The city is great, but if you can be there during what's considered one of the world's most prestigious races, you do. No questions asked.

"It's okay, Mum. Really," I reassure her. "I appreciate it, but honestly, it's not that big of a deal."

It's not that I want to go alone, but I also don't want to make my parents uncomfortable. They're the most important people in my life, and the last thing I want is for them to feel as if I'm going there to look for something they couldn't provide.

She sighs as if she doesn't quite believe me, but lets it go. We catch up for a few more minutes with my mum telling me about a seminar she's attending in Brugge next week. It's called "Sexual Health is Mental Health," and there's supposed to be some new exfoliating lube—whatever that means—in the welcome bags. Never fear, she's more than happy to pass it along to me so I can "experiment."

Ending the call, I head down to the pit garage to get some action shots of the drivers preparing for qualifying round. The rest of the afternoon is a swirl of commotion and camaraderie with Blake and Theo maintaining McAllister's streak of placing pole and second on the grid, respectively.

On race day, I wake up early so I can grab breakfast at the motorhome before I start my day. I'm scrolling through Instagram and eating a buttered croissant when Theo bursts into the cafeteria. The energy of the room is sleepy until his arrival. For someone who doesn't drink coffee very often, Theo always has an abundance of energy. I need at least half of a latte in the morning to even understand the English language, and I need a full latte to speak it.

"I have exciting news," he announces. Placing himself in the seat next to me, he turns his body so our knees are touching.

My entire body flushes at the minute contact. What is this physical response I have to him? His proximity reminds my body of each day I haven't had his hands, breath, lips, on it. It's obnoxious how good-looking he is. Really fucking obnoxious. "You won a lot of points at *Call of Duty*?"

Theo groans loudly, the sound sending heatwaves from my nipples to my other erogenous zones. *What is wrong with me?* Clearly my lady parts are not on the same wavelength as my brain. I need to have a team meeting so my body stops this insane urge to jump Theo's bones whenever he's within a meter of me. Thank God he was gentlemanly enough not to sleep with me when I drunkenly threw myself at him. I'm like a cat in heat with this ridiculous urge to rub my body all over him. Is it normal to react to someone like this? Simply from being in the same space as them?

"You don't win points at COD, princess," he explains slowly. "Well, you do, but it's a currency, not indicating that you're winning or whatever."

I roll my eyes. "Just be happy I know the names of some of your favorite games, babes."

"Name a few."

Well, shit. I didn't think he was going to call me out like that. Um. "*World of War…* or whatever, something like that. *Super Mario Kart, Minecraft…* um, *Halo?*"

"Who needs porn when I can just record you saying, '*World of War* whatever?'" Theo laughs.

I lower my voice to what I hope is a sultry tone. "Can I interest you in a game of *Mario Party?*"

Theo clutches his sides as he laughs. I swear I'd do cart-wheels in my knickers to keep hearing that chuckle. "You trying to seduce me again, Bancroft?"

The emphasis he puts on *again* is not lost on me. "Why do you think I'm trying to seduce you? Because I want to play with your joystick?"

I watch as the pupils of his expressive blue eyes expand ever so slightly, indicating the effect my words have on him. *Shit.* Why did I have to say something like that? I am not this openly flirtatious, especially not with someone whose joystick is something I've been trying to purposefully *not* play with.

Grabbing my coffee from the table, I take a large sip. It's still burning hot, scalding off at least one layer of taste buds, but I need something to cover my lips so he can't see the look of pure horror I'm struggling to contain.

"I'm kidding, Theo," I reassure him moments later when he's still staring at me with undisguised lust. "Drunkenly seducing you in Monaco was a moment of weakness."

A moment of weakness where I told Theo I wanted to suck him like a Tootsie Pop.

He leans his head down, the smell of his cologne invading my personal space, swirling around me in an intoxicating cloak. "Are you saying I'm your weakness, Bancroft?"

"No," I say. *Liar, liar, pants on fire.* "You're… a devil on my shoulder."

"I may be a devil," his lips brush against my ear, his hot breath sending a shiver up my spine, "but you're an angel who so desperately wants to sin."

My chest swells with desire, each breath I take aching independently of the other. I want to taste his lips, swirl my tongue around his mouth, and suck the air right out of his lungs. But that's not something *friends* do. "So, what's the exciting news you have?"

Theo leans back, a smile still playing on his face. He slams papers down on the table, causing my coffee to slosh over the rim of my travel mug. The edges of the papers get stained by the spilled drink, so I quickly pick them up.

"Wait!" He grabs the papers from my hands, clutching them to his chest like I'm going to snatch them away. "Don't. No touching!"

He taps his fingers against the table, taking his sweet time. I roll my eyes at his theatrical performance to build up tension. "Oh, go on then, Walker. No need for dramatics."

Theo sets the papers down once again, but this time, motions for me to pick them up. The first page is a booking confirmation for a four-day stay at a Le Mans hotel with a fancy French name. The second page is an email from Martin with details about a trackside suite to watch the 24 Hueres du Mans. The final few pages are articles on the top sites to see and the best restaurants the city has to offer.

Once I've shuffled through the pages no less than four times, I put them down and fix my eyes on Theo, my eyes widening in confusion. "What is this?"

"We're going to Le Mans."

"I don't understand." My voice is coated in astounded disbelief and the frequency of my blinks makes me feel like I'm twitching. "How?"

"I made it happen. I'm a smarty pants, Bancroft." He flashes me a smile that melts my insides like ice cream on a summer day. "Didn't you know?"

"You thought the phrase was 'the ghost is clear' instead of 'the coast is clear' up until last year." Toying with the wispy tendrils of my hair, I shoot him a skeptical look. "And still can't correctly pronounce *gnocchi*."

He ignores me, continuing to smile adorably. "You can't say no because I already got your time off approved."

"You *what*?"

"I told Rhys I needed social media assistance and asked if he could spare you," he says coolly. "You're good to go."

"And he said yes?" My boss usually requires at least two weeks' notice for any time off to make sure the team has proper coverage. "He believed you?"

Theo tilts his head and grins. "You do realize I make McAllister millions every year, right? Of course he said yes."

"But I'm not going to be working," I point out. "Won't they know?"

"Are you going to narc on yourself?" Theo laughs. "It's okay to break the rules occasionally, angel. We can take some photos at the race if it'll make you feel better."

I nod in awestruck wonder, too overwhelmed to get out a word. The most illegal thing I've ever done is park my car in a fifteen-minute spot for over an hour, so it does indeed make me feel better.

Theo drums his fingers against the table, completely unfazed by my silence. "I made you a playlist, by the way. I'll text it over in a bit."

He says something else, but I'm lost in my own thoughts. I'm going to Le Mans. With Theo. *Oh my God.* I'm only aware of him departing because he buries his lips on the top of head. The lyrics of Taylor Swift's song "Don't Blame Me" float through my head. If Theo's a drug, I'm about ready to open my own damn pharmacy.

A few minutes later, my phone buzzes with a text from Theo. I immediately open it, curious to see what songs he chose for a playlist. He doesn't have bad taste in music, but he tends to gravitate strictly to classic rock and R&B.

playlist for a princess
a playlist by Theo Walker

I Want You to Want Me | Letters to Cleo
Can You | Gooch
Take Off Ur Pants | Indigo De Souza
So I Can | DJ Nas'D
Fuck You | Cee Lo Green
Nice & Slow | Usher
When We | Tank
F**K | The Code
I Wanna Make You Scream | Battalion of Saints
I Want To | Rosenfeld
Rock Your Body | Justin Timberlake
THATS WHAT I WANT | Lil Nas X
I Am | Baby Tate ft. Flo Milli
Craving You | Thomas Rhett, Maren Morris
Baby | Justin Bieber
Come On Over (All I Want Is You) | Christina Aguilera
Yes | Beyoncé
Or Nah | Ty Dolla $ign ft. The Weeknd

It takes me a moment to realize the song titles spell out a message. I suck in air through my teeth, feeling warmth between my legs. I'm an adult, right? I know how to draw boundaries, don't I? Theo is walking, talking sex, so I should be able to enjoy that without letting it affect our friendship, right?

Before I can second guess myself, I quickly put together a playlist for him, choosing the songs so easily, it's like my mind already knew what it wanted to say. I can picture Theo, wherever he is, getting flustered by my response. And God, it turns me on.

walk(er) on the wild side
a playlist by Josie Bancroft

You Right | Doja Cat ft. The Weeknd
Sex with Me | Rihanna
Good as Hell | Lizzo
No Wonder | Barbra Streisand
I Got You | Bebe Rexha
Beggin' | Måneskin
I Don't Wanna | Aaliyah
Fuck Up The Friendship | Leah Kate
Might Be | DJ Luke Nasty
Damned If I Do Ya (Damned If I Don't) | All Time Low
My Answer | Nathan Bell
Maybe | KIDLAROI
XO | Beyoncé
Josie | blink182

Making playlists has always been my way to capture what I'm feeling: sad, happy, confused, angry, betrayed, content. I've never made one for this feeling, though, this out-of-body experience of aching for someone to the point where my core is pulsating without any direct physical contact. It's a new feeling, and I'm not sure if I want to kick myself or dive headfirst and let it consume me.

14

JOSIE

"WELCOME TO LE MANS, PRINCESS," Theo says as we touch down in my birth city.

A smile brings up the corners of my mouth and stays there for the duration of the day. The first thing I notice as we make our way to the hotel is how alive the city is. The sidewalks are packed with pedestrians as police officers guide them through crosswalks because the street closures have caused a buildup of traffic. Colorful street vendors park along the curbs, selling food and specialty items, while cafes leave their doors open to welcome in the influx of tourists. My eyes try to take in everything at once. I unroll the cab window and stick my head out like I'm a dog, enjoying the fresh air on my face as we barrel down an alleyway tucked between tall brick buildings.

"Can we go there?" I ask Theo as we pass a tiny restaurant with decorative lights strung up. Before he can answer, I'm pointing at something else with equal excitement. "Oh! Or what about there? That looks like a cute store."

"We have time, Jos," Theo reminds me with a chuckle. "We can go anywhere you want."

Rather than explore, our first two days in Le Mans are

spent in our safe space: a motorsport circuit. My fake tickets had been for general admission, which naturally, Theo balked at. That's why he had Martin secure us two VIP tickets—which, according to the website, cost about six months' worth of rent for me, and were also sold out and have been for a while.

Not only do we have our own private suite with panoramic views, but we have a dedicated service member to bring us premium catering and drinks from the open bar, and the option to do a helicopter ride over the track. A goddamn helicopter! Like this is the ancient ruins of Greece or something.

We spend time watching practices, meeting some drivers, and getting a tour of the paddock. Unlike the Formula 1 Grand Prix, which are fixed-distance races where the driver with the fastest time wins, the 24 Heures du Mans' winner is determined by the distance driven in twenty-four hours. The kicker? Racing teams must balance the demands of speed as well as the car's ability to run for that long without any mechanical issues. It tests man and machine to their absolute breaking points.

I've never watched a race with Theo. Hell, I've never watched a race that Theo wasn't racing in. The 24 Heures du Le Mans is a new experience in more ways than one because of that. He becomes my personal commentator, telling me about how they've changed the circuit over fourteen times, the four types of engine classifications these cars must have, how the debris from the roads effect the driver. The world sees Formula 1 drivers as insanely fast men who are talented at maneuvering their cars, but people forget just how much they know about the mechanics and engineering behind it, too.

Since this race is a once-in-a-lifetime opportunity for me, I insist on staying for all twenty-four hours of it. In usual Theo manner, he whines a bit, but doesn't put up too much of a fight. I doze off a few times in our suite but manage to catch most of the race. It makes me appreciate the two-hour time limit on the Formula 1 Grand Prix.

Getting a cab to take us back to our hotel proves impossible, so we decide to hoof it. My feet drag across the sidewalk, accidentally kicking stray trash that people have littered. We're halfway back when I stop dead in my tracks. *No fucking way.*

"Theo." I tug on his sleeve to get his attention since he's half asleep and acting like a zombie. "We have to go in here."

He peers in through the glass window of children's toy shop in front of us. "I guess I could get something for Rosalie's birthday."

Theo spoils the living hell out of his goddaughter. For her first birthday, he got her the cutest mini-Chanel bag I've ever seen in my life.

We walk in and are immediately surrounded by shelves lined with colorful board games, new innovative toys, and the latest and greatest in children's literature. It's every kid's dream and every parent's nightmare. I walk past it all, zoning in on the small shelf lined with fuzzy farm animals.

Standing on my tiptoes so I can reach, I carefully pull down a light pink piggy. It's not a large stuffed animal, fitting perfectly in my palm. Two beady eyes stare at me while a snout and a smile hover just underneath. I've never seen these stuffed animals anywhere in London—and yes, I've looked. My own childhood stuffed animal, Mademoiselle, used to be fuzzy and soft like this, but years of cuddles and washing machine trips have left her rather rugged looking. The plushie in my hand looks exactly like Mademoiselle did in the baby photos my parents have hanging around the house.

Theo places his calloused hand on the back of my neck, gently kneading out the tension that's sitting there. "Hey," he says softly. "You good?"

"Hmm?" I lift my head, meeting his piercing blue eyes. His forehead is etched with worry lines as he studies me. I'm sure I look like a proper idiot standing there with tears in my eyes, looking at a damn stuffed animal meant for those "ages 3+."

"Yeah," I say, giving him a small smile. "I'm good. Don't know what came over me."

Theo rubs the pad of his thumb against my cheek, wiping away a stray tear I didn't know was there. "You're crying."

"Tearing up," I correct him. My eyes get puffier than a bao bun when I cry. "Very different."

He narrows his eyes at me. "I don't like it."

"Well, I apologize." I laugh and wipe the skin underneath my eyes to get rid of any emotional evidence. "I used to have a stuffed animal just like this when I was a kid."

Under no circumstances am I revealing that Mademoiselle is still a permanent fixture in my life. I don't travel with her, but she's sitting on my stark white duvet, waiting for me to return from France.

"Yeah?" Theo picks up a stuffed elephant from the shelf, turning it around in his hands. "It's cute. From your parents?"

I shake my head. "Birth mum. I had her with me when my parents adopted me."

Theo squeezes the back of my neck in a comforting motion before putting the elephant back. I follow his lead and place Mademoiselle's twin back on the shelf in between a cow and squirrel.

"We can go now," I announce. "I just wanted to see that. It caught my eye."

I start walking toward the door before realizing Theo's not at my side. Turning back to look at him, he's holding up some sort of princess doll.

"Uh, Theo." I laugh. "You good?"

Theo stares at me as if I should already know the answer. "I haven't picked out anything for Rosalie's birthday yet."

"Oh, I forgot," I admit sheepishly. "Sorry."

Turning to the shop owner, he asks if they have a doll that

has the hair color of the one in his right hand, but wearing the dress of the one in his left hand. As he tries to juggle a third doll in his hand, he says, "You can head outside if you need some air, eh? I'll only be a minute."

In the past few days, Theo's done more for me than he'll ever realize. He's given me happy memories of a place that I've always kept in a shadowed part of my mind, too scared to bring it out into the light. If he wants to decide which princess doll to buy his goddaughter, he can take all the damn time in the world.

WE BOTH SLEEP—IN our separate rooms—for ten hours straight once we got back to the hotel after the race. Theo wakes up crabby and hangry, so we head to a nearby restaurant the hotel manager recommends, and the host leads us to a booth positioned against the window.

"There's got to be some joke about an Englishwoman and an Australian walking into a French restaurant," Theo says with a grin as we slide into the cushioned benches.

"If there's not, I'm sure you can think of something perfectly crude and inappropriate," I reassure him. My eyes light up as I scan the menu. "We should get escargot."

I feel Theo's eyes gaze at me from over the top of his over-sized menu. "You want to eat snails?"

Rolling my eyes, I correct him. "It's not *snail*, it's *escargot.*"

"Giving something a fancy name doesn't change what it is," Theo argues. "It's still a slimy land creature."

"Fortunately for us," I shake my head, "slimy land creature was too many words to fit on the menu."

"You'll eat *that*, but not bananas?"

I've always claimed I don't like the fruit because of the texture, so I see where his confusion lies. But I'm not admitting I've seen too many bananas covered in condoms to ever view them as edible. I flick up my left brow. "Says the guy who refuses to eat the left side of Twix bar."

He sticks his tongue out at me before disappearing back behind his menu. A well-dressed server approaches us to take our drink orders and, in a surprising turn of events, Theo agrees to split a bottle of wine with me.

"To a successful trip to Le Mans," he says, tapping his glass against mine.

"Agreed." I pray he can't see my cheeks flushing in the dim lighting. "Thank you for bringing me."

Theo nods before readjusting the silverware in front of him. "Can I ask you something personal?"

I nearly choke on my drink. Theo's never prefaced any sort of question with permission. He usually just asks me with no warning, leaving me stunned silent or clutching my stomach as I laugh. "Sure?"

He wiggles in his seat nervously. "Why'd you break up with Andrew?"

I'm surprised it's taken him this long to ask, given his propensity to play twenty-questions at any given moment.

"Why do you think I ended things?" I'm the one who panicked while seeing him at Blake's party. If I were Theo, I'd think Andrew broke up with me, not vice versa.

"Any bloke lucky enough to have you would be an absolute idiot to let you go."

A delicious warmth spreads through my body. His sweet words are the key that unlocks the details of my breakup. "When Andrew said he was ready to take the next step in our relationship and move in together, I was initially on board... but then we started talking about what I should bring."

Theo gasps. "And he told you *not* to bring your absurd amount of Tupperware?"

I take a long sip of my wine to buy myself some time. According to the sommelier who picked it out for us, there should be notes of vanilla and ginger. I'm getting notes of wood chips after a rainstorm.

Theo leans back in his seat. "Shit. I was messing with you, Jos. Did he really say that?"

"Not exactly." I sigh. "But when I was deciding what to keep and what to sell before the move, Andrew told me there was no need for me to bring *anything*."

Not my brightly colored floral plates I bought at a flea market with my mum. Not the mismatched mugs I've collected over the years traveling the world with McAllister. Not my cloud-like couch that's permanently dented from where I sit in the same place every time I binge-watch *MasterChef*. Why bring it when Andrew already has perfectly good dishes and a couch?

"It hit me that I was moving into *his* place, with *his* stuff, in *his* favorite neighborhood. Nothing would ever feel like mine, you know?"

I toy with the stem of my wineglass, twirling it between my pointer finger and thumb. Theo separates my hand from my new distraction and rubs his thumb against the soft inside of my palm. My tightly coiled muscles instantly relax at his touch. "I went full quarter-life crisis mode because it hit me that, if we moved in together, I'd lose myself even more," I admit. "I spent so much time prioritizing him instead of myself that I already felt lost. If we started living together, it'd just perpetuate the cycle of my life revolving around his. It made me realize I have no idea who I am when I'm not in a relationship. When it's just me, myself, and I."

Theo nods briefly before grinning at me with boyish charm. I don't miss the way the corners of his mouth twist up with mischief. "I can easily tell you who you are, princess."

"I'm not going to lie, I'm extremely nervous to hear your answer."

"Besides having the best arse and tit combination I've ever encountered," Theo says while leaning forward, "you're extremely self-aware, frighteningly so. You like music so much because it's a way to express how you're feeling when you can't find the right words yourself. You have a sweet smile with an even sweeter tooth, but you're sassy as hell when you feel comfortable with someone. You're also brilliant at your job, although I think you'd be damn good at any job. And despite what you think, you know yourself better than anyone."

I inhale deeply to anchor myself in this moment, right here and now. "I know about you, too."

Theo flicks up an eyebrow before flashing me a smile that could make any woman swoon. And this time, I am the woman who swoons at said smile. "Oi?"

"Mm-hmm." I nod slowly, now stroking the inside of his palm with my thumb. "You have an insane ability to make anyone feel instantly comfortable. You like to know things, not only because you're nosy, but because you want to understand people—what makes them tick; why they are the way they are. It's why you're so open. You're also extremely competitive, but whether you realize it or not, McAllister is more than just a team for you. It's a way for you to stay close to your dad and honor his memory."

The restaurant could set on fire and I don't think either of us would so much as flinch. The noise of side conversations, dishes clanking, servers listing specials—all of it fades away so the only thing I can hear is Theo's shallow breathing and my heart pumping against my ribs.

"I'm sorry you felt like you didn't know who you were," he says, breaking the silence. "But I can't say I'm sorry that it led to the end of your relationship."

I snort and try to pull my hand back, but Theo tightens his grasp.

"No, I mean, you deserve someone who makes you feel like you're the most gorgeous woman in the world, inside and out. Someone who worships the ground you walk on like it's their religion. Someone who makes you a better version of yourself and doesn't just support you, but challenges you, too. And if it took you a quarter-life crisis to figure that out... well, I'm not terribly disappointed about it, Jos. Andrew may be a decent guy, but you deserve way more than decent. You deserve the world."

Um. Shakespeare called, he'd like his soliloquy back.

I don't get a chance to respond before he chuckles and breaks the spell, saying, "Anything else you know about me, Dr. Freud?"

Leaning back into the seat, my hand slips from his grasp. "I also know you're going to let me order slimy land creatures."

"And how do you know that, Miss Bancroft?"

"Because that's how well I know *you*."

I also know that convincing myself I don't want him is equivalent to thinking One Direction was the same once Zayn left—it's just not true. I can tell myself that any desperation I feel for him is just a temporary emotional lapse, but I want more benefits than my health insurance and credit card combined can provide. Sleeping with Theo may be playing with fire, but I'm ready to burn, baby, burn.

15

THEO

I WOULDN'T SAY I'm a selfish guy, but I've never flown a woman I'm not sleeping with somewhere just because I know it'll make her happy. But for Josie? I didn't have to think twice about it. I'd sell one of my kidneys on the black market to keep a smile on her face. God knows the favors Martin had to pull, but I've learned not to ask questions.

We start our first race-free morning at a local patisserie that has tall glass cases filled to the brim with croissants, palmiers, colorful fruit tarts, and golden baguettes. Josie takes her time reading the daily specials written on a black chalkboard behind the counter before choosing a passion fruit and raspberry éclair.

Once we've collected our pastries, we settle into a small table near the open doorway to the kitchen. The scent of berry galettes cooling and chocolate chips melting makes my stomach rumble. I eagerly bite into my croissant as Josie chatters about what she wants to do first. Her itinerary is jampacked with everything from locating the Roman ruins to traipsing down the cobble-stoned alleyways littered with half-timbered homes to checking out the Medieval architecture.

She's pronouncing a church in a French accent that's worse than mine when Martin calls me.

I pick up, knowing he'll keep trying until I answer. "Hey, can I call you later? I'm kind of busy."

"No," Martin says, his voice urgent. "McAllister just moved up all the sponsorship meetings."

"I'm on the phone, too," a voice I recognize as Russell's pipes in. "And I highly suggest un-busying yourself, mate."

Shit. It's not going to be good if Martin called in Russell as reinforcement.

"You're not supposed to surprise someone with a three-way," I mutter, much to the amusement of Josie. "When did it get moved to?"

"Today," Martin says hesitantly.

The croissant in my hand crumbles to small flakes as I crush it in my fist. "You've got to be fucking kidding me."

Josie tilts her head and mouths, "Are you okay?" I force myself to smile and shoot her a thumbs up.

"As much as I love fucking with you, this is not one of those times." Martin sighs through the phone. "The meetings start in an hour. At McAllister's HQ."

My hands grow clammy, the flakes of my crushed pastry sticking to my skin. "Well, that sucks, considering I didn't pack my teleportation pants. How the hell did they get away with changing it so last-minute?"

"Apparently, they did it weeks ago," Martin admits gruffly. "We were just conveniently not told."

On a scale of one to screwed, I'm getting royally fucked up the bum.

"This is fixable, Theo," Russell says hurriedly. "You join the meetings virtually, act like nothing's wrong, and show Avery that he's not getting to you. That you're here to stay. Be the bigger man."

I don't flinch at Avery's name; it's no surprise he's behind the so-called miscommunication of the moved meetings. Missing one isn't great, but also not the end of the world. But missing an entire afternoon of back-to-back meetings with McAllister's biggest sponsors—aka the people and companies whose money secures my ability to race? Not great. Not great at all.

Hanging up the phone a few minutes later, I shoot Josie a pained smile. "Change of plans, angel."

JOSIE IS COMPLETELY understanding about the whole thing, promising she's fine on her own. While that may be true, it doesn't make me feel any better about the situation. Plus, the idea of her walking around a new city alone makes my stomach tighten. I don't like it.

I make her share her location with me, but that doesn't stop me from worrying. I owe Blake an apology for giving him shit whenever he worries about Ella's whereabouts. Knowing bulky guards are protecting her would most definitely calm me down.

To try not to seem like a complete overprotective stalker, I wait until after the first meeting before checking in.

THEO WALKER

> How's it going? Have you tried every flavor of ice cream the city has to offer yet?

Josie responds thirty painstakingly long minutes later by sending me a selfie—her cheeks are wind-burned, hair tied back into a high ponytail, pearly white teeth standing out against the deep pink color of her lips. Grinning next to her is a gray-haired gentleman with wrinkles older than a bottle of wine from the First World War.

THEO WALKER

> I leave you alone for a few hours and you find yourself a sugar daddy?

JOSIE BANCROFT

That's Claude. I'm on a guided tour, and he's
my walking buddy/new friend.

THEO WALKER

Walking buddy? Bancroft, he's ancient. There's
no way that man is walking anywhere but the
nearest bench.

Rather than telling me to "play nice," Josie replies with
another photo of her and her new bestie. They're wearing
matching smiles in front of some ancient-looking church.

We text back and forth a few more times before I focus my
attention back on the meeting. It's mind-numbingly boring to
listen as our sponsors go over numbers, statistics, and ROI.
None of us race for the money. I mean, yes, it's a nice perk, but
you don't spend years dedicating yourself to a sport for a
paycheck. You do it because you love it, because honestly, the
money part ends up being the most frustrating and least
pleasant part to deal with.

The meeting wraps in the late afternoon and I slam my
computer closed with a resounding *thump*.

Fuck Avery. Missing that meeting would've been detrimental.
There's nothing worse than sponsors thinking you're not fully
committed to winning, and therefore bringing in money. Especially when your contract is up in the air.

I take a shower to relieve some tension and am drying off
when someone timidly knocks on my hotel room door.

"I'm not here," I call out. *Aka go the fuck away*.

I'm in a pissy mood, I can't help it. No part of me wanted
to spend my day looking at Avery's face through my computer
screen. Not when I could've been walking behind Josie, taking
in the sight of her arse while she took in the sights of the city.

Another knock comes a few seconds later. *Take a fucking hint.*
"Go away," I shout. "Please."

That doesn't work either, because the gentle knocking goes to full-blown smacks. I swing the door open, ready to yell at whoever it is, but swallow back my anger once I see it's Josie.

"Oh." I rub my forehead to ease the pounding. "Hey."

Josie pushes past me and into the room without saying a word. I shut the door behind me before tightening the towel wrapped around my waist.

When Josie turns around to face me, her eyes roam across my half-naked body and my skin ignites with desire. *Touch me, taste me, tease me.* Brushing a hand through my still wet hair, I stay silent as she continues her appraisal. She somehow looks completely innocent and promiscuous as fuck.

It may sound cocky, but there's a reason I've been included in *People* magazine's Sexiest Man Alive list multiple times. I take care of my body, train regularly with Russell, eat a balanced diet of carbs, proteins, and vegetables, and try to get at least seven hours of sleep a night. The way Josie's staring at me? I'm self-conscious for the first time in my entire life—every part of my body feels exposed.

Neither of us says a word, but the heated tension swirls in front of us like an invisible wall.

"I want you." Her voice is steady, but a wild pink color washes her cheeks.

It's only been six hours since we last saw one another, and nothing about her behavior this morning indicated we'd be doing anything unclothed tonight. I take a small step forward to test the waters. "Did spending time with an old man make you horny for a young one?"

"You should be thanking that old man," Josie says seriously. "He's the reason I'm… applying for benefits. Friends with benefits. Not credit card benefits. Obviously."

My laugh is loud and long. "Do I want to know?"

Josie shrugs weakly, shifting from the balls of her feet to the heels. There's no reason for her to be nervous. All I've wanted to do since we first slept together is have a sequel. I frame her face with my hands, smiling down at her anxious face. She searches my eyes for some indication that I want the same, some reassurance that I want her as badly as she wants me.

I answer her with a kiss that's like London's fog—lazy, thick, and overpowering. Her lips press against mine in equal passion, our tongues dancing and twisting. When her fingers trail across the fuzz leading down my lower abs to where my towel sits on my hips, I let out a deep groan and lean back.

"Are you sure," I take a strangled breath, "you want to do this?"

She bites her full lip in cute nervousness, then slowly tugs the damp towel from my waist. It pools at my feet and my dick springs up, tall and hard like a flagpole. Josie hesitantly wraps her warm hand around me and asks me something, but it goes in one ear and out the other. I'm too focused on how she's slowly stroking me, making me somehow harder than I thought was humanly possible. I'm like goddamn *Iron Man*.

"Jos," I say, panting as she finds a rhythm. "You could ask me to steal the Declaration of Independence right now, and I'd say yes. Can you repeat yourself?"

She bursts out laughing. "Did you seriously just bring up the plot to *National Treasure* while my hand is wrapped around you? Because Nicolas Cage is a total boner-killer."

"Ask me the question again while your hand isn't," I hiss as she swipes her thumb over my tip, swiping away the pre-cum, "jerking me off. Please."

Her hand falls to her side, and I immediately miss the feel of her warm palm against me. "Will you promise me that whenever this ends, we'll still be friends?"

I ignore the prick of pain the words *whenever this ends* elicits and cup her cheeks in my hands. As she looks at me with wide eyes that could melt a glacial snowcap, I momentarily lose my train of thought. I'd steal *any* country's government documents if she fucking wanted me to, hand on my dick or not. "Jos. You'll always be my friend. Sex isn't going to change that."

My breathing becomes quick and shallow as she leaves a trail of wet kisses down my body. She looks up at me when she's on her knees, maintaining eye contact as she licks up the length of my cock. I almost come right there and then. I desperately try to keep my eyes trained on her as I disappear into her mouth, but my head keeps lolling back in pleasure.

Each time I'm about to come, she changes to a painstakingly slow pace to keep me on edge. After the third or fourth time, I thread my fingers through her hair, an unspoken message that she better not tease me anymore.

"Good girl," I moan as she finally takes me deep in her throat. It doesn't take long before I lose control to an earth-shattering orgasm. Pleasure washes through me as I explode in Josie's mouth, letting her swallow my salty release.

I tug her up from her knees, desperate to feel her lips on mine. Parting her swollen lips with my tongue, we get lost in a hungry kiss. I'm not sure how long we stand there before I finally manage to drag my lips from hers and place gentle kisses against her neck. The soft mewling noises she makes have me hard once again, even though I came no less than ten minutes ago.

"Pick a number," I say while unbuttoning Josie's jeans. She's way too overdressed for what we're about to do. "One through five."

"Excuse me?" Josie laughs, shimmying out of her lacy lavender thong. I focus on removing her shirt because I'm desperate to be reunited with the breasts that've taken up an insane amount of my head space these past few weeks. "Why?"

I'm too distracted to answer her. The dusky pink tips of her nipples are beaded in pleasure. I cup a honey soft breast in each hand, gently kneading them with my calloused fingers. Josie's chest heaves as her breathing quickens.

"Number," I remind her. My hands roam everywhere—her heavy breasts, her smooth stomach, her plump ass.

"Two," Josie decides breathily. "Why do I need to choose a number? I'm not at the deli waiting to order cold cuts."

"Cold cuts?" I laugh incredulously. "Nah, baby, that's the number of orgasms I'm going to give you."

I capture her lips against mine with new urgency, gently pushing her toward the bed. Once she's on her back, I take my sweet time exploring her breasts the way I've wanted to. The way I have in my mind every time I've jerked off since we first got together. "Fuck Tom and Jerry. I'm naming your ti—"

Josie interrupts me with a groan. "Do not make me regret this, Theo."

I promptly shut my mouth and go back to stroking her breasts with my hands and tongue until her body's squirming underneath mine for relief. When I slip a hand between her thighs and feel how wet she is, I let out a carnal growl. I drag a finger up and down, feeling how much she wants me. Her body is immediately receptive, and she spreads her legs further apart.

"Theo," she mumbles, arching her back as I tease her. "Don't tease me. Need it."

"Need what, gorgeous?" I move my fingers closer to her entrance, pausing right before giving her what she wants. "Use your words."

"Your… your fingers." Her voice is breathy, firm breasts rising and falling heavily with each strangled breath she takes. "Your mouth. Anything. Please."

She doesn't see my smirk because her eyes are closed in pleasure. "Only because you asked nicely, angel."

I slide two fingers inside her, curling them until I find the rough patch I'm searching for. Josie sucks in a startled breath as I stroke her sweet spot. I swirl my tongue against her clit until she cries out, trapping my head between her thighs. There's nowhere else in the world I'd rather be held captive. Her body spasms uncontrollably as she rides the waves of her pleasure.

"One done," she says, lifting her hand.

My face falls into her stomach. "Are you… are you high-fiving me right now?"

"Trying to! You're halfway to fulfilling your promise." She wiggles her fingers. "Don't leave me hanging, babes."

"I'm an overachiever, Jos," I remind her, slapping my palm against hers. "Two is the *bare minimum*."

Quickly grabbing a condom out of my bag, I roll it on with deft fingers. Josie watches me, her brown eyes filled with undisguised arousal. She parts her legs, inviting me in, and I RSVP with a resounding *yes*.

I stretch my body over hers, resting my elbows on her sides so I don't completely crush her. Entering her again is my own personal nirvana. My instincts tell me to rush after the release I'm desperate for, but I need to last long enough for Josie to be completely satisfied and begging for more. I want to soak in her little moans and whimpers, slowly pleasing her until she's melting in the palm of my hand.

Our bodies move together in total harmony, and each stroke prompts a moan from her that's sexier than the last. She's like a fucking drug—I don't know where or who I am and I don't give a damn. I just want *more*.

"Keep your eyes open," I command, the fierceness in my voice shocking me. "Look at me, baby."

Her fluttering eyes snap open and she captures her lips against mine. Our bodies grind against one another in slow, insistent circles, never missing a beat. It's not long before Josie's whimpering into my neck, tightening around me as another orgasm takes hold of her.

Two for two.

"You feel so good, baby," I murmur into her ear, resting my

forehead against hers. "Been dreaming about your pussy for weeks."

The aroma of her perfume is earthy and floral, sweet and sensual. I lose track of time as I rock inside her. I switch off between brushing my lips against her neck and nibbling on her earlobe, the neglected areas soft and desperate for attention.

It takes me a while to realize the gasping noises hanging in the air are coming from my own mouth. I'm so deep in her that I could get lost, and fuck it, I wouldn't want to be found. My entire body vibrates with need, and I see a kaleidoscope of color as I finally abandon myself to an orgasm, groaning in blissful agony and satisfaction. It sets off a chain reaction and Josie once again shudders around me, stifling a moan by shoving her face into the pillow.

I stay inside her, too spent to move, until she informs me that I'm suffocating her beneath my weight. I slip my now soft cock out of her warmth and roll onto my back, pulling Josie's body so it's pressed against mine.

"Should we harmonize the chorus of 'I Just Had Sex,'" Josie asks, still breathless. "Or would that totally kill the vibe?"

We both start laughing, our bodies shaking against one another.

"I don't think I've ever come that much," Josie admits a few minutes later. "From a man, at least."

A smirk of pride sits on my lips. *Suck on that, Andrew.* What he couldn't do in two years, I did in an hour. And we're just getting started.

"Pick another number," I reply happily. "One through ten."

She lifts her head up, eyes lidded and dripping with pleasure. I love seeing this look on her face, knowing it's me causing it and giving her something no one else can. The way she absentmindedly licks her lips makes my dick twitch again.

"Twelve."

"Good answer," I say before weaving my hands through her hair. "My goal is fifteen."

I didn't think sex with Josie could get any better than it did the first time, but I'm glad I was wrong. We're about to have our own twenty-four-hour endurance race.

16

JOSIE

I'VE HAD MORE collective orgasms in the past few weeks than I have had in my entire life. And I have a seventy-two-year-old Frenchman named Claude to thank.

Seriously.

After our guided tour of Le Mans ended, my walking buddy and I grabbed coffee together. I ended up telling him everything, and I mean *everything*. I never thought I'd say the word "friends with benefits" or "casual sex" to a stranger, especially a man of his age, but my mouth ran like a train with an endless supply of fuel and broken brakes.

And he had rather solid advice for a man who's older than my favorite vintage wine. He said the best way to discover myself is to listen to my instincts. If my gut is telling me to explore casual sex with my best friend, then I should simply go with the flow. Give myself permission to go after what I want.

And right in this moment? I'm not worrying and I'm damn happy.

For the second time this week, I wake up to Theo's naked body pressed against mine. His arm and leg are thrown over me like he's a koala bear, his hard-on resting snugly against my thigh. His lips are parted slightly, nostrils flaring as he breathes deeply. I'm overheated but give myself a few more minutes to enjoy the cuddling before slinking out from beneath him. Theo stirs slightly as I leave my bed, but he's a deep sleeper, so he doesn't wake up.

I should probably nudge him awake to let him know I'm leaving, but he looks so sweet and peaceful. Deciding to leave him be, I quietly slip out my front door and head to SoHo to meet my mum. We have a standing Saturday breakfast date, excluding the weekends I'm at a Grand Prix. We're making our way through an extensive Eater-approved list of the best brunch spots in the city. This morning we're meeting at a new cafe that's been getting rave reviews.

The smell of coffee beans and freshly-baked pastries greet me as I step into the trendy space. I do a quick scan to double-check that my mum's not here before grabbing a table for two next to the counter stacked with chrome espresso machines. My penchant for timeliness did not come from my mum. She's an Aquarius who runs perpetually behind schedule and my Scorpio status explains my need to be punctual.

I order the highly recommended—at least by Instagram— mocha caramel latte and mindlessly scroll through my Pinterest home feed, impatiently awaiting my mum's arrival, when a text from my houseguest pops up.

THEO WALKER

> Did you leave me in your flat without saying goodbye? Is this some sort of weird reverse friends with benefits psychology? Are you playing mind games with me?

JOSIE BANCROFT

> Lol. Didn't want to interrupt your sweet dreams! Also, haven't you learned by now that I'm horrible at games?

THEO WALKER

> That's not true. You're an expert at some games. I'm getting hard just thinking about how well you played with me last night.

> I wish I was between your thighs right now, listening to you moan my name like it's your favorite song.

His sexually charged words send a familiar warmth from my cheeks to the growing heat between my legs. Theo may love being the center of attention outside of the bedroom, but inside it? He's more than happy to let me be in the spotlight. It's like nothing matters but my pleasure. Some of the things he's done with his tongue and hips can only be perfected through lots of practice—and I'm trying not to think about where all his experience comes from in comparison to mine. Sex with Theo could inspire nine hundred R&B songs.

"Darling!" the familiar sound of my mum's voice rings out. "Sorry I'm late. Traffic was horrible. I hope you weren't waiting on me for too long."

My phone clatters to the table as if I've been caught red-handed. I quickly slide it into my back pocket before greeting my mum. With shoulder-length blonde hair, soulful brown eyes, and an easy smile, my mum and I could easily pass for blood relatives. Well, that, and our impressive twin ability to chatter away for hours.

Before I know it, a server's delivering my full English breakfast and my mum's smoked salmon avocado toast.

"So," my mum says, drawing out the "o" so the word seems to last for minutes. "You never told me what you thought of it."

I stare at her blankly. "Thought of what?"

"The vibrator I sent you," she exclaims, not bothering to lower her voice. "The one that stimulates both the—"

"Yup," I say loudly to cut her off. "Got it, Mum."

The newest vibrator she sent to me has more parts than I

know what to do with. The note she wrote with it said, "*I hope this helps you vibe with your body.*" I wish I was kidding. I added it to my ever-growing bin of "toys" she's sent me. I've told her I'm fine with the trusty vibrator I've had since uni, but it falls on deaf ears.

"The most important step in sexual pleasure is knowing your own body," she reminds me. "It's nothing to be ashamed of, Josephine."

I sink so far into the chair that my upper back hits the seat. *Check, please!*

"Can we not talk about this right now, Mum? I'd rather *not* discuss orgasms over an omelet, thank you very much."

"Sex is just as much a part of people's daily routine as eating, darling," she reminds me. "And now that you're single, it's a great time to really focus on your own needs and desires."

"I know, Mum." I sigh, already aware where this conversation is heading. "Communicate to your partner what you like, don't rush foreplay, visit your OB/GYN regularly, experiment with different positions to enhance pleasure."

I've heard it all before. Who needs the religious Ten Commandments when you have the Ten Commandments to Come?

She raises her perfectly sculpted brows. "Are you practicing what I preach?"

"Every one of them." My mouth suddenly goes dry, a betraying flush taking over my cheeks. *Oh fuck.* "I mean, I'm practicing every one of them that applies to me, so the, uh… the one about learning about my body. Studying that one a lot. Soon enough, I'll have a master's degree in it. Don't know if I should add that to my resume or not. May be kind of awkward, if you know what I mean. Marketing manager by day, sexual goddess by night. Yep, yep, yep. You know what they say, practice makes perfect."

A time machine would nice right about now. Or some arsenic. I'd even take a guillotine.

My mum takes a sip of her chai tea latte. Whereas my dad's reactions are exaggerated and honest, my mum can appear diplomatic and neutral at just about anything. She's seen it all in her sessions with clients, so not much can get her to break her cool, calm, and collected demeanor.

"What's his name?"

"Whose name?"

"*His* name. The guy you're seeing."

Shit. "Why do you assume I'm seeing someone?"

A smile shapes her rose-pink lips. "Besides the way you were grinning at your phone when I walked in? I'd say your gift of gab and the way you're flushing are dead giveaways."

Slathering my toast in jam, I avoid eye contact like she's Medusa. "Okay, well, it's not a big deal. We're not seeing one another. It's casual."

"There's nothing wrong with casual sex, honey," she says. "It's definitely… not like you, but that doesn't mean it's not something you can enjoy. You may discover a lot about yourself through it. Explore things you may not in a more serious relationship."

"Exactly!" I nod vehemently. "That's what Claude was getting at, too."

"Is Claude the name of the young man?"

"Claude's seventy-two, and we are definitely *not* sleeping together. Theo's more than age-appropriate, Mum, don't worry. I mean, he's few years older than me, obviously, but he's not in his seventies. God, can you imagine?"

My mum bows her head slightly, a worried frown creasing her Botox-free forehead. "You're sleeping with Theo?"

Oh my God. Is there a muzzle available on the menu?

"Yes," I admit, crossing my arms over my chest. "Can you stop looking at me like *that*?"

Rather than smooth out her expression to "nonjudgmental and understanding," the corners of her mouth droop down further. She's turned from sex therapist to mum-mode.

"I'm an adult. I can make my own decisions regarding my body," I continue, a frown of my own forming. "That's what you always taught me, right?"

"Of course." She gives me a small smile, but it doesn't quite reach her eyes. "But sleeping with Theo isn't casual, darling. It's complicated."

"No, it's quite simple, actually," I argue, my voice getting defensive. "We're still friends. We're just friends who happen to have sex occasionally."

Besides the sex that makes my toes curl and vision blurry, our friendship has remained the same. We laugh *at* one another as often as we laugh *with* one another, and we can talk about everything, anything, and nothing. We just also give into the insane chemistry and temptation now.

"I just don't want to see you get hurt," my mum says cautiously. "Casual sex is only casual if you're not emotionally invested in the person. Theo's one of your closest friends, and you already care deeply for him. Adding intimacy will unequivocally change things. It's an emotional war zone, and you've had no formal training."

"I'm not jumping into a relationship," I explain. "Theo's not looking for anything serious either, so we're on the same page. It's the ideal situation. We're making casual cool, not complicated."

Put that on a bumper sticker.

My mum sets her mug down on the table. Twin lines seem to have carved themselves between her brows as she studies me. "You love deeply, Josephine, and it's one of the things I admire most about you, but are you sure you're going to be able to separate the sex from the friendship? The feelings from the friendship? Or are you going to convince yourself everything's fine when it's not?"

And she's back to therapist-mode.

"I meant it when I said I'm focusing on myself." I fidget with the gold chain around my neck. "And I appreciate the fact that you're looking out for me, but I need you to just trust that you raised me to make smart decisions. And if it turns out I'm wrong, well, then that's my problem."

My mum nods resolutely. "You're right. I just... Well, I hope you're at least being safe and using protect—"

I don't need this speech again. Nope. No, thank you.

"Mum," I groan, cringing both inwardly and outwardly. "Please. I do *not* need another sex talk, thank you very much. I'm pretty sure I can recite it better than you at this point."

She lets out a low laugh, the sound melodious. Picking up her mug once again, she takes a long sip. "Fine, fine. Tell me about work."

"There's not much to tell," I admit with a shrug. "Work is work."

"Sounds rather boring, darling."

I fiddle with the handle of my coffee mug, running my fingers against the smooth ceramic. "No, it's okay. It's just the same as always. Remember how I told you that Lucas mentioned some freelancing work?"

"Mm-hmm."

"He texted me the other day, asking if I was still interested, and I said yes. Can't hurt to at least hear what it is, right?"

"I think that's a brilliant idea, darling. There are too many wonderful possibilities in life to keep doing the same thing if it's not making you the best version of yourself."

"Did you read that quote on Pinterest?"

"No, I just happen to be rather great at giving advice." She grins and flips her hair over her shoulder. "Speaking of which, have you heard of the podcast *Dating and Dildos?* Someone from their team reached out about having me on as a guest."

Oh dear God.

I immediately motion to our server. Screw coffee, I need a mimosa without the orange juice.

17

THEO

GRAY THUNDERCLOUDS MULTIPLY and roll across the sky, covering all evidence that it was sunny an hour ago. I duck into the motorhome a few seconds before the rain starts at full force, blurring the scenery outside the glass windows.

"Walker! Over here," a voice calls out.

I turn around and spot my manager camped out in the front corner of the cafeteria. Making my way over to him, my eyes narrow in on the pastrami sandwich near his right hand.

"Nice job out there today, mate," Martin greets me as I approach. "Your lap time was killer."

I turn a chair around and sit, my chest against the back, legs spread eagle on either side of the seat. "Why thank you, kind sir. You gonna finish that?" Before he can respond, I grab the remaining half of the sandwich from his plate. Chef Albie's deli sandwiches always hit the spot and qualifying tends to work up my appetite.

Martin rolls his eyes but doesn't chastise me. Instead, he pulls out a manila envelope from his briefcase. My McAllister contract. Pieces of lean-cut pastrami fall out of my mouth.

"I've highlighted the areas you should look at," Martin

says, pushing me the document. "And before you panic, remember that we're going to negotiate."

Shit.

Section I. Article II.
[Term Clause]

After completing the one (1) year Contract term, the Contract between McAllister Racing and Theodore Walker automatically terminates, although is subject to the renewal option of Contract to the parties.

Only one year? My original contract with McAllister was for five years. Five. Before I had even driven for them, they knew they wanted me long-term. Now they're only guaranteeing one more season?

Section III.
[Social Media Policy]

The McAllister Racing marketing team will handle [Theo Walker]'s social media [including, but not limited to Instagram, X, LinkedIn, Facebook, TikTok] for all content involving McAllister Racing, their sponsors, and/or their brand-related deals to protect shareholder interest. Furthermore, any social media posts that are deemed controversial will result in a $10,000 fine for [Theo Walker].

C'mon. Seriously? They want to baby proof my account? It's not like I post myself snorting cocaine while wearing a McAllister T-shirt. I don't even like drugs! I've bawled my eyes out every time I've smoked or done an edible.

Section VI. Article X.
[Sponsorship and Endorsements Clause]

McAllister Racing sponsorships supersede individual sponsorships and endorsements. No overlap will be permitted.

Including but not limited to sponsorships in these areas: beverage companies, sportswear brands [footwear/activewear], sporting goods [gear and equipment], electronics maker.

My largest and favorite personal sponsors are sportswear and sporting goods. Not only do they want to screw me out of millions, but they want me to ruin relationships I've worked hard to cultivate. Lovely.

Section XII. Article III.
[Code of Practice]

During pre-race practice and qualifying periods, there will be no restriction on the efforts of either driver. In the designated Grand Prix circuit, for the interest of point aggregation, the Number One car will be expected to finish the race ahead of the second car. For this purpose, the support car will accept that no passing maneuver will be attempted unless the Number One driver has suffered mechanical issues or if given a clear signal from the pits.

My hands shake as I put the contract down. "This isn't a contract, Martin. This is a prison sentence."

It's not uncommon for a team principal to order a car to move aside during a race—whether it's for safety or strategy—but to make me sign something that says that'll be *every* race is demeaning to me and my talent. It's saying I'm not the best and I never will be. It's fucking personal.

"Other than those areas, it's a great offer, Theo." Martin gives me a tight-lipped smile. "You'll receive a nice bonus, plus performance bonuses, and an increased percentage in corporate sponsorships."

"A great offer?" I say loudly. A few people look in our direction, but I don't care. I'm heated. "They're not only fucking locking me out of my accounts, but they're also fucking me out of millions and my existing relationships! And fucking me up the—"

"Theo," Martin says sharply. "Calm down. We're going to counter-offer. When was the last time you ever signed a contract without changing half of the shit on it?"

I take a beat to think about it. "Never."

"Exactly. We'll get this to where you want it to be, okay?"

I cross my arms over my chest. "Good. Because this is completely unacceptable."

This has to be about more than simply my breakup with Christina. You don't slap a two-time World Champion in his peak with contract restrictions like he's a first-year driver still proving himself to the team. Not renewing with McAllister isn't an option, it's just not. McAllister is the best of the best. Everest, Ithaca, and AlphaVite deliver great wins, too, but those weren't my dad's team, McAllister was. I'm not giving up the one thing I still have left of him.

"Why don't you cool it on social media while we work out the details of the contract," Martin suggests. "I don't give a fuck what you post, but let's maybe not live stream yourself from a club this year?"

I roll my eyes. "My fans like how relatable I am."

"I'm not sure what world you're living in, kid, but bottle service at a private table at TAO isn't exactly *average*." He lifts a brow in amusement. "You're aspirational, not relatable."

"I'm not going to change who I am just to get on Avery's good side, Martin. That's bullshit and you know it."

"I never told you to change who you are, Walker, but I do think toning it down a bit won't hurt. Would it kill you to do a Q&A fully clothed and not in your bathtub?"

It wasn't *my* bath; it was the bathtub in some random chick's hotel room last year—the spout was shaped like a snake, which I thought was cool. I don't think that's going to help my case, though, so I keep the information to myself.

"Fine, I'll tone it down. Anything else? Do you think Avery wants me to lick his toes? Wax his asshole?"

Martin ignores my quip and takes a sip of his water. "I'm not interested in what Avery wants. I'm interested in what you want, which is why I'm going to connect with my legal team and come up with a counter-offer. So just lie low, don't do anything stupider than usual, and we'll be fine. *Capisce*?"

Standing from the chair, my entire body pinched with aggravation and tight with resentment, I mumble my agreement before sulking off to the privacy of my suite. Russell stops by after having talked to Martin himself, but I'm not in the mood to discuss it, not even with him.

Before he started dating my mum, back when he was just my dad's old manager and a friend-slash-father-figure to me, I would have texted Richard about this. Or left a long-winded voicemail bitching about how much I hate the politics and contractual bullshit of the sport when all I want to do is race. But now his loyalty is no longer mine, it's my mum's, and the last thing I need is her stressing about me if he repeats anything I tell him.

For the next hour, I lose myself in the F1 racing game. This alternate reality allows me to race for McAllister with no stipulations or strings attached.

A soft knock briefly distracts me as I finish lap twenty-two of the virtual Abu Dhabi Grand Prix. Josie's blonde head pops in a moment later. Her smile softens the knotted rope playing tug-of-war in my stomach. "Hi, can I hide out in here?"

I pause the game, motioning for her to come in. "Only if you tell me who we're hiding from."

She squeezes herself through the crack she's left open before shutting the door behind her. The black T-shirt she's wearing rides up a bit in the front, showing off the toned midriff I ran my tongue over last night. I move the oversized pillow taking up half of the couch so she can join me.

"I'm hiding from Rhys," Josie admits from the safety of her seat. "I think my brain will explode into a million tiny pieces if he asks me how to A/B test a Facebook ad campaign one more time."

McAllister's director of marketing is completely clueless when it comes to the intricacies of social media marketing. He understands the importance of everything, just not how to do it himself. Which is fair, since he has a team for that, but he also asks the same questions an exorbitant number of times.

I offer her the second controller. "Want to play?"

She takes it from my hand and lets me walk her through how to set up her own driver, something I did for her last time. After a ten-minute refresher, we start a new race. It only takes fourteen laps before Josie asks, "Do you want to talk about whatever's bothering you?"

"Ugh," I groan teasingly. "Why do women *always* want to talk?"

Josie smacks my controller out of my hand, but keeps her eyes focused on the screen. It takes me a moment to reel in my surprise and, by the time I've picked up the controller, she's already sped ahead of me.

"You're the chattiest man I've ever met," she says, aggressively pressing buttons. I'm not sure what sort of combination she thinks she's doing, but I can confirm it isn't going to help in any way. "Do you not remember talking my ear off about your uncanny ability to always know when fruit is ripe?"

I scoff at her very correct observation. "And do you remember talking my ear off about why I should put on sunscreen every morning?"

"I stand by that," Josie says vehemently. "Not only does it aid in skin cancer prevention, but it also helps with wrinkles and aging lines. I'm just looking out for you, Walker. You may not realize it, but you're constantly exposed to UV radiation. Even in your handy-dandy little racing helmet. But if you want sunspots and a wrinkly face, then by all means, ignore my advice. Just don't come crying to me and asking for the best anti-aging serum when you're in your forties looking sixty-five."

My lips tilt up in a grin. "Do you want me to walk around with an umbrella to protect myself, too?"

She pauses the game and whips her head to me. "This is no laughing matter. You may think you're above every other man, but you're not above the sun, Theodore Chase Walker. It's a flaming ball of light and fire and… other things."

"Who says I think I'm above every man?"

"You!" She throws her head back and laughs. All I want to do is cover the exposed skin in love bites, each mark a memory of the moans she makes when I suck on the skin. "During the interview with SkySports this morning, you said, 'My race number may be seventeen, but I'm number one at everything else.'"

Sounds about right.

"You make it sound like it's a bad thing." I chuckle. "At the very least, I'm number one at giving orgasms."

"Christ, Walker, are you always going to—" Josie's cheeks turn bright pink and her voice cuts off. "Never mind."

"Always going to do what?" I prompt her. "C'mon, Jos, you can't keep me hanging like that."

She waves me off. "Forget it. It's fine. Can we just go back to playing the game?"

I have a sister and a brain. When a woman says it's fine, it's not fine. It's quite possibly the furthest thing from fine. I once had this chick tell me she was fine, and then she threw a Louboutin heel at my head. Thankfully, my response time is quick, but "I'm fine" almost cost me my vision in my left eye.

"It's obviously not fine," I say gently. "And you know me well enough to know I'm not going to let this go until you tell me. So we can do this the easy way or the hard way, but both scenarios end up with you sharing."

Josie sighs but doesn't say anything. *Looks like we're going with the hard way.*

I start singing "Bohemian Rhapsody" loudly, knowing it won't take more than ten seconds until Josie begs me to stop. She once compared my singing voice to "a chainsaw going through a blender while in a helicopter." And I'm the dramatic one. Go figure.

She claps her hands over her ears. "Fine! Fine! You're making my eardrums bleed."

Ha! Success.

"Now that we have that settled," I say with a grin. "Please finish the sentence. 'Christ, Walker, are you always going to…'"

Josie reaches up to toy with the thin golden chain hanging around her neck. A small "J" dangles from it and she presses it between her thumb and pointer finger. "Remind me that you're more sexually experienced than I am."

My jaw springs open and I blink rapidly. That is most definitely *not* fine. All I can manage to get out is a strangled, "What do you mean? You've been in multiple long-term relationships."

"Sure, but that doesn't mean we were super sexually adventurous or anything. I'm used to rotating through about three positions and calling it a night. Your favorite position is probably called the *Horny Hippo* or something. And I'm sure you've done wild positions with other funky names, like *The Flying Squirrel* or *The Roman Spork*."

She lists a few more absurd names, and I burst out laughing, unable to keep a straight face when she says *The Tuba Twist*. Missionary is my favorite position, but it sounds lame to say that.

"I shouldn't have said anything," Josie says, her face turning bright red. "I made things weird. Let's forget it ever happened. 'Kay? Kay. Sounds like a plan to me. The best laid plans… something. I can't remember the exact phrase right now. Doesn't matter. You're on board with striking this all from the record, right? Because I know you'd rather drink bleach than have that sort of conversation."

She's not wrong that I tend to avoid this type of chat, preferring to roll around in hot coal and broken glass instead. But with Josie, I don't mind. She's always the exception.

"You didn't make things weird," I reassure her. "We should be able to talk about these things with one another. Oi? We're friends, first and foremost. And I want you to enjoy being with me as much as I enjoy being with you."

Josie shifts in her seat. "I enjoy it. Trust me. I just... I just don't want you to think I'm boring because I can't lift my leg behind my head and don't want to do anything while upside down. I'm down to, you know, try some new things, but I'm not trying to break my back playing *Twister* with my body, you know?"

"What kind of sex do you think I've had? You make it seem like I've fucked women while traipsing over a shark-infested body of water."

She nods. "Well, I don't know. It could be possible. Remi told a story on *Dating and Dildos* about a girl she knows who had sex while skydiving."

I chuckle. "I've had my fair share of crazy sex, but that doesn't mean that's all I want, Jos. And full transparency... I'm intimidated as hell by your experience. I'm up against blokes who have had years of experience learning your body and what makes you come undone. So getting you to climax? It makes me feel damn good, angel."

"Yeah?"

"Yep," I confirm. "But if you're interested in trying out the *Crocodile Corkscrew*, we can—"

"Nope. The only corkscrews I need are for wine, thank you very much." She laughs. "Now, can you tell me what's going on with you? And don't say you're fine because you only crack your knuckles when you're stressed, and you've been popping them like damn firecrackers since I came in here."

"You're a clever woman, Bancroft." I laugh, thoroughly impressed. Cracking my fingers is a nervous habit I rarely realize I'm doing. I tap the scar running through my left brow. "You know my scar?"

"Mm-hmm," she says before a smile blooms across her lips. "I believe you said it's from either cage fighting a lion or a failed attempt at using a can opener while blindfolded?"

"Or from skateboarding down the side of a volcano."

Josie rolls her eyes, but the edges of her lips twitch up. I take a deep breath. This is one of the few topics where I fail to find words.

I sigh. "It's from Avery."

Josie's jaw drops, but her eyebrows raise. "As in... James Avery?"

"Yup."

"Did he hit you with brass knuckles?"

It felt like it. The ugly class ring Avery wears immediately flashes into my mind. It's gaudy as hell. Josie runs her thumb over the white jagged skin, and I melt like butter under her touch.

"I dated his daughter Christina." I pause briefly. "Well... she thought we were dating, I thought we were having fun."

"Like we're having fun?" she asks softly, averting her eyes.

"Not at all," I reassure her. "I was in my early twenties and a certified idiot when this happened."

"You're still a certified idiot." Her eyes briefly meet mine and she gives me a quick smile. "So, he punched you because you dated his daughter? That seems excessive."

I sigh. "It ended piss poorly."

I don't blame myself for what happened, but I do know my actions played a part in Christina's spiraling. Once I filed a restraining order, her parents sent her to a health and wellness rehabilitation center in Switzerland, or that's what the rumor mill claims.

Josie traces her pointer finger against the contour of my ab muscles straining against my shirt. "Did something happen between the two of you earlier?"

I don't answer right away. "Avery's had it out for me ever since. And listen, I'm not stupid, I know Blake's the favorite, but I still pull my weight for the team, you know? I'm just as much a part of McAllister as he is. Avery's just been going out of his way to make things difficult for me. It got to me earlier, I guess."

Josie kisses me deeply, helping me momentarily forget what we're talking about. I'm usually the initiator, so it takes me by surprise, but I lean in, letting the taste of her lips calm my rapidly beating heart. Our tongues seek each other out and I briefly wonder if I'm too obsessed with kissing her, but brush the thought away.

She pulls back moments later. "Blake's not everyone's favorite."

"No?"

Her tantalizingly plump lips tug into a cheeky smile. "Nope. I heard one of the engineers likes you better."

"Oof." I let out a low chuckle. "Well, regardless, you're still my favorite."

"Obviously," she scoffs, shooting me a playful wink. "I'm everyone's favorite."

She's not wrong.

I quickly ruffle her hair. "Want to head back to the hotel and order in some food? Maybe watch a movie or something? I don't really feel like going out."

"Sure. Oh!" She claps her hands together. "Can we get sushi?"

"Your wish is my command, princess."

Grabbing my phone off the tiny table nestled next to the couch in my suite, I see a new message from Blake.

BLAKEY BLAKE

Hey. Adler and I are going to grab dinner in a bit. You in?

THEO WALKER

Nah. Gonna hang in tonight. Thanks, though, mate.

BLAKEY BLAKE

Wild Walker choosing to stay in? The world must be ending.

The world isn't ending. My world is just starting to revolve around a blushing blonde with the most kissable lips I've ever encountered.

"Theo?" Josie says as we gather our stuff to leave.

I lift my head. "Hmm?"

A smile lights up her face before she presses her soft lips against my forehead. "You're my favorite, too."

18

JOSIE

ALL LUCAS WILL TELL me about this "freelance opportunity"—which is sounding sketchier by the moment—is that I'll be pleasantly surprised, whatever that means. I meet him at Wells Boxing, a gym that caters to high-profile athletes and up-and-comers. It's like the SoHo house of sports. Lucas has his own performance coach, but occasionally, trains with the owner of the gym, a professional boxer with three titles under his belt.

The door of Wells Boxing is discreet and could easily be mistaken for a service entrance. Painted red with scratches marking up the metal, it doesn't look like it opens into one of London's most exclusive boxing and training gyms. Heavy breathing and grunts echo off the walls as I walk through the door. If I closed my eyes, I could easily be on the set of a porno.

I spy Lucas in the boxing ring that occupies the center of the room. He's wearing a sweat-stained gray shirt that displays his taut, tattooed arms.

I make my way over to him, humming the theme song of

Rocky and side-stepping the personal trainers and men with towels draped around their necks.

"Jos," he calls out with a smile. "You made it."

"I made it," I confirm, holding up my camera to show him I've fulfilled my end of the deal. "Am I here to take thirst-traps for your Instagram?"

Lucas takes a swig from his water bottle before rolling his eyes. He lands somewhere in between Blake and Theo on the social-media-lovers scale. He doesn't accidentally post memes to his story that belong in a private message like Blake, nor does he live-stream himself eating breakfast for two hours like Theo.

"Hardly my style, Bancroft." He huffs out a laugh. Swinging his body beneath the elastic ropes surrounding the ring, he jumps off the elevated platform and saunters over to where I'm standing. "Ready to see something cool?"

"Something actually cool?" I ask with a frown. "Or is this like in Baku, when Blake wanted to show us something cool, and it ended up being a TikTok everyone had seen weeks ago?"

Lucas lets out a long laugh. "He sets the bar pretty low, but this is *actually* cool."

He leads me toward the back of the gym. I'm expecting to stop in the small office tucked away in the corner, but instead, Lucas opens the emergency exit and motions for me to follow him outside. It's a warm night, but that doesn't stop goosebumps from breaking out across my arms as we step into the dark alleyway.

We walk to the end of the alley and make a sharp right before stopping in front of a storefront with metal grates over the tinted windows. It's a quiet street, the only sound coming from our footsteps against the cobblestone. I glance around so I can get a good description in case I need to repeat to the police where I was kidnapped. I've learned a thing or two from watching *Law & Order* with Ella.

"Just trust me," Lucas says, as if reading my mind.

Apparently, we're in *Alice in Wonderland* because we walk through the empty store space and past yet another suspect-looking door at the back. Except this door leads into what's either a den where delinquents run their drug ring *or* a speakeasy that holds illegal gambling.

"Welcome," a silky-smooth voice says from behind us.

I nearly jump out of my Converse, already on edge from the sketchy walk. Turning around, I take in the pure muscle of a man, otherwise known as Kelsey "the Hitman" Wells. With the legendary boxer standing before me, the cogs in my mind begin turning. "Oh my God. Is this an underground boxing place? Like *Fight Club*! Minus the insomnia and Brad Pitt?"

Kelsey's amber-colored eyes sweep over me—not in a creepy or lecherous way, but almost as if he's sizing me up. The mocha color of his complexion contrasts beautifully against his pearly white teeth as he smiles. "No, it's not a secret extension of Wells Boxing, but I see where you're coming from."

"If this were a secret fighting place, I suppose you wouldn't have the need for me to market it." I shoot him a friendly grin before glancing around again. I can't tell if the dust, driftwood, and tools scattered everywhere are because things are being built or torn down. "So, what exactly is this place?"

"It *will* be the most-talked about bar in London," Kelsey says with a chuckle. "Once I finish construction, name the place, finalize a drink and food menu, decorate it, hire staff, and eventually open. Plus, about a million other things."

"Gemini," I blurt out.

I'm met with matching furrowed brows. "Hmm?"

"You should call this place Gemini," I explain, the excitement in my voice evident. "I used to be super into astrology, embarrassingly so. I would read my horoscope, like, every day.

I'm a Scorpio, but a Virgo sun, Aries moon, and Libra rising. Anyway, um, Gemini's are notorious for their two sides—one that they show the world, and then the hidden side, which is their true self. Sort of like this spot. You walk into that smaller room and think it's going to be one thing, say, a record shop or hair salon, and then you walk in *here* and it's something entirely different. The most talked about bar in London, if you will. What you think you're getting versus what you are."

Kelsey glances at Lucas and then back at me. "Lucas was right; you're bloody brilliant."

My friend teasingly nudges me with his elbow. He's everyone's biggest hype man.

Kelsey motions us over to a card table surrounded by folding chairs. I swear, I've seen a painting of dogs drinking whiskey and smoking cigars while playing poker at a table just like this.

Kelsey runs a hand through his corkscrew, caramel-colored curls. "If you're open to it, I'd love for you to take some photos of the space. Get inspired, let your creative juices flow. I don't need a stuffy business proposal, but I'm looking for someone to give me some direction. Find the right voice for the brand. I have a Pinterest board full of ideas, but it's all over the place. I need someone to hone in on my vision and execute it."

I press my leg into Lucas's in a silent "oh my God." Kelsey having a Pinterest board is just about the cutest thing I've ever heard. I *love* that he has a vision board—I have about twenty myself.

"Not to shoot myself in the foot," I say hesitantly, "but don't you already have a marketing agency you use? For Wells Boxing?"

"Yes, but they're too…" He waves his hand, as if the word will magically conjure in front of him.

"Corporate?" I supply.

"Yes. Exactly. Too corporate. They get the job done, but

they don't give it that personal, unique touch I'm looking for. I want creative, provocative, intoxicating. Something that will get people talking, you know?"

Sounds all too familiar. "Makes sense, especially for such a rare space."

Design isn't my specialty, but I know how important ambiance and atmosphere are. The ideas start flowing through my mind like lyrics to a song. Gemini—the unofficial name— has to take *expect the unexpected* to a whole new level. Serve fancy top-shelf whiskey in small inflatable flamingo pool floaties. Feature tater tots topped with caviar at the bar. Hang a disco ball in a marble-filled bathroom.

"Are you looking for someone full-time? I'm not sure if Lucas told you, but—"

"You're a Formula 1 lady." He nods and smiles. "All good. Right now, I'm just looking for someone to help me get this place up and running."

I clench my teeth to stop myself from belting out my favorite Hannah Montana jam, "Best of Both Worlds."

I begin asking Kelsey questions about the bar. They come to me easily, despite the food and beverage industry being wildly different than the motorsport industry. All I have to do is tweak the things I looked for when I did a deep dive into McAllister's marketing plan to find blind spots and solutions.

Has he done a competitor analysis? What will Gemini have that other places don't? What's the sort of crowd he's hoping to attract? What does he want to be known for—atmosphere, food and drink, the music? All the above? What's his timeline?

I'm glad I brought my notebook along with my camera because, an hour later, I've written down six pages of notes and taken over fifty photos.

"Let's link up in a week or so?" Kelsey says as the three of us leave the space. "Talk next steps then?"

"Sounds great!" I squeak out.

When he's out of eyesight and earshot, I lose any ounce of so-called cool I may have. "Oh my God, Lucas! When you said *someone*, I didn't think you meant Kelsey Wells. Are you freaking out as much as I'm freaking out? Why do you seem so calm? This is a stop, drop, and roll kind of situation, babes."

Lucas laughs. "I'm taking it you're interested?"

"Um, duh. Thanks for thinking of me. Do you think tomorrow is too soon to email him a nice little thank you note? Or should I send, like, candy or something? Are fruit baskets still a thing? Or is that too desperate? I haven't had a job interview in forever… not that this was an interview, or even a job. I mean, it is, but it's more of a side hustle, I suppose. Just call me the Hustler. It has a nice ring to it, doesn't it?"

I sing Van McCoy's "The Hustle" as we walk down the alley, toward where Lucas's car is parked down the street. He stares at me with a what-the-hell-is-happening look. I don't blame him. I feel like I just downed a pint of ice cream and am experiencing some sort of sugar high. If my mind is going a million kilometers per hour, my mouth is going double that speed.

My phone vibrates as I slide into the passenger seat of Lucas's jet-black Porsche.

THEO WALKER

Did you turn down plans with me to hang out with Lucas?

I whip my head around, expecting Theo to pop out of the backseat. Instead, I see Lucas's gym bag and an empty plastic water bottle.

JOSIE BANCROFT

Are you stalking me?

THEO WALKER

You didn't answer my text. I thought you died.

His text from a few hours ago read: *How do you feel about Fish and Chips for the girls? Very English-themed.* My lack of response was supposed to be indicative of my displeasure at his newest name for "the girls." Each combination he thinks of for my boobs is somehow worse than the last: Sherlock and Watson. Mario and Luigi. Thunder and Lightning. It's hard to keep a straight face when he comes up with a new moniker solely because his excitement is so genuine.

JOSIE BANCROFT

Reasonable assumption. Death is the only explanation for me not immediately responding to your text.

THEO WALKER

Exactly! So I checked to see if you were in a ditch or something. Turns out you're with Adler.

How in the—? Oh. *Ohh.* I forgot that I'd shared my location with Theo when we were in Le Mans. Oh, my God. Not that I think he's been following my movements, but I'm praying he didn't see that I went to a new Brazilian bikini wax place in Wickham or visited the gelato spot by my flat on back-to-back nights last week.

JOSIE BANCROFT

His friend had some marketing questions.

THEO WALKER

You never answer my questions!

JOSIE BANCROFT

Because your questions are weird, Walker. How am I supposed to know why eleven isn't pronounced onety-one?

THEO WALKER

You say weird, I say creative. Can I ask you a normal question?

JOSIE BANCROFT

We have different definitions of normal, but go ahead.

THEO WALKER

Want to get dinner on Friday?

JOSIE BANCROFT

You're in luck, babes. That's my one free night this week.

It's the first time in a while I've had a jam-packed week of plans. Plans I made, plans I'm excited about, plans with my friends. Plans that in-a-relationship-Josie would have probably turned down or pushed off until they eventually never happened.

THEO WALKER

It's a date, princess. :)

"Who ya texting over there, Jos?" Lucas asks in a teasing tone. "Do you have a new man in your life?"

"Nope," I say a little too quickly. Technically, not a lie, since Theo is, by no means, *new*. We've known each other for years now. "Just texting a friend."

He quickly glances at me, a not-so-subtle *bullshit* look on his face. "I've never blushed at my phone like that from a friend texting me."

"Maybe your friends aren't as good as mine," I say with a wink.

I've never had a friend spend hours between my legs, treating my body like it's the eighth wonder of the world, but here we are.

19

THEO

I PREFER SPENDING the nights I'm not on the road at my house, but Josie prefers her own space. That's why, instead of hanging out at my ten-million-pound, seven-thousand-square-foot house that has both a movie theater and a bowling lane, I'm waiting outside of Josie's one-bedroom, one-bathroom walk-up flat in Shoreditch.

My hands are too full to properly knock, so I kick the toe of my shoe against the door. Her blonde head pops out as I'm rounding up kick three.

"Uh, hi?"

Her voice is hoarse and a pitch lower than I've ever heard it. Probably because I avoid people like the plague when they're sick. I wouldn't talk to Lucas for an entire week after he inadvertently gave me the flu. Then there was the time Russell was drinking tea instead of coffee for a sore throat—which was due to allergies—but I aggressively bullied him to go to the medical tent to get a strep test.

I grin at her, although she can't see it behind the medical mask I'm wearing. "'Ello, gorgeous."

Despite the faded gray pajama set, bright red nose

featuring some sniffling, and paler than usual skin, she's still stunningly beautiful. "I thought you weren't coming over."

When she called me this morning to reschedule our plans, citing congestion and a cough, I told her to rest up and feel better. I was planning on just ordering soup to her apartment as a "get well soon," but then realized if I didn't see her tonight, it'd be another few days before I could. The past five days have been long enough, so here I am.

"I changed my mind," I inform her. "I'll be fine."

"I have a common cold, and you're dressed like I'm radiating toxic waste." She gives my outfit another once over and laughs, the sound raspy. My hands are encased in bright yellow dishwashing gloves, and disinfectant and cleaning supplies are tucked into the large pockets of the bib apron tied around my waist. I'm a sexy version of Mr. Clean.

"Okay, well, once I sanitize and disinfect your flat, I'll be fine."

Her jaw drops. "You're not cleaning my flat just to... Theo... that's absurd."

"Absurdly chivalrous. Now, are you going to be a polite host and let me in or am I going to have to barge past you? I'd prefer option one, as I think the contents of the bags will spill if there's any sort of collision."

She takes the brown paper bags from my hands and peeks inside. "You brought soup?"

"Lots of soup," I confirm. "And crackers."

I'd ordered every type of soup UberEats had available: chicken noodle, minestrone, tomato basil, creamy potato, carrot ginger, lentil, curried cauliflower.

"You don't like soup," Josie points out, opening the door so I can come in. "You think it's a fake food with questionable motives."

"That's because it is."

Soup is not my thing—never has been, never will be. It's

confusing and makes no sense. It's a liquid that we eat. And the little pieces of soluble food? Hard pass.

"Well, I have some whole wheat pasta in the pantry if you want to make that," Josie offers. "Otherwise, I have a frozen veggie pizza in the freezer."

"Sounds good. Now, go back to whatever you were doing while I get to business."

She stares at me momentarily before walking back to the couch. I'm aware that this is a bizarre situation, and she's aware I'm stubborn enough to see it through. Curling up on her couch under a chunky knit blanket, she warily watches me take out my supplies. When she's satisfied I'm actually going to clean and not just move all of her shit around, she resumes writing in the same notebook she carries around every race weekend.

I spray down her counter with something that smells lemony and promises to kill ninety-nine-point nine percent of viruses and bacteria. "I thought you took the day off?"

"I did." Josie simultaneously yawns and shrugs. "I'm just jotting some ideas I have for Gemini."

An unwarranted pang of jealousy hits me like a bullet to the chest. It was nice that Lucas thought of Josie for the freelance opportunity—Kelsey's a solid guy; I've met him a few times when I've boxed with Lucas, and Jos can easily bring his bar to life—but I don't like that my friend has spent more time with her this week than I have.

I walk over to the couch, leaving the spray to soak on the counter. Josie doesn't stop me when I politely grab her notebook. I'm not sure if she just doesn't care or if she knows I'll talk my way into seeing it anyway, and she's just saving her energy.

I flip through the pages—which is hard in rubber gloves— but don't even make it to her Gemini ideas. My hands immediately stop moving when I see "McAllister marketing brainstorm" in her cursive handwriting. There's a long list of ingenious ideas and campaigns—well, I'm sure they're brilliant. There are a lot of technical terms and phrases way out of my wheelhouse: lifecycle engagement, SMART objectives, resource segmentation, reporting and targeting.

I turn the notebook so she can see what I'm looking at and then "ooh" and "ahh" as I make my way through the list. The fact that McAllister *hasn't* implemented these ideas is a crime against the sport.

"Word to the wise," I say with a frown, noting the last thing on the list. "I would remove social media takeover."

"Maybe not with Blake," Josie says with a cute pout. "But you'd be great at it. You don't want to?"

Oh, the irony.

"My new contract has a clause in it prohibiting me from posting about McAllister on my own account without prior approval," I admit, handing her back the notebook. "So I don't think they're going to like the idea of me taking over the actual McAllister account."

Josie's lips part. "Excuse me?"

I shrug like it's no big deal, even though it's been eating at me. It's not unheard of for athletic teams to manage their drivers' or players' social media, especially if their antics tend to attract public attention, but it is unheard of for *me*. Half of my brand is my outgoing personality and candidness. I have hundreds of thousands of people tune into my Twitch streams and weekly workouts.

"Is that even," she pauses to sneeze into a tissue, "legal? Because that's major bullshit, babes."

"It's complicated. But yes, it's technically legal."

Formula 1 contracts are under strict lock and key—not even the media knows the details of them. Hell, if you Google my name, I make anywhere between eight million and forty-five million. I earn seventeen million a year, excluding performance bonuses and personal sponsorships, although McAllister is trying to slash those.

"Is this because of you-know-who?"

"Hmm?" I tilt my head before putting two and two together. "Oh, Avery? You can say his name; he's not Voldemort, angel."

She shakes her head. "If he put that clause in your contract, he most definitely is."

Can't disagree with her there. If Avery was out of the picture, then my contract would already have been signed, sealed, and delivered.

"Have you showed these to Rhys?" I ask, desperate to change the subject. There's no need for Avery to occupy any more of my headspace.

Josie pulls the blanket tighter around her shoulders like its protective armor. "Not yet. Waiting for the right moment, I guess."

Giving her a taste of her own medicine, I belt out the chorus of Kelly Clarkson's "A Moment Like This." Serenading a woman isn't my usual go-to, nor should it be based on the way Josie's trying not to laugh at my nails-on-chalkboard singing voice.

She sticks out her hand and wiggles her fingers once I'm through singing. I hand back her notebook, despite my urge to get into the working mind of Josie, going through and analyzing every page.

"Back to cleaning," I announce. "Time to make this place sparkle and shine like a goddamn gem."

Josie rolls her eyes, but her lips curve into the smile I've come to know so well. Considering the size of her flat, it doesn't take me too long to sanitize and sterilize to my complete satisfaction. Taking off my mask and cleaning gloves, I toss them into the trash before joining Josie on the couch. After an extra-lengthy workout with Russell this morning, my tight muscles sing in joy as they sink into the comfy material of her couch.

When Josie still hasn't curled up into me after five minutes, I grab the clicker and pause the movie. "Excuse me, miss. Why aren't you cuddling me?"

Josie tilts her head up at me and laughs. "I didn't know if you wanted me to. I'm trying to be respectful of your boundaries since I'm under the weather."

I reach out to brush a stray piece of hair away from her face. It's warmer than usual, probably due to a low fever. "I appreciate it, but I definitely want cuddles."

"Good," she says, snuggling up against me. "Thanks for coming over. And cleaning. I know you prefer to not be around people when they're sick."

"You're not people," I say simply. "You're you."

I've always been super vigilant about not being around germs, viruses, infections… anything that could trigger a flare-up of my dad's MS. After he suffered a particularly bad relapse when I was sixteen, my dislike for germs spiraled into a neurotic fear of any sort of illness-inducing exposure. My parents strong-armed me into therapy for it so it wouldn't impact my career and I've gotten better, but if given the choice, I tend to err on the side of caution. Except with Josie. None of my usual rules apply to her.

Josie presses her warm lips against the underside of my jaw, rewarding me with a few quick kisses. My dick still stirs in my pants at her touch. It's like I'm eleven-years-old again and unable to control a boner that's popped up at the most inopportune time. I shift my position to try to hide the fact that I'm getting semi-hard, but Josie's quick to take notice.

She swallows back a smirk. "Looks like someone wants to say hello."

Fuck. I didn't come here with sex or seduction in mind, but my brain seems to have forgotten to relay that message to my nether regions.

"I swear I'm not here for anything but PG activities. My dick just has a, uh… very unhealthy obsession with your body. But don't worry, he's going in a time-out." I point a finger at my crotch and scold it, "Bad, Theo Jr., *bad*."

Josie giggles at my weirdness. "According to my mother, orgasms are actually very good at boosting your immune system while you're sick."

Maybe Theo Jr. doesn't need to go in a time out after all. "Yeah?"

"Mm-hmm. She dropped off a vibrator earlier with a lovely little note."

My jaw drops. "No, she didn't."

Josie nods and sighs, motioning to a small notecard tucked beneath a candle on her coffee table. I pick it up, bouncing my legs as I scan the card.

Josephine,
You know what they say—an orgasm a day keeps
the doctor away.
Seriously. It's scientifically proven.
Feel better and happy masturbating, darling!
xx,
Mum

Aggressively loud laughter rips through me, and I topple over onto my side. I reread the note three more times, but it just keeps getting better every time I do. Josie plays with my hair as I attempt to get ahold of myself.

"This is gold, Bancroft," I howl, my abs constricting. "And she gave you another vibrator?"

Josie's shown me the large plastic container under her bed

that houses the various vibrators, dildos, lube, anal beads, and sword-looking things her mum has given her over the years.

"It's called the *Buzz Lightyear*," Josie admits with a small smile. "Not only does it have seven vibration settings, but it glows in the dark."

I lose my cool all over again. I'd break my fingers before I ever let my mum say the word *masturbation* in front of me, but Josie seems relatively unconcerned, used to her mum's intrusion on her sex life.

"Can we watch a horror movie or something?" I ask, still laughing. "This vibrator talk is just making my predicament worse."

Thankfully, Theo Jr. manages to stay on his best behavior for the rest of the night, even when Josie takes a shower before we head to bed. Yep. I'm sleeping over. Even though Josie swears she changed her sheets this morning, she does it again just to make me feel better.

I shoot Martin a text as I snuggle into Josie's warm, clean bed.

THEO WALKER

Any update on the contract?

MARTIN THE MANAGER

Not yet, but it's only been two weeks. You know this can take months.

THEO WALKER

I'm impatient.

MARTIN THE MANGER

I'm aware. I was there when the server told you your plate was hot, and you ignored him and burnt the fuck out of your fingers. Almost missed a race because your hands were out of sorts.

THEO WALKER

> In my defense, he didn't clarify it was "you'll literally get third-degree burns and scream" hot.

MARTIN THE MANAGER

> Just keep your Gucci knickers out of a twist, eh? No need to prematurely burn yourself this time around.

THEO WALKER

> Only Lucas wears Gucci. Mine are Tom Ford. But I'll try.

Josie pops her head out of the bathroom with a mouth full of toothpaste thirty minutes later. She starts talking but I have no idea what she's trying to say. Holding out a finger, she disappears from sight. The moment she's gone, I place my phone face-down on the bedside table. It feels slimy, but Jenna's in town and has been persistently calling me for the past twenty minutes. The hornier she gets, the more nude photos she sends. I told her I was indefinitely busy, but she's not taking the hint.

"Are you discovering a new scientific element or something?" I call out. "You've been in there for five hours."

Her skin care routine has more steps than an Ikea furniture instruction manual. She probably puts sunscreen on before bed to protect her skin from the moon's dangerous glow.

A moment later, Josie slides into the other side of the bed. As I move my arm to wrap around her, I'm reminded of a *very* important question I have to ask her. "Why didn't you tell me you wanted to have a threesome?"

Josie's mouth immediately falls open, her upper lip curling back. I'm glad the bedside lamp's still on so I can watch how horrified she seems by the idea.

"Absolutely not," she says abruptly. "I don't know where you got that idea, but—"

I cut her off by showing her the plush piggy that's been

concealed behind my back. It was hidden underneath the pillows, and I only discovered it when I went to switch them because I like the flatter one on top.

"I wonder if this counts as a *ménage à trois*," I tease lightly. "You, me, and Miss Piggy."

Her cheeks flush bright pink and she lunges for the piglet. I hold my arm up so it's out of her reach.

"Theo!" Her lower lip pushes forward. All I want to do is nibble on it, common cold be damned. "Give me back Mademoiselle!"

Mademoiselle? My arm briefly bends as unrestrained laughter pours out of me. Josie takes advantage of my lax muscles and pounces on me. Being straddled by a bombshell with a low-grade fever while I'm holding her stuffed pig named Mademoiselle hostage isn't how I ever imagined myself spending a Friday night, but here we are.

When Josie reaches up to grab her prized possession, she accidentally grinds against my cock. The soft moan I let out as she continues to wiggle around makes her pause briefly. Suddenly, she begins moving her hips in a very strategic manner. I'm Play-Doh—complete and utterly at her mercy as my cock hardens under her touch. She easily recaptures Mademoiselle and rolls off me.

I'm now uncomfortably turned on, but what else is new? It happens every time I'm thinking about or around Josie. I rest my hand on her hip, but she smacks it away. "Leave me and Mademoiselle alone."

"Jos." I chuckle, snaking my arm around her. "I think it's adorable that you still sleep with a stuffed animal."

"Lots of adults sleep with their childhood stuffed animal," she huffs. "Almost forty percent of the population, according to studies."

"I believe you." I press slow butterfly kisses along her

shoulder blade before letting my lips take their final place on her neck. "It's sweet."

Despite her quiet grumbling, I can hear her breathing become shallow as I continue to tease her neck with my tongue. Knowing I turn her on just as much as she turns me on makes my head spin.

"Is *Mademoiselle* the one you got from your birth mum?" I pronounce the name with a French accent.

Josie turns around and when her eyes meet mine, my brain gets fuzzy. "Yes," she says simply.

I press my lips against her collarbone. "This is a horrible segue, but do you want to go to Rosalie's birthday party with me in a few weeks?"

I ended up buying my goddaughter all three dolls I was comparing at the store. It's not like I don't have the money for it.

Josie scrunches up her nose. "Why is that a bad segue?"

"Because it's Peppa Pig-themed."

She smacks me in the arm, an adorably angry pout on her face. "Sod off, Walker."

"Please?" I ask in a whiney voice. I love my goddaughter but quite frankly, I'd like to drop kick Peppa Pig into the depths of the Atlantic Ocean. I don't know what it is about that damn pig, but she drives me up a wall. I find her insufferable. "Did I mention there's going to be an ice cream cake?"

Her features relax slightly at the mention of this. "I'll think about it."

We both know that's a yes. Josie rolls her eyes at my wide smile and flicks off her bedside lamp. My body immediately finds hers in the dark and I wrap my arms around her, feeling the smooth warmth of her skin. Her still damp hair holds the intoxicating mix I associate with her, and I nuzzle into it.

"Jos?"

"Hmm?"

"Do you want Mademoiselle to sleep on your side or mine?"

She kicks my shin with the heel of her foot under the blanket. "You're not going to have a side if you keep up your teasing, Walker."

That shuts me up immediately. Besides landing pole for a race and the *Crocodile Corkscrew*, spooning is now one of my favorite positions. And I don't want to lose that privilege anytime soon.

20

JOSIE

I NEVER THOUGHT I'd compare myself to a rotisserie chicken, but thanks to the Singapore heat, that's exactly what's happening. I chug ice water in the cafeteria, but sweat it out almost immediately. So much for staying hydrated. Theo walking around shirtless isn't helping my body temperature go down, either. Sweat just adds to his raw sexual appeal.

"I'm in love," Ella announces. She sits in the chair across from me and rests her chin in her hands.

Despite the fog my brain seems to be caught in, I still manage to sing the opening lines of "I'm 'N Luv (With a Stripper)."

"David Green is not a stripper." Ella laughs, her dimple winking. "Although I'm sure he'd look good in minimal clothing."

I've never personally met David, but I know damn well who he is considering I've married and smashed him in multiple games of Bang, Smash, Dash in the past year. Besides being the youngest team principal in Formula 1 history, he's also the most attractive. AlphaVite is flourishing under his leadership and came in second for last season's Constructors' Championship, beating out Everest.

"You interviewed him?"

"Yes!" Ella wiggles her shoulders in excitement. "He was *so* sweet. He even gave me an AlphaVite hat, although I think Blake will go into cardiac arrest if he sees it."

Blake thinks anyone who's near Ella is automatically in love with her, but he's been very chill about her spending time with other teams. He understands its part of her job and is just happy to have her at the Grand Prix with him. Wearing another team's merchandise is where he draws the line, though.

Ella fills me in on her interview, adding in details she knows I'll appreciate—like the fact that David enjoys cooking and prefers workout classes to running outside. She also points out that he's single. He's thirty-seven, which is a bit out of my age range, plus I can't handle sleeping with more than one person at a time. Not that Ella knows I'm even sleeping with one person.

I tune in and out of the conversation, my mind circling back to my conversation with Rhys from yesterday morning.

"Josephine!" Rhys greets me. His straw-blonde hair is slicked back like he's in Grease. *If he were holding a cigarette and wearing a leather jacket, he'd for sure be a John Travolta groupie. Instead, he's in his classic uniform—a white McAllister polo, black slacks, and bright white trainers. A classic 'dad uniform,' minus the kids and minivan. "Come in, come in."*

I slip into the sleek conference room titled Progress, praying it's a good omen.

"Got your email," he says with a smile. "And love where your head is at. Always driving innovation."

"That is the motto, right?" I smile and sit in the padded desk chair next to him.

McAllister may drive innovation, but this room may also drive someone to a psych ward. It's like a creepy shrine to Blake and Theo.

Every available wall surface is plastered with their photos. Blake's feature a stoic look of determination, whereas Theo's feature his carefree, boyish smile.

"All of your ideas are great." I sense a but coming, and right on cue, he continues, "But our marketing plans for the rest of the season are locked in."

"What about implementing them next season?"

"You know how the big guys feel. There's no need to rework the wheel if it's driving just fine."

Rhys is technically one of those big guys, but whatever.

"Earth to Jos?" A finger snaps wildly in front of my face. "You good over there?"

I take a long sip of my water. "Mm-hmm. Just overheated, I think."

She nods sympathetically. "I feel you. I'm drained. Plus, I slept like shit. This hotel has the world's hardest beds, don't you think?"

"Not comfy at all."

I hate lying, but my only other option is to admit that I can't relate because Theo's bed is heavenly. He not only has his own sheets, comforter, and pillows sent to every Grand Prix ahead of his arrival, he has a Tempur-Pedic mattress topper flown in, too. We've come up with an unspoken agreement that in London we stay at my place, but at races, we stay in his hotel room.

I force out a yawn to back up my fib. "Sorry about spacing. What were you saying about AlphaVite's marketing plan? They want to do driver-cam vlogs?"

Ella entertains me with stories of her interview until it's time to head to the pit. It's thankfully a night race, so it's cooled down a bit by the time we leave the air-conditioned cafeteria.

Blake starts in pole and keeps his position until he crashes in lap twenty-seven and is forced to retire early. If there wasn't steam coming off his body because of the heat, there'd be steam pouring out of his ears in anger. Harry Thompson better hide unless he wants to face the wrath of Blake.

Blake and Harry exiting the race leaves Theo with a massive opportunity to win. And he does by a whopping seven-point-four seconds. It's not his first podium win in Singapore, but it is his first first-place win and the celebrations begin the moment the podium ceremony is over.

Rather than go to a club, we swap out flashing strobe lights for a dive bar where neon beer signs cover the walls. Heading to a table toward the back, I pass inebriated patrons yelling at one another over the loud music, making it hard to hear my own thoughts. Maybe that's for the best.

"Shouldn't drive innovation apply to all aspects of the company?" I push Rhys, not ready to give up on the brilliant—if I do say so myself—ideas I'd sent him in a very lovely presentation. "Not just the engines and technology?"

Rhys gives me a weighted smile. "Listen, Jos, you're one of the best. And I know the whole team appreciates your work, but as far as our share-holders are concerned, we're crushing it. We're generating revenue, and just because our campaigns don't include influencers or TikTok, doesn't make them any less successful, you know?"

I nod dutifully. What else am I supposed to do? Throw a fit? Storm out of here? Stomp my feet until I get my way?

"I'll bring some of these up at the next director's meeting," he compro-mises. "I just don't want you to get your hopes up."

I settle in a seat between Ella and a driver she's inter-viewing for her podcast next week. The two of them talk to one another while I sip my drink, thankful I don't have to participate in the conversation. Between my unsuccessful meeting with Rhys and the sauna I've been in for the past three days, I'm emotionally and physically drained.

My eyes wander around the bar, noting things I like and dislike. Since Kelsey's approval—and complete obsession—of the brand guidelines and content strategy plan I sent him, it's been full steam ahead. Now my brain is constantly cataloging new ideas for the bar, especially in comparison to the places I've been to while traveling with McAllister.

Will we feature local beers on tap to ingratiate ourselves into the neighborhood? Do we want to do any cross-promotions with neighboring stores? Should we give into the alcoholic seltzer trend or explicitly stick to a more traditional beers, liquor, and wine menu?

Half an hour later, my phone buzzes with a text from Theo. He's sitting only a few seats away but is in conversation with Lucas about something or other. I've been too distracted to eavesdrop.

THEO WALKER

> Everything peachy, princess? Awfully quiet over there.

I glance up to find him staring at me with hypnotic intensity. The soft, questioning look in his eyes contrasts with the sharp downturn of his lips. The urge to run my fingers through his hair and wrap my arms around his neck comes on so suddenly, I forget to breathe.

JOSIE BANCROFT

> Meet me in the bathroom?

Theo's face goes from concerned to confused to completely turned on in the span of three seconds. This is not my style, *at all*. But I don't care. Right now, all I want is Theo. His body, his hands, his lips. The perfect distraction. I don't wait for his answer, instead standing from the table and mumbling something about getting a new drink.

There's a large crowd hovering in front of the women's bathroom—because of course there is—but no line to get into the men's. *Fuck it.* Maybe it's my buzz, or the heat, or the intense desire to have Theo kiss away every ounce of frustration I'm feeling, but *fuck* it. I push open the door, praying he's not far behind me.

The sound of the lock clicking into place behind him as he walks into the bathroom emboldens me. I pull him in by his belt loops, our thighs pressed against one another. Theo lets out a noise that's half-chuckle, half-groan. "Bathroom sex, angel? Didn't think you'd—"

My lips crash into his in a demanding manner. Theo doesn't question my sudden neediness. He meets me halfway, parting my lips with his wet tongue, tangling it with mine. I run my hands through his smooth hair, and he moans deeply in response.

The kiss doesn't alleviate the craving I have for him; it makes it worse. It's a battle of desire, except we may explode in flames before we find out who wins. I suck his bottom lip into my mouth to nibble on and sate my ache.

I need him. Need this.

Theo places his hands on my hips and effortlessly lifts me, placing me on the edge of the sink. My breath hitches in my chest as he scrunches my skirt up around my waist and teases my lace thong to the side. I spread my legs and when he glides a finger against me, I lean into his touch, desperate for it.

"Always so wet for me, gorgeous," he groans deeply. "Love getting you all worked up like this."

I don't think he'll ever *stop* getting me worked up like this. My body is a fuse begging to be lit by his flame. I'm glad the music in the bar is loud because I can't stop the noises that slip through my lips as he slowly twists two fingers inside me. I'm fighting for my breath as he massages the sensitive spot inside, the heel of his hand rubbing against my clit.

Theo tugs the end of my ponytail so my neck's exposed and swirls his tongue around the sensitive spot right above my collarbone. He sucks the skin harshly, but I don't care about the deep red spots that will no doubt mark my skin.

"Do you know how goddamn sexy you are?" Theo murmurs into my ear. "Want you all the damn time. Can't ever get enough of you."

My legs shake as the familiar tightening in my stomach spirals south. The soul-shattering intensity of my climax is overwhelming. It's a rush so intense that it grabs a hold of me and doesn't let go. But the moans slipping through my lips quickly turn to strangled gasps as tears that have been sitting latent beneath the surface fall down my cheeks like a torrential storm.

I cover my face with my hands as my chest caves inward. *Hi, and welcome to my own personal hell: crying after an orgasm!* Unrestrained sobs wrack my body, every one of my limbs feeling thick with embarrassment and emotion.

Theo's voice is laced with concern. "What's wrong? Are you hurt? Did I hurt you?"

My throat aches too badly to get a word out, so I just shake my head *no*. He reaches out and cups my cheeks with his calloused hands. "Say something. Please. You're freaking me out, baby."

God only knows how I look. I'm not a cute crier, far from it. My face gets splotchy and red, like I'm having some sort of allergic reaction. My eyes focus on Theo's face—the deep blue of his eyes, the frown marking his usually smiling lips. It just makes me cry harder.

Theo doesn't say anything else. He simply wraps his arms around me as I crumble against his sturdy body. He murmurs sweet nothings into my ear, stroking my back in a soothing motion. His arms around me feel like a weighted blanket, and my breathing eventually steadies to a pace that wouldn't make a doctor panic.

"Are you oka—"

He's cut off by someone aggressively smacking the bathroom door, and my head jerks up at the interruption. The man is *not* happy about the door being locked and shares some not very nice words to tell us this.

"Piss off, will ya?" Theo shouts. "We're busy."

"Screw somewhere else!" a gruff voice yells back. "Some of us need to take a piss!"

"We're trying to repopulate the earth because there's an impending apocalypse, so fuck the fuck off, you douche canoe."

I half-laugh, half-sniffle. "An apocalypse? Really, babes?"

"I will break this door down," the guy screams.

Theo blows a puff of air out of his cheeks. "Do you know who Blake Hollis is?"

There's a long pause before the voice says, "Yes."

"Well, he doesn't like when people give his friends a hard time, so I suggest taking a piss in the goddamn women's bathroom or I will personally have Mr. Hollis remove you from the premises."

Pressing my face into his chest, I let loose a long laugh. *Did he seriously just use Blake as his guard dog?* We hear the man swear loudly, but thirty seconds later, the shadow of his footsteps disappears from beneath the door.

"I look like a marshmallow." I sniffle, lifting my head up. "I'm all puffy."

Theo presses his lips together to stop his lips from curling up. "I've always had a weakness for s'mores."

I laugh as Theo wipes my remaining tears with the back of his hand. I thought this would make me feel better, not make me bawl my eyes out on a bathroom sink post-orgasm. "God, what the hell is wrong with me?"

"There's a laundry list of things wrong with you, angel." He chuckles. "You call lizards baby dragons, you don't like bacon but think chunky peanut butter is acceptable, and you thought the *Game of Thrones* series finale made sense. Oh, and don't even get me started on the fact that you think orange Starbursts are the best ones."

"You refer to mayonnaise as *egg butter*!" I argue. "And think that duels should be brought back as a legitimate form of fighting."

"Well, you eat waffles *without* syrup."

"You refuse to eat raisins because you think they look like tiny nut sacks," I huff. "And I meant something's wrong with me because I just cried after… coming."

Even saying it makes my cheeks sting. This is, hands-down, the most embarrassing sexual experience I've ever had.

"I once cried after a blowjob," Theo says, completely serious. "If it makes you feel any better."

I truly can't tell if he's kidding or not. "Wait, what?"

"This chick went down on me after eating super spicy food. It was so painful; it felt like fire ants had crawled up my dick and were attacking me. I swear to God, I thought it was about to fall off, Bancroft. I called Russell in hysterics."

Slapping my hand over my mouth, I desperately try to swallow down a giggle. "That does make me feel slightly better."

Theo grins as he laughs. "So at least you got a good orgasm out of your cry. All I got were blue balls."

I wipe my cheeks with the back of my hands as he spreads his fingers across my bare thighs. "Can I have a re-do later?"

"Absolutely." Theo swipes his tongue over his lower lip. "But I'm holding Theo Jr. hostage until you tell me what's going on."

"It's stupid," I mumble.

He shakes his head. "Not if it made you cry."

"I'm just…" I pause, trying to come up with the right word, "discouraged, I guess. I finally met with Rhys to discuss the stuff you saw in my notebook, and he more or less told me that we can't do any of it. The same shit he always says. And I've worked with Kelsey for only a few weeks, and he's given me free reign to try new things out and think outside the box.

It's making me realize that McAllister may value the work I do, but not enough to take any of my ideas into consideration and implement real changes, you know?" I shrink into my shoulders, wanting to hide from his almost-accusatory stare. "So yeah, frustrated."

"I had no idea you felt this way, Jos," he says, his voice softening. "Why didn't you say anything sooner?"

Because I didn't realize how frustrated I was until I started working with Kelsey. Because I'm worried if I do tell you these things, I'll become too dependent. Because I'm falling for you, even though I know I shouldn't be.

I can't tell him any of this, so instead I say, "Because you live and breathe McAllister, Walker."

He nods pensively. "Yeah, but I came out of the womb knowing I wanted to race for them. This has always been my dream, and I get to wake up every morning and live it. I don't mean to discredit your work because you know I think you're fantastic at what you do, but I don't think McAllister is necessarily the end all, be all for you."

My shoulders slightly relax as he gives it an encouraging squeeze. "No?"

"I mean, if you start freelancing for another team, I will go full-blown Blake, but other than that, no. You're smart, talented, very skilled—in and out of the bedroom. Kelsey's lucky to have you for the next few months. And honestly? I think it's rather selfish of you to not share your talents with more people. So, side hustle your heart away, baby."

His approval means a lot to me. Not because I *need* it, but because I value it.

"Well, maybe not *all* of your talents," he amends. "I'd like that thing you do with your tongue to be specially reserved for me."

I rest my head on his shoulder, nodding with a laugh. "The tongue thing is all yours, babes."

"Good." He gently kisses my head before grabbing me by the waist and helping me off the sink. "Now, can we get out of here? God knows the last time they cleaned these counters. Christ, I can't believe we almost had sex in a bathroom. What are you doing to me, Bancroft?"

The same damn thing he's doing to me. I'm supposed to be focusing on myself, not complicating my life by falling for Theo, yet I no longer have any idea where the invisible line between purely platonic and strictly sexual falls.

21

THEO

I JOLT up to the sound of someone ringing my doorbell at rapid-fire speed. I'm running on minimal sleep thanks to a delayed flight back from Singapore. Looking at my phone, I see it's only seven-forty-two. *What the fuck?* Throwing on a pair of sweats, I head downstairs. The hardwood floor is cold beneath my feet and sends an unwelcome shiver through my body. I should check the peephole, but I'm too desperate to stop the goddamn EDM song my doorbell's conducting.

Swinging open the door, I find my sister standing with a massive suitcase next to her. She's a mini version of our mum —except for the blue eyes we both inherited from our dad— with her wavy, dark brown hair, a nose no plastic surgeon could find fault in, and dimples that wink with her ever-present smile. And right now she's giving me our mum's infamous stare of calm reproach.

"What are you doing here?" I ask, dumbfounded.

She puts her hands on her hips and raises a singular eyebrow. "You're kidding me, right?"

I rub the sleepiness from my eyes. "Uh. No?"

"Did you forget that I'm having an existential crisis and desperately need a holiday?"

Charlotte has just one semester of university left before graduation and has no idea what she wants to do afterward. Considering she's changed her major three times and collects hobbies like Pokémon cards, I can't necessarily say I'm surprised. Not that I'd ever tell her that. Nope. I'd like to have kids in the future, so I'm keeping that observation to myself.

"I didn't forget, Char, but you told me you were arriving tomorrow," I reply slowly.

"There was an earlier flight available," she says with a frown. "I texted you about it."

There's no way I would've given her the green light to arrive the day I got home from a race, but I don't mention that. "No big deal, Char. I'm glad you're here."

"I swear I did, Theodore." She starts scrolling through her phone to find the text. Glancing up a few moments later, she bites her lower lip and mumbles, "Oops. I texted my friend Thea instead of you. I didn't notice since, ya know, it's only a letter off. Shit, I'm sorry. I—"

I burst out laughing since I did the same thing earlier this year, although it was my team principal on the receiving end of a dick pic.

"C'mere, kid." I pull her in for a long hug, resting my chin on the top of her head. I place my hands on her shoulders a few seconds later. "How about you freshen up while I get dressed and then we can head to breakfast? There's a new spot down the street we can try out."

Her dimples flash as her grimace dissipates. "Perfect. I'm starving." She walks past me and into my foyer, saying, "Oh! What's the dress code of this place?"

"It's breakfast, Lottie. Wear pajamas for all I care," I state, rolling my eyes. The world is Charlotte's runway and I say that with complete seriousness. The woman dresses up to grab her prescriptions from the pharmacy.

"Okay, so cute-casual." She flashes me a thumbs up before rushing up the stairs to get ready in a guest bedroom.

I text my friends and let them know that Lottie's joining our dinner plans. I could reschedule, but they all get on well and having plans will help fight the eleven-hour jet lag.

I sigh when I notice a purse at the bottom of the stairs and a pair of shoes haphazardly piled at the front door, blocking the coat closet—where the shoes *should* go. I love my baby sis, but it's going to be a *long* week.

THE WARM WOOD floors and sleek lighting of the restaurant make me feel like I'm at a spa. A spa that just so happens to serve spicy salmon on crispy rice and steamed dim sum with a garlic-infused vinegar dipping sauce. Given its close proximity to Josie's apartment, she meets us for a quick drink before our dinner reservation. I spot her sitting at the large central bar, seated on one of the stools as she chats with the bartender. No surprise she's first to arrive.

"'Ello, princess," I greet her. "Fancy seeing you here."

Josie's eyes light up as she looks at me, a heart-melting smile traveling across her lips. Before she can give me a proper hello—one that I wish involved a lingering kiss—Charlotte squeals and throws her arms around Josie's neck.

Over the years, the two of them have developed a friendship completely devoid of my existence. They text frequently and comment on one another's Instagram posts more than they comment on mine. Granted, I have millions of followers while they don't, but whatever.

"Thank God you're here," Josie says conspiratorially as we settle into the two seats next to her. "Do either of you know what the bloody hell a dynamic low-intervention wine is?"

Charlotte picks up the drink menu, scanning it quickly although we both know she's going to order wine. "No idea about that, but their cocktails have house shrubs in them... which sounds rather interesting, eh?"

The bartender hands over two glasses of wine and a cosmo —obviously mine—and we do a quick toast to Charlotte's visit.

I intertwine my free hand with Josie's under the table, desperate to feel her. To be close. We haven't seen each other much over the past few weeks due to busy schedules and free time that doesn't overlap. She came to Rosalie's birthday party but spent more time doing somersaults and cartwheels with the four-year-olds than hanging out with me. I miss her... way more than a friend should. This weekend is the Hungarian Grand Prix and after that is summer break, so I'll be in Australia for the month. Four weeks without Josie; four weeks with Richard. Worst fucking trade off of the century.

"Sorry I can't stay for dinner," Josie says with an apologetic smile. She's going to a comedy show with some friends later and, while it's great that she's spending more time with them, I selfishly wish she could stay the whole night.

"I'm glad you could at least make drinks," Charlotte reassures her. "Have you been here before?"

"No." Josie shakes her head. "But I've had their ginger carrot soup, and it's to die for."

She rests her hand on my thigh under the table and gives it a quick squeeze. Her nails are painted light pink, the color of ballet slippers. I wonder when she got them done, considering they were lavender the last time we saw one another.

"To die for because it's so horrible," I correct her. "Highly *don't* recommend."

"You got Theo to try a soup?" Charlotte asks bewilderedly. "Did you hold a gun to his head?"

No, but she did promise to let me see the Buzz Lightyear vibrator. And hinted that she'd let us introduce it in the bedroom.

"I just asked nicely," Josie says. "I was sick, so he felt bad saying no. He was a very good nurse."

Charlotte's drink lands on the table with such a loud *thump* that I flinch. "You're telling me that you got Theo to *eat* soup with you while you were *sick*?"

I mumble under my breath that you can't eat soup as Josie nods with a laugh. Charlotte—being the ever so subtle sister she is—gapes at me with her mouth slightly ajar. She attempts to pry for more details, but Josie changes the topic of conversation. I'm sure my sister will hit me with an M16-level interrogation the moment Josie leaves.

The two of them chat as if I'm not there, but I don't mind. I'm too distracted, anyway. The way Josie's rubbing her thumb over my knuckles is getting me worked up. I want her hands all over me. Gripping my thighs as she swirls her tongue around me. Pressed against my chest as she rides me. Hands in my hair as she kisses me.

The bartender approaches us, but rather than ask us if we want another round, he hands Josie a new glass of wine. "From the gentleman over there," he says, nodding to a bloke at the other end of the bar.

"Oh, um, thanks." Josie gives the fucker a small smile and a quick wave. "Cheers."

Fuck no. Hell fucking no. I know this move. I've done this move plenty of times before. I don't realize how tightly my fingers are gripping her thigh until she shifts uncomfortably in her seat. The bloke may be wearing a green shirt, but I've turned into the green-eyed-monster.

Thankfully, the glass remains untouched for the duration of Josie's time with us. The moment she leaves, I wave over the bartender. "Can you please tell the *gentleman* that sent over this drink that my *friend* is allergic to grapes and can't drink wine?"

He looks down at the empty wineglass Josie had spent drinking the past hour. Didn't really think that excuse through, but instead of trying to back it up, I push the glass forward, indicating that he should take it.

"Theodore." Charlotte giggles and waves off the server, taking the glass of wine for herself. "Stop glowering at the poor man."

"I'm not glowering," I huff, averting my death-stare from the man in question. "Blake glowers; I glow. I'm like a damn Coppertone sunscreen or some shit. Stop being dramatic."

She rolls her eyes. "You're dramatic, I'm… cinematic."

I snort. "More like problematic."

She sticks her tongue out before taking a sip of her drink. "All I'm saying is that I've never seen you jealous over a woman. It's endearing, big bro."

"It's not a woman," I argue. "It's Josie."

Charlotte lets out an obnoxiously long laugh. "Oh, yeah. Real nice. I'm sure she'd *loooove* to hear you say that."

I elbow her in the arm. "You know what I mean. It's… it's Josie. She's my best friend. Of course, I'm going to be protective of her."

"Your best friend that you just so happen to be banging."

I choke on my cocktail. *How in the hell does she know that?*

Charlotte grins at me, clearly pleased that she's thrown me off. I think sisters sometimes feel the need to stir the pot for no reason. Hell, I suppose brothers act that way, too. I've certainly started my fair share of shit with her over the years.

"I'm not twelve," she reminds me. "The sexual tension was so palpable, it was almost pornographic. I'm surprised you don't have drool all over your chin, honestly."

"Are you done bullying me?"

"Me bullying you?" Her jaw drops. "Do you not remember locking me in the basement when I was five because I accidentally sneezed on you?"

Accidentally my ass. Her aim had clearly been directed at

me. It's been seventeen years, and I still remember the incident as if it were yesterday.

"Whatever," I huff. "Can we move on?"

"Nope. I'm just getting warmed up, and this is the most fun I've had all day. Tell me what's going on with you two. Are you friends with benefits? Casually doing it? Exclusively doing it? Boyfriend-girlfriend? Ready to meet the parents? Looking at engagement rings? Picking out baby names?"

Has she always been this annoying? Christ. "Uh… I'm not sure."

There's nothing casual about what we're doing, that's for sure. We've had hot and heavy sex, but we've also—and it freaks me out to say this—made love. And I didn't hate it… I fucking loved it. There's something satisfyingly intimate about having sex with someone you deeply care about. It makes the orgasm ten times better, but it isn't even about the orgasm, it's about connecting. Friends don't have the kind of sex we had, that much I know. What I don't know is if I'm ready to admit what that means.

"Okay, well, what do you *want* it to be?"

"Is that relevant? Career comes first. Remember?" The line rolls off my tongue with practiced precision. Even though figuring things out with McAllister is my number one priority, that mantra tastes sour on my tongue.

"I'm focusing on my career," Charlotte mimics in a deep baritone. "I'm literally breaking out in hives because that's such a lame answer, Theodore."

She holds out her arm to show me her invisible allergic reaction. *There's no way people think I'm more dramatic than her, right?*

"Josie's an integral part of your career, you dummy," she continues. "The two of you travel together for every race. You'll never find another woman *more* focused on your career. So your bullshit answer won't work with me."

"Yeah, but—"

"There's no *but*. You're being ridiculous. Dad had a career *and* a family. I'd say he was pretty okay. And no offense, but Josie's way out of your league. I'm your sister, so I'm forced to like you, but the fact that she *willingly* hangs out with you… Lock that in, Theodore. Seriously."

I raise my brows. "Ever consider law school?"

"Why? Because I just shot down your line of defense in three sentences?"

"Because you turn everything into an argument," I mutter.

When I spy Blake and Lucas, I practically leap into their arms, grateful for the reprieve from twenty questions. We're led to a table tucked in the back corner of the restaurant, away from the prying eyes of the other patrons who are craning their necks to get a better look at the Formula 1 royalty gracing their presence. We all know better than to argue with Blake when he requests privacy.

The moment my sister sits down, she grabs Lucas's bicep and leans in to get a better look. "Ohh. I like this tattoo, Lucas. New?"

A grin of appreciation breaks across his face. "Yeah, thanks. Surprised you noticed it."

Blake and I exchange a look because neither of us spotted his new ink, despite being in close proximity to him all the time.

Charlotte flashes him a twinkling smile, her blue eyes filled with mirth. "You've got great arms. Women take notice."

Nope. Absolutely not.

"You can't just touch people like that, Charlotte," I snap, not liking her flirty tone one iota.

Charlotte scoffs and rolls her eyes. "Why not? Is he going to die of cooties?" She turns her head to Lucas and raises a brow. "Is your body disintegrating at my touch?"

"No." He lets out a throaty chuckle. "And you're not one to talk, Theo. You're the king of invading personal space."

"Am not."

"Yes, you are," Blake says, flagging down a server so he can order a drink.

Lucas flicks up a blonde brow and takes a sip of his water. "Hmm. Remember when you broke into my hotel room while I was showering and proceeded to have a conversation with me, completely ignoring the fact that I was ass-naked? Or the time you whipped off your briefs to show me your dick because—"

"Okay, okay!" I shout, raising my hands. "Sorry for wanting to make sure it wasn't about to fall off."

Turns out it was a side effect of taking Viagra for fun. My bad.

"You're so weird, Theodore." Charlotte props her chin in her hands. "Maybe I should get a tattoo."

"You're not getting a tattoo," I decide with finality. No way in hell.

"I don't remember asking you." She flips me the bird before turning to Lucas and Blake, she says, "Okay. Let's discuss. What do you guys think about Theo and Josie? He should get over his dumb *career comes first* bullshit, right?"

She's dead to me. R.I.P. Nice knowing you, Charlotte!

When neither of them answers, she grimaces and mutters, "Oops. You guys didn't know, did you?"

I'm too scared to look at my friends, unsure of how they're going to react. I focus my attention on my drink, watching bubbles float to the top as I slurp it up in large gulps.

"Ha!" Lucas says suddenly, hitting his hands against the table. "Pay up, Hollis."

Blake throws me a quick eye roll. "You just lost me a grand, arsehole."

My jaw opens and closes. "What are you talking about?"

"There's like twelve different bets going on, mate," he replies with a nonchalant shrug. "You and Jos, huh? Care to fill us in?"

"We've been seeing one another," I reply lamely.

"You've mastered the art of over-sharing, Walker," Blake argues, his brows creasing together. "You tell me how often you bloody fucking manscape. And that's all you're going to say about it?"

I shrug. "My manscaping schedule is a perfected science. You should be *honored* I shared it with you."

Lucas drums his fingers against the table. "Dude, we know the first porn video you ever jer—"

"Can we maybe *not* talk about that?" Charlotte asks, her nose screwing up in disgust. "Please and thank you."

"Is that seriously the only insight you're going to give us?" Blake continues. "Just that you're seeing one another?"

For the first time in my life, I don't want to say anything else. What Josie and I have is ours. It's not that I want to keep her a secret, but I want to keep us private. And quite frankly, I don't know what to tell them. We're friends who have sex? We're not together but act like we are? That, even though we're both single, I want to strangle any man who even so much as looks her way and don't care about any other woman but her?

"I lied before." Charlotte throws her arm around my shoulder. "*This* is the most fun I've had all day."

I shrug her off before daring to make eye contact with my friends. A very pregnant pause ensues where Lucas and Blake have a telepathic conversation, staring at one another without saying a word. I don't like being on the outside, not sure of what they're thinking, and I let it be known by aggressively clearing my throat.

Blake runs a hand through his messy hair. "Don't take this the wrong way, but if you're Josie's rebound, what happens when she wants a relationship?"

His words send a wave of nausea through me. I may not be

Josie's boyfriend but I'm sure as fuck not just her rebound. Right?

"Who says we're not both happy with how things are?"

"You may be," he continues, "but how long does that last? You can't be in a situationship forever, mate."

"It's not like that."

Blake takes a sip of his drink, studying me coolly. "Yes, it is. If you're more than friends but not a couple, that's the literal definition of a situationship. Textbook case. Don't be dumb."

Before I can say anything, Lucas cuts in, "I don't think Blake's trying to be a dick." He chastises Blake with narrowed eyes. "All he means is that Josie does relationships. Serious, stable, monogamous relationships. And sooner or later, she's going to want to be in another one. So where do you fall into that?"

"There's a lot more at stake than just than just a romance, you know?" I admit cautiously. "I don't want to lose her friendship because a relationship may not work out."

Blake nods in understanding. "I get that, but do you honestly think you could go back to being *just* friends now?"

He's right, and I know it. The mere thought of Josie talking to me about other men or asking advice on what a text from some bloke means sends acid through my veins.

Charlotte takes a sip wine. "So, are you cool with being a rebound or you going to stop making excuses for why you can't be in a relationship?"

I don't know the answer to that, but I do know I'm not willing to lose Josie.

22

JOSIE

SUMMER BREAK MEANS four uninterrupted weeks of no travel. Four weeks of falling asleep in my own bed. Four weeks of sleeping in until ten a.m. on the weekends. Four weeks of having a normal schedule.

It also means four weeks without Theo.

I don't realize how seamlessly he snuck his way into the weekly routine I've carefully crafted and curated until he isn't at my Tuesday spin class with me, complaining about his balls losing circulation. We text and FaceTime, of course, but Australia is eleven hours ahead of London. He sleeps while I'm awake, and I'm snoozing when he's up and active, and that makes it a little difficult to catch up when you're on complete opposite schedules.

Luckily for me, I've been more than busy enough to keep myself occupied. I only work three-day weeks during the break —a nice tradeoff for working race weekends—so I've had lots of time to dedicate to Gemini, which is now the official name of Kelsey's bar. Instead of spending my days off sleeping in and spending time with friends, I'm combing through the dark depths of the internet to locate an old-timey gumball machine that would look perfect in the bar.

Walking into the room that disguises Gemini's entrance, a smile lights up my face. Gibson and Fender guitars hang on the walls while bin upon bin wait to be filled with records. A glass-top counter occupies the right side of the space, housing limited edition albums and rare finds. Kelsey loved my suggestion to turn the entry space into a record shop, so I've been sourcing items to make it a reality. He fully trusts my best judgment to test and try what works best. It's a nice change of pace and one I'm taking seriously.

Kelsey calls out my name from one of the barstools as I enter the bar itself. It's still dimly lit, with low lights and neon signs, but now decor is starting to bring the space to life. A bright blue jukebox is nestled in the back corner and red leather barstools sit against a brass foot rail at the walnut wood bar.

Kelsey holds up a massive faux oil painting of his bulldog, Hamilton, dressed up as a king. After finding an Etsy shop that turns pet photos into portraits of distinguished historical figures, I knew Gemini wouldn't be complete without a few. There's nothing better than a Dachshund wearing knight's armor or a Great Dane dressed as Henry the VIII.

"You may need to order another one of these," he says with a pleased smile. "Because my daughter wants this one for herself."

His large frame makes it look like he's sitting in a chair meant for children. Despite his intimidating size and the fact that his nickname insinuates he's a killing machine, Kelsey's surprisingly mellow. His voice is rich and soft, and he always acts as if he's just walked out of a Zen meditation session.

"Happy to." I laugh. "I'm glad you like it."

He nods emphatically as I slide into the seat next to him. We work in comfortable silence for the next few hours with the occasional off-handed comment or question. Working on the website copy, I struggle to write Kelsey's bio. The world knows who he is; there's page after page on Google about him—the early stages of his career, his boxing stats, all his fights, his failed marriage. I know more about his childhood than I remember about my own. Glancing up, I say, "Question."

"Answer."

"What made you want to open this place? Professional boxer to business owner is a big jump. I mean, I know Wells Boxing is a business, but it's more in the line of your career. Not that owning a bar can't be your career. I just, um… well, they're very different is all. Not that I think different is bad. And tons of celebs have opened places. Hugh Jackman, Ryan Gosling, Lady Gaga. But why not start a protein powder business? Or activewear line? Something you're more familiar with. Granted, maybe your great-great-grandfather owned a pub or a food truck—wait… were food trucks around then? Regardless. It *could* be part of your history and that's why you wanted to. Who knows? Well, you do. Suppose I should let you answer the question now." I bite down on my lip to get myself to stop speaking.

"It's a fair question." He chuckles and drums his fingers against the table as he thinks. After a minute of silence, he replies, "I've been boxing since I was a kid, but I'm fifty-one now. I'm ready to try something *new*. It may be out of my wheelhouse, but I'm determined enough to make it work. And if it doesn't? *C'est la vie.*"

I don't speak French, but I know enough to understand that famous phrase.

"This place will definitely work out," I reassure him.

"Yeah?" He lifts his brows, a smile playing on his lips. "How do you know?"

"Because I'm just as determined to make it happen."

. . .

I'M dead asleep later that night when my phone rings not once, not twice, but three times. The only person who has this persistent strategy—even when we're in the same time zone—is Theo.

"Hello?" I answer groggily.

"'Ello, angel."

"It's," I hold out my phone to look at the time, "two in the morning, Theo."

"But it's a Friday night," he argues. "I thought maybe you'd be out or something."

I'm too tired to roll my eyes, so I just sigh. Even when I do go out on a Friday night, midnight is my cut off. One a.m. if I'm feeling extra rowdy. "I was out cold, not out at a bar."

He pauses before saying, "But you're up now, right?"

"Yes." Turning on my side, I press the phone against my ear. "What's going on?"

He makes some sort of grunt-slash-choking noise. "I hate Richard living in my house."

Any annoyance I have fades. Theo's discomfort over his mum's boyfriend moving in with her has come out in full force during this visit home. If anyone saw his texts to me when Richard moved where the spoons go in the kitchen, there's a slight chance he'd be arrested. "What'd he do?"

"Well, for starters, he's *there*," Theo says with a *hmph*. "Which is annoying of him."

"Absolutely horrible." I gasp playfully. "How dare he!"

Theo laughs, although it doesn't have the same depth as his usual one. "The worst part is that Charlotte doesn't think it's weird at all that our mum's now *living* with him. He was our dad's manager, for fuck's sake. It's so messed up, yet I'm the only one who cares."

"Have you tried speaking with Charlotte about it?"

He makes a noise of non-committal. "She says I'm being melodramatic."

"And your mum?"

"I don't know what I'd say to her," he says quietly. "It's… it's hard enough, you know? Watching them together."

My lips curve into a frown. "I'm sorry, babes."

There's a long pause. "It's okay, angel. How were things at Gemini today?"

"Good." I can't keep the smile off my face. "Kelsey loved the dog portraits I ordered."

Theo lets out a long laugh. "I'd be worried if he *didn't* enjoy a Husky dressed as a colonel."

"Mm-hmm," I say, fighting back a yawn. "He started interviewing some chefs, too."

A loud *ohh* filters through the phone. "Anyone good?"

"Well, I hope they're all good." I giggle. "But I'm not really sure who's in the running."

"He's doing something without you?" Theo gasps noisily. "Hell must have frozen over."

Marketing may be my area of expertise, but I've become Kelsey's right-hand woman. He asks for my opinion on everything from drink names to bar staff uniforms to what kind of lock the bathroom doors should have.

"I've got enough on my plate," I reply. "But I am going to the tasting in a few weeks when he hires someone."

"Good. You deserve it." Theo chuckles. He waits a beat before adding, "Am I keeping you up? Do you want to go back to bed?"

"I'm okay," I admit. "It's nice talking to you rather than listening to you talk to your twelve million Instagram followers in a live video."

"You said you didn't watch any of my content!"

My cheeks heat in the darkness of my room. Of course I watch it. Theo's a one-man show who doesn't need any props or co-stars. But he also has an ego bigger than most, and it's never been my job to feed it.

"Whatever," I huff. "I want to hear more about Australia. What have you been doing?"

"Well, the other day, Ri—"

"No Richard. I want to hear about *you*."

Theo sighs deeply. "Fine, fine. Your wish is my command, princess."

I close my eyes as he recaps the adventures he's gone on while home. Dune-buggying across muddy hills. Playing rugby with childhood friends. Checking out a few microbreweries. I'm lulled into a deep sleep by the steady warmth of his voice.

23

THEO

I'M DYING SLOW, painful death caused by one too many push-ups. One month without Russell whooping my arse, and it's like I've never worked out in my life. I went on a lot of runs in Australia—anything to excuse myself from being in Richard's presence over break—but nothing like the intensity of Russell's workout regimen.

"Forty-five, forty-six, forty-seven…" Russell counts like a drill sergeant. "Forty-eight, forty-nine, fifty."

I lie face-down on the mat and let out a muffled groan. My arms feel like uncooked spaghetti. If Jos were here, she'd sing the opening lines of Eminem's "Lose Yourself." We're only thirty minutes into our session, and I'm ready to tap out.

"Can we be done?" I whine from the floor. "Please?"

"Nope. Not even close, bud," he says. "Are you ready to focus now?"

"I am focused," I argue, rolling onto my back. "Laser-focused."

"On staring at the wall, maybe. But you're definitely not focused on this."

How am I supposed to concentrate when McAllister

responded to our counter-offer two hours ago? They only compromised a little bit, so now personal sponsorships can remain in place, but they can't overlap with specific products or services. So, if a McAllister sponsor wants us to promote shoes, I can no longer work on a shoe collaboration with Pegasus. The worst part is that they won't back down on the Number One car—aka Blake—finishing every race first. No exceptions.

"What's next?" I sigh, standing up. "Can it be something less torturous? Maybe something that doesn't make me want to jump in front of a moving car?"

"It's not my job to watch you half-arse things, Walker. So do it right, and we won't have to spend the rest of the morning arguing over how much training you still have to do."

I grumble to myself as I start doing kettlebell squats. Russell reaches over and adjusts my body, so my shoulders get pushed back a bit. "Ten more reps. Then we'll get started on chest flys."

Fucking hell. I try to stand straight so I can argue with him, but he smacks the back of my head. I'm immediately back in position.

"I could sue you for damages, you know," I complain as I bend my knees. "Emotional and physical harm or whatever."

He snorts loudly. "You're more than capable of harming yourself, mate. You're going to pull something if you don't keep your shoulders back. Let's go."

An hour later, I'm lying flat on my back on the floor once again, forcing my lungs to fill with oxygen, when a ball of fur pounces on my face. I'm momentarily suffocated until it moves off me and I get a leathery paw on my cheek instead.

What the fuck?

Sitting up, I find Blake grinning at me with undisguised amusement. He lets out a quick whistle and the fluff in question hops over to him with a wagging tail and flopping tongue.

He looks like a tiny UGG boot with his curly caramel-colored fur.

"Uh… is that a dog?"

"As opposed to what? A peach pie?" Blake rolls his dark eyes. "Yes. Obviously, it's a dog, Walker."

"Whose dog is it?"

He stares at me like I'm an idiot. "Mine."

"Let me rephrase." I cough into the crook of my arm to clear my throat for dramatic effect. "Why do you have a dog?"

"Because it's my dog," he says with a frown. "I'm not sure what you're not understanding. Ella and I got a dog. This is that dog. The dog is now ours. We are the owners of this dog."

"Holy shit." Blake Hollis has a dog. Two years ago, he couldn't even take care of himself, and now he's taking care of a living, breathing ball of… fluff. I look at the pup stationed at his feet and tap the floor to coax him to come back over.

He prances over, ditching his dad. *Wow.* Don't think I'll get over Blake being a dog dad anytime soon. Stopping in front of my feet, he lunges at my shoelaces. "Wait, I thought you weren't training until later? What're you doing here now?"

Blake gives me a guilty shrug. "As much as I like Poppy… I need a little peace and quiet."

After spending summer break in New York—where Goldy successfully testified in the trial that put away the fucker who assaulted her last year—her best friend Poppy flew back to London with them to visit for the week. She's in Portugal with the team for the Grand Prix this weekend before she heads back to New York.

"You want to play with Champ for a bit while I warm up?" Blake asks, walking over to the barbells.

I stare at him for a moment before rolling onto my side as I laugh. "You named your dog Champ… as in Champion?"

It's a cute name, despite the fact that it sounds rather cocky.

He takes a large sip of his water and Champ's ears perk up at the sound of the crinkling plastic water bottle. Not super environmentally friendly, but after a shitty practice three years ago, Blake threw his metal water bottle at a wall and shattered a fuck-ton of glass. They've baby-proofed him with plastic.

"Yes. Champion Bagel Hollis-Gold."

I struggle to breathe once I hear Champ's middle name. "Bagel?" I cough out. "You're fucking with me." This is the best thing I've heard all day. It almost makes up for McAllister's shitty updated contract.

"No," Blake grunts. "And I suggest not giving me any more shit if you'd like your face to remain unbroken."

I pick Champ up and press his little black nose against my own. "You have bigger balls than your daddy. Did you know that, Champ? Your mummy neutered him and keeps them in her purse."

Blake chucks his water bottle at my head. If that had been his metal water bottle, my skull would be in pieces all over the gym floor. I'm grateful for McAllister's foresight. Champ aggressively licks my nose, so I place him back in my lap. I let out a yelp as he latches onto my finger. This thing is more lethal than Blake's attitude. I pry his tiny jaw open, but apparently, that's me challenging him. "Champ. No."

He nips at my arms, but every time I put him back on the floor, he jumps onto me like it's a game. I accept the fact that my body is a chew toy and let him climb all over, his tongue happily hanging out the side of his mouth.

"Question for you, Blakey Blake."

The weights he's using clank against the floor, the sound causing Champ to momentarily stop his assault on my exposed skin. How can something so small have teeth so sharp? Christ.

Blake turns to me. "Theo, for the last time, I am not measuring my dick. Stop asking."

I roll my eyes, although his reaction isn't that unwarranted.

I don't know why he's not curious how scientifically big his dick is considering it's a third leg, but whatever. "I was going to ask when you knew you wanted to get serious with Ella."

"Oh."

I flip Champ onto his back so I can give him a belly rub. "So? What made you want to go from fuckboy to lover boy?"

Blake chuckles at my words, taking a seat on the bench nearest to him. "I realized that being the one to make her laugh or smile made me just as happy as kicking your arse during a race."

Blake tilts his head as he studies me. "You know, prying isn't my style, but friends with benefits with Josie doesn't make sense. It's like you're saying she's good enough to fuck but not good enough to have feelings for, which we both know is total bullshit."

"I'm not—"

"Let me finish. Relationships aren't a walk in the park, but being with Ella is the single-greatest thing that's ever happened to me. I had zero interest in getting married and having kids until her. And now? I have a bloody list of baby names I like, mate. I wouldn't trade what we have for all the World Championship titles in the world. And in case you forgot, I have six of those."

How could I possibly forget that he has the highest number of championship titles of any driver ever?

"You're right."

Blake starts to speak, no doubt gearing up to argue with me, but quickly stops himself. "I'm right?"

"Mm-hmm." I scratch Champ behind the ears. "But don't get used to it."

"I won't." He chuckles. "I have a girlfriend, Walker. That means I'm never right."

"Sounds like a personal problem, Blakey Blake."

Rolling his eyes, he stands back up. "So what's the plan?"

The plan is to convince Josie this is more than just a fuck or a fling for me. This is now a forever sort of thing.

I SEE Josie around the paddock and hotel, but it isn't until we're watching a movie alone in her hotel room the night before the race that I carry out my plan. And then blow it all to hell moments later when I open my mouth and state, "You're a cat."

Josie's face scrunches up adorably and she tilts her head. Tugging at the strings on her jumper—that features my last name and number, thank you very much—she says, "What?"

"You're my cat."

Nice, Walker. Way to clarify things.

"Is this your way of saying you want me to role play as a cat," Josie muses unsurely. "Because, um, I'm not sure how I feel about that. I mean, cats are cute and all, but I'm more of a dog person and—"

"No, let me start over." I take a deep breath, hoping my mind will stay in one lane and not do its typical routine of trying to fit twelve topics into one sentence. "Blake once made me watch this god-awful documentary on cats. In my defense, I had just taken an edible, and he could've asked me to stare at a wall and I would've agreed. It was actually a pretty good doc, though. I ended up crying over this little kitten named Annabelle who… you know what? Never mind. The point is, that it went on and on about how cats rub against objects to claim ownership. You're like a cat. Now that you've rubbed on me, I'm one of your belongings. I don't think I ever stood a chance."

Josie opens her mouth but doesn't say anything. Instead, her fingers tug at the delicate gold chain on her neck. "Um, okay. Well, thank you. I think?"

Not off to a great start, Walker.

"I don't want you seeing other people," I try again. "Or me. I don't want either of us seeing other people."

"Oh." She pulls her necklace so hard I worry she may break it in half. Really not off to a good start. "To be honest, I thought that we were already kind of exclusively hooking up. But, um, I guess we never really clarified, so I guess it's fine if you've been doing your thing or whatever. I haven't been seeing anyone else, though. I've been focusing on myself and all that. Kind of rules out the whole dating thing, you know?"

My heart hammers in my chest at her words. "But aren't we dating?"

"We're friends with benefits. I mean, that's what you suggested and what we both agreed to."

"Is that all we are, though?"

Josie blinks up at me, her brown eyes narrowing as she searches my face. "I-I don't know."

"You don't know if we're dating or not?"

"I'm confused, Theo. Why are you asking me all this?"

"Because I want to be with you, Jos." For good measure I add, "As more than just a friend you have sex with."

Her pouty mouth widens into an "O," but she doesn't say anything. At the very least, I was expecting her to launch into some speech about how she doesn't want to date me, but I wasn't prepared for silence. That's quite honestly the worst-case scenario. Neither of us tend to do well with extended periods of quiet.

"Well?" I prompt impatiently. "What're your thoughts?"

Grabbing a clip off the coffee table, she twists her hair and locks it into place. "Okay, well, um… I'm not quite sure what to say, honestly. You caught me off guard, Theo. Give me a second to process, yeah?"

The past few months haven't been enough time?

My mouth goes dry from the mix of adrenaline and embarrassment and anger, and it's hard to get any words out.

They stick in my mouth, fighting to stay there, but I force them out. "We can go back to being friends or whatever. It's clear you don't like me as more than that. Forgive me for thinking you could possibly see me as boyfriend material."

"Theo, that's not—"

I interrupt her before she can finish her sentence, responding with a burst of unwarranted aggression. "I've always said my career comes first, but can you not see how important you are to me? How much I like being with you? We hung out while you were on your deathbed with a cold, for Christ's sake, Josie. I wouldn't even do that for Blake or Lucas, and they've been my best mates forever. What else do I have to do to prove that I'm serious about us?" I snap at Josie's silence, my usual confidence fading into uncertainty. "You know what? Fine. If all I am is your personal pleasure palace, then so be it. I'm more than happy to live up to my title as a paddock play-boy. Why try to fight nature, right?"

Josie presses a hand to her cheek but doesn't say anything, so I quickly retreat out of her room. I need to catch my breath and figure out where the hell I veered off, made a U-turn, and then crashed into a barrier.

THE MOMENT the door to Ella's hotel suite opens, I barge past her and into the spacious living area. Plush, squeaky dog toys are scattered around the floor and a small crate is tucked away near the tiny en suite kitchen. I tiptoe through an array of colorful toys to find a bare spot on the plush carpet. Sitting down, I pat the floor in front of me. Champ stops chewing on the end of a dinosaur-shaped toy and parades over to me, covering my face in much-needed puppy kisses.

I glance up at Ella. "Is Blake here?"

"Nope." The door shuts with a soft *thump*, and she makes her way over to me. Situating herself on the oversized gray couch, she says, "He's playing poker with Lucas."

"And Poppy?"

As if on cue, Ella's friend waltzes out of the bathroom. She's visiting from New York and, let's just say, she's made the paddock her own personal dating service. I've concluded that her theme song is "Man Eater" since the power Poppy has over the opposite sex is impressive. Men have willingly gone back to her apartment after dates—fully knowing they're not getting any action—just to change her smoke detector batteries or fix her washing machine. Considering she eats men for breakfast, her opinion on my current predicament may be helpful. Or hurtful. That's up in the air.

I draw in a deep, audible breath. *Here goes nothing.*

"I've been sleeping with Theo. And yes, the Theo I'm talking about is Theo Walker. The same Theo Walker who had a debate with an ESPN reporter on why using conditioner before shampoo better moisturizes your hair. And he just told me that he wants to give things a real shot, and I didn't know what to say. I can't just make a snap decision about a relationship like that, you know? This isn't like deciding if I want one or two scoops of ice cream. Do I want to be with him? Yes, of course. He's my best friend. But this year was supposed to be about doing things for myself, not getting into another relationship. So, now I have no clue what I'm supposed to do about any of this, and I need your help."

The minute I'm done speaking, I bury my head into Champ's scruffy neck, feeling exposed and on display. I abhor confrontation and Theo put me in the spotlight in the worst way possible. Hence why I asked for a minute to breathe, although that led him going off on me.

Poppy claps her hands together. "Told you so! Pay up."

I glance up to find her auburn eyes narrowing at Ella expectantly. Ella's completely oblivious to her friend. Instead, she gapes at me in dawning astonishment before tossing a throw pillow in my direction. It smacks me in the head before landing softly at my side. Champ leaps onto it before turning in a few circles and curling up into a ball. *Such a little tater tot.*

Ella tucks a strand of hair behind her ear. "What the hell! Why didn't you tell me?"

"Oh c'mon, El," Poppy cuts in. "You're the world's worst secret-keeper."

"Am not! I'm just not a good liar. *Very* big difference." Ella grabs another pillow and throws it at Poppy before swiveling her head to me again. "You know I wouldn't have told anyone, right? Not even Blake."

"Yes, yes, I know," I reassure her. "I was trying to figure things out on my own. Us out. How I felt. Feel."

Ella's rarely at a loss for words, but she continues to stare at me with a slack jaw and wide eyes. *Lovely.* Not exactly the support I need right now. Poppy pours us each a glass of wine to ease the confused tension in the room. The liquid reaches the rim, threatening to spill over if the glasses are disturbed.

"Since your news seems to have broken Ella," Poppy says with a pointed eye roll, "I'll take over. Is Theo the only guy you're sleeping with?"

I nod. "Yes."

A simple look from Theo and my pulse skyrockets. He has complete control over my body and all it takes is a sweet smile, a lingering kiss, or a caress of the arm. He's ruined all other men for me and the wanker knows it.

She crosses her long legs like she's conducting an important interview. "Are you going on dates with other people?"

"Um… no."

Poppy sighs. "You have to have a roster, Josie. That way, you don't catch feelings for anyone."

"That sounds complicated," I admit. "What if two of them have the same name and you accidentally text one instead of the other?"

"I don't save anyone's number unless they've made me orgasm at least five times total." Poppy shrugs as if this should be a well-documented fact. "Do you guys text all the time or just when making plans?"

"The former," I squeak out faintly. If I'm not with Theo, I'm either on the phone with him, texting him, or most likely thinking about him.

"Okay." Poppy nods slowly. "And if you—or he—found out

the other person was sleeping with someone else, what would happen?"

The mere thought of *anyone* touching Theo the way I have —the way I *do*—makes my stomach churn. I'm not a particularly jealous person, but I'd ask Kelsey for private lessons if it meant keeping the Insta-models at bay.

My silence to her question is answer enough.

She slowly claps her hands together and smiles widely. "Well, congrats! There's no need for you to freak out."

"No?"

She shakes her head, her raven-dark hair brushing against her shoulders. "Nope. The decision's already made. Theo's your boyfriend."

Her words send a flutter of warmth to the pit of my stomach. *Shit.* I groan loudly into Champ's scruffy neck. This is the *one* thing that wasn't supposed to happen. Under any circumstances. Whatsoever. How do you figure out who you are when you're tied up in a relationship? "Why do I suck at being single?"

Ella interrupts my pity party. "Before you spiral, keep in mind that you can't compare Theo to any of your exes or previous relationships."

Can too, because I'm doing it right now.

I lift my head. "Why not?"

"Because in your other relationships, you neglected things you loved for their benefit, without getting the same things in return. You're selfless, not selfish, Jos. And that's amazing, but you tend to focus on others before yourself," she explains. "Think about it. Does Theo ever make you feel like being your own person and spending time with him are mutually exclusive? Even when you were just friends?"

I don't even have to think twice about it. "Never."

In past relationships, I've felt like I had to give up *something* to make room for *someone*. But with Theo, it's different. I can spend time with him and not sacrifice spending time with myself. He gives me space while still always being there for me.

"Exactly," Ella says. "Stop overthinking things and trust your gut, Jos."

My conversation with Claude rushes through my head. *Trust your gut, Josephine. No one knows you better than you, whether you've realized that or not. With the right people, you won't have to worry. You'll just know.*

"Plus, Theo's Theo. He's not on the same playing field as any other guy. He talks about his dick in the third person, and he still thinks the phrase is 'Florida ceiling windows' and not 'floor-to-ceiling windows,' but that's why we all love him, you know?"

A lightness fills my chest as I think about the man whose playfulness camouflages the pensive side of him. A man whose easy smile brightens any room he walks into and sets my entire body ablaze with a single unassuming stare. "You're right."

"I know." She grins at me, her dimple popping up. "I'm always right. Just ask Blake."

AS I WALK BACK to my hotel room, the sound of someone crooning a very horrible rendition of Justin Bieber's "Sorry" echoes off the walls. That someone is a blue-eyed, tone-deaf Australian with a complete disregard for every other hotel guest. I have no idea how to even *begin* dissecting what's going on.

"You singing backup for the Biebs?" I call out as I approach him. "Or just trying to burst my eardrums?"

The moment he spots me, he jumps to his feet like a kangaroo and sweeps the hair from his forehead. "I thought you were inside and just ignoring me," he admits. "Figured singing was a surefire way to catch your attention."

"It definitely caught someone's attention." I laugh, nodding toward the couple staring at Theo from the other end of the hallway.

Opening the door so we can talk in private, I motion for Theo to follow me. I can feel him breathing down my neck as I make my way to the couch, the smell of his cologne flooding my senses. Sitting down, he leaves zero space between us, pressing his thigh against mine. Sparks of electricity crawl across my skin—an automatic reaction to being near him.

"I'm sorry for walking out earlier." His lips tremble around the words, making his nerves clear, despite his calm demeanor. "I got overwhelmed and panicked and, well, as you can see, I'm not very good at this."

I tuck my knees up to my chest and look at him. "At what?"

"Admitting to my best friend that I want relationship benefits, too."

An accidental giggle breaks free. "Is that what you were doing? Because, if I recall correctly, you mildly accused me of using your penis as my personal pleasure palace."

Placing his hand on my knee, he gives it a light squeeze. "Sorry 'bout that, angel. Don't know what I was rambling on about. I was so nervous, I temporarily blacked out."

Resting my hand on top of his, I run my thumb against his knuckles. The tips of my fingers barely go past his middle knuckle. "I wasn't saying I don't want to be with you, Theo. But you came to me knowing what you wanted. You had time to think about it. I didn't. I needed a moment to catch my breath. I never make big decisions without thinking them through, and you know that."

"Have you had enough time?" He rubs his free hand up and down his bouncing legs. "You know… to think?"

I answer by teasingly elbowing his arm. "Is this your subtle way of reminding me how impatient you are?"

Shoulder pushing back, his back straightens. "No. This is

me telling you that you're worth the wait. If you need time to think it over, that's cool with me."

Taking a deep breath, I lean back and study the man— sometimes man-child— I've been spending my days laughing with and nights cuddling next to. Stubble pricks at my fingertips as I trail them against his movie-star jaw. Theo's eyes follow my every move, watching me with an intensity that makes my cheeks burn. "Are you sure this is what you want? A relationship?"

"I want to be the one whose arms you fall asleep in. And if I'm not next to you, I want to be the one you're thinking of when you lay in bed at night. I want to be the person whose touch you crave when you wake up. I want to be the one you look for in a crowded room, and the one you want to send memes to on Instagram. I want you and only you. I love you, Jos."

I cup his cheeks, feeling the warmth of his skin on my palm. "Well, the good news is that I love you, too. A wild amount."

I'm not sure who leans in first, but when our lips meet, it's like my world is suddenly put back on its axis, turning in the right direction. Theo snakes his tongue in my mouth and tangles his fingers into the hair laying over the nape of my neck. A small whimper of content slips through my lips, and Theo eagerly accepts it.

Leaning back, I gently place my hands on his chest. His lustful eyes roam up and down my body. My legs, my waist, my chest, my neck, my lips, my face.

"If we do this—"

"We're doing this."

"We're doing this," I agree with a nod. "But on one condition."

Theo laughs from deep in his throat. "Is the condition that I give you endless orgasms?"

"That's a given, babes."

"Unlimited cuddles and back scratches? Constant compliments about how fucking fantastic your arse is? A new nickname for the girls?"

I laugh and hold up my hand to stop him. "Those are all great, but not what I was thinking. The condition is that, even if you're my boyfriend, you're still my best friend, too. That doesn't change."

That can't change.

"Agreed. Is there a contract you want me to sign? Any other terms I should be aware of? Do I get a bonus if I buy you flowers every week?"

As his friend, I shoot him an annoyed eye roll. As his girlfriend, I cover his lips with mine to force him to shut up. He eagerly licks into my mouth and soon we're stumbling over to my bed, desperate for one another. Theo peels off each piece of my clothing with expert care, admiring the exposed skin beneath as the material falls away.

I can't get over how gentle his big hands are as he caresses my naked body. He knows every curve, every dip, every inch of skin better than he knows the circuits he drives on. He cups my breasts, squeezing and massaging them like he's never seen or felt them before. My nipples tighten as he teases the bare tips, running his tongue over them like a man possessed. Tortured sighs turned to moans as his teeth get involved, marking my pale skin.

"Lay down, baby," he instructs, his voice husky. "Need to taste you."

I nearly collapse backwards onto the bed, already lightheaded with desire. As he strips out of his clothing, my need only escalates. Muscles ripple down his arms, his rounded shoulders, his toned stomach, his strong legs. His chest is wonderfully broad, with a tuft of coarse hair set in the middle.

It's an overwhelmingly sexy silhouette made even better by his straining erection.

He looks down at his cock, a playful smirk marking his lips. "Wild, isn't it? How much of an effect we have on one another?"

Feeling bold, I say, "All words, pretty boy. Let's see if you can walk the walk."

The smile on his face disappears out of sight as he moves between my legs. Theo parts me with his thumbs before tracing his tongue against the folds, humming in pleasure at my taste. His mouth moves in synchronization with my moans and the movements of my hips. I'm almost embarrassed by how quickly he gets me to the point of no return. I grab the white sheets in my fists, mumbling his name as my climax sweeps through me. Theo continues to lick and suck my center until I'm squirming under his touch, too sensitive for more of his magical tongue.

With a satisfied grin tugging at his lips, he scoots off the bed and grabs his pants, fumbling around to find the condom that's always hidden in his wallet. We usually have sex in his hotel suite because "Egyptian cotton is more sensual," so I don't keep any on me.

Theo lays back on the bed and rolls the condom over his impressive length. My breath hitches in my chest as I slowly lower myself onto him. His hands cup my arse for grip as I ride him, using my hips to say everything I don't know how to. I'm a whimpering mess as he massages the sensitive spot inside me, the pad of his thumb rubbing against my clit while his other hand pinches and tugs at my sensitive nipples.

"Theo," I gasp, my breath getting caught in my chest.

He places a quick kiss on my lips before sitting up and holding me against him. "I know, baby, I know."

Our bare chests press against each other, providing more heat to the already stifling room. Theo drags his lips down my jawline to my neck while he grips my hips, moving them to grind against his. I throw my head back and enjoy the affection he's giving my body, along with the slow but deep thrusting done by his hips.

My body feels like a boiling pot of water, a slow build ready to overflow at any moment. I moan with reckless abandon, clinging to his body as the delicious rush of another orgasm edges closer. Theo's body is an aphrodisiac that controls every fiber of my being.

"You're mine." He leans in, fiercely searing his lips against mine. "Mine, Josie Bancroft."

My climax rolls through my stomach, sliding south until I'm contracting around Theo, writhing like a snake in his lap. It's like a volcano is erupting inside my veins, my coiled muscles relieving themselves of the tension my arousal created.

Thrusting up harder and faster to prolong my orgasm and catch up to his own, he emits those little noises he always denies making when he gets close. Knowing he's on edge, I rake my nails against his back, listening to the hiss of breath between his teeth. Moments later, I feel him pulse inside me, swears coming from his lips accompanying his shattering release.

"This is my favorite place to be," Theo says as we lay cuddled in my bed sometime later.

I roll onto my side so our noses are practically tip to tip. "In bed?"

"With you." He flashes me a sultry smile. "You're my biggest adventure and my safe space all rolled into one gorgeous girl with a fantastic rack."

"That was very sweet until you brought my tits into it."

"Chip and Dale deserve recognition," Theo argues with a pout.

I bury my face into his chest so he can't see the grin I'm failing miserably to hide. Then again, it's Theo—I'm always wearing a smile around him. He is my favorite person, after all.

25

THEO

SILVERSTONE IS ALWAYS A MASSIVE RACE. It's McAllister's home race, as well as Blake's. This year it also happens to be a race that James Avery—and his family—will be attending. The thought of having to see Christina again after so many years makes my stomach churn like butter. If only time would speed up and allow me to rush through this weekend. Hit fast forward on my worst nightmare sneaking out from the depths of my mind and unfolding in front of me.

The cherry on top of the very stressful sundae is that Josie's parents will also be at the Grand Prix. I've met the Bancrofts before at previous races, but haven't spent much one-on-one quality time with them. Her dad scared the living shit out of me before we became official, so there's no doubt he'll intimidate me ten times more now.

It's going to be a weekend of kissing one man's arse while avoiding another's entirely. *Oh, what fun.*

The sheets rustle as Josie rests her head on my chest, snuggling into me. "Morning, babe. How'd you sleep?"

I kiss the top of her head. "I slept alright. What about you?"

"Liar, liar, pants on fire," Josie hums. "You were tossing and turning the entire night."

I'm well-aware of this, but I hadn't meant to keep Josie awake. "Sorry about that. I didn't mean to keep you up."

She rolls over so her chin is resting in the middle of my chest. Toying with the small patch of chest hair, she asks if I'm okay.

"Mm-hmm. No dramas. Big race, is all," I reply coolly.

"Your pants are still on fire, Walker."

"I'm not wearing pants," I cheekily remind her. "Or did you forget last night?"

Her nose digs into my chest as she hides her face. Josie was so desperate to get my pajama pants off me last night that she ripped them straight down the seam and they're now in the trash. I laughed for thirty minutes straight at how flushed her cheeks were.

"I would never forget my newfound Hulk-like strength," she mumbles, embarrassed. "Plus, you're practically rubbing your dick against my leg."

She's right about that. My dick wakes up a little before me, excited for morning sex to start my day. I've completely given up on any type of coffee—there's no need for it when Josie's moans are the only alarm clock I need. "Are you not going to say hello back to him?"

"Stop referring to it as him." She giggles. "It freaks me out."

"He turns you into a freak, maybe, but I don't think he—"

My teasing is interrupted by Josie giving my right nipple a titty twister. I yelp at the suddenness of the pain. "You're going to pay for that, Miss Bancroft," I tell her, my eyes darkening with desire. I flip over so she's pinned underneath me. "You know that, right?"

She nods quickly, her lips parted ever so slightly. I'm

pressed against her and can already feel how wet and ready she is for me. *Fuck.*

Theo Junior is rewarded for his morning alertness in no time.

"Let's just skip the race," I mumble into Josie's neck as we lay there in a post-sex haze. "Stay in your flat all day, making love and having orgasms."

"That sounds lovely, babes, but they'd notice if you were gone since, you know, about one hundred and fifty thousand people are here to watch you race."

One hundred fifty thousand and *three* people, if you include the Avery family. One hundred fifty thousand and *five*, if you include Josie's parents, too. I debate texting Blake for one of his emergency anxiety pills, but decide against it. I don't need anything affecting my performance.

"What's going on?" Josie asks, her lip screwing up into a pout. "Talk to me, baby."

Hmph. Josie's smart. She knows I'm more pliable after sex, especially if she uses a pet name. My new nickname should be Whipped Walker because she's truly mastered the art of seduction.

"Did you purposefully tempt me?" I ask, lifting my head and glancing at her with disapproval clear on my face. "That's not fair."

She laughs, her body vibrating against mine. "Did it work?"

I grunt and relax against the calm feeling of her hands running up and down my back. My tension soon begins to dissipate under her touch. As much as I don't want to talk about Christina, the image of her confronting Josie—saying God knows what about me—is even worse.

A few minutes later, I rip off the Band-Aid. "Christina may be there."

She briefly pauses her massage. "Christina Avery?"

"Yep."

"Oh." She presses her lips against my shoulder. "You can tell me what happened, you know. I'm aware that you've slept with most of the female population, so it's not that big of a deal. I can handle it. And I've already stalked Christina on social media, so I know what she looks like. I won't be jealous or anything. Not that she's not gorgeous, because she is. Her hair is Pantene-commercial worthy, so I'm jealous of that. I just meant I'm not, like, worried you'll rekindle anything and run off with her or whatever. I trust you."

"Good, because what I have with you, I don't want with anyone else. You're it for me, baby." I pause as the full impact of her words hit me. "Wait, how did you stalk her? Do you follow one another?"

Christina's profile is private. Trust me, I've checked.

"Oh, uh, no. She has a public TikTok account, and I watched some videos," Josie admits, her cheeks flushing. "Are you upset with me? I didn't mean to overstep or—"

Tucking a piece of hair behind her ear, I reassure her I'm not. I don't blame Josie for being curious; I've visited Andrew's profile quite a few times since they broke up just to keep tabs. Josie's way out of his league: looks, personality, humor, all of it. He's a decent-looking guy, but my girlfriend's a knockout. She said herself that's she's the full kit and caboodle.

"We started seeing each other during my last season with Ithaca," I reveal with a resigned sigh. "We were both in Milan, and a mutual friend in the party circuit introduced us. She knew I wasn't looking for anything serious when we got together."

Josie flicks up a brow. "And she was okay with that?"

They always said they're okay with it, but they never really were.

"Or so she said, but after a month or two, it was clear she wasn't. Things started getting intense. She'd show up at Ithaca's headquarters to bring me lunch. She texted me all the time and would freak out if I didn't answer, despite knowing how busy I am. Every time she noticed I liked something, she took it to another level. She saw I used citrus-scented shampoo and conditioner, so she changed her perfume to a similar fragrance. I showed off my AC/DC album collection and the next time we hung out, she was wearing one of their concert shirts. If I made an off-handed remark about craving a cookie, the next day there'd be an entire basket full of every type of cookie at my front door—chocolate chip, oatmeal raisin, snickerdoodle, sugar cookie. It was a lot.

"I should've ended it before I did, but I was traveling all the time and ignored how invested she was in me. I thought it was a girlish crush she'd get over, but then she told me she would move to London to be closer to me when I moved there for McAllister. I knew I had to end it then, but when I did, she told me she was pregnant. Five weeks."

Josie's face blanches and her eyebrows pinch together, slowly shaking her head as she processes my words. I can tell she's too shocked to say anything, so I keep going. I want to tell her the full story. I *need* to tell her everything.

"When James found out I got his daughter pregnant," I point to my scar, "shit got ugly. I told her I'd support whatever she wanted to do, but a baby wouldn't change my feelings about being in a relationship with her. It wouldn't fix anything because nothing was broken; we just weren't compatible. I didn't even know who she was because she was too busy trying to be who she thought I wanted."

I draw in a shaky breath, surprised by how emotional I'm getting. Josie sits up and brushes her lips against mine, momentarily calming my nerves. She's like an inhalation of oxygen, warming the icy memories of what happened in Milan.

"Turns out she wasn't pregnant," I say wryly. "I went to an appointment with her. No signs or traces of a pregnancy. She made the whole thing up. I honestly have no idea what her plan was or how she thought things would play out because you can't come back from something like that."

I feel Josie's eyes on me, searching my face for answers I don't have. Maybe Christina was hoping a baby could convince me we were meant to be? That I wouldn't care that she manipulated me? I don't know. Lying is one of the few things I don't tolerate, ever. It's a breach of trust in the highest regard.

"I cut off all communication, and I thought that'd be the end of it. When she wouldn't stop calling and texting and showing up wherever I was, I filed a restraining order. Didn't know what else to do, you know? From what I heard, she took some time off from school and checked into a Swiss wellness center afterward."

"Bloody hell," Josie murmurs pensively, almost to herself.

"Mm-hmm."

I focus on her dresser, which is filled with perfume bottles and a few framed photos: her and Ella in Barcelona, a McAllister team photo from the Austrian Grand Prix, her parents grinning next to her at university graduation. I make a mental note to frame a photo of us to add to the collection.

Josie rests her palm against my chest. "You should talk to her. Say hi."

Shock bolts down my spine. "What—and I mean this in the nicest way—in the actual fuck?"

She bites her lip in a valiant attempt to not laugh at my flustered response. "I'm not saying take her out to drinks and have a heart-to-heart, but if you see her, I think it'd be good for you to clear the air. Get some closure."

I stare blankly. "Did you not hear me the first time when I said *what in the actual fuck*?"

She places a chaste kiss on my lips to settle me. "It's just… God, this is so embarrassing to say, but I've been the girl in a relationship who's insecure and loses who she is for a guy, okay? The girl who changes who she is without realizing how damaging it is."

I stay quiet, wanting to know where she's taking this. Besides Andrew, I don't know much about Josie's other exes. I can't even think of their real names because I mostly refer to them as *Officer Fuck Face* and *Deputy Dick Head* in my thoughts.

Josie sits up and crosses her legs, her knees grazing against my side. "In Year 10, I auditioned for the school play. Keep in mind, I have no theatrical talent or background. The only reason I auditioned was because this Year 12 named Gregory was the student director, and he was *so* cute. My friends and I all had the biggest crush on him."

"Ah, *Sergeant Simpleton*," I mutter to myself. Forgot about him.

"Hmm?"

"Never mind. Sorry. Did you get a role?"

"Nope," she acknowledges with a shrug. "No surprise there, since I'm not well-suited for memorizing lengths of Shakespeare's work, but Gregory offered me the director's assistant position. It was the best-case scenario because I didn't have to act, but could still spend time with him."

"I can't imagine you enjoying directing. At all."

She raises her finger in the air in an *aha!* kind of way. "Exactly my point. I find Shakespeare mind-numbingly boring, yet I spent *four* months going to play practice every day after school just because of Gregory. Logically, it makes no sense, but I had a crush on him, and he liked theatre, so I pretended to as well. We ended up dating for over a year, and I pretended to *love* plays the entire time. To this day, I can talk about *Death of a Salesman* in-depth all because of that."

"Wow," is all I manage to say.

"And don't even get me started on the fact that, when I was dating Andrew, I would miss brunch with my mum to watch *golf* with him and his brother. Golf, Theo! I hate golf. It's the most boring sport. Watching someone put away their dishes is more interesting than that."

Andrew's name is like nails on a chalkboard, sending goosebumps across my skin. "I'd never make you watch golf, angel. Promise."

Josie rewards me with a breathtaking smile. "I know, but that's the thing. Andrew didn't *make* me; I did it because it was something he liked and I wanted to, I don't know, be a part of that, I guess?"

She runs a frustrated hand over her face as if washing away the memory. I hate that she *changed* for them—compromised her own wants for what she thought they needed. Anyone who doesn't love Josie for exactly who she is, is an idiot who doesn't deserve to have her in the first place.

"What Christina did is messed up, and I'm not condoning it at all, but I do think you'll feel better if you at least see how she's doing," she admits quietly. "When else will you ever get the chance to?"

Tapping my fingertips against my lips, I consider it. The worst that happens is that I'm in the same position I am in now, right? It's not like her dad can add another dumb clause into my contract if she still hates me.

Right?

AT FIRST GLANCE, Mr. Bancroft looks like some type of body builder-slash-mobster-slash-professional-boxer. Seriously. I'm almost positive he could snap my body in half like a pistachio shell with two fingers. If he told me he was Kelsey Wells's bodyguard, I'd believe him.

Josie waves off my concern that he's going to put a hit out on me. It may be dramatic, but he stares at me like I'm his worst nightmare come to life. I may as well be. I'm not sure what father in their right mind would want their only daughter

—their only kid—to date a guy whose antics have been featured in the tabloids around the world. I feel a desperate need to redeem myself and prove I'm worthy of her, but so far, it's not working.

I got her parents added to the list for tonight's gala, but Mr. Bancroft seems entirely unimpressed. None of the high walls with crown moldings, the impressive floral centerpieces, or the waitstaff dressed in black and white filtering through the crowd passing out Veuve and caviar seem to *wow* him. The only thing that warms him up a bit is when he meets Lucas, who happens to be his favorite driver. *Of course.* God forbid he shows any type of interest in the driver who just so happens to worship the ground his daughter walks on.

Grabbing a flute off the tray of a passing server, I quickly take a sip. I wasn't planning on drinking much, but I need something to loosen the chokehold Mr. Bancroft has on my tongue.

"Josie said you'll be watching the race from the paddock this year." I shift my weight from one foot to the next. "That should be fun."

By the way her dad appraises me, you'd think I said something serial-killer-sinister instead of sincere. Watching the race from the paddock is a VIP experience that costs more than some people make in a year. I may get my form of thanks in a body bag.

Mrs. Bancroft replies with a warm smile, "We're very excited, darling. I was hoping to make it to the qualifying round tomorrow, but I have an emergency session with some clients."

"No dramas," I reassure her. "The race is where all the good stuff happens, anyway."

Unlike next year, where I'll be constantly bowing down to Blake.

Her silky-smooth hair bounces as she nods. "Speaking of

the good stuff, did Josephine ever share the package I sent for the two of you?"

"Mum," Josie mutters under her breath. "Can you not do this right now?"

I'm too curious to let it go. Josie doesn't like presents, but me? I love gifts. A lot. "What package?"

Mrs. Bancroft narrows her eyes at her daughter, clearly displeased she's been withholding from me. "I sent the two of you some goodies to try out. Josephine can confirm, but I believe it was a panty vibrator, a cock ring, and a double dil—"

As if rehearsed, Mr. Bancroft shouts, "Caroline!" Josie turns white as a ghost, and I spit champagne all over myself. Never in a million years did I think my girlfriend's mum would buy me a cock ring. Quite frankly, never in a million years did I think I'd hear my girlfriend's mum even say *cock*.

Mrs. Bancroft laughs, the sound light and airy. I'm glad she finds it funny because if I thought Mr. Bancroft hated me before, reminding him I do indeed have male genitalia has made things twelve times worse. Josie shoots me an apologetic smile before I excuse myself from the conversation, waving to my champagne-soaked navy dress shirt.

I'm opening the restroom door when a familiar voice calls out my name. I turn around slowly, silently praying that someone else has the same exact voice as her. Of course, my prayers go unanswered. That seems to happen a lot around the Avery family.

Christina Avery stands before me, looking as gorgeous as ever. Her dark eyes are almost identical to her father's, albeit less menacing, and the red dress she's wearing hugs every curve of her hourglass figure. She still has loose, buoyant curls that resemble a lion's mane, and they bounce as she makes her way over to me.

"Christina. Hey."

"Promise I'm not stalking you," she says, holding her hands up. "Again."

I'm not sure if it's too soon to laugh or not, so I just give her a small smile. Having to file for a temporary restraining order on a twenty-year-old woman is not something I'm proud of, but at the time, I didn't have another option.

Taking a deep breath, I square my shoulders and stand tall. I can do this. If Josie has faith in me, the least I can do is try to have a conversation with her.

"So, uh, how are you?" I ask awkwardly. "Been a while."

We're now face-to-face, so I take a step away from the bathroom door. I don't *think* she'll shove me in there and torture me, but that's not a risk I'm willing to take. Waterboarded by toilet water is not how I want to spend the rest of the night.

"I'm good. How about yourself?"

A single bead of sweat drips down my back. "I'm… with someone."

Maybe my nickname should be What the fuck, Walker?

"I'm not here to flirt with you, Theo," she explains with an uncomfortable laugh. "I saw you walking this way and figured I should come over to apologize."

I tilt my head like Champ does whenever Blake crumples up his water bottles. "Apologize?"

"Uh, yeah. I'm not sure if you remember or not, but I faked a pregnancy and then continued to show up to your house unannounced. Pretty positive that qualifies as legally batshit crazy."

How could I forget? "Oh. That."

"Yeah," she says lightly, her cheeks flushing pink against her tanned skin. "I'm sorry. That wasn't okay. *I* wasn't okay."

Whatever I was expecting from this conversation, it wasn't an "I'm sorry." A bitch slap or a glass of water being thrown at me are more like it.

"I appreciate it," I say after an extremely long, tongue-tied pause, courtesy of me. "And I'm sorry, too. I should've realized you weren't okay with the kind of casual I was looking for. It wasn't my intention to lead you on or give you false hope."

Josie's right. It feels good to say that. Really damn good. Maybe Blake's onto something with the whole "boyfriends are never right" thing.

Her lips curl into a grateful smile. "I appreciate that, thanks."

I wipe my clammy hands against my pant suit to distract myself from the silence between us.

"Your dad still hates me," I blurt out. "A lot."

Like hates me so much, he may've accepted this job just to ruin my career.

She doesn't disagree with me, which makes the pit in my stomach sink even deeper. "Our relationship went downhill after everything in Milan. It's easier for him to blame you than to take any real responsibility for what happened."

My brows scrunch up. "How was he responsible?"

"Things at home were really shitty when we first got together," she says, looking away. "Found out my dad was cheating on my mum, and I ended up in the middle of their fighting. You were the only *stable*, consistent thing I had at the time, and when you tried to end things, I freaked out. My therapist calls it 'anxious preoccupied attachment;' I just call it embarrassing."

I stare at her, dumbfounded. I may not have wanted to date her, but it wasn't like we had sex and that was it. We did the whole pillow talk thing, too. "You never said anything."

"I definitely did." Christina lets out a low laugh like it's no big deal. "You tend to like when things are on your terms, with you at the center. My family drama didn't really fit into that box."

Ouch. Her words slap me across the mouth before wrapping

around my throat, humbling me to the highest degree. I may like attention, but that doesn't mean I'm incapable of letting other people have their moments in the sun.

"I've grown a lot since then," I say defensively. I mean, I have a girlfriend, for fuck's sake. How much more personal growth can a bloke have?

She nods. "So have I. I'm only here as a sign of good faith to my dad that I'm ready to rebuild our relationship."

A deep breath I hadn't realized I was holding rushes out. "I thought you were here for me," I admit with a shrug. "To tell me I'm a horrible person or something."

"Cocky as ever, I see." She gives me an easy smile. "I should probably head back in there, but it was good seeing you. I'm glad you're doing well."

"Yeah, you, too," I murmur.

Walking into the bathroom, I splash cold water against my face and repeat my new mantra: Christina is the past and Josie is my future.

Now I just need to figure out which of those categories McAllister falls into.

26

JOSIE

FROM THE DECK of the Walker family residence just outside of Melbourne, I watch as the sun fades from a vibrant red to a dull yellow. The conversation around me plays like background music as I snuggle further under Theo's arm as the soft seaside landscape disappears from the final rays of light hiding behind the sea. It's a perfect, peaceful night before the craziness tomorrow's race will bring.

He presses his lips against my temple as he listens intently while his mum and sister discuss a new boutique that's opened in town. He's been unusually quiet today, not even taking the bait when Charlotte regaled us with a story that ended with her spending the night locked in the home decor section of a department store. There's no doubt in my mind he's keeping to himself to avoid lashing out at Richard. Every time his mum's boyfriend speaks, his protective hand resting on my thigh subconsciously squeezes tighter. We've made it through the day with minimal snarky comments, and I pray we can finish off the night in a civil manner, too.

"Josie, Theodore said you've been doing some freelance

work," Mrs. Walker says. She pokes the flames in the fire pit with a stick and they roar upward, as if reaching for the sky.

"Yes," I say, flushing under the attention. "I'm helping out with some marketing projects."

Charlotte shoots me a supportive smile. "Social media and that kind of stuff, right, Jos?"

"Yes, lots of brand building: content creation, developing promotional campaigns, SEO for the website. Those sorts of things."

I've never worn so many hats in my life. Gemini's flexing a creative muscle that's been stiff with inactivity at McAllister.

"And this is *freelance*?" Mrs. Walker asks with a hand over her chest. "Not even your full-time job?"

Theo kisses the top of my head. "My princess is a true marketing genius, eh?"

"Then can she try to get your social media accounts under control?" Charlotte teases. "Because your thirst trap Thursdays are getting a little ridiculous. And don't even get me started on your sweaty Saturday posts. Who in their right mind wants to watch you exercise with Russell? All you do is grunt."

Although neither of them will ever admit it, Charlotte takes after Theo with her lack of filter, need for adventure, and role as the life of the party. It's probably why Theo constantly worries about her. He morphs into a mother hen around her, which is rather cute.

Theo blows air out of his nose. "Josie happens to enjoy when I gr—"

I dig my nails into his leg to stop him from finishing that sentence. It's like his mind permanently resides in a gutter full of sexual innuendos.

"That's great, Josie," Mrs. Walker says, bringing the conversation back to safe territory. "Although it does sound rather stressful. And that's coming from the woman who raised these two."

Theo chuckles, but Mrs. Walker's right. It is stressful—more stressful than I was anticipating. I'm frustrated that McAllister continues to undervalue my work and ideas, and I'm frustrated that there aren't enough hours in the day to do everything I want for Gemini.

"You good?" Theo murmurs softly. "It's getting late."

"'Course." I give him a small smile. "You?"

He clandestinely rolls his eyes to where Richard's arm is wrapped around his mum's shoulders. I'll take that as a no. As if his ears are ringing, Richard says, "Theo, your contract is up at the end of the season, right? Have you given any thought to next year?"

Oof. Abort mission, buddy. Take cover. Not only are contract negotiations top secret, but it's one subject Theo does *not* enjoy discussing. The most he's told me is that Martin's "ironing out some details," and even then, his whole body stiffens like he's under siege. I've told him to fight the social media clause, but that's as much as he'll let me say before he changes the subject.

Theo gives a brief nod of acknowledgement but doesn't say anything in response. I watch as Richard's smile falters, unsure of how to proceed. It's been like this the whole night. Richard offering an olive branch and Theo snapping it in half with a single look. Theo used to like Richard quite a bit. It's his role as their mum's boyfriend that he doesn't seem to agree with.

"Do you think you'll re-sign?" he tries again.

"Why wouldn't I?" Theo snaps. "Think I'm not a good enough driver?"

Oh boy.

"Contracts are complicated," I interject, as if I know *anything* about sports law. "Lots of...details. And, um, other things to sort through. Legal jargon and big words. But Theo's manager is great so I'm sure he'll work through everything."

Legal jargon and big words? Jeez, Josie, way to wow them with your intelligence.

"Well, you know I'm happy to talk anything through," Richard says with a nod. "Take a look before you cross your T's and dot your I's."

I try to change the subject, sensing Theo's brewing emotions, but I don't get the change to before he snaps, "Yeah, sure. Just like before, right?"

"Exactly," Richard agrees, not at all catching onto Theo's fighting words.

I would not describe the laugh my boyfriend lets out as nice. If anything, it's a little maniacal, especially when he adds, "You seriously think anything can be like how it was before?"

"Nothing's changed, Theo," Richard says, his calm voice more likely irritating Theo than balancing him.

"*Everything's* changed," Theo yells, throwing his hands up. "Look around you, Richard. My dad's not here. You *are*. Ever since you two started dating, everything's changed. Instead of being a friend to me—hell, a friend to my dad—you're dating my mum and acting as if that position was always rightfully yours. Are you that fucking blind that you don't realize things can never go back to the way they were?"

Silence covers everyone like a blanket—the only noise the crackle and hiss from the flames before us. Theo's leg shakes at rapid-fire speed against mine, his nervous energy ready to erupt and cause the heat of the fire pit to look cool in comparison. I've heard Theo swear, curse, and yell, but I've never seen him as visibly agitated as he is now. The vein in his neck pulses and he clenches his jaw so tightly, I'm nervous his teeth will crack.

"Take a deep breath, Theodore," Charlotte says sternly. "Richard and Mum are allowed to be happy."

"Of course they are," Theo says flatly. "Can't have Dad, so

may as well go for the next best thing, right, Mum? His best friend?"

"Don't talk to your mother that way, Theo," Richard says, raising his voice. "If you have a problem with me, then take it up with me. Not her."

"Hey, Richard?" The sharpness of his voice makes me shift in my chair. "Fuck off."

"Theo!" Mrs. Walker cries out. Tears threaten to spill down her round cheeks and she looks upward, as if heaven will have the answer on how to handle this. "Have some respect. Please."

He whips his head around so he's facing his mum again. His lips thin with rage—they're pursed so tightly the color in them is fading. "Respect? Don't talk to me about respect, Mum. You—"

"Theo," I interrupt him. "Take a walk and cool off."

Charlotte's simultaneously fighting off tears and the urge to throttle her brother. "Jesus. Why can't you let Mum be happy? Dad's gone. Being an asshole isn't going to change that."

"Oh. Wow. Thanks for the update. I had no idea Dad's gone since none of you talk about him. *Ever.* It's like he never existed."

"That's not true," Charlotte says fiercely. Her voice is harsh, but a shakiness has edged its way in.

"Isn't it? I work my arse off three hundred and sixty-five days a year to make sure Dad's legacy lives on. What do you do? Oh, right. You welcomed Richard in like a goddamn understudy for Dad. Well, enjoy. I hope you're all *really* happy."

Theo bolts from his chair and stomps across the deck without another word. I wait a few moments before noiselessly excusing myself to find him.

Part of me wants to locate him, drag his arse back, and make him work things out with his family. But the other part of me—the realistic side—knows that's not an option. I can support him, but in the end, this is his fight, not mine. Family are the people who love you at your worst just as much as they do when you're at your best. It can be an uncomfortable reality.

I find him pacing the driveway with his shoulders hunched forward. My heart sinks as I study him—his sharp cheekbones stained with tears that glisten against the moonlight. I'm not sure how much time passes before he notices me. Once he does, he silently makes his way over to me, draws me into his arms, and buries his head into the crook of my neck.

"That was a shit storm, eh? Made my mum cry," he murmurs after a minute. "Are they alright?"

"They will be." I run my hand up and down his back, loving how tight and toned he feels against my palms and fingers. "Are you okay, baby?"

Theo doesn't respond right away, and when he does, his voice is low and laced with uncertainty. "I've never lashed out like that."

An unspeakable pain grips me by the throat. There's nothing I can say or do to make him feel better. It's the worst kind of heartbreak. I want to put him in a bubble where nothing and no one can hurt him. Wrap him up so tightly that he forgets about his pain and only feels a calm and everlasting bliss. Instead, I just press my forehead against his and whisper, "I'm sorry."

"Do you think I'm a terrible person?"

I nod. "Yes, but only because you sleep with socks on."

"Cheeky." He chuckles. "What about them? Do they think I'm horrible?"

Shaking my head, I rub my hands up and down his arms. "No, Theo, they don't. They may want to kill you sometimes, but they still love you."

"I sure as hell make it difficult."

"Loving you is easy, baby." I chuckle into his chest. "The hard part would be trying to stop."

27

THEO

MY BEDROOM IS PAINFULLY QUIET, and it's not the peaceful kind of quiet where you can easily fall back asleep. It's the loud silence that leaves you alone with all your thoughts. The kind that gets you so worked up that you overthink and reevaluate.

When counting sheep for the thirtieth time fails to lull me into a peaceful slumber, I quietly slip out of bed and head downstairs. What a fucking shitshow the past twenty-four hours have been.

Filling a kettle with water, I place it on the stove to warm up. Maybe a cuppa will calm my intrusive thoughts. My contract is all that's been on my mind as I tossed and turned. Well, that and making a complete arse of myself to my family. There's no doubt I'll have to go on an apology tour after the race, starting with my mum and ending with Richard. Thank goodness I keep my own flat here in Melbourne, because spending the night at my childhood home after that fight would've been… uncomfortable, to say the least.

"Care for some company?"

Josie stands at the entryway to the kitchen wearing one of

my McAllister shirts, the letters on the front so faded they're barely visible. My racing heart immediately slows down. "What're you doing up, princess?"

She walks over to me, kissing my shoulder before settling onto the stool to my right. "I could ask you the same thing."

"Couldn't sleep," I admit. "Sorry if I woke you."

"Six-hundred count thread bed sheets aren't nearly as comfortable when you don't have anyone to cuddle with."

"Poke fun all you want, but you know my sheets are superior."

She laughs while picking up her phone, reading the messages that are lighting up her screen. I nearly ask who she could possibly be texting at this hour before remembering the different time zones.

Suddenly, she starts saying "oh my God" repeatedly while she taps away, her nails creating a *clackity-clack* noise. I wiggle in my seat, wanting to be let in on what's going on. My FOMO gets worse when it involves Josie.

I rest my head on her shoulder, reading her messages with Kelsey. *Hmph.*

KELSEY WELLS

Are you around next Saturday for a tasting? Would love to get your millennial feedback on some dishes.

P.S. Jamie is consulting on the menu.

Jamie Wolff, in case that wasn't clear.

JOSIE BANCROFT

OMG. How did you get him!? Did you have to sell him your kidney?

KELSEY WELLS

> Have to get his name tatted on my forehead,
> but it'll be worth it. I showed him the cocktail
> menu, and he has some great ideas for
> pairings.

JOSIE BANCROFT

> LOL. Yay! Can't wait. I'll come hungry.

"Who's Jamie Wolff?" I ask with a furrowed brow.

"He was the runner-up on season seven of *MasterChef*!" Josie squeals. "His whole thing is elevated street food. On one of the episodes, he made this burger with a coffee rub and caramelized onion that was positively *to-die for*. It sounds odd, but the flavors worked and the judges nearly pissed themselves at how good it was."

My smile grows as she gives me an in-depth explanation of the dish. I love how she talks about the burger, as if she had actually tried it. Hell, I feel like I've tried it thanks to her descriptions.

"Look at you, getting all chummy with your fellow foodies." I chuckle. "It's too bad the tasting's not during the week, though."

Josie tilts her head, her blonde waves moving to the left as she does. "Why?"

"The Dutch Grand Prix is next weekend."

"Bloody hell." Closing her eyes, she runs her hands over her face. "I didn't even think about the race."

I could never forget a race... it's what my life revolves around. It's what hers does, too.

A deep sigh comes from her chest. "I have a lot of time off I haven't used."

"Isn't it a little last minute?"

That's what she told me when we went to Le Mans. McAllister asks for at least two weeks' advance notice.

"I'm sure I can convince Rhys to make an exception," she says, almost to herself. "Plus, this is a once in a lifetime opportunity, you know? When else am I going to be invited to a menu tasting with a *MasterChef* contestant? And it'll be good for me to be there. Bars are all about the experience and the food is obviously a big part of that. I want to make sure the dishes are unique enough to make us stand out but also not too fancy that it'll turn the average bloke away. We have to toe the line of being good food, but not four-course sit-down meal good."

Us? We?

"So, you'd be missing work for other work? Isn't that, like, against the rules or something?"

Her shoulders lift into a shrug. "It's not like I'm missing the race to help Catalyst or something, babes. And how I spend my time off is none of McAllister's business."

But it's my *business.*

I look down so she can't see the way my lips have settled into a petulant pout that refuses to leave. Everything she's saying makes sense, but that doesn't mean I like her missing a race. Josie's not only my girlfriend; she's my support system. She's the final person to wish me luck before I hop into my car, the only person whose laugh can make me feel better after a shitty practice, and the person who cheers the loudest when I win. Blake may be the fan favorite, but I've always been Josie's favorite.

"Hey," she says, cupping my cheek and forcing me to look at her. She thinks her brown eyes are dull and boring, but they're not. They're the color of my favorite hot cocoa topped with cinnamon. They drive me wild. "Are you upset?"

I shrug. "I'm going to miss you, is all."

"I'll miss you, too, baby. But it's just *one* race," she tells me. "You'll be so busy, you'll hardly notice I'm gone!"

Not likely. "Will you still watch?"

"Don't be silly. I haven't *not* watched a race in years. It'll just be from my television instead of from the pit garage."

That last part is the part I don't like. "And you'll be at the next race, right?"

"Of course. Why wouldn't I be?"

The same reason you won't be at this one. Your priorities are elsewhere.

She looks at me with a fraught plea in her eyes. *Fuck.* I know she wants me to be okay with her missing the race, and I am. Well, I'm trying to be. This is important to her. And I'm not like Josie's exes.

"Just making sure." I shoot her an understanding smile to ease her nerves. "The tasting will be amazing. I'm jealous."

"Don't worry," she promises. "I'll send you *lots* of photos."

I'm not sure which Grand Prix will be worse; tomorrow with my family mad at me or next weekend's with Josie not in attendance.

THE CLACKING and grinding as engineers with tools in hand work on my car pounds in my head. *Thump, crank, whoosh.* I take a small sip of the coffee Blake brought me, but immediately spit it back into the cup. When I do drink coffee, I like the taste disguised by milk and artificial sugar. I thought drinking it black would jolt my system awake, but no such luck.

"Stop acting like it's motor oil," Blake scoffs. He takes a sip of his twin coffee, not even flinching as he swallows. *Gross.*

"Don't disrespect motor oil. That tastes way better than *this*."

Blake rolls his eyes before nodding at the entrance of the garage. "You know she was coming?"

I shake my head. My mum's wearing an old McAllister shirt—from my dad's racing days—but the number and last name still work. She steps over kidney-shaped oil stains on the concrete as she makes her way over.

"Hey, Mrs. Walker," Blake greets my mum as she pulls him into a hug. "How're you?"

"Blake," she lightheartedly reprimands. "How many times am I going to have to tell you to call me Laura?"

He shrugs sheepishly. Blake's known my mum forever, but he feels weird about calling her anything but Mrs. Walker. She should take it as a compliment. Not everyone earns the respectable miss, missus, or mister from Blake, who refers to most people by their last name or as "that fucker." Hearing him call Ella pet names will forever sound foreign to me.

"Probably about a hundred more times."

I place my motor oil coffee on the workbench behind me, needing to free my hands so I can crack my knuckles. "What're you doing here, Mum? The race isn't for a few more hours."

Turning to me, she says, "I was hoping you had some free time to chat."

"We have a press conference in five," I admit with a frown. "Are you—"

"I'll get it pushed back," Blake says, as if it's no biggie. "Is an hour enough time?"

Before either of us can respond, Blake strolls off to work his magic. And by magic, I mean he'll come up with some insane excuse as to why we have to postpone the conference. He's a good friend, especially because we both know moving a press conference is going to piss off a lot of people with tight deadlines and strict schedules. He may not care what people think of him, but I do.

I lead my mum up the stairs to my suite on the second floor. It's a tight space, only big enough to hold a desk, two-seater couch, and mini fridge, but it's home away from home.

"This looks like your childhood bedroom." My mum

laughs to herself. "Minus the race car bed and *Power Ranger* posters."

Looking around, I see what she means. Video game cases are stacked on every available surface, and McAllister memorabilia is tacked on the walls. The protein powder and weights are new, but besides that, it's got the same vibes as eight-year-old Theo's room.

She takes a seat on the couch, crossing her legs in a ladylike manner. "We should talk about last night. I never let your dad start a race if we were in a fight. Old habits die hard, I suppose."

"Yeah. Probably." I'm nervous that if I say anything else, I'll end up shoving my foot in my mouth. Again.

"I didn't realize you were so upset about Richard and me being together," she reveals, shaking her head. "And I need you to know that my love for your father is irreplaceable, honey. Richard doesn't change how I felt about him. How I *feel* about him. I'm not effacing any of the memories we created; I'm simply making new memories with someone else."

I stare at my hands like they're a long-lost Picasso that's just been rediscovered. "With Richard."

"You used to like Richard," my mum reminds me. "Quite a lot, if I remember correctly. He and Dad took you to your first rugby ga—"

"But do you not see how weird that is?" I say, brasher than intended. "He was Dad's *manager*, Mum. His best friend. They were together every day, and now you're with him."

"Theodore, you're making it seem like we were having an affair."

Shrugging, I avoid eye contact. "Well. Were you?"

"Theodore Chase Walker." My mum's voice is so stern that my back automatically straightens. "I didn't go through twenty-two hours of natural labor with you to sit here and have you accuse me of nonsense."

"Sorry," I mutter, shame heating my cheeks. "I know."

"I loved your father, and I loved our life together." She reaches out and clasps my hands in hers. "There's no rulebook on how to handle grief. And I miss your dad. Every single day."

"Yeah?"

"Yes. And do you want to know what's so nice about being with Richard? I can talk to him about your father. We're able to share memories and tell stories and help one another heal. It's nice having someone I can relate to on that level."

The tears come without warning. One second, I'm dry-eyed and the next, I'm sobbing so fiercely, I can't catch my breath. I collapse into myself, my chest heaving as hot tears race down my cheeks. My throat becomes so thick, I can barely swallow.

"Oh, honey," my mum murmurs. Wrapping her arms around me, she holds me as I tremble uncontrollably. We stay like that until the unmistakable sadness loosens its grasp around me. I'm winded by the time I can sit up and breathe without feeling like I'm choking.

"Feel better?"

"Yeah," I admit, wiping my face with the back of my hands. "A little. And I'm sorry for what I said last night. I didn't mean to yell at you like I did. It's just weird for me to see you with someone Dad was so close with, I guess."

"You've got to admit, he's better than Jim, though."

I snort loudly. Before Richard, my mum dated a bloke named Jim, who was… interesting. He moonlighted as a ventriloquist, and not a very good one, if that says anything. "The grocery store clerk was better than Jim, Mum."

She chuckles and ruffles my hair. "And next time, come talk to me instead of bottling it all up, okay? This is a weird transition for all of us, but we'll get through it together."

"It's weird for you, too?"

"Absolutely." She laughs and pats my cheek. "Living with someone new after *twenty-seven* years of marriage is a huge adjustment. Did you know Richard likes his dishes to soak overnight before putting them in the washer?"

She throws me a pointed look, which makes me laugh. One of my dad's biggest pet peeves was when one of us left our dirty dishes in the sink. We always happened to forget, and he got stuck either hand-cleaning them or placing them in the dishwasher.

"Dad's probably rolling in his grave right now." I chuckle. "He'd hate that."

"Probably," she agrees with a laugh. "And we do talk about your dad, honey. You're not in Melbourne to hear it, but I promise, we do because he's a part of us all."

He's also part of McAllister.

"And he'd be very proud of you, Theo. We all are."

Taking a deep breath, I lean back into the couch. "I haven't re-signed my contract yet."

My mum raises her hands to her cheek in mock surprise. "I gathered that from your zero to one hundred behavior last night."

Embarrassment floods my cheeks, although I know she's teasing me. "Things are complicated. There are some clauses I don't agree with, and McAllister's being difficult."

"Ah, is that the *legal jargon* Josie was referring to?"

"Something like that." I sigh. Jos was only trying to save Richard from my wrath and stop me from losing it, but she knows nothing about contract negotiations.

"Are they not offering you enough?"

She's not being malicious, but her words sting more than they should. I could quit racing tomorrow and still be set for life. I've been smart with my money and I have invested wisely. I do splurge on certain things like my travel sheets and private plane, but those are necessary for my mental health. "C'mon, you know I don't care about that, Mum."

"Then what is it?"

I run my hands over my face. The last thing I want to do is open Pandora's box before a race. Quite frankly, Pandora needs to suck a dick and fade into obscurity. I'd like things nice, neat, and clean with no dramatic blow ups, thank you very much.

"Don't worry about it," I reassure her. "Everything will sort itself out."

I don't want to talk about this anymore. Or ever, for that matter. Flashing my signature carefree smile, I pray she believes me. God knows I don't believe myself.

28

JOSIE

LOOKING AROUND GEMINI, I try to remember how it looked when I first stepped foot inside—dusty, dim, and sparse. Now it's the perfect mix of comfort and classic. Ambient twinkle lights glisten off the mirrored wall behind the long oak bar, and bottles of fancy wine, local craft beers, and every whiskey brand known to mankind line the shelves. Tufted leather booths line the exposed brick walls and mismatched light fixtures hang from the high ceiling: a vintage Busch beer chandelier next to a gold starburst pendant.

"We don't need the bang bang shrimp *and* the shrimp tacos," Kelsey muses aloud. "What do you think?"

I glance down at my notebook—the pages are smudged with oil and aioli. "I think I'm going to need to be rolled out of here. Any way I could get a free membership to that gym of yours?"

Leaning back into the booth, Kelsey lets out a low laugh. He knows I'm right, considering we just ate a week's worth of meals in three hours. Jamie made us full-sized plates of every bar bite imaginable. A queso dip with salted fingerling potatoes. Mussels and frites. Chipotle mac & cheese. Smoked apricot barbecue wings. And Jamie's take on fish and chips? Tempura-battered cod and sweet potato fries with a spicy wasabi tartare dipping sauce. How do you not eat all of that? You have to. Honestly, it'd be rude to leave any morsels left on the plate.

Thankfully, my sweater is long enough to cover the fact that my jeans have been unbuttoned for the past thirty minutes. "I say we do the bang bang shrimp," I add. "If I were religious, I'd want to be baptized in that sauce."

Kelsey grins at me. "Bang bang it is."

I shoot him finger guns. *Bang bang.* The corner of his mouth quirks up as he closes his own grease-stained notebook.

A text from Theo pops up on my screen and momentarily distracts me. There's only an hour time difference between Zandvoort and London, but based on our constant game of text tag and missed calls, it seems like a much larger gap.

> **THEO WALKER**
>
> Just saw you called. Was in a meeting. :/

> **JOSIE BANCROFT**
>
> It's okay! How was practice?

> **THEO WALKER**
>
> Eh, fine. Pace was off. You around now to chat?

> **JOSIE BANCROFT**
>
> At Gemini. I'll call when I leave!

> **THEO WALKER**
>
> Have a sponsor event in a bit. Chat tonight?

Kelsey clears his throat, the raspy tone making me glance up. "I want you to work with me full-time."

My phone slips from my hands and clatters to the table dramatically. "What?"

"I want you to work with me," he repeats with a chuckle.

"Call it a gut feeling, but we've created something special here, and this is just the beginning. I want to open more spots that are about more than just what's on the table—places where people feel completely at home while still experiencing the joy of dining or drinking out."

"Wells Drink Hospitality," I blurt out.

Kelsey's brows curve downward. "Hmm?"

"That's what you should call the hospitality group," I clarify. "Think about it. Your last name is Wells, obviously, and it's *way* too convenient that well drinks happen to be the bread and butter for bars. Hence—"

"Wells Drink Hospitality," he repeats back. "See? This is why I need you full-time. I can't even name places by myself."

Excitement blooms in my stomach and a million questions come flying out at once. The first one obviously being: are you kidding me? Kelsey answers each one of my questions with the practiced precision of a boxer. He's direct, honest, and every response packs an exciting punch.

"I'd be remiss to not try to steal you away from McAllister. And with me, you can expand and grow your role into what you want and build your own team," he continues. "Take some time to think about it, okay?"

All I can do is nod and say, "Sure."

I FINALLY GET ahold of Theo right before I go to bed. The moment he answers the phone, we both start talking at rapid-fire speed. If anyone were eavesdropping on our conversation, they'd think we're speaking gibberish or on drugs. God knows Theo's the more impatient of the two of us, so I let him speak first. I need his full attention for my news, anyway.

"My tire strategy sucks," he says agitatedly. "They want me to switch to medium tires on a one-stop strategy. At Zandvoort! It's bad enough that Pirelli didn't produce altered tires to handle the tracks' banking, but switching me to that? The wear and degradation are going to kill my speed."

The Grand Prix in Zandvoort has recently been redeveloped, meaning the data to formulate tire strategy isn't as exact as it should be. Though the team should know enough that soft to hard tires is the move, not soft to medium.

"That doesn't seem like Andreas."

Theo snorts. "It seems like Avery, though, right?"

Ah.

"Your strategy could easily change," I remind him soothingly. "Especially if the weather causes more degradation than expected. How was qualifying?"

"Fine, but I was on *soft tires*." He mutters something to himself, but his accent and low tone make it hard to make out what he's saying. "I wish you were here, Jos. You make everything better."

His words send a guilty flush to my cheeks. I'd be lying if I said that the tasting wasn't worth missing a race weekend, which in Theo's eyes is akin to blasphemy.

"I miss you, too." I cradle the phone against my ear and cuddle deeper into the warm embrace of my bed. "Is there anything I can do to help?"

"There is one thing you could do," he suggests with a low chuckle. "If you're up for it."

"Mm-hmm?"

I hear his breath hitch. "You can tell me what you're wearing."

Oh.

Oh my god.

Um.

Does he want me to tell him what I'm actually wearing to bed or should I lie and say something sexy?

"That blue cotton pajama set," I admit quietly. "With the white trim on it."

"I like that one. Always feels so soft against my skin, yeah?" His voice is an octave deeper, a dead giveaway that he's turned on. "Wish I was there right now, spooning with you. Well, we wouldn't really be cuddling."

"No?"

"Nu-uh," he replies huskily. "I'd be balls-deep in that pretty little pussy of yours, making you moan my name as you come all over my cock."

A wave of desire crashes into my core, quickly rolling through my veins like a drug. What the fuck do I say to that? *Cool! Amazing! Smashing!* Even with all the traveling I did, I never had phone sex with any of my exes—I never felt the need to. And even if I did want to, I wasn't nearly bold enough to initiate it. I don't want to mess this up by saying the wrong thing.

"You'd like that, wouldn't you, princess? Me rocking into you and rubbing your swollen clit with my fingers."

Bloody hell. His words are so intimate and primal that my chest heaves as I fight to control my breathing. "Ye-yes."

"I'm so hard, Jos. You're all I think about."

My body vibrates to the thump of my heart. "I don't really, uh, know… how to do this. Phone sex. I don't know if I'm going to be very good at it. Haven't really explored this particular avenue before. Or street. Boulevard. Whatever you want to call it. Masturbation station."

Theo laughs softly. "Well, all you have to do is tell me what you want and how you're touching yourself. For example… right now, I'm stroking my cock, thinking about how good your pussy feels. How fucking warm it is, because you're always so wet and ready for me."

My cheeks flush at the brazenness of his words. "Oh?"

"Mm-hmm. Are you wet right now? Do you want to touch yourself, angel?"

"Yes," I squeak out. Theo's words get me more riled up

than I thought was humanly possible. He's awakened a fire in me, and I'm desperate to let it consume every inch of my skin.

"Do it, baby," he coaxes.

I sigh as I press softly against my clit, pleasure coursing through my body as I slowly stroke myself. "I'm, well… um, touching myself."

No shit, Sherlock. Christ. What is wrong with me? That's so un-sexy. Should I pretend I have bad service and just end the call and hide out in a hole for the rest of my life?

"Details, baby," Theo says, amusement lacing his words. "I want you to tell me exactly how you're touching yourself. What are you thinking about?"

"You," I admit, my voice breathy. "I'm thinking about you."

"What're you thinking about me doing?"

"I'm pretending it's your fingers rubbing against me. Slowly teasing me until I can't take it anymore."

He moans into the phone. "I can't wait to be inside you. How fast do you think I can make you come when I see you? Hmm?"

My response is immediate. "Fast."

He laughs deeply. "It's because my cock was made for your pussy, yeah? Always feels so fucking good."

"Ah-huh." I can barely get the words out, the excitement over what we're doing overwhelming my senses. I feel my stomach start to burn, my orgasm edging closer with every second that passes.

"Don't get shy on me now, gorgeous. Tell me what else."

"I'm thinking of your fingers filling me," I whisper.

"Fuck, that's hot, baby. Slide a finger in for me."

He doesn't have to tell me twice. I whimper quietly into the phone as I caress the spot inside me. This is better than any solo self-pleasure session I've ever had.

"Do me a favor," Theo says huskily. "Go get Buzz Lightyear."

I've toyed around with Buzz—no pun intended—and surprisingly, I like him a lot. Not that I would ever admit that to my mum. *Nope. Don't think about your mum right now, Josie.*

Rolling onto my side, I open my bedside drawer and pull Buzz out of his protective case—which, yes, is shaped like a rocket ship. He's royal purple and green, and made of high-quality silicon that gives him a silky feel.

"Okay, I have him. It. I have it," I say, clicking the button three times to get to my favorite setting. "It's turned on."

And so am I. Theo coaxes me on how to touch myself. What he wants me to do. What he wants to be doing to me. I'm a mess as I near my orgasm, moaning his name into the phone like I'm a phone sex operator who does this for a living.

"Fuck, I'm so close, Jos," he says in a strained voice. "Come with me, baby."

That's all it takes. At his words, I come undone, arching my back deeply, eyes screwed shut as I ride the wave of electricity flowing through my body. The throaty noise he denies making filters through the phone as he comes. I smile at the sound, knowing that even thousands of miles away, I'm still the one making him unravel.

"Christ, Jos. That was…"

"I know." My chest rises and falls as I try to catch my breath. "You're good at phone sex."

Closing my eyes, I imagine his smile—not cocky, not conceited, but content. For a moment, there's only heavy breathing coming through the phone.

"This was my first time," he says.

And just as my heart rate was starting to go down, it skyrockets once again. His first time? Theo's smile may not be cocky, but mine sure as hell is. I like being one of his firsts, especially since he probably doesn't have many left.

"Well, wow," I finally stammer out. "Color me impressed, Walker."

"Eh, no need to be impressed. I just know what I want."

My heart skips a beat. "Me?"

"Always you, baby. I'm—"

He's cut off by loud, muffled voices and intense banging. "Shit, Jos. I've got to go. Call you later, yeah? Love you, angel."

"Mm-hmm. Love you, too."

My news will have to wait.

EACH DAY in Zandvoort without Josie seems to be just a little longer than the last, and my anticipation reaches new heights as I near my return date to London. Knowing it was just *one* race weekend of many is all that kept me sane. Especially with Avery lurking about, making offhand remarks about my "sub-par" performance. *Fucker.*

Josie appears on my doorstep ten minutes after I'm back from the airport. An all-encompassing sense of lightness floods through me as I hold her—it's a rejuvenating shot of adrenaline straight to my heart and head. Our lips connect, savoring and exploring as if the four days apart were four years. *God, I fucking missed her.* One Grand Prix without her was one Grand Prix too many. She leans back and briefly nestles her cheek against my chest.

"Hi, angel," I murmur into her hair. "Missed you."

Josie smiles up at me. "How much?"

I take the clip out of her hair, running my hands through her blonde locks. "I lost a game of *Halo* because I couldn't stop thinking about you."

"Wow." She whistles softly. "That's a lot."

"Mm-hmm." I tug her inside with interlaced fingers. My hand stays clasped with hers as we walk to the living room and settle on the couch, our limbs intertwined like some tantric yoga position.

"I want to talk to you about something big." Josie grins widely and claps her hands together adorably. "*Very* big."

"What is it?" I have no clue where this conversation is going, but I'm dying to know what has her this excited.

Her narrowed eyes suddenly shine with delight. "Kelsey wants to start a hospitality group. Well, he's technically already started one. I'm not really in the know with that side of the business, but anyway. The even *more* exciting part is…" she drums her hands against my thigh, "he asked me to be the head of marketing!"

A shiver runs over my skin like a ghostly touch. "Full-time?"

She nods. "Yes. There's no way I could work for him *and* McAllister *and* help Ella out with the podcast. Although El may be hiring her own team soon, but still."

"Are you accepting it?" I couldn't keep the edge out of my voice even if I wanted to. "I thought you only wanted to consult."

That's what you told me.

"I haven't decided. Originally, yes, it was simply freelance, but this is an unreal opportunity." She shrugs nonchalantly, as if her words aren't crashing over me like waves during a storm. "I'd be able to build out my own team and everything. Can you imagine me being someone's boss? I mean, I technically boss you and Blake around, but this is an official boss title. Cool, right?"

"I, uh—"

"And listen to this!" Josie says, her eyes lit with excitement. "When I was at Gemini the other day, I was craving ice cream. I mean, when am I not craving ice cream? But I was *really* craving it then, more than usual. But I was also craving a cookie. It got me thinking. What if we created an artisanal ice cream *sandwich* shop? Customers could choose their cookie—snickerdoodle, sugar, chocolate chip, fudge brownie—and then whatever ice cream flavor they wanted. Kelsey says if I come up with a real proposal, we can discuss it! Doesn't that sound to die for?"

Josie leaving McAllister isn't part of my plan. I need her.

"Theo? Are you okay?" Josie rests her hand on my forearm. "You look like you're getting a root canal, for Christ's sake."

Usually, I'd laugh at Josie's ridiculous comparison, but I'm too focused on reeling in the red-hot betrayal swirling through my veins. My throat burns and I readjust myself, causing her legs to fall out of my lap. "You'd be leaving me."

A carefree laugh slips through her lips. "I wouldn't be leaving you, babes. I'd be leaving McAllister."

They're one and the same. "And you're fine with that?"

"You yourself said that McAllister isn't the end all, be all for me," Josie says, the casualness of her voice turning to confusion. "You encouraged me to share my talents with more people."

"Key word being *share*, not use them all somewhere else," I snap, anger flashing in my eyes. "When did he offer you the job?"

"After the tasting. I tried to tell you on the phone, but there was never a good time." Josie's smile falters. "Why are you upset? I thought you'd be happy for me."

"Well, apparently I don't make you happy if you want to leave me."

"Of course you make me happy. Don't be ridiculous," she says hastily. "I-I just think this could make me happy, too. I have a chance to create something really cool from the ground up. Not only a company that I believe in, but one that believes in me, too. This has *nothing* to do with you. I promise."

"It does if you're leaving McAllister." My voice cuts through each word with razor-sharp precision. I slink further down the couch to put some space between us. "It has everything to do with us."

"I love you and what we have together," she says firmly. "No job is going to change that."

Taking a deep breath, I nod absentmindedly. Almost as if her words are just that, words. "You leaving McAllister will fundamentally change our relationship. Change *my* life. If I sign McAllister's contract, who's going to handle my social media? I was only fine with that if it was *you*. You can't leave. You just can't."

Now it's Josie who moves back to put space between us. "So you want me to turn down a really amazing offer because it means I'd have a life of my own outside of Formula 1? Outside of you?"

"Formula 1 is *our* life! It's *us*, Josie. How do you not see that?"

Her wry laugh makes the hairs on my arms stand up. "Since when is our relationship dependent on me working for Formula 1? You're being unreasonable, Theo."

"You saw how we barely spoke last weekend. You couldn't even find time to tell me something *huge*. It'll be like that every weekend. Living two completely separate lives. I can't do that. I won't, Josie."

My words hang in the air between us, sucking up the oxygen and making it hard to breathe. The way Josie's shoulders turn inward sends a chill through me. As if I'm not the first man who's let her down, and I won't be the last.

"I always knew your career came first for you… I just didn't realize it had to for me as well," she says, her voice scarily detached. Rather than hot cocoa, her eyes look like quicksand, telling me that I've fallen and there's no escape route. We're not making it out of this situation without one of us drowning. "So this," she waves to the space between us, "doesn't work for me, either."

I don't say a damn word. I couldn't even if I wanted to. Everything I should say catches in my throat, unable to get past the massive lump forming.

Josie walks out without a backward glance. I'm not even worth another look. An unbearably sharp pain takes hold of my body that seems to stretch on forever. It takes me a moment to realize it's not a heart attack, it's just a broken heart.

30

JOSIE

A WEEK after I tell Theo we're through, I meet him at my favorite ice cream parlor. Neutral territory, except for the fact that the employees know my name and order by heart. Well, they know Theo's name, too, but only because he's been here with me a few times. And probably because his face graces the front of tabloid magazines every week.

I pass the glass case filled with dozens of flavors as I make my way to the two syrup dispensers Theo's camped out by. *God, he's gorgeous.* Brown hair brushed away from his face, stubble marking his chiseled jaw, blue eyes so beautiful, I could drown in them. Every person in the shop stares at him with their phone cameras playing amateur paparazzi. I don't blame them. He's breathtakingly beautiful. He's also so used to the attention that it doesn't even register for him.

"'Ello, angel," he greets me, a lopsided smile appearing on his lips. "Thanks for meeting me."

Theo's called and texted me so many times in the past few days, I thought my phone was going to self-implode. I didn't answer him until now, knowing my emotions were too raw to have a productive conversation.

I don't get a word in before Marco—my favorite employee —thrusts a bumpy, freshly-made waffle cone into my hand. Two scoops of chocolate chip cookie dough ice cream sprinkled with gummy bears sit on top. My go-to order. He gives Theo a kid's size cup of vanilla ice cream with rainbow sprinkles, even though he has a stellar memory and is fully aware that Theo likes pistachio ice cream with chocolate sprinkles. It's like he *knows* Theo acted like a child and, therefore, should be treated like one.

Marco scoffs at our attempt to pay for our treats. "On the house," he says, throwing me a wink.

Even if Kelsey gives the go-ahead on pursuing my ice cream sandwich shop idea, I'll always be loyal to this place. This kind of customer service earns allegiance.

Theo chuckles at the staff's familiarity with me—it never fails to amaze him. Who needs bottle service when you can have ice cream shop service? I'll take that over bottles of Veuve any day of the week.

"I want to apologize," Theo says as I dig into my ice cream. He rubs the back of his neck with his free hand. "I was a selfish prick, Jos, and I'm so sorry."

I lick the sugary mix of smooth ice cream and bits of cookie dough to buy myself some time. I've rehearsed what I want to say a million times, but now I can no longer remember a single word. This is why I didn't get a real role in my school's play production: stage fright.

It takes me a few more moments to find my voice. "You really hurt me. I told you about an opportunity I'm excited for, and the only thing you wanted to know was what it meant for you."

Theo nods. "I know. I wasn't sure what to say, and I overreacted, Jos. I acted like what I wanted is more important than what you want, and that wasn't fair of me. There's no excuse for my behavior."

"You could've said you were happy for me. That it's an amazing opportunity," I say softly. "That it may be an adjustment, but that you'd fight for us."

Theo rests his elbows on the table and searches my face. His blue eyes are glassy, tears threatening to spill down his cheeks. "You're right. That is what I should've said because I *am* happy for you and it *is* an amazing opportunity. And even if I'm terrified of losing you, I sure as hell am going to fight for us. You're the best thing that's ever happened to me."

Confusion floods through me, making me lightheaded. "What do you mean, you're scared to lose me? What would make you think that might happen?"

Theo swipes at his eyes and turns to the wall to shield his face from the onlookers. "Because if you leave McAllister behind, then maybe you'll leave me behind, too. You'll realize that I'm not your favorite person. That there's someone else who can love you better than I can."

I'm not used to seeing this vulnerable side of Theo—walls stripped down, heart completely exposed, waiting for me to nurture it or rip it to shreds. I'm suddenly not in the mood for my ice cream anymore.

"I couldn't leave you behind even if I wanted to," I say gently. "We promised we'd always be best friends, yeah?"

The hopeful spark in his eyes fades and makes my stomach churn. "Is that all we are, Jos? Friends?"

I don't want to say it out loud, but I have to.

"I think friends is what's best for us both," I admit quietly. "At least for right now. When you reacted that way, it broke my heart. And I started second-guessing if it was a silly idea. If you were right. If Formula 1 is, and should stay, my life."

A strangled noise comes from Theo. "I'm an idiot."

"I'm not disputing that," I say with a small smile. "But I have to decide what I want my future to look like on my own, without worrying about how you—or anyone else—will react. I've gone from one relationship to the next, but now is my chance to be alone and figure myself out for a change. I owe myself that much."

"And while I'm sorting out my own stuff," I add, "you can decide if McAllister is the right team for you, whether I'm there to handle your social media or not."

He flinches at my words. "Don't... don't give up on us," he says quietly. "Please, Josie."

I grab his hand in mine and give it a squeeze. It's sticky from the ice cream dripping down, but Theo doesn't seem to mind. He intertwines our fingers, gripping my hand so tightly, I'm nervous I may lose circulation.

"I'm not giving up on us, Theo," I promise. "The farthest thing from it. I'm giving us a chance. But I need to figure things out for *me*, not the me that's in a relationship. I've always put other people first, and for once in my life, I need to put myself first to prove that I can handle the big stuff alone."

Theo nods slowly, letting my words sink in. His death grip on my hand gradually relaxes and blood rushes to my hand. *Christ.* I sometimes forget how much muscle he has. Personality of a golden retriever, muscle mass of a goddamn German shepherd.

"Okay, angel." He pauses before nodding. "If you think this is what's best... I trust you, eh? I won't give up on us, either. I mean it when I say I'm going to fight for us."

I release the deep breath I've been holding hostage in my chest. I expected Theo to argue with me, to dig his heels into the sand and push and plead until he got his way. To scream, kick, and fight his way back into a relationship. Because that's Theo. A few years ago, he talked Blake out of getting arrested for trying to undress a cop he thought was a stripper. He has a way with words that few have blades sharp enough to fight.

Instead, he's respecting my space and listening to what I need. He's giving me hope that we can work out.

He's letting me choose myself.

31

THEO

EVERY TIME I TURN AROUND, my heart plummets when I realize Josie's not here. She hasn't made a final decision about Kelsey's offer yet, but she did request this race weekend off and her absence is glaring. And not just for me; Wes threatened to smack Blake in the head with a fire extinguisher if he didn't stop acting like an "entitled brat" and Ella had to step in to play referee.

Spending time apart from Jos is unwittingly forcing my hand. Without her smile or laughter to distract me, I have no choice *but* to think about my contract. The end of the season is quickly approaching. To sign with McAllister or not to sign with McAllister, that's the question twenty-first century Shakespeare would be asking.

My radio snaps me out of my thoughts. "How you doing, Walker?"

I roll my eyes, thankful they can't see behind my helmet. I've kept to myself this weekend, opting out of additional fan encounters and interviews. I'm not sure who knows about my breakup-slash-break-slash-time-out and who doesn't, but I don't give a shit. I can't think about that. All I can think about is winning. It's all I can allow myself to focus on. Because when my mind wanders, it always finds its way back to Josie.

"Fine," I reply.

"Everything good?"

"Mm-hmm."

The voice on the other side snickers. "Um… this is Theo, right? Not Blake? Want to make sure we didn't press the wrong button."

I snort at the comment. My one-word answers are reason for concern. "Yeah. I'm all good, mate."

"Alright. Good luck out there."

Josie should be the one wishing me good luck.

Taking a deep breath, I rest my hands against the wheel, letting the familiar smell of burning rubber and fuel calm me. The race is business as usual, until lap forty-seven, when McAllister fucks up. Big time. They pit Blake early because they're worried his tire degradation won't last through the final stretch of the race. They may be right, but now he's running over the same piece of track as me in the final third of the Grand Prix. That means our strategies are overlapping, and I'm two-point-five seconds ahead of him.

"Don't hold up Hollis," the guys from the pit wall instruct. "Pull back."

Rage churns inside me, resentment clouding my thoughts. Does Blake have a better chance of winning the Drivers' Championship this year? Yes, probably. But this may be the last year I'm able to willingly fight for it.

I ignore the radio. Fuck it.

Switching gears as I head into the next turn, I brake a second early, using the downforce to open the exit of the corner and gain acceleration heading down the next straight. Thompson is ahead of me, taking a curve at an impressive speed. Kid's honing in on his instinct, I'll give him that.

"Walker, do you copy?" I hear Andreas's tense tone through the radio. "Pull back. We need you to fend off Adler."

"Andreas? Are you saying something?"

"Yes!" he shouts. "Stop holding up Hollis, for fu——"

"All I hear is a really weird crackling," I lie, the chaos of my rage taking over. "Something must be off with my radio."

Why shouldn't I be able to hold my own pace? I'm here to race, not be a goddamn pawn piece to Blake's King. I continue to ignore my radio for nearly half a lap more. As we go into turn ten, Blake underbrakes, forcing me to pull back so I don't ram into the barricade.

Biting back my frustration, I maintain my position, not edging any closer to Blake. God knows I've pissed off the pit wall enough. The crackle from my radio simply tells me, "Keep Adler and Fraser at bay."

The minute the race is over and I'm out of my car, Andreas is on my ass. I tune him out—something I've become relatively proficient at over the years—as he admonishes me for my unsportsmanlike behavior. *Whatever*. Blaming my radio, I brush it off as an unfortunate accident. Blake won regardless. Can't he just let it go?

I head to the press conference alone so I can avoid Blake as long as humanly possible. There's no way in hell he's going to let me off the hook so easily. As his competition, I didn't do anything out of the ordinary, but as his teammate and friend, I drove like an absolute asshole. My only saving grace is that I placed third and Thompson placed second, so he acts as a buffer between us at the table. My human shield.

It's no surprise when the first question of the press conference is aimed at me. "How do you feel about the outcome of today's race?" a reporter asks. "You had a chance to secure a first or second place win, but were told to stand back for Blake."

"There's a lot of times when we have to play as a team," I

say, each word eating at me. "This race was one of those times. We need to win both titles—Constructors' Championship and Drivers'. If Andreas thinks Blake is in a better position to help secure McAllister those wins, then that's the situation. My radio was going in and out, so it took me a little longer to realize the strategy shift."

"Are you still in contention for the title?"

I won't be next year if I sign the contract.

I give a half-assed smile. "Aren't we all?"

"Let me rephrase," the reporter says. "Are you allowed to fight for the title? Or are you being told to stand back for Blake to clinch his seventh win?"

He may as well have given me a stake and asked me to shove it through my heart.

"We all want to win—races, points, championships. My goal is to go into every race bringing in as many points as I can for the team."

This seems to satisfy the reporter, at least for now. What about when they ask next season? I can't openly say, "I signed away my right to beat Blake just so I could stay on the team." It feels just as pathetic as it sounds.

"Blake!" a SkySports writer asks. "How do you feel about what happened during lap fifty-three?"

Blake moves his chair closer to his microphone. "Uh. It happened. It's over. What more is there to say?"

For once, I'm glad Blake doesn't give too many details during interviews. He hates press conferences as much as I hate going to the doctor.

"Did you know that Theo was told to back down?"

Blake rolls his eyes. "Were your ear plugs in when I said, 'Why the bloody fuck isn't he letting me pass?' on the radio?"

"So you were upset with Theo not giving you back the lead?"

"Listen." Blake sighs, narrowing his eyes at the pesky

journalist. "Theo's a great teammate, and I highly doubt he went into the lap with anything but good intentions. Sometimes we're put in a position where we have to put the team first, ahead of our own desire to get the most points for the Drivers' Championship. Does it suck? Sure. But we want McAllister to get the maximum number of points. That's key."

The room is eerily quiet. That may be the most Blake's said during a press conference in years. Little does he know, the sucky position he spoke about is where McAllister wants me to reside permanently.

Thankfully, the reporters move on, asking Harry about his last-minute strategy change. The moment the press conference wraps up, I'm out of my seat and out the door. Blake is hot on my heels as I walk back through the paddock. He leaves just enough space so I'd look like an arse if I yelled at him to leave me alone.

That changes the moment we're in the privacy of McAllister's motorhome.

"So, are we going to talk about what the fuck happened out there?" he asks, not bothering to lower his voice.

"You said it yourself," I snap, not turning around as I stomp up the stairs to the second floor. "It happened, it's over. What else is there to say?"

Blake scoffs at the fierceness of my tone. "What the fuck is up with you? Is this about the breakup?"

"Fuck off," I mumble, walking into my suite.

This is one time when visitors are not welcome in my room, but Blake doesn't seem to give a shit. His tall frame takes up the space of my doorframe. "Seriously, Theo. What the bloody hell is going on? You've been a dick to me the past week, and I have no idea what I did wrong. You fucking railroaded me out there."

"It's a race, Blake," I grunt. "I'm *so* sorry I didn't make it easy for you to win. God forbid I try to get points for myself, yeah? Now can you get out? I'd like to be alone."

Blake shakes his head in disbelief. "We're going to talk about this, Walker. This isn't you."

"No, we're not." I take a step forward, shoving his chest. It feels really fucking good. "So get the fuck out of my room."

Blake lets out a sharp laugh. "You really want to go this route? Because I'll—"

The palm of my hand connects with Blake's cheek, and a resounding *smack* vibrates through the room. *Oh fuck.* I glance at Blake, wondering if I can slip past him and down the hall before his fist dislocates my jaws. I've held him back from many bar fights over the years, but I've never been the victim of his right hook or left jab.

"Did… did you just bitch slap me?" he asks with wide eyes.

I take a step back. "Um… yeah?"

His shoulders shake as his laugh rumbles through his chest. He leans against the doorframe, using it to hold himself up. I'll take this reaction over a broken nose any day of the week.

Blake wipes tears from his eyes. "Didn't want to punch me instead, mate?"

"And risk breaking my fingers before the end of the season? Hell no, Blakey Blake." I shake my head as my anger makes way for exhaustion. "I am sorry about that, though. Don't know what came over me."

He gingerly touches the bright red mark covering his cheek. "I'm quite proud of you, mate. It was a long time coming, although I usually know what I did to deserve it. This time, I'm not so sure. So why don't you tell me what the hell is going on with you?"

I fall back onto the couch and rest my elbows on my thighs. *Where the fuck to even begin?* "Everything."

32

JOSIE

I PASTE a smile on my face despite the urge I have to crawl under the nearest table. While some girls—and Theo—have a birthday month or a birthday week, one day is *more* than enough for me. As much as I absolutely love celebrating other people's birthdays, I tend to dislike my own. There's too much pressure. Coordinating friends for a dinner, opening gifts in front of people, coming up with a half-assed answer to someone asking if all my wishes have come true. *No, Linda, my wish to become a stay-at-home dog mum millionaire did not come true.* The only thing I ever do is dinner with my parents and that's more for them than it is for me.

The hostess leads me to the table with a bundle of nylon balloons that say, "Happy Birthday!" and "Birthday Girl" in a bright, bold font. Apparently, nothing says Michelin-star dining more than matching polka-dotted hats.

The balloon-buyer greets me with an ear-to-ear smile. "Happy birthday, darling!"

Of course, the one time a year my mum's on time is my birthday, and that's only so she can set up the table to look like a decoration store had a buy-one-get-one sale.

I lean down and kiss her cheek before giving my dad a quick side hug. Pushing away some balloons, I slide into the open chair. "I thought you promised we could keep things under the radar this year."

"This is your mother's version of low-key." My dad chuckles. "Not a single "Birthday Girl" sash in sight. Do you feel any older? Any wiser?"

I laugh and shake my head. He asks me the same question every year, and every year I give him the same answer in response. "I feel the same as I do the other three hundred and sixty-four days of the year."

A server swings by our table to take our drink orders and waves to the empty seat across from me. "Waiting on one more?"

I pick up my menu to give my hands something to do so they don't tug at my necklace. The fourth seat, which was originally meant for Theo, is painfully empty. He's staying true to his word and respecting my space. Yet every time my phone buzzes, a part of me wishes it's a text from him asking if it's normal to spend five hundred pounds for extra lives in *World of Warcraft*. And every time I discover a new artist on Spotify or find a new restaurant I want to try, my fingers itch to dial his number so I can tell him. I didn't realize how loud the silence of space could be.

"Just the three of us," my mum informs him. "We're celebrating our daughter's birthday."

As if he can't tell.

I hum "We Are Family" under my breath as my mum orders a bottle of wine and some appetizers. I wait until our glasses are filled to share my news. Unlike my birthday, this is something I'm eager to celebrate, despite its bittersweet nature.

"Before Mum makes her annual 'Cheers to staying positive and testing negative' toast," I say with a pointed look, "I have a rather exciting announcement to make. I accepted Kelsey's job offer and gave McAllister my two-weeks' notice."

"That's lovely, dear." My dad's brows lift just enough to raise alarm bells in my head. "And this is what you want, yes?"

I narrow my eyes at what he's insinuating. McAllister will always hold a special place in my heart, but leaving is the right decision for me. It wasn't until taking a step back from them—and Theo—that I realized I was letting my comfort undermine my desire to challenge myself. Now Johnny Nash's "I Can See Clearly Now" plays in a constant loop in my head like a theme song. "This has nothing to do with Theo or our breakup. You know I would never let—"

"He's being protective, sweetie," my mum intervenes before I can launch into defensive mode. "We know this decision didn't come lightly, and we're very proud of you."

"Right-o." My dad taps his wineglass against mine. "Have you gotten the contract from Kelsey yet?"

I sigh. "I know the drill. I'll send it over to you before signing anything."

He grins his approval. "Well, then congratulations, Josephine. What a lovely announcement. A great way to start the first day of a new age."

The rest of dinner is harmless enough, despite the three-tier birthday cake that comes out and features a multitude of sparklers. I'm very ready for my birthday to be over, but when I arrive back at my flat, a sparkly bag with crumpled tissue paper sticking out greets me. A card with "Angel" scrawled in Theo's doctor-like handwriting is taped to the front. I pick it up off the floor before taking it inside with me.

Theo's gotten me a wide range of gifts for my birthday over the years—everything from a Cartier bracelet that cost triple my monthly rent to a waffle-maker. Andrew was not a fan of Theo buying me expensive jewelry, no matter how many times I explained not to read into it. Theo doesn't think about

money the way average people do. I take the tube when Uber
has a surcharge, whereas Theo once took a helicopter across
London because he was too impatient to sit in traffic during
rush hour. To him, there's not much different between a David
Yurman ring and a plastic one you'd get out of a gumball
machine.

The card isn't sealed because Theo finds licking envelopes
"an infestation of bacterial growth" so it's easy to open. My
eyes scan over the note he's written.

> Happy birthday, princess.
> You may not like to celebrate today,
> but it just so happens to be the day
> my favorite person was born.
> I love you.
>
> —Theo

Bloody hell. I'm a sucker for a sweet card. I place it on the
kitchen table before taking out the tissue paper covering the
gift. Inside, I discover a brown plush bear with floppy arms and
an adorably stitched nose. Running my hands over the fluffy
paws, I realize it's the same texture and material as Mademoiselle. Tears spring to my eyes when it hits me. It's the bear we
saw at the toy store in Le Mans.

My heart is so full of love, I worry it may explode. Slipping
my phone out of my pocket, I hit Theo's name on my list of
favorite contacts. It rings twice before he picks up.

"'Ello, birthday girl. You get my gift?"

"Theo... I don't know what to say," I choke out. The bear
sits tightly in my arms, and I worry about accidentally decapi-
tating it. "How did— When did— What?"

He laughs softly. "You really thought it took me twenty minutes to pick out a princess doll for Rosalie?"

"Yes! You once spent close to an hour deciding which toothpaste to buy."

"In my defense, the ingredients were in Arabic, and I wanted to be sure it had gum protection." Theo's voice gets unusually shy. "You like her, yeah?"

"Best gift ever. And it's a *him*, not a her." I pause as I consider a name. "Monsieur."

Theo's deep laugh brings an uncontrollable smile to my face. "If Mademoiselle and Monsieur weren't the cutest names for stuffed animals, I'd seriously regret getting you another man to cuddle with."

Walking over to my bed, I place Monsieur in his new spot next to his fluffy cousin, Mademoiselle. "Thank you, Theo. Seriously. It means the world to me."

"You mean the world to me," he says softly. "Happy birthday, Jos."

33

THEO

THE AFTERNOON SUN shines through the window, heating the otherwise cool room. I hold up my hand to shade my eyes from the bright rays hitting me. It's a surprisingly warm day in Sochi. I can switch seats—the paddock conference room has more than enough—but I need to spare my energy for this conversation.

Russell and Martin sit across the table from me like this is some sort of high-level, top-secret debrief—which, I guess it sort of is. I ignore their intense gazes and click on my text exchange with Josie. No new messages.

"We need to chat about the latest revisions in the McAllister contract," Martin says. "You can't keep avoiding it."

"Yes, I can," I argue. *Revisions, my ass*. They took out a few words that held no meaning. The things I give a shit about—what they *know* I care about—have stayed the same.

Russell rolls his eyes at me. He's still slightly pissed at me for accidentally saying "shit" in front of Rosalie last week. She's now incorporating it into almost every sentence. He says I need to watch my language, but I think he should be proud his daughter is such a quick learner.

"Do I need to knock some sense into you, Walker?" Martin huffs.

"I can do it," Russell volunteers with a grin. He leans back in his chair, the pleather squeaking from the movement.

I make an imperceptible sound under my breath.

"Nothing has changed," I grunt. "The contract still sucks. Avery still sucks. They still want me to suck."

Neither disagrees with me. "I've pulled out every stop in the book, Theo," Martin says, sounding defeated. "Worked with lawyers to update the language, tried to find loopholes… McAllister won't budge."

Avery won't budge because he holds a grudge. They should teach that rhyme in Rosalie's school.

"They could be willing to make more changes to the contract once the year is up," Russell adds. "But you need to decide if you can deal with *this* contract."

The thought of having to deal with renegotiations like this *again* next year makes me nauseous, like the time I ate two boxes of Sour Patch Kids in a row. I don't *think* I'll throw up, but I wouldn't hedge any money on it, either.

"Fuck," I mutter.

"Let's review your other options." Martin's ability to switch gears is impressive. "Who do you want to start with?"

"Whoever."

Martin sighs. I know that sigh. It's his 'what am I going to do with you' sigh—the one he makes when I'm not making his life easy. "We're coming down to the wire, mate. The press is only going to get more inquisitive about where you stand on negotiations. We've got to start making some decisions. Decide who you want to drive for."

McAllister is still the end goal, but I don't know if I can come to terms with what that means for my career. Slipping my phone into my pocket—but not before making sure it's on full volume—I give my manager and performance coach my undivided attention. We've met with Catalyst, Porsche, and AlphaVite, and they've all extended offers. As much as I want to re-sign with McAllister, it does feel good to be wanted.

"I vote we take Catalyst out of the running," Russell kicks things off.

I nod. "Agreed. Their team principal is meh."

Martin picks up his Montblanc pen, crossing them off the list of teams who have offered me a contract. "What about Porsche?"

I shrug. "No strong feelings either way."

"I'll leave them as a maybe." He nods and draws a big question mark. "And AlphaVite?"

Lucas's current driving partner, Mateo Bertole, is retiring from Formula 1 after the season, leaving an open seat on the team. I'd be making a few million less than I am now, but their new team principal has a clear plan for AlphaVite's future— one that's equally rooted in leadership and partnership. There's a lot of room for growth, and at least I know I'd get along well with my driving partner.

"It's a good contract," I admit as I drum my fingers against the table. "And I like Green."

So does Josie. AlphaVite's team principal David Green is her Formula 1 crush.

"They also switched to a Mercedes-produced engine," Martin points out. "It's definitely upped their competitive edge."

I nod thoughtfully. They came second in the Constructors' last year, which surprised the hell out of everyone, even them. "Competitive enough to win more championships, though?"

"With you behind the wheel?" Russell nods. "No doubt in my mind, mate."

"And AlphaVite's headquarters aren't too far of a drive from London, which is convenient," Martin adds.

My phone lets out a short *beep* and I nearly break my hand

trying to wrestle it out of my pant pocket. *Fuck*. It's from Ella. I'm a guest on her podcast this week, and we're recording in her hotel room later. Given my always running twenty minutes behind schedule timetable, she wants to confirm I'll be there *on time*. And risk a scolding from Blake? Fat fucking chance.

Martin coughs loudly to recapture my focus. Somehow, he knows I'm no longer an active participant in the conversation. "Can you focus again, please?"

"Yes."

"I was saying," he raises his eyebrows as if he doesn't quite believe I'm listening, "we should see if they'd go up half a mil more if you bring on Pegasus as a team sponsor."

"No."

Russell's eyes widen at my snappy tone. "Any particular reason *why*?"

"They're *my* sponsor." Even I cringe at how bratty I sound. Taking a deep breath, I explain, "I've been with Pegasus for over ten years. I'm not gambling my relationship with them just for more money."

I'm also not gambling away another piece of my dad. Pegasus was his sponsor, and now they're mine. No team is taking another damn thing away from me.

"If you sign with AlphaVite, we'd ensure your personal sponsorship supersedes the team sponsorship, yeah?"

"He's right," Russell agrees. "And Pegasus is Team Theo. That's not about to change."

I nod. "Alright. Ask them about it. Is that it? Are we done?"

"No, we're not done, Theo." Martin sighs. "But considering your attention is that of a toddler who just snorted a Pixie stick, we can pick back up tomorrow. Deal?"

"Cool." I nod as if I'm going to be any less unfocused tomorrow. "Do you blokes mind if I have the room? I have a call to make."

Martin rubs his smooth head and the Rolex encased around his wrist flashes in the sunlight. "Everything... good?"

"Yep. No dramas, mate."

I may die of heart palpitations before the call is over, but sure, everything's good!

"Anything I need to know about?" His eyes nearly disappear as he squints at me. "As your manager—"

"It's a personal call," I reassure him with the flick of a wrist. "Nothing work-related."

Russell lifts his brows but doesn't comment. I've never been one to shy away from sharing every detail of my personal life, especially with him, so his suspicion is warranted.

It takes twenty minutes for me to work up the nerve to hit the little green call button on my screen. It's just a casual, friendly phone call. No biggie. Part of me prays it goes to voicemail.

"Hello?" a familiar voice says. "Theodore?"

I roll my eyes. "No. Santa Claus."

Why is my first reaction always to be a dick to him?

Richard chuckles. "Definitely Theodore. Is everything okay? I'm not with your mum right now. She's—"

"I was, uh, actually hoping to talk to you about something," I stammer awkwardly. "Off the record."

"Oh?"

"I don't want my mum to worry, is all," I quickly add.

There's a brief hesitation before he consents. "Sure. What happens on this call, stays on this call. Just like Vegas."

My laugh comes without warning. My dad and Richard's Vegas trip from way back when is legendary in the sense that no one knows what happened, except for the fact that Richard is no longer allowed in the state of Nevada. It's unclear whether they didn't remember much of the trip or if it was so raunchy they couldn't fathom spilling the details.

"What's going on?"

"Well, first, I want to apologize about what happened in Melbourne. I said some uncalled-for shit and I'm sorry."

"You've already apologized, Theodore," Richard says, his words marked with confusion.

I take a deep breath. "Yeah, but um… this time I mean it."

Deep, loud laughter comes through the phone—just as I think it's going to end, it lingers. My original half-arse apology to him was to appease my mum, and not because I actually felt bad for being a dick. Call it maturing or realizing that the things I say in the heat of the moment have long-lasting, unde- sirable consequences, but I *do* mean it now.

"Well, apology accepted. *Again.* You are your dad's son through and through, you know that, right? Always able to make people laugh, whether you mean to or not."

A sheepish smile spreads across my face. Most people compare me to my dad in terms of my driving—not as many people can look at our similarities strictly as dad and son. "Mum says you talk about him… together."

What was once weird to me now gives me a small sense of comfort.

"We do," he admits cautiously. "He was a big part of both of our lives. And I'd never try to replace him, Theo. He's your dad and he loved you more than anything."

I crack my knuckles against my thighs. "Do you think… I mean, what are your— Shit, uh… well, did my dad always know he wanted to drive for McAllister?"

There's a long pause before Richard says, "He almost signed with Giovani."

My head jerks back at his statement. *What?* "Giovani? They haven't been around in," I attempt to do the math in my head, but give up, "years."

They were a pretty good team, comparable to today's Porsche, that had the potential to be great, but just couldn't seem to get there. They lost their funding a few years after my dad's retirement.

"If your dad had signed with them, I'm sure their luck would've changed," Richard notes. "But McAllister offered him a contract a few days before he signed with Giovani."

"And he obviously chose McAllister," I finish for him.

"Not obviously," he corrects me. "Your dad was torn. Giovani was offering more money, but he liked the team over at McAllister better. There was more room to grow. More of a chance to make a name for himself. Ultimately, that's why he chose them."

"Why didn't he tell me?" I ask, dumbfounded. "I thought he was always ride or die McAllister."

"He loved McAllister with all his heart, but I'm sure he would've been just as happy at Giovani. Or with any team, for that matter. Your dad would've entered a damn golf cart in a Grand Prix if it meant he could race."

I smile to myself at the image. "But he always encouraged me to land a spot driving for McAllister."

"Because that's what *you* wanted. From the moment you knew your dad drove for them, you were a McAllister man, Theodore. And yes, it's special that you get to drive for your dad's team, but trust me when I say, he would be just as happy with you driving for another team. It didn't matter to him as long as you were happy." He pauses before asking, "And are you? Happy?"

A film of sweat coats my body at his innocent question. Puffing up my cheeks, I blow out a deep breath and tell him everything. And I mean everything. Once given the chance to explode, I'm like Mount Vesuvius, spouting and spitting destructive fire. He stays quiet as I ramble and rage about Avery. My contract. The clauses.

I rest my head on the table once I'm through, not giving a flying fuck about the germs. A sick day doesn't sound that terrible—at least it'd be an excuse to lock myself away from the world and their questions and opinions.

"I don't know what to do," I mumble.

"You have to do what's best for *you*," Richard says carefully. "And from what you've told me, that may mean you driving for another team. If you drove for Everest or Ithaca and they offered you this contract, would you sign it? No, you wouldn't. You wouldn't have even bothered counter-offering. You'd already be knee-deep in negotiations with another team."

"I've met with other teams," I defend myself weakly.

But they aren't McAllister. If Josie were here with me now, she'd be singing "I Want You To Want Me" by Cheaptrick.

"I know McAllister means a lot to you, but I promise there's bigger and better things besides them. My advice? Stop focusing on if McAllister wants you or not and start thinking about if *you* want *them*. You're a goddamn Walker, and any team would be lucky to have you."

34

THEO

I STOMP MY FOOT, really leaning into the whole toddler-throwing-a-tantrum attitude I've had all morning. "I don't want to go."

"Dealing with you is like having a kid I didn't ask for." Russell throws his hands up. "If you don't mind a fine, then by all means, skip out on the press conference."

Fuck fuckity fuck fuck. I forgot about the FIA's tendency to fine drivers for missing mandatory media interviews. God knows Blake has enough of those to keep his lawyers busy for the rest of their lives.

I frown once again. "You know what they're going to ask me."

The same shit they've been spouting at me all weekend. *Will you be re-signing your contract with McAllister? What's the holdup with your contract negotiations? Are you considering switching teams? Who else has offered you a contract? There are rumors you've met with other teams, care to comment on that?*

"You've had media training," he reminds me, his voice losing its sliver of annoyance. "You know how to answer the questions, Theo. It's nothing new."

Media training requires giving diplomatic answers with a blank face. I've never been known for my subtlety, or filter for that matter. Giving them a cookie cutter answer is akin to admitting guilt, and I tell Russell as much.

"It'll look worse to skip out," he replies. "They'll start digging. And if anyone approaches McAllister, who knows what they'll say."

Shit. He's right. The ball is in my court; it has been since they gave their final counter. Taking a deep breath and pasting on a smile, I waltz into the press room like it's any other post-qualifying press conference. As predicted, they start off with a doozy, not bothering with any of the niceties.

"Theo! Theo!" an ESPN reporter shouts. "McAllister had some recent internal management changes. Is that what's been holding up your contract negotiation?"

Oh fuck.

Blake leans in and simply says, "Yes."

"Oh, um, that question was directed at Theo," the reporter clarifies. "Not you, Blake."

Blake shrugs and takes a sip of his water. "Well, if I had to guess what's holding up Theo's contract, it's that the internal management changes at McAllister suck. They hired a piece of shit for their CEO, and he's going to run the team into the ground."

Every nerve in my body pinches, like crabs are hanging off every available surface of skin.

"Um. Blake? Shut the fuck up," I mumble. Now I know how Ella felt last year when Blake accidentally shared her secret to millions of people on live television. It's like watching a dumpster fire and not having any water to put it out.

He pretends not to hear me as he scans the room with a scowl. Reporters shout questions over one another, trying to ask the follow-up questions that are bound to be replayed on every sports show for the next few days.

"Blake, what gripes do you have with the CEO?" a woman from SkySports shouts. "Do you think he's not leading McAllister in the right direction?"

I kick Blake's shin under the table, hoping to distract him, but he doesn't even flinch. *Fuck.*

"I think James Avery presents a potential risk to the integrity of Formula 1 as a whole, not just McAllister. That's what happens when you care more about the money than the honest outcome of the competition. His actions go against the very definition of the word sports and if—"

My hands shoot out in front of Blake, knocking his microphone off the table. It falls to the ground with a loud *thud* that everyone hears since the room's gone completely quiet. I'm not sure who's more startled by my actions, though I think it's me.

What the fuck is he thinking?

"We need to talk," I murmur under my breath.

"Uh, I'm kind of in the middle of something, mate. Like saving your contract."

"Meet me under the table. Now."

Without a second thought, I sink down into my seat and onto the floor, slithering underneath the black Formula 1 tablecloth covering the table and crouching on the scratchy green-and-gold-patterned carpet.

"Walker, I'm not getting under the table with you," Blake hisses. His dark eyes move back and forth from me to the roomful of reporters. "We're at a goddamn press conference."

"Unless you want me sharing what happened in Barcelona," I say, throwing him a pointed look, "I suggest you crawl under this table with me."

Barcelona involved a cop Blake thought was a stripper. Not a story that should be shared, probably ever. Mumbling something about how he wants to strangle me, Blake pushes back his chair and joins my impromptu hide-out. It's an extremely cramped space meant only for legs, not two full-grown men.

"What the fuck are you doing?" I ask, keeping my voice low. "You're going to get sued for slander or defamation or whatever the fuck it's called. I hate Avery more than anyone, but I'm not going to let you risk your career just to start shit with him."

"Nothing I said was untrue." Blake shakes his head. "He's spot-fixing based on the clause in your contract."

I blink slowly. Gambling has never been my thing, but even I know that ensuring a certain result in a prop bet is *very* illegal. "Excuse me?"

Blake huffs. "I have proof that he's been in contact with sports wagering sites to make a buck at your—and McAllister's—expense."

"How in the hell do you know this? Did you hack him?"

Blake shrugs. "Yes. Well, no, not me personally. Jesse Adler did."

My jaw nearly hits the floor. Lucas doesn't talk to his brother Jesse anymore, so for him to reach out for this? To code and hack and do cool shit for me? Holy hell.

"Paul and I came up with a plan," Blake says firmly. "It's all going to work out. You can re-sign your contract, and Avery will be gone. It's a win-win for everyone."

"Who the hell is Paul?" I ask, struggling to keep my voice down. "I told you not to tell anyone, Blake."

He narrows his eyes. "My therapist."

I know now's not the time to dig into this, but old habits die hard. "His name is Paul? I always envisioned him as more of a William or a Gregory. Does he look like a Paul?"

"What the hell is a Paul supposed to look like, Theo?" Blake gives me a perfected eye roll. "You know what? I don't want to know. Can you just let me expose Avery so you can re-sign your contract and we can move on from this?"

I pause and shake my head. "I'm not sure I'm going to re-sign with McAllister." My voice sounds way more confident than expected.

Blake's head shoots back so violently, it slams against the underside of the table. A barrage of colorful swear words fly from his mouth. "Why the hell not? Is this because of Josie?"

"No, it's... I mean yes, but no. Part of why I love McAllister so much is because of her, but now that she's not here..." I take a deep breath, knowing once I say it, I can't take it back. "I wonder if my dedication to McAllister is holding me back from other opportunities. Maybe it's time to let go and try something new. Drive for another team. Focus on me instead of what everyone expects from me."

What I thought my dad wanted for me.

"Wow," he mutters. "Um, shit. Well okay. Paul and I didn't really prepare for that outcome."

It may be dark under the table, but the telltale sign of his shallow breathing indicates how anxious my comment has made him. The last thing we need is for him to have a panic attack under a table mid-press conference.

"Deep breaths, Blakey Blake," I say, lowering my voice. "No matter what team I drive for, you'll still be the person to help me get my dick out of a water wiggler."

He groans. "Oh God, I forgot about that."

Rosalie had left a water wiggler—a brightly colored vinyl tube filled with liquid and glitter and beads—at my house, and I wanted to test out if it was like a FleshLight. I figured it'd be easy since the kid's toy is slippery and squishy, but it was not. Blake ended up having to use a kitchen knife to cut through the material. It was almost a second circumcision.

"You nearly carved your initials into my manhood," I scoff. "That's not something you easily forget."

"Who puts a children's toy on their manhood for fun? Do you know how bloody—"

"Uh, hey," Lucas says, his blond head peaking underneath

the tablecloth. His green eyes dart back and forth between us. "You guys nearly done? It's getting a little crowded up here, and I can only talk about qualifying for so long."

I turn to Blake. "You good?"

"Can I still get rid of Avery? With or without you, I don't want that bloke anywhere near this sport."

I haven't seen angry Blakey Blake in quite some time. Wish I had a bag of popcorn. "Let loose, mate."

My legs are stiff as I crawl back out, taking my seat once again. The amount of people in the room seems to have doubled since we disappeared. Lucas shoots us a questioning look before sharing, "Every news organization called backup during your tea party."

"Sorry 'bout that," I apologize into the mic, holding up my hands. "Blake wanted a blowie, but I was explaining to him how inappropriate that is at a press conference."

Blake grabs my microphone since his is still laying on the floor like a crime scene victim.

"As I was saying," he says, straightening his back, "the FIA explicitly prohibits participating in sports wagering activities, yet James Avery is providing information regarding McAllister's team strategy to outside parties."

The questions come at rapid-fire speed, making it impossible to hear what anyone is saying. For once, I'm happy to sit back and let Blake handle all the talking. Taking out my phone, I check my texts.

MARTIN THE MANAGER

I don't go to one race and the press conference turns into a zoo? For fuck's sake.

THEO WALKER

Let's meet once I'm back in London.

MARTIN THE MANGER

You make a decision while in your makeshift
fort with Blake?

THEO WALKER

A few of them, actually.

35

JOSIE

A CRISPY TATER tot with legs greets me by running full speed into my shins. Champ's tongue hangs out of one side of his mouth while a fuzzy tennis ball occupies the other. He drops the ball expectantly at my feet as his tail wags so furiously it could double as a personal fan. Readjusting my bag so none of the contents spill out, I grab the ball and lob it down the empty hallway.

"Hi!" Ella's head pops out of her office. "I have doughnuts. And coffee."

I belt out a raspy chorus of Andrew Gold's "Thank You For Being a Friend." This early Tuesday morning call time isn't ideal, but it's the only free slot Kelsey and Ella both had in their busy schedules. Kelsey being a guest on an episode of *Coffee with Champions* is part of our PR-plan for opening month. He won't be here for a bit, but Ella wanted me to go over her questions ahead of time.

Plus, I need ample time to grill her about what in the absolute hell that press conference was.

Walking into her office is like entering a sports museum. Paraphernalia decks the walls, but besides a few European *foot-*

ball teams, all the jerseys and posters are American teams I've never heard of. I grab a chocolate-frosted doughnut and a cup of coffee from her paper-covered desk before settling into the lounge chair in the corner. Before I can take a bite, Champ once again drops the ball at my feet.

"No balls inside, Champ," Ella says in a tone that's hardly reprimanding. Surprisingly, Blake's worse at disciplining than she is. He can make reporters and engineers cry with a single look, but saying no to Champ is nearly impossible for him. Ella nudges a plush cupcake toward him as an alternative. "Play with one of your other toys."

"What's the little man doing here? I thought he lost his privileges."

Champ may be adorable, but he's an absolute rascal. Ella's recording studio is right next to her office, and the multi-colored patch cords snaking around and connecting the many consoles, mixers, and interfaces are all things for him to chew or piss on.

"Figured you could use some fluffy love," Ella informs me with a grin. "And Blake has meetings all day, anyway, so I'm on doggie duty."

"Meetings with McAllister?" I ask, not bothering to be coy.

"Mm-hmm."

I've never been on the receiving end of one of Blake's angry rants, but I've witnessed enough of them to know that William McAllister had better prepare for war. He deserves every bit of venom Blake sends his way. How could he let Avery manipulate Theo's contract? I thought the social media clause was bad… but this? What was revealed during that press conference was just the tip of the iceberg of how they tried to manipulate Theo. It makes my stomach sink thinking about how they used his love for McAllister to convince him he should sign a contract that took away his talent.

Ella leans back in her chair and teasingly rolls her eyes.

"He tried deleting his Instagram yesterday because he was annoyed by all the comments he was getting. Couldn't figure out how to do it, so he just turned his phone off instead."

Wes texted me that I should be glad I left before this happened because it's a madhouse. All of McAllister's marketing efforts have shifted to crisis mode. It's probably for the best that I no longer work for them; there's no telling if I'd accidentally change an Instagram caption from *"Red suit, red car, red helmet, ready to win"* to *"Red everything. Ready for revenge."*

Ella takes a sip of her coffee, and I say coffee very loosely. It's essentially almond milk with a splash of coffee. "Have you talked to Theo?"

I shake my head. Theo's been completely ignoring my calls and texts, not even responding with a brief "we'll chat soon" or "ttyl." Guilt eats away at me, knowing that I left him to deal with this on his own.

Leaning back in the chair, I take an aggressive bite of my doughnut. "Why didn't he tell me what was going on? Doesn't he trust me? I'm his… *was* his girlfriend."

Glancing down, I find Champ innocently chewing on my shoelaces. *Lovely.*

"It has nothing to do with trust, Jos." Ella picks Champ up and places him in my lap. I really did need some puppy love. "He knew what you'd say if he told you. That he'd be an idiot to sign it, and he should drive for another team. Think about it. If Theo reacted poorly to *you* leaving McAllister, God only knows how he'd react if you told *him* to leave."

"But I could've been someone to talk to," I argue. "I know how to be objective."

Ella laughs and shakes her head. "No, you don't, Jos. And Theo loves you for it. You've always been his biggest fan. He's an amazing driver—"

"He's a *phenomenal* driver."

Okay, now I see her point about not being objective.

"Yes, he is. But Blake's like Tiger Woods or Steph Curry."

She looks at me expectantly, but I just shrug. "Who?"

"Are you kidding?" Ella rubs her hands against her face. "Tiger Woods is undoubtedly the best golfer! He's won eighty-two PGA Tour events and has the lowest career scoring average ever. And Steph Curry may be one of the greatest point guards *ever*. He's the reason teams now routinely utilize the three-point shot. And his wife Ayesha—"

"Sorry, babes, but you lost me at 'are you kidding?'" Sometimes I forget that Ella's background is sports journalism. Her knowledge extends far beyond Formula 1, and she can easily chat with anyone about obscure stats that no human should have memorized.

She sticks her tongue out at me. "Let's go with David Beckham. He's British and plays soccer. Does that work?"

"Unfamiliar with soccer," I tease. "What's that?"

"*Football*," Ella huffs. "All I'm saying is that every sport has an all-star. You could know nothing about the actual sport, but you know that *one* name. That's Blake for Formula 1. His talent is once-in-a-lifetime legendary. And yes, I'm his girlfriend, so I'm also a bit biased, but you've seen him drive. He's—"

"Bloody impressive."

There's no denying Blake is Formula 1's favorite. And not just because he's handsome and elusive; he's genuinely that good. He consistently delivers in all areas: defending and overtaking, tire management, attack strategy.

"Exactly," Ella agrees. "But Theo's always been *your* all-star. Since day one, he's been your favorite. He's never had to compete with Blake for your attention or affection."

I finish my doughnut before nuzzling into Champ's soft coat. "They took the clauses out, though, right? He can do his own social media? And not be Blake's bitch?"

Ella raises a brow but lets the comment slide. "They did, but as far as I know, he still hasn't signed."

My thoughts swirl around my head so quickly that it makes it hard to see straight. "I need to talk to him."

I don't know when or how that's going to happen, considering he's dodging my calls like one of the bad guys in his video games. And not only is it the Saudi Arabian Grand Prix this weekend, it's also Gemini's soft opening.

"Are you finally done being single?" Ella asks with a chuckle.

I shoot her a cheeky wink. "I've always sucked at it, anyway."

I've had enough time on my own. I can be alone, I know that. And I don't *need* Theo, but I sure as hell *want* him. I want his loud laugh when I send him funny TikTok videos or burst into song. I want his weird two a.m. comments about how it's odd that peeing in a urinal isn't considered public indecency. I want to tell him about my day while I watch him kill dragons or build some sort of virtual fort.

He's the Monsieur to my Mademoiselle. Good on their own, but even better together.

36

THEO

ANOTHER TEXT from Martin comes in, but I don't bother reading it. Just like I've ignored the other seventy-five texts I've received today. I don't need to justify or explain my decision to anyone. It's my life. And right now, this is exactly where I want to be.

I've heard Josie talk about Gemini enough that walking in shouldn't be as awe-inducing as it is. The entry is a record shop, minus a cashier and cash register. My eyes zip and zoom around, not knowing where to focus. CDs from the 2000s and first-generation iPods sit in a display case, artist and band posters are tacked to the walls, and shiny instruments sparkle under the lighting.

The floorboards covered by a Persian rug creak under my weight as I explore the space. I briefly sift through a bin of vinyl records and laugh because only Josie would position The Beatles and Megan the Stallion next to one another.

Taking a deep breath, I head toward the *real* entrance of Gemini. Goosebumps ripple down my arms. I haven't seen Josie in five weeks. Five weeks without her smile that feels like a hug. Five weeks without her hair fanning across my chest as she cuddles me in her sleep. Five weeks without her lips on mine. Five weeks without my best friend. My person. My heart.

I push through the door with an alarming amount of force and briefly worry that it's about to fall off the hinges. Stepping forward, I'm greeted by Kelsey standing behind the bar holding a knife. In his defense, he's cutting lemons and limes, so it makes sense, but still, the sight is frightening.

Kelsey lifts his head. "Theo? What're you doing here?"

"I'm just, uh—" I crack my knuckles, and take it all in. "Wow. The place looks amazing."

He wipes his hands on the apron tied around his waist before waving me over. I keep my eyes focused on the knife that's still within his arm's reach as I head over to the bar.

"All Josie," he comments. "Assuming you're here looking for her?"

"Yeah."

"She's in the back, but should be out in a minute or two."

"I just want to wish her luck tonight," I explain awkwardly. "Let her know how proud I am of her."

Kelsey slides a glass of water across the bar. "She watched all your races religiously, you know. We both did. She even had me rooting for you instead of Lucas for some of the races, but don't tell him that."

Rubbing my neck, I shrug. "Well, Jos is a McAllister fan through and through."

"She's a *you* fan, mate," he corrects me. "Don't think she knows McAllister even has another driver."

There's no use trying to fight my smile. "I'm a Josie fan, too."

"I hope the two of you work things out soon, because I don't know if I can listen to one more of her Taylor Swift playlists."

"Hate to break it to you, mate, but they all have Swift on 'em."

He groans and takes a sip of his drink. "I should've guessed. The—"

A voice I'd recognize in a chorus of thousands interrupts whatever Kelsey is about to say. I whip my head around and the breath gets sucked right out of my chest. Josie stands there in a svelte green knit dress, looking positively radiant. She's a rare flower—so breathtakingly stunning that it's an honor to even look at such beauty, both inside and out.

"What are you doing here?" Josie rushes over to me and jabs her finger into my chest. "Are you aware there's a Grand Prix tomorrow?"

As if on cue, my phone buzzes in my pocket. Probably another text from Martin. Or Blake. Or Russell. Or one of the million people who have been blowing up my phone all day, asking where I am. All I told my team was that something came up and McAllister needs to call up a reserve driver. Blake's probably torturing the poor bloke right now.

"I am."

Her eyebrows furrow. "You're missing qualifying."

"Yep."

"You can't race if you miss qualifying," she says rapidly.

"I'm well aware, angel. I've driven in Formula 1 for quite a while now."

Voices of staff arriving through the back entrance filter through the room. My timing could not have been worse, but Kelsey saves the day and offers to let us chat in his office. It's hardly an office considering the small space barely fits a desk and a chair, let alone two people, but at least it's private.

Josie's lips part slightly as she stares at me in utter confusion. "What are you doing here, Theo?"

"This is a huge night for you, babe, and I wanted to support you. Show you how proud I am of you."

"I... I thought you were mad at me," Josie says quietly, her eyes downcast.

Now it's my brows that dip forward in confusion. "Jos, what could possibly make you think that?"

"You've been ignoring my calls and texts for over a week. I thought you were upset I made you deal with," she waves her hands in front of her, "everything on your own. I wasn't there for you, and I should've been."

"No, Jos," I reassure her with the shake of my head. "You needed to focus on *you*. And the time apart made me focus on my own shit. It's what I needed, too."

As much as I want to spend the next hour filling Josie in on everything that's transpired over the past week, this is her night, not mine.

"But I really fucking missed you," I add.

"Missed you, too, baby." The familiar pet name loosens the tension in my back. Josie rests her hands on my chest and my rapidly beating heart goes wild at her touch. "And I don't want any more alone time. I want you. I want *us*."

My aim wasn't to speed up Josie's timeline, but I'd be lying if this wasn't the best-case scenario. "Oi?"

"Oi," she says in a terrible Australian accent. "I love you."

Grinning like an idiot, I say, "Thank fucking fuck."

I bow my head and tenderly press my lips against Josie's. My tongue finds hers and we explore each other with soft caresses, with no care in the world. There isn't the slightest doubt in my mind that I'm the luckiest man alive.

Josie pulls away first. Brown eyes meet blue, both filled with magnetic intensity. "Why didn't you tell me?"

"I kept holding out hope that things would change," I admit. I run my fingers through her hair, loving the way her blonde locks feel soft against my skin. "And when they didn't, I was embarrassed, I guess. Hurt that a team I invested so much time in didn't care."

"Theo." She cups my face in her hands. "If there's anything to be embarrassed about, it's how horribly you sing in the shower. And you yourself said it. You're number one at everything, especially at giving me orgasms. But your team should know that first and foremost—not the orgasm part, I meant the part about you being the best."

I cover my lips with hers in a silent thank you. "Love you so much, angel. I thought I lost you, eh?" I murmur against her lips. "It hurt worse than getting kicked in the nuts."

Josie's head flings back as she laughs. "You get that off a Hallmark card, Walker?"

"Pinterest." I run my palms against the material wrapped around her waist. The voices filtering through the crack in the door are getting hard to ignore, so I ruefully suggest, "You should probably go greet some people, yeah? Socialize and schmooze?"

She deserves to be celebrated for the hard work she's put into Gemini. Hell, she deserves to be celebrated every day for simply being her. Josie clasps her hands behind my neck and tenderly works her fingertips into the base of my skull. Her soft touch is my Achilles heel and I grit my teeth to block a moan from slipping out. "I hate when you use logic, Walker."

"I'm a smarty pants, Bancroft." I chuckle. "Or did you forget?"

"You didn't know the plastic applicator was supposed to come out when a woman puts in a tampon," Josie reminds me. "You've also referred to salt as 'white pepper' on numerous occasions."

"That happened *twice!*"

She rolls her brown eyes. Damn, I missed her being annoyed with me. I missed everything about her.

"You'll stay?" A flicker of nerves passes through her eyes. "For the party?"

My fingers dance across her shoulders. "Of course, princess. There's nowhere else I'd rather be."

. . .

THE PARTY LASTS until nearly two in the morning. It's by far the latest I've ever stayed up the night before a race, even one I'm not racing in, but my body is on high alert. I tried, and failed, to keep my PDA to a minimum, but I'm stuck to her like a magnet.

Once the last guest leaves, Kelsey and Josie dissect every aspect of the opening.

"Do you think people had a good time? They liked everything?" Josie swivels her head to me. "What did you think?"

"I think it was brilliant. The food was outstanding. I get why you freaked out over Jamie Wolff. He lives up to the hype."

Russell's going to have to whoop my arse back into shape after all the bang bang shrimp I ate.

"You were brilliant, Josie," Kelsey adds.

Her cheeks flush under his praise. She made the right choice. Jos deserves to have a job—and boss—who appreciates the hell out of her.

"Why don't you two head out of here? I'll make sure everything gets locked up for the night."

Josie tilts her head. "Are you sure? We can stay to help. It's not a problem, Kelsey."

He looks at my hand, which is lightly rubbing Josie's bare arm. "I think this one is eager to get you alone."

I've never loved another man so much.

We're barely through the door to Josie's flat before my hands start removing articles of clothing. I need to be as close to her as humanly possible. Tell her she's all I ever want. Taste the warmth of her lips pressing against mine. Feel her body desperate to be joined with mine.

I press my lips against her collarbone and gently pepper her chest in kisses until her breathing quickens. I grab a condom from her bin of eclectic sex toys and then fit myself on top of her, and our limbs tangle together in all the right places. There's no need for foreplay, and I easily settle deep inside her.

"Jesus Christ," Josie moans.

I grin cheekily. "Nah, just me."

Her laughter turns to gasps as I begin rocking into her. I wish I could make a playlist out of all the noises she makes. Josie wraps her legs around my waist to pull me deeper, and I happily oblige. Our moans fill the air as we give each other what we're hopelessly craving. Josie writhes beneath me, rotating her hips against mine as I dip my head down and gently suck on her pert nipples.

"You feel so good, princess," I rasp.

Josie lifts my head by grasping my jaw and greedily sears her lips against mine. I could kiss her forever. Hell, I plan on kissing her forever. I melt into her touch and bask in the feel of her under me, touching me, loving me.

Littering kisses across her exposed skin, I feel her involuntarily clench against me. I brush back her hair so I can watch her face as she comes undone.

"Come for me, baby," I whisper against her lips. "Let me feel you."

Her orgasm consumes her, and she arches her back, lustfully moaning. I don't let up and pound into her until the twist in my belly gets closer and closer to my own release. Deep guttural noises come from my chest as my orgasm rolls through me. My arms tremble from holding myself up, but fuck if it's not the most magical feeling in the goddamn world. The Disney World of sex, if you will.

It's only been a few weeks since I've been with her, but that time made me forget how good she makes me feel. How good I make her feel. It's like I've hidden our lovemaking deep into my subconscious to help me survive our time apart. And now that we're reunited, it's overwhelming. Slow tears fall from my eyes as I cradle Josie's face. My beautiful angel. What the hell did I do to deserve her?

"Oh my God. Are you okay?" Josie stammers, her words rushed. "Did I break your penis? Because it's possible; my mum told me. I know the penis isn't actually a bone, despite the word boner, but it's more of a pressure overload than a break, anyway. Do—"

I kiss her deeply so she stops her insane but adorable worrying. "I'm just happy, is all."

"I'm happy, too," Josie says, her eyes fluttering as exhaustion finally sets in. "Want me to sing Pharrell's 'Happy' for you?"

I flop onto my back and pull her on top of me. She settles against me like she's done thousands of times before. Usually, Mademoiselle is tucked underneath a pillow, but now she's snuggled comfortably next to Monsieur to the left of my head. Josie doesn't bother hiding her stuffed animals anymore.

"What about 'Walking on Sunshine'?" I suggest.

"Or 'Can't Stop the Feeling'?"

We go back and forth, listing off feel-good songs until Josie dozes off, her warm breath hot against my chest. Even in a bed with low thread-count sheets and permanently dented pillows, I'll sleep better than ever just because I'm with her.

That's what Josie does. She makes everything better. Every cup of coffee and matcha latte tastes more delicious when I'm drinking it next to her. Every song sounds better when she's singing it because it's so completely her. Every story I tell is funnier when she lets one of her giggles loose. She makes the most mundane, everyday type of shit exciting. She's the love of my life. And here, with her, is exactly where I belong.

37

JOSIE

I TURN onto my side and reach out, only to find the other side of my bed empty. My muscles tighten as I momentarily wonder if last night was a dream. Did Theo *not* come to Gemini's opening party? The sudden *bang* and *thump* of things falling in my bathroom reassures me that Theo is indeed here.

"Babe?" I call out. "You there?"

My words cause some sort of volcanic explosion, because that's the only explanation for the subsequent noises that come from my bathroom. *What in the bloody hell is that man doing?* Before I can get out of bed to check that my makeup isn't shattered on the floor, Theo comes waltzing out. Just like the first time we slept together, he's completely naked and utterly happy about it. Unlike the first time we slept together, I can now study his gorgeous frame without an ounce of embarrassment. I've never met someone so comfortable in their natural form—not that I'm complaining.

He walks over, swinging his dick like a helicopter, and slips under the covers with me. "Morning, gorgeous."

"Morning, handsome." I snuggle against the hard warmth

of his body. Muscular arms wrap around me, trying to pull me even closer. "Should I be scared to go into my bathroom?"

When he doesn't answer right away, I nudge his rock-hard abs.

"I organized it," he says quickly. "How'd you sleep? I slept like a rock. Well, a very rock-hard rock, if you know what I mean."

The only part of that sentence I focus on is the word "organized." This is what I get for sleeping in. Before I can demand an explanation and answers, he gives me a pout and says, "I even took before and after photos."

I'm not sure if I should laugh or cry. "What's wrong with how my things are organized, Theo? Please tell me you didn't throw anything away."

"For starters, none of the labels are facing the same way," he says defensively. "How do you know what anything is? I only threw out expired medicines and face creams."

I smack his arm. "Why'd you do that? You can use medicine for, like, two years after it expires, babes. Google it."

"No, you can't," he groans. "And if you don't properly shut your toothpaste, bacteria will spread and multiply."

I shove my face into my pillow so I don't say anything I regret. This is what happens when Theo is left unattended for too long. *Chaos*.

He presses a kiss against my forehead. *Such a boyfriend move.* "I'm just preparing you for when we eventually live together because your lack of organization is *not* going to fly, princess." Theo nuzzles his face into my neck. The rough feeling of his scruff against my skin tickles, and I squirm underneath him. "I'll be the best roommate ever. I cook, I clean, I make you orgasm, *and* I watch all your shows with you."

"You don't stop chattering during my shows. It took us two hours to get through a thirty-minute sitcom because I kept having to rewind."

He purses his lips in thought. "But it makes me more lovable."

"It does. You're very, very lovable." I place a few kisses on his stubbled jaw. "Should we turn on the race?"

Theo's started in almost one hundred and fifty Grand Prix. This morning marks the first one he's missed in nearly eight years.

"Weird hearing you say that, eh?" Theo chuckles. "But nah, I'm okay. I've had my fill of Formula 1 this morning. Finalized the details of my contract."

Ah. That explains why he was up early enough to organize my entire bathroom.

"Everything's sorted now?"

He nods with a satisfied smirk. "Yep. You're looking at AlphaVite's newest driver."

The noise that comes out of my mouth is half actress-being-scared-in-a-horror-movie and half actress-being-surprised-in-a-cute-way-in-a-romcom. Theo waits as I bombard him with question after question, not giving him any time to answer one before jumping to the next.

"Slow down, baby." Theo kisses my forehead again. "Yes, I'm happy with my decision. Yes, McAllister is about to go through a PR nightmare. Yes, I'm taking a pay cut, but I'll still be able to buy you unlimited ice cream, so don't worry. And yes, it was completely my decision. It's what I want. AlphaVite is an opportunity for growth and new challenges. And even with the clauses in my McAllister contract gone... well, fuck them. I'm petty."

My petty, perfect man.

I leap out of bed and rummage through my closet until I find what I'm looking for. It's buried beneath the rest of my F1 attire, which is mostly McAllister shirts and hats, but it's relatively easy to spot, considering it's the only blue item in a sea of red.

Theo laughs loudly when I reappear wearing my gifted AlphaVite baseball hat. "Why the hell do you have that? Have you been hiding it?"

"David gave it to Ella when she interviewed him," I admit. "She re-gifted it to me because—"

"Blake would have had a fucking hernia if she wore that," he finishes for me. "It looks sexy on you."

Jumping back into bed, I straddle Theo and place my hands on his chest. "Blue is going to look *super* sexy on you. Much better than red does."

He gasps playfully. "You don't think I look good in red?"

"You always look good—which is quite annoying, by the way—but red is a tough color to pull off. Blue compliments your eyes and complexion more." I take the cap off and place it on his head to illustrate my point. "There! You look perfectly gorgeous."

"You're perfectly gorgeous."

My cheeks flush as I smile. "Thank you."

"Now that we've determined we're the most perfectly gorgeous couple," Theo says with a grin. "How shall we spend the day? Besides millions of orgasms, of course."

"Do you want to come—"

"Yes. I thought we just clarified that part, angel."

I roll my eyes. "You didn't let me finish! What—"

"I always let you finish." A boyish grin pulls at his cheeks. "Quite proud of myself for it, too, eh?"

Fighting the urge to laugh, I press my hand over his mouth, so he stops interrupting me. "Do you want to come to brunch with me and my parents, you horny Aussie?"

THEO SHIFTS NERVOUSLY as my parents make themselves comfortable across the table from us at the restaurant. The moment my boyfriend is around my dad, he seems to forget the entire English language, including how to greet someone. He mumbles some incoherent "hello" before downing half a glass of juice.

Opening her menu, my mum peers over the top and casually asks, "How was the makeup sex?"

Orange juice sprays out of Theo's mouth and onto the white table in front of us. *And we're off to a fantastic start.* My dad pretends he doesn't hear the question, knowing he'll get dragged into choosing sides if he does.

"Oh my God, Mum," I hiss. "We're in *public*. And that is absolutely none of your business."

She waves me off with the flick of her hand. "Making love after an emotional separation is gratifying, Josephine. It's a healthy way to reconnect and bond with your partner. Nothing to be embarrassed about."

"Caroline," my dad interjects after an intense staring contest. "Why don't you talk to Josephine about this in private? Later, hmm?"

He nods to Theo, who looks white as a ghost. *Poor bloke.* He better buckle in for a lifetime of this kind of questioning. He hasn't even heard my mum talk about pregnancy sex or childbirth.

She sighs dramatically. "Fine, fine. Tell us about the party. Was last night a smashing success?"

My mum and dad wanted to come to Gemini's soft opening but had already committed to attending a charity gala. I think it worked out for the best because the last thing I needed was to spend the whole night stressing out that my mum was telling people about some new dildo or lube.

Before I can get a word in, Theo remembers how to speak in front of other people and starts filling them in at rapid-fire speed. Pride sits on his face as he tells them about the appetizers, the guest list, the decor, the drinks, everything he can remember. My dad's features soften slightly as he listens to Theo animatedly applaud and admire me.

"It was very sweet of you to miss your race to be there for Josephine," my mum comments.

"Josie's the only trophy I need," he says before blanching. "Not that she's a trophy. I mean, she is—she's amazing and deserves to be on a pedestal. But I meant she's not, like, property. I'll take the title of her boyfriend over the World Champion title any day of the week, though. Wow. It's hot in here."

Instead of wrapping his hands around Theo's neck, my dad simply nods. "I hope McAllister didn't give you too hard of a time for missing the Grand Prix. Especially after the bullshit with your contract."

Theo gives him a tentative smile. "Yeah, and I just signed a new contract with another team, so there's not much they could do, anyway."

My mum presses her hand against her chest. "Josephine didn't tell us! Congrats, Theo. That's very exciting."

"I just found out this morning," I cut in.

"During post-coital pillow ta—"

"What team?" my dad, thankfully, interrupts my mum.

"AlphaVite," Theo announces. I give his thigh a quick, supportive squeeze under the table. His new contract won't be announced until next week, but telling my dad he signed to his favorite team will definitely earn him some brownie points.

"They're a great team." My dad nods in approval. "What do you think about their engine change?"

"So far, it seems fantastic. The wing design seems to have really helped with porpoising as well, which was always their biggest issue in previous cars. Have you ever played the Formula 1 video game?"

My dad shakes his head. "I haven't played a video game since Pac-Man first came out."

Before I can beg Theo not to go into a twenty-minute, in-depth review on it like he's a video game reviewer with a YouTube channel, he does just that. My parents look at him in equal parts confusion and amusement. Their one and only child preferred dolls over driving games.

"We can play together sometime," Theo offers excitedly, his smile wider than a cartoon chipmunk. "If you want, I mean."

I hold my breath as I wait for my dad to respond, only releasing it when he gives Theo a simple, but firm, "Okay."

Theo grins like he won today's Grand Prix rather than simply made progress with my dad. He grabs my hand under the table before talking about his other favorite video games... all nine hundred of them.

As a server delivers our food, he turns to me and murmurs, "Have I told you how much I love you?"

I lean into his feather-light touch. "Not in the past ten minutes."

"Well, I love you. More than anything, angel."

"I love you, too," I say softly. "And thank you for being here. I know this isn't a usual Grand Prix Sunday for either of us, and it won't be the new norm, but it means a lot to me."

Theo responds by singing the chorus of Frankie Vallie's "Can't Keep Me Eyes Off of You." A smile stretches across my lips and doesn't leave for the rest of brunch. Hell, I never think it'll leave. Not with Theo by my side. He's my favorite person, my best friend, and my lover all rolled into one ridiculously loud, dangerously handsome man. And he's mine, forever.

38

THEO

BLAKE NEVER PLAYS video games with me before a race. *Ever.* He claims it takes him out of the "zone." I don't know what that means, but in the five years we've driven together, he hasn't once picked up the extra controller in my suite to play a round of anything with me.

Today is different.

It's the last race of the season, and my last race as a McAllister driver.

Blake's thumbs rapidly click the X button, trying to maneuver his player away from mine. If he'd been playing with me regularly, he'd know he should be hitting Y instead. In two swift moves, I annihilate him like I will at the race later. Hopefully.

I'm going into the last Grand Prix in pole position, but in all honesty, I think Blake purposefully held back in order to let me secure it. He's already won the Drivers' Championship, so winning this race won't mean as much for him as it would for me. I told him he better go full fucking throttle because if I do win, I want it to be because I earned it, not because he has a soft spot for me.

"How do you feel?" Blake asks me. His leg bounces at an insanely fast speed, shaking the couch with his nerves.

"Like a bag of M&Ms," I admit. "Mixed emotions."

"M&Ms are technically all the same flavor," he says with a sheepish look. "And I only know that because Ella has told me about ten times."

I snort. Classic Goldy knowing random snack facts. "Mixed feelings nonetheless."

"Mm-hmm." Blake clenches his jaw. "I'm sure."

"Are you going to cry?" I ask with wide eyes. I'm not one to talk, considering I recently cried post-sex, but he doesn't know that. "It's totally fine if you are, but I just want to know so I'm prepared to—"

Blake punches me in the arm. "Nah, but I am going to miss you."

"I'll be just a few motorhomes away," I remind him. "And you'll like Cooper. He's a stand-up bloke."

Cooper Fraser, McAllister's reserve driver who's filling the open spot on the team next season, is in for a world of fun. Blake's my best mate, but he's not an easy fellow to impress, and he doesn't like newcomers. Or when people challenge him. Or about nine hundred other things. Thank God for Goldy.

"We'll see." He shrugs noncommittedly. "I'm going to head to my room to call my sister. See you on the grid?"

"Mm-hmm. Tell her I say hi."

Like a revolving door, Russell enters the room as Blake leaves. He's holding a box with a bright red bow on it, and I light up like a candle during a blackout.

"You got me a gift, Russ? How sweet! You do know my birthday isn't for a few more weeks, though, right?"

He rolls his eyes and chuckles. "From Charlotte, mate. Not me. I'm just the delivery man."

Eagerly ripping into the wrapping paper, I find a brand-new shiny red helmet. It's the same high-grade carbon fiber design as my other helmets, made for speed and safety, but this one features photos of some of my favorite memories and moments with McAllister. Winning my first Drivers' Championship, Blake and me at our first podium win as teammates, a team photo from the Australian Grand Prix, sitting on Russell's shoulder after I clinched a win in Singapore, Lucas and me spraying champagne at one another. There's even one of me and Jos from a few years back, way before I ever knew how much she'd mean to me.

"This is amazing," I breathe out. My sister has a knack for design and has been creating my helmet designs for years, but this one takes the cake.

"We should get a shadow box for it so you can keep it in your AlphaVite suite next season." Russell knocks his knuckles against the helmet. "Rosalie loved the shirt you bought her, by the way. Blue's her favorite color."

Russell's wife sent me a photo earlier this morning of Rosalie wearing an AlphaVite shirt that looked more like a dress on her tiny four-year-old frame. She reassured me it'll fit better by the start of next season.

"She told me sequin is her favorite color," I remind him with a grin. "And that her favorite flavor is rainbow."

Russell lets out a deep laugh. "She's got an imagination, that's for sure. You ready to head down?"

"Mm-hmm," I confirm. "I want to get a few pics of me with the car before the race."

He ruffles my hair in response. "There's the Theodore I know and love. Let's do it."

I find Josie at a café table with Ella and Wes on my way to the garage. She flew in last night to be here for my final McAllister race, and I appreciate that more than I can say. While she won't be at every Grand Prix with me, she's going to try to come to as many within reasonable flying distance as she can. I'm not worried. We'll make it work. We're us.

I kiss the top of her head. "Hey, princess."

"Hey, babes. Where are you off to?"

"Grabbing some beauty shots with my car."

She lifts her camera and raises her brows. "Want me to take them? For old time's sake?"

"Let's do it." As we walk out toward the garage and pit lane, I murmur, "I thought of a new name for your tits."

She throws her head back and half-sighs, half-laughs. "That's what you're thinking about right now?"

"It's what I'm *always* thinking about," I remind her. "How do you feel about Sweet and Spicy?"

"I…" She gives me a meager shrug. "Well, actually, it's not horrible. I've heard worse."

"Is that a yes?"

My girlfriend—fuck, it feels good to say that again—doesn't have time to confirm before reporters are in hearing distance and start bombarding me with questions. It looks like the tourist crowds outside of Buckingham Palace. McAllister's already announced a new CEO—someone who's less of an evil douche canoe—so I'm hopeful they'll lay off with those sorts of questions. Not my zoo, not my monkeys.

"Walker! Walker!" they all shout. I nod at someone from the *London Daily* and the rest of the group simmers down.

"What made you sign with AlphaVite? There are rumors that multiple teams extended you a contract."

"My girlfriend told me that blue is a sexy color on me," I answer with a wink. "Well, she told me I look sexy naked, but if I have to be wearing clothes, that blue brings out my eyes."

I receive an immediate elbow into my ribcage, courtesy of Josie. "Hope you enjoyed seeing Sweet and Spicy for the last time ever."

My lips somehow twitch up higher.

"But in all seriousness, AlphaVite is a strong team. I've always had a lot of respect and admiration for them, and I'm ready for a new challenge. I'm excited to work with David Green. And Lucas, of course."

"How do you feel about leaving McAllister?" someone else asks.

Josie intertwines her fingers with mine and gives my hand a hand a quick squeeze. Taking a deep breath, I say, "They were my dad's team, and getting to race with them the past few years has been an honor. I'm extremely proud of everything we've achieved together."

This time, I give Josie's hand a squeeze. "McAllister also introduced me to the love of my life, and while I'm forever grateful for that, I'm ready to build my own legacy, with her, both on the track and off."

EPILOGUE
JOSIE

Twelve years later…

OPEN-MOUTHED KISSES MAKE their way down from my neck to my chest. Theo rocks his body against mine, his hardness rubbing against my core through our thin pajamas.

We both freeze at the soft knock at the door. *Eloise*. If it were one of the boys, they wouldn't bother with knocking, but Eloise is a rule-follower. How a little girl so polite and proper shares genes with my in-your-face husband is truly a mystery.

"Have kids, they said…" I laugh under my breath. "It'll be fun, they said."

Groaning quietly, Theo rolls off me before adjusting himself through his sweatpants. "Later?"

"It's a date." I wink as I pull the thin strap of my tank top back over my shoulder. "You can come in, darling. The door's open."

A moment later, her blonde curls appear in our doorframe. Besides the hair, she's all Theo with her gorgeous blue eyes and easy smile. "You're up!"

Theo glances down at his crotch and whispers, "Not anymore," which has me elbowing him in the side.

Patting the empty spot between us in bed, I say, "How'd you sleep, lovely?"

"Good." She scrambles up into the bed, burrowing between us. "Look, Mum! I found a new bracelet. It even buzzes."

I glance down and nearly pass out at the sight of her new "bracelet." *I'm going to kill my mother.*

"Is it sparkly, Lou Lou?" Theo asks, leaning over to get a look. The poor bloke is still under the impression she's about to show him some of the costume jewelry Aunt Charlotte got her.

"Isn't it pretty?" Eloise holds up her arm to show him the bright blue vibrating cock ring she's wearing as an accessory. It's untouched and unused, but that doesn't make it any better.

You'd think by now my mum would quit giving us things to spice up our sex life, but nope. The cock ring is the last gift of many that we've received at family brunches throughout the years. At least she has the courtesy to put her "special surprises" in gift bags, so I don't have to explain what they are to my three impressionable young children. *Or so I thought.*

"Oh my God," Theo chokes out. His face flushes a shade so red, I momentarily worry he's stopped breathing. "Can I see that?"

He doesn't wait for an answer before he slides the cock ring off her wrist, clicking the button on top to stop the vibrating. "This is actually Mummy's bracelet, Lou Lou. It's very special to her, so I'm going to put it away so we don't accidentally break it, okay?"

She sticks out her lower lip in disappointment. "But you said caring is sharing. So you *have* to share the bracelet with me. Those are the rules."

"Christ Almighty," Theo murmurs under his breath as she throws our parenting rules back at us. "Do you want some ice cream? I'll even give you extra gummy bears on top." It's a fair offer to distract her from the confiscated 'bracelet'.

"Crew likes ice cream," Eloise announces in a serious voice. Well, as serious as a four-year-old can be. "It's his favorite. Vanilla with sprinkles and Oreos on top. He told me so."

Theo shoots me an unhappy look. Eloise's infatuation with Ella and Blake's eight-year-old son Crew is adorably cute to me, but horrendous to him. It doesn't help that Crew's a carbon copy of Blake—down to the broody attitude—although he always goes out of his way to include Eloise whenever we get together.

"Can we invite him for ice cream?" Eloise asks. She tilts her head and smiles at Theo, knowing that usually has him melting at her every request.

"He's on holiday with his family," I remind her.

"Oh." Her brows furrow together in worry. "But he's coming back, right?"

"Unfortunately," Theo mumbles under his breath.

I smack him in the stomach, which is still chiseled with a six-pack after all these years. "He's a child. Be nice."

"She's too young to have crushes."

I don't bother arguing because there's no changing Theo's mind about Eloise's interest in Crew. I'd love for Ella to be my in-law, but we've got years and years before that's in the cards.

"How about we go out for breakfast instead?" I suggest, tucking a stray curl behind her ear. "You can get chocolate chip pancakes."

"And then ice cream for dessert?" The last thing Eloise needs is a sugar overload this early in the morning, but as she reminds me, "Daddy said I can have ice cream and you can't break a promise, Mum—that's what you told me. And maybe Uncle Kelsey will be at Milkman, and we can say hi to him. Then he can let me name a new flavor like last time, right?"

Yeah, she definitely got her love of ice cream from me.

Milkman is the ice cream sandwich shop Kelsey and I opened about five years ago. My brainchild has well-exceeded expectations, and we launched two more locations last year. "Mm-hmm. Why don't you go get the boys?"

"They're playing video games," she says with a little huff. "They won't listen to me."

The twins—Archie and Oliver—are currently addicted to the F1 driving game. They love playing as their dad and practicing their skills since they're both "going to be World Champions when we grow up." They have a whole plan where they're going to form their own team so they can be driving partners. How that's going to pan out with their ultra-competitive natures, I'm not sure, but I'm trying not to borrow trouble.

"I bet they will if you tell them about the ice cream," Theo prompts. He ruffles her hair, which has her giggling as she speeds out of the room to get her big brothers.

"Ice cream, Theo?" I ask with a raised brow. "Really?"

"She was wearing a *cock ring*, angel," Theo says, throwing up his arms. "What was I supposed to do? Her crush on Crew is bad enough; the last thing we need is to be having the birds and bees talk with her this young."

I burst out laughing because, as traumatizing as this entire situation is, it's also hilarious. "I need to have a serious talk with my mum."

"We gave her three grandkids," Theo says with the shake of his head. "I don't know what more she wants from us."

"Another one?"

Theo waggles his eyebrows. "You know I'm down, baby. More mini-mes and yous? Hell yeah. I think—"

He's interrupted by Archie and Oliver running into our room, chattering a million miles an hour. Eloise talks over them, asking, "Why did they get to name *two* ice cream flavors, and I only got to name *one*? That's not fair, Mum."

Oliver smirks at his sister, his dark brown eyes twinkling with mirth. "Uncle Kelsey likes us better."

"Yeah, we're cooler than you, Lou Lou," Archie chimes in.

It's no wonder she likes Crew so much when these two tease her endlessly.

"There's two of them and one of you," Theo points out.

She purses her lips and then nods, accepting this answer. Archie rolls his eyes. "Whatever. We're still cooler than you."

"Drop the attitude," I warn in what Theo's labeled my "Mum voice."

My husband nods in solidarity. "Or you can say goodbye to your Xbox."

We rock at this whole parenting thing.

"Sorry," the boys mumble under their breath.

"Alright, everyone, get dressed." Theo sits up and claps his hands together. Glancing at me, he asks, "Where do you want to go to brekky, princess? Ladies choice."

Eloise takes a step forward and holds out her hand. "That's *my* nickname, Da. I'm your princess."

I tuck my chin into my chest to hide my laugh. She's such a daddy's girl.

"What should I call your mum then?"

"What about queen?" Oliver suggests.

Archie high-fives his twin. "Yeah. Mum's definitely a queen."

Eloise twirls with her hands in the air. "And in the storybooks, the princess's mum is always a queen."

"You happy with that nickname, *queen*?" Theo teases, pressing a light kiss on my shoulder.

I grin, looking at my family with a full heart. "I couldn't be happier."

THANK YOU FOR READING!

Thank you for reading DRIVE ME WILD! If you enjoyed Josie and Theo's story, please consider leaving a review or sharing it with your friends.

Stay up-to-date on all of my future releases and get an exclusive bonus epilogue by subscribing to my newsletter (www.carly robynauthor.com/newsletter) and following me on social media (@carlyrobynauthor).

ACKNOWLEDGMENTS

To my mom, your love, support, and unwavering belief in me have been at the cornerstone of everything I've ever achieved. Thank you for being my biggest cheerleader and number one fan.

To my agent, Claire Harris, thank you for absolutely everything. Whether it's answering my late-night emails with the subject line "help, I'm spiraling," to calls explaining my never-ending questions, you're such a rock in this wild publishing world, and I couldn't do any of it without you.

A massive thank you to Taryn Fagerness at the Taryn Fagerness Agency and Olivia Fanaro and Mirabel Michelson at UTA, as well. I'm so grateful for all the work you do behind the scenes to help the Drive Me series get into the hands of people who love the story as much as we do. And thank you to my publishers worldwide—City Editions, Fischer, General Press, Michael Joseph, Sperling, and Rosman—for helping me share this story with readers near and far.

To Danielle, who has seen so many versions of covers and branding designs, that it's a miracle you still respond to my texts. Thank you for hyping me up, no matter how little the win is, and supporting me through thick and thin.

To my beta readers—Kara, Wren, Ashley, and Rukhshar—thank you for all your comments, critiques, and encouragement. You helped shape this story, and I appreciate the time and care you took in ensuring Jos and Theo got the happily ever after they deserve.

To you, the reader, who chose to spend your time with these characters and their journey. I hope this story brings a smile to your face and that you now have a new book boyfriend and book bestie.

To Josie and Theo, thank you for letting me tell your story. To say it was fun is the understatement of the year—you two had me giggling at every word I wrote. I'll forever be obsessed with you. Without you, this book would just be empty pages.

And last but certainly not least, to me. I'll forever be proud of you.

Loved *Drive Me Wild*?

CARLY ROBYN

DRIVE ME
crazy

Read on for an extract of the first
book in the series, *Drive Me Crazy*...

NURTURING WRITERS SINCE 1935

ONE
ELLA

IT'S SO cold out that my nips could be classified as weapons of mass destruction. I walk down the sidewalk, shivering against the biting chill as a light layer of snow dusts against my shoulders. My winter jacket is a lot better at making me look like an extra-fluffy marshmallow than keeping me warm.

Buildings stretch toward the night sky and cast eerie shadows onto the cars careening down the street at a breakneck speed. When I first moved to the city—hell, even a few months ago—the sight of the skyscrapers and classic yellow taxis brought a smile to my face. Now they serve as mocking reminders that the concrete jungle thoroughly whooped my ass. And not in the kinky spanking kind of way. More in a that-hurt-so-badly-I'm-never-sitting-again way.

I would've been more than happy to ghost everyone in Manhattan, but Poppy insisted on a proper send-off. It's the only reason I'm dragging my ass to her place in twenty-degree weather. When I finally arrive, I'm so focused on thawing my frozen fingers that I walk straight into a Hot Wheels piñata.

Oh my God.

Poppy's entire Midtown apartment has turned into a race

car enthusiast's wet dream. Signs reading "Yield to Party" and "Race in Progress" cover the walls, and checkered flags hang from the ceiling. The only thing indicating this isn't a four-year-old's birthday party is the excessive amount of alcohol in the kitchen.

I spy my best friend through the red, black, and white balloons floating around aimlessly. My mouth falls open, but no words come out. She's propping up a life-size, custom cut-out of Formula 1 legend Blake Hollis with his arm draped over some unknown woman. A woman who just so happens to have my face photoshopped over hers. *Lord help me.*

Blake looks gorgeous as per usual, but nothing ruins a pretty face more than a bad attitude. It's no wonder his team wants to have a biography written and released in less than a year. He needs as much good PR as he can get after last year's train wreck of a season.

I'm studying the display, contemplating how I'd look if I were supermodel tall with boobs faker than Monopoly money instead of five-foot-two with run-of-the-mill B-cups, when Poppy pulls me in for an organ-crushing hug.

"Ella! What do you think?" She twirls in a circle, arms above her head. "Perfect, right?"

"It's perfectly on theme," I agree, taking another bewildered look around. It's over-the-top, but then I wouldn't expect anything less. Poppy has the impressive ability to hyper-focus on a project to the point where it surpasses even the highest of expectations. It's annoying as hell when her projects happen to be my love life and floundering career, but I'll admit her apartment looks good. I wouldn't mind turning Blake's cardboard body into some type of dart board, though.

Jack bounces over from where he's sitting on the couch. He looks like he just walked off the cover of a billionaire romance novel with his perpetual smirk. He greets me with a one-armed hug before turning to Poppy. "Can I be done blowing up balloons?"

"I thought you loved blowing." Batting her piercing blue eyes, she flutters her lashes innocently. "That's why I gave you that job in the first place."

"Ha." He rolls his eyes, a teasing quirk at the corners of his mouth. "I do. I just prefer it be muscular blonds with daddy issues instead of balloons."

The conversation snowballs into Jack's latest dating mistake on a long list of many. He'll probably be Poppy's new project once I'm gone. I swallow the lump in my throat, trying not to focus on how much I'm going to miss them.

As if she can sense the chink in my armor, Poppy sighs dramatically and says, "It's not too late to back out and look for another job in New York."

I'm not sure how many times we can have this conversation before my head implodes. Two more times tops. Maybe. I throw my arm around her shoulders and gently shake her.

"It's definitely too late for that. I'm going," I confirm. A cold thrill goes up and down my spine. "And it's a phenomenal opportunity."

When I reached out to my mentor, George Phillips, for advice after leaving PlayMedia, I'd been expecting some career guidance. Instead, he offered me a job to be his feet-on-the-ground co-author for Blake's authorized biography. I haven't done much writing since my podcast, *Coffee with Champions*, blew up and I'm excited to get back to my roots. After what happened, the thought of podcasting, or even being in a recording room, makes my body flood with panic. I don't want to be constantly reminded of that. But writing? That's a safe space. It doesn't hurt that I'll be halfway around the world, either.

"Fine," she huffs, crossing her arms over her chest. "But

then you have to promise me you'll find out how many *Sports Illustrated* models Blake's slept with."

I hit a balloon floating by at her and she quickly swats it away from her raven black hair to avoid any static aftermath. Poppy's not big on sports, but she's big on celebrity gossip, and Blake's one of the athletes whose prowess has earned him international notoriety and prestige.

"Those aren't the questions he's going to want to answer, Pop," I tell her. Blake's extremely private. There's also a slight chance I'm already on his bad side after comparing his partying last year to Paris Hilton circa 2006. I don't think asking the McAllister driver his body count is going to earn me any brownie points.

"You're no fun." She sticks out her lower lip. "At least confirm the rumors that he has a huge dick."

"I'd like to know that one, too," Jack agrees with an aggressive head nod. "Honestly, if you could make a comparison chart of every driver's dick size, I feel like that would be really beneficial to us all."

Resting my face in my hands, I let out a groan. "Can I please have a drink before either one of you says *dick* again?"

A wicked grin spreads across Poppy's lips as she leads me into the kitchen. She's created a menu of drinks and snacks with Formula-One-themed names. I take a small sip of my McAllister Martini, cringing as the strong taste burns my throat. This isn't a martini; it's a hangover in a glass.

"I hate him," Poppy announces to no one in particular. "It's *his* fault you're leaving."

She says it so casually that it takes me a moment to realize who she's talking about. Connor Brixton. She refuses to call him by his name. I wish she wouldn't refer to him at all. *Adios, au revoir, and arrivederci, motherfucker.*

"I left PlayMedia of my own accord," I remind her. Digging my fingernails into my palms, I shrug my shoulders. I didn't have much of a choice, but at the end of the day, I quit; they didn't make me leave. "Can we not talk about this?"

"Ella, c'mon. You left—"

"Poppy," Jack warns, cutting her off. "We're supposed to be having fun and clearly Ella doesn't want to discuss it."

I shoot him a grateful look, but he and Poppy are staring each other down like parents in a bitter custody battle. Now would be a great time to snack on some Pit Stop Popcorn or Crash Test Chips, but they're on the other side of the counter.

"You're right. Sorry," Poppy acquiesces after a minute. She focuses her attention back on me. "Do you think Blake's listened to your podcast?"

My shoulders tense, but I don't bother reminding her that it's no longer my podcast. "I'm assuming he's looked me up. It's not hard to put two and two together."

"I'm sure he knows it was all in good fun," Jack reassures me.

I didn't say anything untrue or outrageous about Blake on my show, but I did poke some fun at his messy performance last year. My podcast was listed under sports and comedy for a reason. How could I *not* make a joke about him driving into more panties than wins? I'm praying George is right and Blake won't care that I made a few subjectively funny remarks about him.

"Pop, should we give El her present?" Jack changes the subject. "Before people arrive?"

He sips his drink, a Jump Start Gin and Juice, with a glint of mischief in his eyes. Poppy disappears, arriving back momentarily with a gift bag covered in race cars. No shocker there. It's filled with a variety of fun tchotchkes, but it's the last few items that really surprise me.

"Condoms." I blink rapidly. "You got me condoms."

I take a closer look and see the phrase *Save Fuel, Ride a Driver* embossed on the foil wrappers. My drink sputters out of my mouth, nearly hitting Poppy's chest.

"So?" Jack asks, staring at me with undisguised amusement. "What do you think?"

"That you two are certifiable." I hold the roll out in front of me. The ones in red foil are apparently cherry flavored. *Yum.* "I don't think I'll be using these, but I appreciate it."

Formula 1 drivers are infamously known as fuckboys. *No, thank you.* I'm twenty-seven years old. If I still felt like playing mind games and faking orgasms, I could walk into any bar within a five-block radius of my apartment. I want to be swept off my feet, not swept under a rug after a one-night stand.

"One final thing," Poppy says, pulling a lipstick out from the bottom of the bag. "Open it!"

I'm praying it's not a bright red color because regardless of what she says, it just doesn't work with my complexion. My eyes widen as I twist the bottom of the tube. I was way off base considering it's a goddamn knife.

Poppy claps her hands together. "Now you're protected from STDs *and* attackers!"

"Condoms to screw men"—I laugh, twisting the tube so I don't accidentally stab myself—"and a lipstick knife if they try to screw with me."

Jack chuckles with a wink. "London's not going to know what hit 'em."

"Neither will Belgium," Poppy adds. "Or Australia. Or Japan. Or any of the other places you're traveling to."

I clink my red plastic cup against hers in agreement. Twenty-one cities in fifty-two weeks. If that kind of time and distance can't help me move on from what happened, I'm not sure what will.

He just wanted a decent book to read ...

Not too much to ask, is it? It was in 1935 when Allen Lane, Managing Director of Bodley Head Publishers, stood on a platform at Exeter railway station looking for something good to read on his journey back to London. His choice was limited to popular magazines and poor-quality paperbacks – the same choice faced every day by the vast majority of readers, few of whom could afford hardbacks. Lane's disappointment and subsequent anger at the range of books generally available led him to found a company – and change the world.

'We believed in the existence in this country of a vast reading public for intelligent books at a low price, and staked everything on it'
Sir Allen Lane, 1902–1970, founder of Penguin Books

The quality paperback had arrived – and not just in bookshops. Lane was adamant that his Penguins should appear in chain stores and tobacconists, and should cost no more than a packet of cigarettes.

Reading habits (and cigarette prices) have changed since 1935, but Penguin still believes in publishing the best books for everybody to enjoy. We still believe that good design costs no more than bad design, and we still believe that quality books published passionately and responsibly make the world a better place.

So wherever you see the little bird – whether it's on a piece of prize-winning literary fiction or a celebrity autobiography, political tour de force or historical masterpiece, a serial-killer thriller, reference book, world classic or a piece of pure escapism – you can bet that it represents the very best that the genre has to offer.

Whatever you like to read – trust Penguin.